Wildwood

Wildwood

Drusilla Campbell

KENSINGTON BOOKS
http://www.kensingtonbooks.com

KENSINGTON BOOKS are published by

Kensington Publishing Corp.
850 Third Avenue
New York, NY 10022

All Kensington titles, imprints and distributed lines are available at special quantity discounts for bulk purchases for sales promotion, premiums, fund-raising, educational or institutional use.

Special book excerpts or customized printings can also be created to fit specific needs. For details, write or phone the office of the Kensington Special Sales Manager: Kensington Publishing Corp., 850 Third Avenue, New York, NY 10022. Attn. Special Sales Department. Phone: 1-800-221-2647.

ISBN 0-7582-0293-8

First Kensington Trade Paperback Printing: February 2003
10 9 8 7 6 5 4 3 2 1

Printed in the United States of America

For AWC, PLC, and the RBR

Acknowledgments

A number of people have read all or parts of *Wildwood* through its various incarnations. At the beginning there were Marion Jones and Peggy Lang; at the end I counted on Judy Reeves and Susan Belasco Hayhurst and my editor, Ann LaFarge, for their insights and opinions. The Women of Arrowhead supported and sustained me as did Art Campbell. If he ever got tired of talking about *Wildwood* and its characters, he kept it to himself. A special thanks to my sons, Matt and Rocky, who believed in me and kept the computer running. And to my agent, Elly Sidel, for her honesty, determination and friendship.

I am grateful to Dr. Robert Slotkin, Dr. Chris Khoury, and Dr. Dale Mitchell and his nurse, Adele, each of whom patiently answered my questions about the physiology and possibilities of midlife pregnancy, the emotional effects of abortion, and the varieties of Post-Traumatic Shock Syndrome.

Though *Wildwood* is entirely fictional in both its story and characters, Betty Balch, Judy Hanshue, and Jill Derby will recognize bits and pieces of our shared childhood within its pages. Bluegang Creek no longer exists. The city's fathers and mothers and the state of California covered it with concrete and asphalt decades ago, but generations of Los Gatos boys and girls remember its pristine beauty and the summer days spent sunning and swimming and growing up on its rocky banks.

Wildwood

Summer

That week no new polio cases were reported in Rinconada so most kids swam at the town pool. For practically the first time all summer, Bluegang Creek belonged to the birds and the squirrels and the crawdad—and a twelve-year-old girl sunbathing on a flat rock with her old Brownie shirt tied at her midriff like Debra Paget, painting her toenails with Tangee Strawberry Sundae polish, waiting for her two best friends.

Hannah Whittaker twisted the top off the polish and took a deep breath. Strawberry Sundae smelled forbidden, grown-up and cheap—like ankle bracelets and pierced ears and the music she listened to on that Oakland radio station. The show was called *Sepia Serenade* and she didn't know what *sepia* meant until she looked it up. Brown. Hannah Whittaker, the Episcopal minister's daughter, closed her bedroom door and listened to Negro music down low so her parents wouldn't hear.

She steadied her right foot, lifted the brush from the polish, let it drip, then brought it gingerly over to her big toenail and painted a perfect stripe of pink. Toes were easier than fingernails. Of course it didn't matter if she did a good job or not since she had to pick it all off before she went home. If her mother saw her painted toes, she'd catch it.

Hannah had always understood that she and her mother were not alike. This made her feel bad because if a girl wasn't like her mother, who *was* she like? She wanted her mother to love and admire her but there seemed no way this could happen unless she made herself into someone she was not, a carbon copy of her mother.

Hannah had explained this to her friends, Liz and Jeanne, and they knew exactly what she meant. Sometimes she felt like they lived right inside her head and if they were captured by Communists and tortured and their tongues cut out they would still be able to communicate. That was what it meant to be best friends.

Hannah's mom thought they all spent too much time together. She didn't approve of the way Liz was being brought up, half neglected. She said intellectuals had "no business" having children. She wouldn't even say what she thought of Jeanne's parents. Just rolled her eyes. Hannah's mother divided her world into two columns, those people who met her standards and those who did not. Women and girls were always either ladies or not. Ladies did not paint their toenails except with clear polish and where was the fun in that?

Fortunately, Hannah's mother was easy to fool.

Hannah had headed down to Bluegang right after breakfast when Liz called and said she had the new copy of *Secrets*, snitched from Green's Drugstore. It wasn't like they wanted to steal; they had to. In a town like Rinconada they couldn't even pay a quarter for a confession magazine without word getting back to someone's mother.

Hannah hummed a few bars of a song she liked, "Bebop Wino." She loved the beat and the smoky sound of the music on *Sepia Serenade*, but most of all the words which, even when they didn't say anything, implied so much. "Shake, Rattle and Roll." "Money Honey." "Sixty-Minute Man."

Dirty songs, songs about sex, the dark side of the moon.

If nail polish was cheap, confession magazines were unadulterated trash. Hannah wasn't sure what her mother meant when she said *unadulterated*; it was one of her favorite words and bad for sure. *I Married My Brother. Forced to Love—Forced to Pay. My Secret Shame.* The stories were never as good as the titles, which sent little ripples of expectant heat through Hannah's stomach.

Liz always kept the magazines because her mother never investigated her bedroom the way Hannah's did. Hannah stole nail polish and lipstick from Woolworth's and hid them in her bookcase behind boring old Nancy Drew, and she had to remember to carry them to school with her on Tuesdays because that was the day her mother dragged out the Hoover and all its attachments, the furniture polish, the vinegar and ammonia and the basket of rags and cleaned house like she expected a visit from an angel. Jeanne mixed cocktails when they slept over at her house. Last weekend they'd tried out Manhattans, which tasted the way Tangee nail polish smelled.

Hannah heard the crunch and rustle of deep oak leaves, the snap of a branch and looked up, expecting her friends. Instead she saw Billy Phillips on the hillside above her, standing on a saddle of roots from the big oak that had been undercut by high water some winters before.

"Hubba-hubba," he said.

Billy and his mother lived next door to Hannah and went to her father's church. Hannah's father said Mrs. Phillips wanted Billy to be an acolyte but the ritual was too challenging for him. He was a tall, heavyset boy who should have been in high school but had been held back. He wore his hair slicked with grease like a pachuco, but he was white and Episcopalian like Hannah. With his chewed-down fingernails he picked at the clusters of white-capped pimples on his chin and forehead.

"Your girlfriends ain't comin'," he said. "I seen 'em up by the flume."

"You lie."

Billy grinned. Without a shirt on, his pale torso looked soft and feminine. She tried not to stare at his pointy pink nipples. He looked more like a girl than she did.

"Pool's open," he said. "How come you didn't go? I seen you there another time. You swim good."

She shrugged.

"That friend of yours, the one with the braces? She's a good diver."

"She took lessons."

"I could dive from here." Billy teetered on the edge of the root saddle, giggling.

"You better be careful."

He made a face.

She caught the Tangee bottle in her fist and slipped it into the World War II khaki pack that held lunch.

"Whatcha got?"

Peanut butter and jelly sandwiches, oatmeal cookies and bananas, but it wasn't Billy Phillips's business.

"How long ago did you see 'em?" she asked.

"Couple hours."

"Now I know you're lying, Billy. We were just talking on the phone then."

Billy patted the pocket of his blue jeans. "I got something."

She rolled her eyes.

"Betcha can't guess what."

"Betcha I don't care," she said. "Whatever it is, you probably stole it."

"Takes one to know one."

"What's that supposed to mean?"

"Mrs. Watson at Green's Drug told my ma you and your girlfriends'll probably end up in San Quentin the way you snitch stuff."

"She never."

He laughed.

"Shut up, Billy. You don't even know what you're talking about."

"Don't you want to know what I got?"

Hannah said, sarcastically, "I could not care less."

"What if I said it was something of yours."

"You'd be lying."

"What if I said it was outa your bedroom."

"You've never even been upstairs at my house."

His laugh sounded like he was gagging for air.

She stood up. "You can just show me what it is or you can leave, Billy Phillips. You're not even supposed to be down here."

"It's a free country. Who says I ain't supposed to be down here?"

Hannah had heard her mother say if Mrs. Phillips was smart she'd never let Billy out of her sight. "Are you sure they were going to the flume?"

"That fat one—"

"She is not fat!"

"The one with hair like Nancy in the comics. She had smokes in her pocket."

"You make me sick the way you lie."

Billy looked up into the branches of the oak. "I bet if I was to climb up there, I could jump clear out to where the water's deep."

Hannah buckled her brown leather sandals and gathered up the army pack, slinging it over her shoulder. "You do that and then write me a letter. I'll try to remember to read it." She leaped across the space between her rock and the shore and scrambled up the path.

"Where you going?"

"Crazy," Hannah said. "Wanna come along?"

He grabbed her arm.

"Get your cooties off me!"

He squeezed her wrist so her bones hurt.

"I'm gonna tell."

"Yeah? Well, I could tell your ma some things about you and your girlfriends."

"You better let me go, Billy." Hannah wanted to ask him what he knew but more than that, she wanted to get away from him. Their raised voices had attracted the attention of the crows. A pair scolded them from the branch of a sycamore across the creek.

"I seen you down here actin' like movie stars with your shirts tied up around your chi-chis."

He grabbed at the Debra Paget front of her shirt and yanked it undone. With her free hand, she tried to hold it together. In her ears, a ringing began like the song of the cicadas.

"You're in big trouble now," Hannah said, tugging away from him. "I'll tell my father."

He grabbed for her again; and she kicked his shin and told herself not to be frightened—it was only dumb old Billy Phillips—but panic nipped at her anyway. She kicked again, but he was ready for her and stepped back so she lost her balance and would have fallen if he hadn't caught her wrist again.

"I seen you plenty of times down here when you didn't know I was lookin'."

"You can go to jail for that. That's spying." She snarled the worst thing she could think of. "Commie."

"Look in my pocket. Go ahead. I dare you."

Her fingers were numb and tingled.

"You're hurting me."

"Put your hand in there," he said.

"I don't want to." She began to cry.

Billy snorted. He shook her hard by the arm and she hiccupped. "Put your hand in."

Her fingers touched the frayed edge of his denim pants pocket.

"What you think you're gonna feel? Mr. Pinky?"

"Shut your nasty mouth, Billy."

"You want me to let you go, you gotta . . ."

Hannah squeezed her eyes shut and put her fingers into his pants pocket up to the middle knuckle. She felt something silky.

"Go on."

"My underpants!"

It was one of her Seven Days of the Week panties. Her mother had printed her name on the elastic band with a laundry marker when she went on the day camp overnight. She thought of her mother, hanging out the wash and talking to Mrs. Phillips over the fence, thought of Billy's hands on her shirts and shorts and underpants. She didn't think, she just shoved the panties back at him.

"You stole these off the line, you dirty creep. I'll tell your mother. You're gonna get in so much trouble—"

His hand clamped over her mouth. "Wanna see Mr. Pinky spit up?"

She bit his palm. Surprised, he jerked his hand back. Her first scream rang through the woods.

Up in the field by the old chicken coop, Jeanne and Liz stopped walking. Liz was plump with her dark hair cut in a Dutch-boy style. Jeanne, a full head taller, chewed on a pigtail and talked through a mouthful of braces.

"That was a scream." Jeanne's Ss whistled.

Another scream, like diesel brakes on the long, snaky grade down from the summit; and a murder of crows burst from the canopy, cawing.

"That was Hannah," Liz said.

"Come on," Jeanne cried and ran into the trees at the edge of the ravine; and after a moment, Liz followed, slipping and sliding sideways down a steep trail through scrub oak and manzanita and thickets of pungent bay and eucalyptus trees.

A third scream ripped through the wildwood and then another, deeper.

Jeanne yelled, "We're coming, we're coming!"

At the bottom of the hill they found Hannah in tears, her shirt half open and filthy, leaning against the trunk of an oak tree. She looked at them accusingly.

"He said you guys went to the flume."

"Who?"

"What's the matter with you? Why were you screaming?" Jeanne tossed her braids back. "We were just this minute up by the chicken coop."

"Are you okay?" Liz asked. "Do you need to go to the hospital?"

"He said you had cigarettes." Snot ran out of Hannah's nose and along the line of her lip. She licked it away. "Billy Phillips."

"What about him?"

Hannah pointed down over the root saddle, down the path and onto the Bluegang rocks.

Liz inched her way to the edge of the overhanging roots. "Wow!"

Billy Phillips lay sprawled on his back on a boulder, his head at an odd angle, his arms and legs splayed.

"His mom's our cook," Jeanne said.

"What happened?" Liz asked.

"I . . . pushed him." When Hannah cried, her whole body moved, up and down, pumping up the tears.

Jeanne grabbed her by the shoulders and shook hard.

"Stop being a bully," Liz said. "She's scared and you're makin' it worse." She reached around Hannah and hugged her. "You want us to go home with you so you can tell your mom?"

"Are you stupid? You know her mother, how she gets. And what about the nail polish? That's gotta come off before we—"

Hannah looked down at her toes.

"But he's hurt—" Liz said.

"He isn't hurt, you stupe, he's dead," Jeanne said. "This isn't like a story, in a book, it's real and she's in big trouble."

Hannah sank to the ground and huddled against the trunk of the oak.

"Are you sure?" Liz peered down at the body on the rocks. "There's lots of blood on the rock. We should go down and look, huh?" The way his head was turned, they couldn't see his eyes. "He might be in a coma." Liz had read of such things.

"He had my underpants. They were in his pocket."

"Yuck."

"How'd he get them?" Jeanne asked.

"He stole them, I guess. Off the clothesline."

"Is that why you killed him?"

"I didn't kill him!"

Jeanne peered over the bank another time. "Looks suspicious."

"I didn't mean for him to fall. He was touching me and saying nasty stuff."

"Boy, if this ever gets out, your family, your entire family, is going to be completely ruined. You'll have to leave town."

The three girls looked at each other.

"She didn't mean to do anything. It was an accident, like self-defense."

Jeanne snorted. "It's not like he was trying to kill her." She crouched on the edge of the hillside and picked at a scab on her knee. "This would destroy your parents. Probably ruin your father, you know that, don't you?"

Hannah didn't know anything except that she wanted to be away from Bluegang.

"Him being a minister means his family's got to be perfect or the congregation fires him."

The way Jeanne said it left no room for doubt.

"I just wanted him to stop touching me."

"Your mom'll have a heart attack."

"I'm sure it'll be okay." Liz's round, serious face in its squared-off haircut looked almost adult. "I read in a book where this woman—"

"I told you before, this is real life." Jeanne thought a moment. "When the police find out she was down here alone painting her toes with stolen polish, *in public,* they'll say it's no wonder Billy Phillips acted funny. Haven't you ever heard of girls asking for it?"

"Asking for what?"

"You know."

They looked at each other again. Below them Bluegang sang over rocks and gravel and sand on its way down to the Santa Clara Valley and the San Francisco Bay; and in the deep pools the trout and crawdads dozed in the shadows of boulders and above it all crows perched in the oaks and sycamores and alders and bays, translating everything the girls said into squawks and caws.

Liz said, "I still think we should tell a grown-up."

Jeanne crouched before Hannah. "If you tell someone, it'll be just like on *Gangbusters.* The police'll want to know everything Billy said and what he did and there'll probably be photographers from the paper and no one's gonna care if you're crying or embarrassed or anything like that. I bet you have to stand up and tell everything in court. With a jury and all."

"He said bad things."

"And the judge'll want you to say 'em out loud for the jury."

"But I didn't do anything."

"You expect a jury to believe you? You're a girl."

"What's that got to do with it?"

"The church'll have a big meeting and they'll vote and you'll have to move out of Rinconada. Maybe go someplace like Georgia or Alabama."

Hannah blinked and wiped her tears. A smudge of dirt and snot and tears spread from one cheek, under her nose to the other. "All I want is for it to be like it never happened."

Jeanne thought a moment. "Maybe it can be." She stared down at Billy Phillips. "We could just go away and leave him."

"You don't mean it. You know that's wrong, you know it." Liz's plump cheeks colored. "Besides, dogs might get him. There's coyotes around here . . ."

"Someone'll find him. They'll just think he fell over."

"What about his mother?" Liz said. "She's only got one son."

"What're you talking about her for?" Hannah sprang up in outrage. "What about me? He said he was going to make me do something . . . nasty. I don't care what happens to him. I wish coyotes *would* get him. I wish I could forget about this forever. I wish I could hit my head on the rocks and get amnesia."

"Like *Young Widder Brown*." Liz nodded as if she now understood perfectly.

"Yeah, well, if wishes were fishes our nets would be full. My dad says in real life people don't get amnesia." Jeanne tossed back her braids. "Actions have consequences and he says we have to take what we get and make the best of it." She glanced down at her Mickey Mouse Club watch. "If we're gonna leave we better do it before anyone comes along.

"We'll say you fell. We'll say we went up to the flume and you fell off at that place where the boards are rotten. You could say you saw a snake, a big one and it really scared you and that's how come you were crying. And you could walk through the poison oak on the way home. You'll swell up like I do and no one'll blame you for being miserable."

Half way up the hill Liz stopped and pointed at Hannah's feet. "What about her toenails? Her mom'll see—"

"I don't care!"

Painted toenails and confession magazines and cigarettes were not important anymore. All that mattered was getting away from Bluegang and never coming back. Maybe then Hannah could forget Billy Phillips. Maybe if she lay down in the poison oak and rolled over and over, the poison on the outside would drive out the poison she felt on the inside.

At the top of the hill, Liz and Jeanne put their arms around her in an awkward hug. She wanted to believe Liz when she said, "It'll be okay. It'll be like it never happened."

When Hannah got home her mother was in the kitchen fixing dinner, a pork roast with applesauce and summer squash and bowls of Jell-O chocolate pudding with sprinkles of coconut on the top.

"I'm not hungry," Hannah said on her way across the kitchen.

"You will be by dinnertime. Have you done your chores?"

Clean the upstairs bathroom bowl, scour the sink with Bon Ami, fold the towels in the special way her mother said was the only way to fold towels.

"I will."

"Come back here, Hannah." Mrs. Whittaker laid her palm across Hannah's forehead. She was a tall almost-pretty woman with soft curly hair and wary eyes. "You look flushed. Do you feel all right?"

Her mother worried about polio, all the parents did. If a kid got a fever or felt stiff or had a bad headache, the doctor made a house call that very night. Mostly it was too much sun or sugar, but sometimes it really was polio. The summer before two boys in Hannah's class had been attacked—this was the way grown-ups always spoke of the disease, like it was an enemy soldier. One of the boys would have to live in an iron lung the rest of his life. The other was half-crippled and could never lead a normal life. That was the worst thing about polio, and another thing grown-ups always said: once you got it, you could never lead a normal life.

Hannah hardly thought about polio, or about anything going on in the world. There had been a war in Korea and when grown-ups weren't talking about being "attacked" by polio they worried about the The Bomb and Communism; and it seemed to Hannah that being an adult meant being scared all the time. Hannah mostly thought about school and her friends and how she couldn't wait to be a teenager. That was about as far ahead as her imagination carried her—though occasionally she wondered if anyone would ever want to marry her and what kind of a house she'd live in and what would it be like to do "it." There were so many things more urgent to Hannah than polio and bombs and Communists.

"I want you to take a couple of aspirin and nap a while," Mrs. Whittaker said. She looked Hannah up and down.

Hannah tried to curl her toes under.

"You've been painting your toenails."

Hannah stared at her feet and the ten pink dots.

"Oh, Hannah." Her mother sighed and sat down at the kitchen table. "What am I going to do about you?"

"It's only polish, Mommy. I can take it off."

"I know you can take it off and you will, believe me, you will. That's not the point."

The point, Hannah knew without listening, was that there would be a time and occasions in the future for painting her toes. When she was grown she could paint them green if she wanted to.

But she was too young now. She needed to try to understand how it looked to people to see a little girl with painted toes; she should be aware of the kinds of assumptions people made just on appearances.

"You never want anyone to think you're not a lady, Hannah. A young lady now. A grown lady soon enough."

Hannah wondered if her mother would ever understand that she did not care about being a lady any more than she cared about polio and Communism. She wanted to yell out how much she hated gloves and girdles and those hats with dinky veils. But the way her mother bent her head and passed a hand over her face, the dejected slope of her shoulders, stopped her and filled her with shame. She thought about Billy Phillips lying dead on the rocks at Bluegang and about the terrible things he had said to her, and she had to believe that what her mother had said was true. She had painted her toenails and tied up her Brownie blouse and Billy Phillips . . . assumed. It was her fault. The police would say so, the judge too.

"I'm sorry, Mommy," she said and meant it.

Upstairs as she lay on the bed with a washcloth across her forehead and a glass of cold water—her mother was a loving nurse—Hannah could not stop her mind from going over and over what had happened. And then she remembered her Saturday panties.

Jeanne sat in the kitchen eating the slice of peach cobbler the school cook, Mrs. Phillips, had left for her. It felt very peculiar eating the cobbler and thinking about Mrs. Phillips making the crust and all and her son lying dead, probably. She was glad Mrs. Phillips had gone home for the day and Jeanne didn't have to look at her face and answer her questions about what kind of a day she was having.

She couldn't stop thinking about the way Billy looked lying on the rocks, but instead of trying to put the image out of her mind, she went over every detail. She saw the way his legs were sprawled and the zipper down on his pants. Maybe someone would find him and think he fell when he was peeing. She had watched the boys from her parents' school having pissing contests and could just imagine Billy Phillips arcing his pee out over the oak root saddle like a fountain. When she watched the boys, she never saw their you-knows but she'd once seen her father's when she walked in on him in the bathroom, and he was so stewed he barely saw her. The next day she went to the library after school and looked up penis in a medical book. There were about a dozen pictures of men who had venereal disease and one had the elephant's disease and the underneath part of his thing had swollen up so it looked like he was sitting on a basketball. Jeanne had decided the penis was the ugliest of any body part and she was really glad she didn't have one and that she hadn't seen Billy Phillips's. She finished her cobbler, washed her dish and left the dining hall. Bells rang every hour at Hilltop so she knew it was after three. Too soon to go home.

Jeanne's mother had fallen off the water wagon again so she had a pretty good idea what awaited her at home. Mrs. Hendrickson would be sitting in the little den with a book open on her lap and a tall glass of water beside her. It wasn't really water; it was vodka, only Jeanne wasn't supposed to know that except one time she had sneaked a taste.

Instead of going home she walked around the far side of the rose cloister, across Casabella Road and scrambled up the hill to the flume that had until recently carried water from the reservoir in the Santa Cruz mountains to the town below. She hoisted herself up and walked along until she had a clear view of the Santa Clara Valley. The calendar in the school kitchen had a view of the valley at blossom time: from Rinconada to the San Jose foothills, nothing but prune plums and apricots in bloom. Under the picture it said, "The Valley of Heart's Delight." In August all Jeanne could see were trees and green and a few streets and houses. In the distance—exactly eleven miles from Rinconada according to the sign at the town limits—she made out a half dozen medium-tall buildings in San Jose and beyond the little city the rolling eastern foothills the color of late summer gold.

The hills looked like breasts. Jeanne didn't have any yet. She hadn't started her period even. But she knew it would be soon. She had looked up puberty at the library and found out that the few hairs sprouting under her arms, which she carefully kept cut back with scissors, meant she was on the edge of, just beginning, puberty and pretty soon she would have to buy Kotex and a belt and remember to bring an extra one to school or she'd bleed all over everything like what happened to one of the girls in her class last year.

She would be glad to start her period even if it did mean she couldn't swim or go on hikes or ride her bike for five days out of every month. The sooner she grew up the sooner she could go to Cal and get away from her parents. Her brother Michael had gone to Stanford and Jeanne didn't think she could stand to walk where he had, maybe sit in the exact same classrooms as he.

No one ever said so, but Jeanne knew Michael and his buddies had been drinking when their car hit the abutment on the Bayshore Freeway. Three years had passed since he died and she still felt angry with him because he had broken his word to her. She remembered a time when she was small—only six or seven and he was in high school—and she told him he shouldn't drink beer or he'd end up being like their father. Michael had laughed and promised her he would never do that. The lie was bitter in her memory. Jeanne had vowed she would never be more than a light social drinker. She would never be like her parents.

She lay down on warm boards over the flume and folded her hands behind her head. There were a few clouds, harmless white puffy things in funny shapes. An elephant, a face with a big nose, one looked like a penis. She started thinking about Billy Phillips again. Something dug away at the edge of her memory. She chewed on the end of her braid as she tried to think. It was important, whatever it was.

The evening of the day Billy Phillips died, Liz Shepherd tried to tell her parents what had happened. Twice she went into the study where her parents worked after dinner. She had practiced her speech, not wanting to waste their time. *A bad accident had happened. Hannah got scared. Billy Phillips did something nasty* . . . Her father read in his Eames chair and her mother sat at the desk correcting papers.

"Yes, Liz?" She liked the way her father looked at her over the top of his glasses with his eyebrows raised a little. Long after he was gone, she remembered that look and missed him.

Her mother asked, "Are you ready for bed?"

"Can I talk to you? Both?"

Her father's gray eyes smiled, but her mother said, "Can't it wait, Liz? I'm going to be up late as it is."

The incident at Bluegang lived in her, squirming and twisting and knotting her insides, invading her lungs so she could hardly breathe. She should have insisted. Liz knew it then and she knew it later, but at the time she could not override her mother's chilliness.

"Tomorrow," her father said, still smiling. "We have an appointment for a conversation. You and I."

"At breakfast, Liz," her mother said. And then, "Close the door after you, dear."

That night her mattress had lumps and ridges she had never felt before and the fluff in her pillow bunched up and got hard. Her stomach cramped but three trips to the toilet didn't help. She heard the screams and the crows and imagined Billy Phillips struggling to climb up out of the canyon. But he was dead, wasn't he? She could not recall if his eyes had been open or closed, and the more she thought and worried the more likely it seemed that he wasn't dead at all. There had been a mirror in her pack. She should have gone down and held it in front of his mouth.

On the floor below her turret room she heard her mother and father turn out the lights and close their bedroom door. For a while the sounds of something classical—her parents never listened to music with words—drifted up from below. Usually the sound of that peaceful, boring music put Liz to sleep but not this night. This night she was wide-awake as a coyote prowling backyards in the moonlight, hunting cats. She imagined a coyote sniffing around Billy Phillips's comatose body. Maybe he'd had candy in his pocket and the sugary smell would make the wild dog burrow. She imagined Billy Phillips teetering on the brink of consciousness, trying to breathe, trying to make a sound and the dog shoving at him with its wet nose and its sharp teeth and claws.

Liz sat up and reached for the clock on her bedside table: 11:45. Not so late really. Sometimes she stayed awake until midnight reading and listening to *Sepia Serenade.* But she didn't want to listen or read tonight. She could not get the image of the hungry coyote out of her head and the more she thought, the more sure she was that Billy Phillips was still alive, alive and in pain and struggling helplessly.

She should have checked to see if he was breathing. She should have stood up to Jeanne. She should have insisted that they get help. She should have made her parents listen to her.

She pulled her shorts on over the bottoms of her baby doll pajamas and dragged a shirt out of the pile of dirty clothes on the floor of her closet. She carried her sandals in her hand as she crept down the ladder steps from her room to the second floor of the house. The hall floor creaked under her feet but her parents were sound sleepers and it didn't matter even if they woke up. They'd think she was going to the bathroom again.

Years later she would think about how she ran up Casabella Road that night, about how strong and healthy she had been at twelve and how she had taken stamina and energy for granted. She would remember the security of those times. The confidence. When had rape and abduction and molest entered her consciousness as more than words? They certainly weren't there when she was twelve, not as real events that happened to girls like her.

At the vacant lot, she left the road and sped across the field to the hill down to Bluegang making a wide detour around the spooky chicken coop. She'd come this way a hundred times. She might have been able to find the path through the wildwood by starlight alone but tonight there was a half moon and that was more than enough light for her to see the break in the oaks, the worn away dusty path down the hill. Moonlight came through the canopy in dapples, like stepping-stones. When she was halfway down the hill she saw someone standing in moonlight by the rocks. She froze where she was and squinted. After a second she relaxed.

"Hannah?"

The figure looked up.

"Jeez-Louise, you scared me. What are you doing here?" Liz slipped down the hill sideways and fast, filling her sandals with dirt and throwing up dusty clouds. She skirted the saddle and roots of the great oak and half-slid down to the rocks. She got as close as four feet from Billy Phillips's body and stopped. He lay as they had left him hours before. On his pale flaccid chest his nipples stood erect, frozen forever in a moment of terror. One arm flopped at his side; the other stretched out, palm up.

"He's dead," Hannah said.

His eyes were open.

"My panties—"

Liz had forgotten all about them.

"They have my name on them."

Liz stared at the body on the rocks.

"They should be in his pants pocket."

"You looked?"

Hannah nodded.

"You touched him?"

"His pocket."

"And they aren't there?"

Hannah shook her head. In the moonlight the shadows made her face look long and tired, as if drawn in chalk and charcoal.

Liz thought a moment.

"You probably got confused."

"Where are they then?"

Liz knew where this conversation was going.

"You think they're under him?"

"Maybe," Liz said.

Hannah folded her arms across her chest and shoved her hands into her armpits. After a moment she said, "I can't turn him over." She looked at Liz. "Will you do it?"

"Me?" Her stomach rolled.

"But what if they're under there?"

"You said you saw him put them in his pocket."

"Yeah, and they're not there now. I told you that." She stared at Liz. "Someone took 'em."

"Why?" It was an easier question than *who?*

"You think someone watched? Saw what happened?" Hannah looked back up the dark hillside.

Liz looked up too. She thought about Hilltop School. The boys there often broke school rules and sneaked down to Bluegang to swim and smoke and catch crawdads. For a while they kept a secret clubhouse in a cave farther up. It was possible one of them had watched Hannah shove Billy Phillips off the oak saddle onto the rocks.

"Why would they take your panties?" Liz asked.

Hannah lifted her shoulders and let them drop. She murmured under her breath.

"What?"

"Blackmail?"

Liz started to laugh, looked down at Billy Phillips and stopped herself. "There's no such thing in real life. Only in cities. Only bad people."

"How do you know that?"

Because Liz would rather read novels than play outdoors, because she lived on Casabella Road in Rinconada, California, because she had looked hard enough at the new world for one day.

"I bet Jeanne came down here and got them."

"How come?"

"She probably remembered and—"

"No."

Liz stared at the back of her friend's head. The wild mass of blonde curls and tangles, silver in the moonlight.

"She would have told me. She would have called."

"It's late."

"Not that late. Not even midnight yet."

Jeanne loved the telephone.

"She called me at two in the morning when her dog died."

Liz looked down at Billy Phillips. His right arm lay awkwardly with the palm of his hand facing straight up and the fingers curved toward the calloused palm as if about to grab something. She wished they had at least closed his eyes earlier but it was too late. From books she knew his eyeballs were dry and dusty now. Pretty soon they would start to wrinkle up and fall back into their sockets. His mouth was open, and she remembered a song from third grade: *The worms crawl in, the worms crawl out/ The worms play pinochle on your snout.*

"We gotta go." Liz knew if she didn't get away from Bluegang and fast she would be caught there forever. She imagined Billy Phillips's hand grabbing her ankle, pulling her down to lie beside him. She clambered back up the hill.

Hannah did not move.

"We have to get out of here." Liz held out her hand.

"It could have been a tramp, huh?"

"If you don't come now, I'm leaving you." It wasn't true. She would not abandon her friend, not ever and they both knew it. It was the kind of thing tough-minded Jeanne would say. "Jeanne's got 'em. I bet she shows 'em to you tomorrow."

But she didn't and early next morning when it was reported that two boys with fishing poles had discovered the body and run into town to tell Sheriff Bacci, Hannah Whittaker's Saturday panties were not mentioned.

Florida

"Water walls," Liz Shepherd said. "I'm standing on the balcony and I can't even see the building across the street." She held the cell phone out over the abyss. Fifteen stories down the swimming pool was a blue baguette. "Can you hear it?"

Hannah Tarwater sighed from California. "Bring it with you. Please."

"California's got enough natural disasters without importing hurricanes."

"Is it windy?"

"Mostly just wet." In the bathroom Liz had hung her drenched raincoat over the tub. Her boots were in the tub leaving muddy prints. "We've had more than an inch already."

"Everything's so dry here. I've practically abandoned the garden."

They made trivial conversation; the important questions hanging in the air like wash on a line stretching coast to coast.

"I'll pick you up," Hannah said. "Look for the woman having a hot flash."

"Still?"

"The doctor says a few women have it bad despite hormone replacement. I seem to be one of those."

Liz tried to read Hannah's voice. False cheer? Hard to tell with her, even after decades of friendship.

"The up side is I'm saving a fortune on blusher."

They could go on like this for hours. They could pirouette around and about one hundred subjects, silly and profound, twirl through menopause, family, gardens, clothes and makeup, animals, world affairs, God, and never once come down off their toes long enough to talk about Bluegang. After so many years wasn't there something deeply, even dangerously, strange about this determined silence? Gerard said there was.

More desultory conversation and then Hannah had to go off to a place called Resurrection House where she was a volunteer. Something about crack babies. She was always taking care of someone or something. Mother to the world, that was Hannah. Liz walked back into the hotel room, closed the sliding door, and picked up her room key and purse and went out into the hall and down to the elevator.

The hotel had more amenities than most villages in Belize where Liz and Gerard lived. On a wet and windy night she could buy a wardrobe for a family, liquor and salsa and gourmet sausage, books and souvenirs and laxatives, without ever leaving the hotel's protection. She stepped out of the elevator and fitted her dark glasses over her ears. The fluorescent midday dimmed to a murky twilight. In the drugstore she bought a plastic spray bottle, the kind used to spritz hair or sprinkle clothes back when housewives still stood at ironing boards.

A garish sign in Spanish and English in the window of a hair salon caught her eye: NO APPOINTMENT NECESSARY. Reflected next to it she saw herself. A tallish middle-aged woman, thin and long muscled after a tubby childhood. Her features—even her nose— seemed miniaturized in contrast to her thick dark hair like a chrysanthemum gone wild.

The salon's Cuban manager—her elided accent was easy to identify—warned Liz the electricity might go off at any time. Did she really want to get her hair done in the middle of a hurricane?

"I'm no' workin' by flashligh', ya know."

"I'll risk it."

Now that she had noticed it, her hair seemed like a blind, a bosky hideout, and she couldn't wait to escape it. She was soul-sick of hiding. Besides, a haircut always lifted her spirits, gave her confidence, which she needed for what lay ahead. But later when she stared at her image in the mirror over the bathroom sink the swingy dark hair shaped to the curve of her jaw didn't do it. She felt no more up to what lay ahead than she had an hour earlier though certainly the cut improved her appearance. And at least she wasn't hiding anymore.

She walked out onto the balcony, unscrewed the spritz top of the bottle she had bought and held it out beyond the balcony's shallow overhang. The hard rain almost drove it out of her hand. For several moments she stood with her arm outstretched, getting wet to the shoulder, filling the plastic bottle with rainwater. Afterwards she screwed the top back on and put it in her purse, standing it upright so it wouldn't leak.

She lay on the expanse of bed that faced the window, folded her hands across her stomach and thought about the week ahead.

Liz had been back to Rinconada fewer than a dozen times since college graduation almost thirty years ago. Her parents had retired from the state university system and moved to La Jolla in Southern California where Liz had visited them only twice before they died, within months of each other. But despite distance and time her friendship with Hannah and Jeanne had endured. They met two or three times a year on more neutral territory, spoke often on the phone; and now they had long, searching conversations electronically. Rinconada had become a kind of destination of last resort, a place she went only because she knew it was expected of her occasionally. The town of her childhood was gone—the blossoming trees and one-lane roads, vacant lots alight with wild mustard—smothered in silicon, buried under new houses and chic stores up and down the main street where once she and Hannah and Jeanne had been known by every proprietor.

The Three Musketeers. Battle, Murder and Sudden Death. The Unholy Trinity.

Gone utterly yet she knew that behind and beneath the new architecture, the widened roads, she would encounter the geography of her childhood. A thousand matinees and Friday nights at the movie theater on Santa Cruz Avenue, the high school's wide lawns, Overlook Road where they went to neck and drink beer. And Bluegang. Bluegang right in Hannah's backyard.

Her eyelids grew heavy staring at the steel-colored wall of water, but she did not want to sleep. She sat up and turned on the bedside light. Where was her novel? Was it too early to order room service? Why did they always hide the menu?

She walked back to the window.

Somewhere, between the two buildings across the street, there was a view of the ocean; but she had only glimpsed it for an hour before the rain began. She shouldn't have left Belize at all with a tropical storm in the forecast. This one, Claudette by name, had been promoted to a hurricane while she was at the doctor's office that afternoon. By the time her plane took off tomorrow, the worst would be over.

She liked hurricanes in the same way she half-enjoyed earthquakes when she was a girl and the house shook and grumbled and books fell off shelves in her father's study. There was nothing she could do about natural disasters except live through them. She wasn't expected to take responsibility for anything so she needn't feel like a failure for doing nothing.

If there had been a way to avoid this trip to Rinconada she would have taken almost any detour before confronting the path down the hill through the wildwood's bay trees, gums and oaks to Bluegang. But Gerard had said, "You cannot run the rest of your life." He knew what she was going through. Mornings when he walked into the kitchen and found her seated at the big worktable drinking her third cup of coffee, sitting where she'd planted herself in the middle of the night because dreams had awakened her as they did several times a month, staring at the whorls in the worn surface of the worktable as if by following the lines they would lead her to a place where Bluegang wasn't, on those mornings he saw the struggle knotted in her. He would kiss the top of her head and leave her alone. He cared but what could he do? She might have endured the dreams if they were the only disturbance; but Billy Phillips, his grieving mother, and she and Hannah and Jeanne hugging at the top of the hill had become her daylight companions too. Walking down to the quay to buy fish, Bluegang was with her; browsing at the booksellers the memory came in and all at once she couldn't read, couldn't concentrate, couldn't think of anything but that dead boy.

"Something's eatin' at you," Divina the fortune-teller said. "Best get it out, like a worm, 'fore you waste."

There were details she recalled clearly now, which she did not remember noticing at the time. A line of dirt around Billy Phillips's neck. His mouth open a little, as if death had caught him in midcry. That was what she heard in her dreams. That cry. That plea for help. What she saw was a coyote.

Gerard said it was impossible that she was the only one having a reaction to the Bluegang experience. "You cannot put such things from your mind forever," he told her, sounding very much like his psychiatrist father. Under different circumstances she would have noted this aloud and he would have sputtered defensively. But why tease when she knew he was right? He said Hannah and Jeanne would probably be grateful for the chance to talk about what happened to them. Liz didn't think so, but she'd let him talk her into flying out to California. She had to come to the United States anyway for the other business—which she also didn't want to think about. It was hard work, not thinking.

Had she hit on a new definition of middle age? Was it the time when the secrets of the past and the mistakes of the present came together and made life miserable and sleep impossible? Maybe this was why some people died early. Middle age took so much energy to survive they had none left for old age.

Thursday

Hannah Tarwater woke at dawn when a mockingbird trilled its lyric from the top of the eucalyptus tree outside her bedroom window. Through the half-open shutters she glimpsed another cloudless October sky and sighed. Last year the Santa Clara Valley had less than fifteen inches of rain, the year before just barely twenty. There hadn't been a drop since early March, not even a sprinkle. She thought of Africa, of Oklahoma, of California lifted by the wind and deposited around the world, grit from her own garden drifting down over Mexico.

She reached behind her to the combination radio/tape recorder and pressed the rewind button. When the whirring stopped, she pressed play and after a moment the sound of distant thunder and rain falling on leaves filled the shadowed bedroom. She closed her eyes and dozed a little.

Dan stirred and reached for her. Pulling her back against his chest, he nuzzled the nape of her neck and growled.

From down the hall an alarm's nervy scream was followed by a feeble ding-a-ling as the clock hit the floor.

"Eddie's awake," Hannah said.

They listened for the ritual noise of their teenage son's rising: the bedroom door flung wide, the bathroom door assaulted, the clang of the toilet seat hitting the tank, the torrent of pee. Flush. Clatter.

Dan tightened his embrace, cupping Hannah's breast in his large warm palm. He kissed the nape of her neck.

She asked, "How's your schedule look?"

"Routine. Big bellies and bawling babies."

"Heaven, right?"

"Wrong." He hugged her so tight she gasped. "This is heaven." His hand slipped down the curve of her hip and between her thighs.

She elbowed him gently. "What's going on down there?"

They heard another door open, footsteps, several sharp raps on the bathroom door, and listened to their seventeen-year-old daughter, Ingrid, announce to her younger brother that he would vacate the bathroom instantly if he knew what was fucking good for him.

Dan groaned and rolled onto his back. "That girl's a Marine."

"Hard to believe she was once a sweet-tempered baby. She was so quiet in the mornings, I sometimes forgot we had her. Remember how happy she was to lie in bed and play with her toes?" Hannah felt Dan's body tense but she couldn't stop herself. It was like picking at a wound, taking perverse pleasure in the pain. "And the way she used to talk to herself, making all those little nonsense noises with little question marks at the end? Remember, Dan?"

"Don't start this, Hannah."

"I'm just remembering."

"You know what I mean."

"You loved her."

"I still love her." In the shadowed room his eyes were cobalt blue. "I love Eddie too."

"You loved being a Daddy."

"And I still do."

"I don't mean teenagers. I mean babies and little ones."

Dan groaned again and closed his eyes, cutting the line between them, disconnecting the fuse. Depression dived into bed beside Hannah, ignored Dan and tucked around her in the bedclothes, nuzzled up. Tears sprang to her eyes and she was suddenly furious.

There had been a time when she could wangle anything she wanted out of Dan. When he was a homely, shy and bony boy in medical school Hannah knew he couldn't believe his luck that she loved him. Back then all he wanted to do was make her happy and keep her that way. Now, she asked herself, did he care? Did he give a good goddamn how she felt since time and good bone structure had turned him into a middle-aged hunk? His shyness had become a soft-spoken charm both men and women found attractive; and no one called him bony anymore. God forbid saying he was homely. The cowlicky brown hair, his hawkish nose and square jaw, these made a strong Yankee face, friends told her. *You're so lucky, Hannah. You got one of the good ones.* They didn't know how mulish he could be. Pigheaded and half-blind.

"It's not like we're too old, Dan. I know that's what you think but it isn't true. Fifty isn't the same as it was for our parents. Besides, when I talked to the child advocate she said the court would waive the age requirement under the circumstances."

"Jesus Christ, Hannah, you've been talking to the advocate?" Dan pushed back the bedcovers, swung his legs onto the floor and sat up. "How many times do I have to say it? I don't want another baby."

"But if you'd only come over to Resurrection House and take a look." She knelt on the bed behind him, wrapping her arms around his chest, resting her cheek on his shoulder. Angry still but trying not to be, trying not to let it show. "If you'd just hold her . . ."

"I don't want to hold her. Or see her. I don't even want to hear her name."

Angel.

Dan shrugged free of her, rested his elbows on his knees and held his head in his hands. "You're driving me crazy with this, Hannah. I can't take much more."

Hannah put a plate of cinnamon toast before Eddie, neat little triangles overlapping like shingles. "You can't go to school without breakfast. How do you expect to play football if you don't eat?"

"Maybe he doesn't want to play football."

Ingrid stood by the back door and applied mascara while she waited for her ride. She was a strong athletic girl with her mother's wild blonde hair and her father's deep blue eyes spaced far apart. Healthy skin and perfect teeth, the smile that gleamed: she could have been an ad for the American Dream, Hannah thought. Ingrid would have been identified as American on any street in any foreign port.

Ingrid said, "Maybe he wants to be a computer nerd 'til the day he dies."

"Shut up, Gridlock."

"Of course he wants to play football."

"Ma—"

"Eddie, trust me on this one, okay? Finish your oatmeal and eat your toast. Your body needs fuel. Even to move a joystick. Can I drive my car without gas?"

He stared at the toast as if it were contagious.

Tires crunched on the driveway. Ingrid grabbed her backpack and slung it over her shoulder. "I'm outa here."

Hannah watched her long-legged daughter swing up into the open Jeep's passenger seat and kiss the driver. Mix Hannah Whittaker with Dan Tarwater and you got this lithe and confident, smart-mouthed, sexual creature. Children were the strongest argument she knew of for the existence of God.

"Home by six," Hannah called. "Aunt Liz'll be here."

Ingrid jabbed her thumb in the air as the Jeep roared out the driveway.

Back in the kitchen, Eddie stood in front of the open refrigerator eating leftover pepperoni pizza and feeding the crusts to Cherokee, the family's Irish setter.

Hannah reached around him for the milk and poured a glass. "At least drink this. And sit down. People who eat standing up get high cholesterol."

He took the milk from her, slammed the refrigerator shut with a backward kick and slumped in his chair. In shorts, his bare legs seemed to stretch halfway across the kitchen and the dark hair on them looked coarse as string.

Hannah leaned against the sink and watched him drink. The milky mustache on his upper lip made an unattractive contrast to the one starting to grow there naturally.

"Did you wash your hair this morning?"

"You always ask me that."

"It doesn't look like it."

"I got oily hair, Ma. I can't help it." He muttered *shit* under his breath and she pretended not to hear.

Pick your battles, she thought. Living with teenagers taught a mother to think strategically. Or it should. Lately she couldn't keep from picking at Eddie. Everything about him got under her skin and bit hard.

She squirted scouring glug into the sink and took a brush to the persistent coffee stains. Pregnant with Eddie, the smell of the stuff and its bilious blue-green color was all she needed to make her throw up. Now she enjoyed using it, took satisfaction from watching it foam up and the porcelain sparkle.

I am really pathetic.

She laughed aloud.

"Can you drive me to the card show tomorrow?"

"You've got school."

"If I wait until Saturday all the good deals'll be gone."

"You're not missing school for a sport card show." Sometimes she scrubbed so hard the muscles across her shoulder tightened up like rubber bands on braces. "You've already got thousands of cards."

"They're an investment, Ma."

"That's what you tell me." She rinsed the sink, turned and looked at her son.

He had pimples across his forehead like a relief map of the Sierras. Like his oily hair and incipient mustache and the dark hair on his legs, she disliked this sign of hormone activity. For some reason they put her against him. "Anyway, I'm always at Resurrection House on Fridays." She held out his napkin.

He ignored it and wiped his mouth on his sleeve. "All you ever think of is that place."

"They count on me three days a week, Eddie. I may be a volunteer, but it's still a job." She waved the napkin in front of his face.

He grabbed it and shoved it in a sterling silver ring with his initials on it. "Big deal," he said.

"It *is* a big deal. If it weren't for me and a few other women, the babies at Resurrection House would never get held or talked to or rocked. . . . When Angel came out of the hospital the drugs her mother used had practically destroyed her nervous system. I had to make her a special—"

"Yeah, I know." Eddie headed for the door. "You told me about a million times."

"Do you have your homework?"

"Gee, no, Ma." He grinned and crossed his eyes. "I forgot." His braces gleamed in the sunny kitchen.

For an instant Hannah saw in her tall awkward son a baby boy with a wicked grin, and her heart stopped. She reached out to touch him, but he ducked away just in time.

The phone rang as she was pouring soap in the dishwasher. She picked it up and held the receiver under her chin while she wiped the counters and straightened the bowl of flowers on the butcher block.

"I heard Paco's Jeep." Jeanne Tate lived and worked on the next property up Casabella Road: Hilltop School. She called Hannah almost every morning from her office.

"His name's Frank." Ingrid's beloved had been ordinary Frank Pinelli until last year when he began calling himself Paco. Hannah knew the affectation irritated her illogically. She shouldn't care what the kid called himself so long as he behaved around Ingrid. Maybe that was the problem. She knew he wasn't behaving himself and neither was her daughter and she didn't want to think about it.

"What time's the flight?" Jeanne asked.

"Around noon. I have to check."

"Well, it should be interesting."

"It should be." Hannah imitated her friend's dry tone.

"Almost five years. I checked my old calendar."

"We've seen her plenty in between."

"I think it's a little peculiar. She stays away—makes a point of staying away . . . Now all of a sudden and with no warning, she announces she's coming home. Don't pretend you're not curious."

"Who's pretending?" Hannah knew perhaps too much about Jeanne's life, but about Liz's she didn't know enough. She hadn't even met the Frenchman she lived with. Gerard. Older and the son of a famous psychiatrist. Maybe he didn't really exist. Liz had made him up. She had always hidden herself inside books and imagination. She knew how to lie. They all did.

Jeanne said, "I have to hang up in a minute. Parent interview. New kid all the way from Wisconsin."

"How's Teddy?" Teddy Tate, Doctor of Education, and Jeanne's husband. Together they owned and ran Hilltop School.

"He has a headache. He's lying in bed right now with an ice pack on his forehead."

Hannah couldn't manage to feel sorry for Teddy.

"It's the dry weather. He's had them on and off for weeks. Today's the first time he's stayed down. He's being stoical mostly. Up and around, doing his projects, chasing his tail."

"Better his own, than someone else's." It was a mean thing to say. "Sorry, Jeanne. Tell me about the Wisconsin kid."

"Busy now."

"Jeanne, I said I was sorry."

"I know you're sorry." *Implication: sorry comes easy for you, Hannah Tarwater.* "Are we still on for Saturday night?"

"Did you hear me? I said I was sorry. You know the way I talk, I say—"

"And I assume we're both welcome?"

"Jesus H. Christ."

"Just checking, Hannah. Just checking."

The phone line clicked dead.

Hannah stared at the receiver in her hand.

She was fifty years old; was there any hope at all she would ever learn to keep her mouth shut? She was mad at Jeanne for being touchy. Mad at herself for making a joke at the expense of the esteemed Dr. Theodore Tate—renowned horse's ass. Every woman in town knew he was a lech; was it possible Jeanne didn't? Somehow Hannah had never found the nerve to bring the subject up because since childhood Jeanne had been able to intimidate her. Hannah was also mad at the kids and mad at Dan. Mad at Liz too. She knew how Liz would look when she got off the plane, all strong and striding and confident. Almond-tanned. While every other woman in the English-speaking world fretted about overexposure to the sun's rays, the genes of some long-ago Sephardic ancestor put lucky Liz at low risk for melanoma. This irritated Hannah and she didn't care why because it just did. Thank heaven she didn't have to explain it to anyone because she hadn't a clue. She had always been moody but in the last couple of years she had begun to fear the sunrise, not knowing what darkness awaited her, what illogical anger or resentment. And then someone would tell her how good she looked, and she felt like a cheat. There she was, apparently a woman with her world in full bloom. Fifty and still mostly blonde, her skin good and barely lined, her body straight and slim and strong. A woman to be admired and envied. Right? Hah. God, she hated her moods. The way they stormed in and took over her life. Even as a kid, she could wake up feeling cheery as a red apple and in an hour, for no reason she could ever identify, everything went wormy with anger or dread.

After five years away, Liz had suddenly announced she was coming back to Rinconada for a visit. When Hannah asked her why, she waffled around, wouldn't say anything specific. That vagueness was all it took to set Hannah's imagination going. Liz had cancer, Hannah was sure of it.

"Why are you coming?" Hannah couldn't help asking when Liz called her from Florida to talk about the rain. Liz had laughed.

"Because I love you. And I miss you."

And I have cancer and I'm going to die and I don't want to tell you in a letter. On the phone the word was right there, *cancer,* waving on the line like a pair of blood-red panties.

Hannah walked to the window and stared down the garden to the pool and below it to the barn and paddock and the line of trees that marked the slope leading to the creek. The view further depressed her: autumn flowers sparse and stunted, a film of dust on every leaf and blade of grass. More than three years without a season of generous rain had stressed even the stoic eucalyptus. Against the sky, they drooped in bedraggled silhouettes like a line of dirty mops.

"Please, God, make Liz okay and let her bring the rain with her." Hannah rested her forehead against the window glass. Like the parched earth she felt abandoned, uncared for and depleted.

Reflexively, her mother's critical voice played in her head. *You have so much, Hannah. It's a sin to want more when others have nothing.*

Her father had taught her to make an alphabetical gratitude list. He said it was what he did. *Even a priest in the Episcopal Church has his down days, Hannah. The thing is, not to give in.*

First up: A.

Angel.

I am grateful for Angel because she smiles at me and holds out her arms to me, because there are things I can do for her that no one else can.

B.

Baby.

Angel. I'm grateful for the smell of her skin after I bathe her and for her heart I can hear when I press my ear to her chest.

C: child.

Angel. I am grateful for the soles of her feet and her long toes.

D: daughter.

Angel.

Jeanne Tate's brain was like an old-fashioned oak desk fitted with niches, and drawers and cubbyholes. Moments before a parent conference it was fruitless to wonder about the mystery of Liz's visit or let Hannah irritate her, so she squirreled her questions and feelings away and didn't think about them after that. It was as if they didn't exist at all.

Most of the parents Jeanne Tate interviewed were younger than Simon Weed; and she couldn't always conceal her contempt for the yuppie moms and dads who appeared in her office wearing gold and smelling expensive. Yuppie. The word was dated now—or so Hannah told her every time she used it—but to Jeanne it best described the parents who parked their sleek cars in front of the school and then had to be told to move them to the parking lot behind the gymnasium as if they couldn't read the sign that said NO PARKING, as if they were exempted. Hard bodied, glowing with affluent good health, cell phones ringing, palms stuck to miniature computers that told them where they were supposed to be and why: couldn't they walk the little distance up the hill from the parking lot like everyone else?

Simon Weed might be older than most parents but Teddy had read aloud his credit report. He was another Silicon Valley millionaire, might even be a billionaire, Jeanne supposed. Such numbers became meaningless after a while.

Teddy had already begun to talk about pressing him for a contribution to the computer center Teddy was positive the school needed in order to stay competitive. That's what Teddy did; he asked people for money and they gave it to him. The school was richly endowed because Teddy was a born fund-raiser and funds were everywhere in the Santa Clara valley. Happy Teddy, a boy in a world where every day was payday, where the skies rained dollars, not raindrops.

Weed might not be the easy touch Teddy thought he was. Jeanne saw that he had been cut from a different loaf than the rest of the zillionaires. For one thing, he had followed the signs directly to the lot, and Jeanne liked that. She also liked the paunchiness around his middle and the telltale line bisecting the lenses of his wire-rimmed glasses. Here, for once and all the way from Wisconsin, was an imperfect specimen, a real human being. She felt disposed to like his child as well.

"My company's out here. Since I always seem to be working it makes sense to have Adam here too."

Jeanne agreed and asked him a few more questions about his business—electronic somethings, she had only the vaguest idea what a transistor was, let alone a chip, or this little thing Simon Weed was explaining to her—but she knew how to nod intelligently. She was very good at that.

"Adam was born almost three months premature," Weed said. "He's got a little brain damage—enough so I've learned not to expect too much from him. He can get Cs, no question, but he has to work mighty hard. His last experience was pretty, well, pretty pitiful." He looked guilty. "Public school." Weed slapped his driving gloves across his palm as if he could punish himself.

"If a child works hard at Hilltop," Jeanne said, "his grades will reflect that effort." She heard the pedant in her voice and wished she could take the words back, start again. Speak the truth for once. *We'll take good care of him. He'll be safe here. We'll be kind. You won't regret giving him to Hilltop.*

What came out instead was, "Mr. Weed, I try to be sympathetic with public school educators. They don't have an easy time of it, and sometimes children like Adam fall between the cracks." She cringed at the cliché but kept going. "It's sad how many children miss out in life for that very reason. But that doesn't have to happen to Adam."

"I don't want him coddled."

In Jeanne's experience all parents wanted their children coddled, fussed over, and given special privileges; but she smiled at Simon Weed and pretended she believed him. "Here at Hilltop, Dr. Tate and I believe no good comes of hiding the truth from children, no matter how unpleasant or challenging that truth happens to be." Weed looked agreeable to this so she went on. Words came easily, always. In graduate school when she was writing Teddy's papers for him, she had to stop herself from writing too much.

She said, "In Adam's case, he will have to acknowledge the fact of his brain damage for the rest of his life and age eight isn't too young to start. We won't make excuses for him but we also won't punish him for what is certainly not his fault. We will teach him to make good use of the talents and abilities he has."

"Mrs. Tate, I love my son. But he's . . . sensitive. And losing his mother like he did last year, well, he's pulled back from me. I can't tell what he's thinking anymore. And he spends too much time alone. He has a way of . . . disappearing, sometimes for hours at a time. What I'm trying to say is, he needs a lot of attention." Simon Weed took off his glasses and rubbed the bridge of his nose. "He's never been a gregarious child, but he was close to his mother. She taught him to ride. He wasn't very good at it, but it gave him pleasure. Then he had to be the one to find her . . ."

"Perhaps you should tell me what happened." Jeanne resisted a strong temptation to reach across the desk and touch his hand.

Simon Weed looked startled by her request and she thought for a moment that he would refuse. "He went down to saddle his mare." He spoke so softly Jeanne could barely hear him. "She was right there in the barn, hanging from a crossbeam."

Jeanne imagined a horse hanging from the barn roof and scolded herself for being perverse.

"Afterwards, I tried to get him to talk about it, but he clammed up. Sometimes I wonder if he's forgotten it completely."

Jeanne looked at the picture of Adam Weed on her computer screen. A boy with a pinched face and dull eyes separated by two deep vertical creases. She sensed the effort it took for him to look out at the world and not inward to his pain, to keep from imploding, from shrinking to a dot no larger than a period on a page.

"Children forget in order to protect themselves. It's actually very healthy."

"But he's got to remember sooner or later, doesn't he? I don't want him to grow up twisted, Mrs. Tate. When I die, he'll be a rich man no matter how well he does in school. But I want him to have a life . . ."

"And there's no reason he can't have a good one. None at all."

Simon Weed shifted in his chair. "How does a father know he's doing the right thing? I told him we were coming here and he cried. He begged to stay with me." He shifted again, his discomfort so intense Jeanne felt it come across the desk at her like a blast of heat. "I think he might need . . ." Weed struggled with the word, "psychiatric help."

Jeanne didn't approve of psychiatrists, particularly not for children, although she knew this was an old-fashioned attitude, one she had inherited from her father along with the rest of the Hilltop Method. She remembered him saying once that no child had problems so severe they couldn't be cured with fairness and discipline. Over the years, a handful of troubled boys had tested Jeanne, but never enough to tempt her away from her father's opinion.

"Give Adam a little time and he'll find his place at Hilltop. He'll be in the junior dorm, sharing a room with one other boy. His housemother is Mrs. White. Sooner or later, he'll open his heart to her. All the boys confide their problems to Edith. I'm tempted to do it myself." Jeanne laughed to dispel any suggestion that she might actually have problems. "We also have a brother system at Hilltop. Every boy in primary has a big brother assigned to him. This is someone he can go to when he needs help with his homework or if he thinks another boy's bullying him or if he's just lonesome for home. I've chosen Robby McFadden to be Adam's big brother. This afternoon Robby will introduce your son around, give him a tour of the campus, find him a gym locker—"

"I'd feel better if you—"

"Tomorrow I'll get acquainted with Adam myself. I promise." Jeanne stood up and held out her hand. "Trust me, Mr. Weed, your son will do well at Hilltop. This is a very special place."

He placed his chair back against the wall with an orderliness that delighted Jeanne's heart.

"I'll be flying between San Francisco and Tokyo from now until Christmas." He handed Jeanne his business card. "You can always reach me at that number. If I'm not available, my secretary can find me. I'll tell her to put through any calls from you right away."

He stopped and pointed out the window at three boys lugging buckets across the front lawn for the school. "What are they doing?"

Jeanne walked around her desk and stood beside him. "We've been in a drought for the last three years, and we've learned to save water any way we can. Last year we issued a bucket for every shower stall and the boys fill them with the warm-up water. Rather than waste that water letting it run down the drain, the boys are assigned particular plants around the school to water. Thanks to them, the basic shrubbery and the rose cloister that was here when my parents bought the school have never looked better."

She saw that Simon Weed approved of this.

"It's another example of the Hilltop Method, Mr. Weed. Facing facts and making the best of reality whether it's pleasant or not."

Simon Weed looked at her with admiration.

Jeanne felt herself blush and became suddenly shy. "Credit my father and husband. Most of the good ideas come from them."

"I was hoping I could meet Dr. Tate."

"He'll be sorry to have missed you."

Simon Weed pointed to the framed diploma on the wall between the window and the office door. "You went to graduate school at Columbia, I see."

"In the dark ages, yes."

"My wife was there too."

A frisson of anxiety tightened Jeanne's back.

"Journalism."

"It's a wonderful department," she said, moving toward the door.

"I knew your husband had a Ph.D. but I didn't know you did. Was that mentioned in the brochure?"

"No," Jeanne said. She put her hand on his shoulder, eased him out of the office. "A printer's error. We didn't catch it in time."

In the hall Simon Weed said, "I'll miss him."

Jeanne saw that he meant it, and knew that despite his disadvantages, Adam Weed was a fortunate child. So many of the parents who brought their boys to Hilltop couldn't wait to be rid of them and back to their own lives. Jeanne watched these parents as they left her office. She watched them through the window, climbing into their illegally parked BMWs and Land Rovers, speaking into cell phones, poking at their small computers.

"I'll call you," she said. "Try not to worry."

She watched him walk away and returned to her office. She saw he had left his driving gloves on her desk. Absently, she slipped the gloves on and held her hands before her, turning them slowly palm to back to palm again. She held them to her face and inhaled the smell of leather and worn-in dirt and Simon Weed. She imagined they were still warm from his hands.

In the bottom drawer of her bedside table, Jeanne kept another pair of gloves wrapped in tissue paper and tied with a length of frayed pink hair ribbon. Those gloves were not expensive like Simon Weed's, not hand stitched of supple leather, not meant for driving. They had a yellowed fleece lining and were intended to warm a young man's hands on a frigid Berkeley afternoon when a wet wind from the northwest scoured the streets. Across the leather palms dark stains marked the leather leash of a yellow Lab, all muscle and high spirits and determined to drag the man—a graduate student—down the street to the patch of green the neighborhood called a park.

Jeanne had traced her son on-line and been surprised by how easy it was to run down the whereabouts of an adopted child. Perhaps if she had known how quickly and almost casually this could be accomplished with the help of the Internet, she would not have had the courage to try. But on a rainy afternoon, working late and finding it impossible to concentrate on the monthly report to the board, she had finally done what had occurred to her a hundred times before. Why had she called up her search engine and typed in *adoption search* on that particular day? Maybe she had been feeling lonely or nostalgic or regretful. Maybe Teddy had been more difficult than usual. She could not remember; it didn't matter. She had done it, begun the process; and Jeanne rarely stopped something once she'd started it. The search for her son became her own exciting secret.

To find him so close, fifty miles to the north, practically a neighbor . . . She had not been sure what she felt then. Gladness, relief, a new dread to add to the others?

For a time it had been possible to put James, now called Mark, out of her mind. She had that kind of mind; it did as it was told. But she dreamed of him sometimes and there were boys at Hilltop whose names and faces tweaked her memory. According to the tracer's report he had graduated from NYU and become a graduate student at UC. But what did he study? And what kind of personality did he have? Was he funny, impatient, thoughtful? The strong silent type or garrulous and talkative? Not married, the report said. But maybe in love? Gay or straight?

One afternoon she told Teddy she had an appointment in San Jose and left school early. She drove to Berkeley and parked outside the tiny bungalow where her son lived. She had no particular intention, and in this her behavior was so completely unlike her that if Hannah or Liz had heard about it they would have declared the story fiction. Logical Jeanne. Orderly Jeanne. Jeanne who would not tolerate loose ends or indecision parked her car in front of the house and turned off the ignition. She wrapped herself in her heavy wool coat and scrunched down behind the wheel like a private investigator in a film noir. She found the NPR affiliate station but turned it off after a few minutes. The talk intruded. If I am going to do something as peculiar and risky as this, she thought, I want to do it with full concentration.

After a while a man came out of the house leading a dog on a leash. He wore a navy blue parka and a black watch cap tugged down to cover his ears. Absolutely, this was her son. The glimpse she had of his handsome profile was like sighting Teddy at twenty. If someone had told her this was not her James she would have fought to prove it was.

She uttered a choking cry and began to weep.

The Lab tugged on the leash like a comic book dog, dragging its complaining, laughing master after him. The sound of the young man's voice thrilled Jeanne. He turned into the park. She wiped her eyes, got out of the car and followed him. It was cold. Her damp face stung and her hands trembled. She shoved them deep in the pockets of her coat.

The park had a jungle gym, a soggy sandbox, a few benches and a picnic table with an overturned trash can beside it. James/Mark unhooked the Lab's leash. The dog took off after the birds pecking at the trash can, got distracted and started digging in the trash himself.

"Rontu," James/Mark called. "Get outa there."

Rontu ignored him and grabbed a fried chicken box and shook it, scattering bones and papers around.

"Jesus Christ," the young man yelled. "Goddamn son of a bitch. Sit, Rontu, goddamn sit!"

The dog looked up and dutifully sat, head hung low. James/Mark laughed and rubbed its ears, murmuring something. Jeanne couldn't hear him; but she knew he was saying, "Good dog, good dog."

James/Mark leashed the dog again, took a plastic bag from his pocket and removed his gloves, tossed them on the picnic table. With his hand in the plastic bag he picked up the mess Rontu had made. Neat, Jeanne thought. And responsible. *My son.* She thought her chest might burst with pleasure. She wanted to help him but the fear he would recognize her held her back. Was there a son and mother recognition gene? What would she say? How would she explain? If he knew the true story he would never forgive her.

James/Mark righted the trash can and turned away, walking toward the far side of the park. Jeanne thought it would look too obvious if she followed him. He would turn and look closely at her and then, the possibility of recognition. She watched his straight back and long strides all the way across the park. When he turned the corner out of sight, she sat down at the picnic table and held her face in her hands.

This was her son and Teddy's. And she had been right to give him up. She could see immediately that his adopted parents had done a fine job of raising him. Look how wonderfully well he had turned out: an intelligent and responsible man with a sense of humor.

Better than we could have done.

Beside her elbow, his gloves. She picked them up and looked across the park where she had hoped to see him return. If he did she would say: *You left your gloves.* And he would grin and say, *Yeah, thanks.* No, he might see the similarity in their eyes or high cheekbones. Worse, he could recall her voice from his infancy. She had sung him a lullaby her grandmother taught her: *Stay little wave, stay little wave, Shy one stay on the shore.*

She slipped her hands inside the gloves and walked back to the car wearing them and crossed the street to lay them on the bungalow's square porch where he would find them. But at the edge of the ragged lawn she stopped, turned back to the car and drove home.

It wasn't stealing. James/Mark was her son, her blood. And Jeanne had always appropriated items belonging to the people she cared about. Cuff links from her father's dresser. A neatly folded, embroidered handkerchief from her mother's purse. Not to use, to hoard and hide. When Hannah's daughter, Ingrid, was born Jeanne took a little ribbon headband, pink and pale yellow, the quintessence of femininity for a bald-headed baby girl. A frivolous thing. But it had relieved the anger and envy Jeanne felt whenever she thought of Hannah and her newborn.

Now she touched her cheek with Simon Weed's gloves. The leather was soft as baby skin. She felt no envy for Simon Weed. Nothing about him made her angry, nor did she want power over him. Jeanne didn't know why she wanted his gloves but it was not in her character to dissect and microanalyze motives. She wanted them. She would put them in her desk where she could sometimes take them out and slip them on. If he came back for them they would be there, but he was a rich man. A pair of worn gloves meant nothing to him.

Jeanne went into the office adjoining hers and told the school secretary, Ann Vickery, that she was going home before taking her lunch with the boys in the dining hall.

"Simon Weed forgot his gloves," she said. "They're in my top drawer if he calls."

Teddy refused to eat the school food but the presence of one or the other of them was expected in the dining room. Today was Thursday; she was scheduled to sit with the eight-year-olds and watch them drip ketchup down their chins. She left the administration building by a side door.

Though larger now, with a new gymnasium and outdoor amphitheater, Hilltop School was not much changed from the days when Jeanne and Liz and Hannah—nine or ten at the time—hid in the bushes outside the dorms and spied on the boys undressing. Or when, a few years later, they shared a crush on a senior-school boy whose father was a famous movie star. Jeanne's parents, Wade and Vera Hendrickson, had bought the land and buildings during the war from a departing religious order for—as Jeanne's father always said with smirky cleverness—a hymn. The old buildings were of stone and stucco with heavy tile roofs; and though Hilltop was decidedly nondenominational, an atmosphere of latent Romanism clung to the place in the form of religious arcana cut in the arches and windows and doors of the older buildings. Here and there along the paths that unified the forty-acre grounds, stone slabs had been sunk between the flagstones and etched with pious Latin phrases. What had once been a chapel was now called simply the Meeting House, but the stained glass windows and carved Stations of the Cross contradicted the plain Yankee name.

Jeanne remembered Hilltop's lean years when her parents taught every subject themselves and borrowed money to keep the school open. Nowadays Jeanne turned away dozens of prospective students for lack of space. According to the Hilltop Method, small classes were essential to good schooling—as were facing facts, standards of responsibility, and teaching boys to start at the beginning and move forward logically, step by step, sticking to the task until completed. A strong work ethic, Wade Hendrickson had often said, was more important than a college education.

It wasn't a sophisticated pedagogical theory; in the Sixties and Seventies it had been derided as backward and stifling. But with the back-to-basics movement, Hilltop had actually become trendy. It didn't hurt that Hilltop had the test scores and bank balance to prove its method worked.

Jeanne crossed the yellowed lawn to the flagstone path that entered the walled rose garden and divided the one hundred plants into concentric circles, a kind of simple labyrinth where once, Jeanne supposed, the nuns in their floating robes had strolled, whispering their rosaries. They had left behind, trapped within the walls, a meditative calm. In the midst of the garden crouched a lion-footed stone bench. She stopped beside it a moment and inhaled the fragrance of the blooms. *Ragged Robin, Eglantine, Damask Rose, Etoile d'Hollande*: she loved the old-fashioned names and blowsy cabbage blossoms that reminded her of buxom old ladies in silk. The roses in the cloister bloomed while the grass outside the wall yellowed and died.

In a photo taken when she was six or seven, still in pigtails, of course, and a dress with puffed sleeves—didn't all little-girl dresses have puffed sleeves in those days?—her brother Michael stands at her side, his hand on her shoulder. He is so much taller than she, her head only reaches the middle of his chest.

Jeanne clearly remembered the occasion of the photo. Seconds before her father snapped it, she had been whining because her organdy dress scratched her arms and neck. The old black-and-white photo still shows, just above Jeanne's smile, the slight shadow on one cheek where her mother slapped her.

Teddy and Jeanne's home lay beyond the rose garden and through a hedge of pink oleander bushes that loved the drought. The single story frame-and-stucco house had been designed in what used to be called California ranch style. Judging from the French chateaux and Elizabethan fortresses now being built in the hills around Rinconada, the California ranch style was currently out of favor. But Jeanne loved the house and could walk through it blindfolded, for apart from college and the years when she and Teddy were in Manhattan, this house with its deep-silled, shuttered windows and cool rooms was the only one she had ever lived in. She walked toward the sound of a television blaring.

On the bed, Teddy Tate silenced the TV with the remote.

"If your head hurts, you shouldn't watch the set. It's a strain on your eyes." Jeanne went into the bathroom and came out brushing her shoulder length brown hair. "I think you should see a doctor. There's medicine for a sinus condition." She twisted her hair into a knot at the nape of her neck.

"You look like a schoolmarm," Teddy said.

"That's what I am."

"Wear your contacts."

"The air's too dry."

"You're a good-looking woman, Jeanne. Why don't you do something with yourself?"

Jeanne went back into the bathroom and wiped down the counter and basin.

Teddy called from the bedroom, "Have you seen my Waterman?"

"You shouldn't be straining your eyes by writing."

"That pen cost more than two hundred dollars."

"Don't lie flat. It'll make the sinuses worse. You need extra pillows."

"I haven't seen it since last week."

"Close your eyes."

"You took the audiotapes."

"I'm returning them to the library this afternoon when I take the littlies in the van." She slipped a twisty around her hair and made a bun tight as a fist. "You could listen to music. Would you like me to find the classical station for you?"

Teddy mumbled that he would and closed his eyes.

Jeanne thought it was unfair of the Universe that men aged so handsomely. At fifty-two Teddy's polished, preppy good looks had hardened, lost the sweetness that was there when he was young. Now he was just plain turn-around-and-gawk handsome. His strong chin and nose gave him the look of a man of character, someone to be relied upon in a pinch or a crisis. This no longer struck her as ironic.

She turned the radio dial. "I met Simon Weed this morning. He seems like a nice man. He told me his wife committed suicide. Hanged herself in the barn and the boy found her."

"Another traumatized child." Teddy groaned. "Lucky Hilltop School."

"He noticed my diploma."

"So? It's on the wall." The music was Wagner. "Turn it down, Jeanne. I can't take Valhalla this morning."

She looked at the telephone answering machine on the table next to the radio. She enjoyed talking on the phone, enjoyed being free to speak without being observed. But she resented the demands of the answering machine and would sometimes let twenty calls accumulate before pressing the play button. In her otherwise responsible personality, this was an aberration about which she could seem to do nothing. Did it signal something fundamentally unsound in her? A flaw she had been unable to eradicate?

Only one call today.

"Your sainted friend." Teddy had never liked Hannah.

"What did she want?"

"I didn't talk to her, Jeanne."

"Did she leave a message?"

"I don't know why we have an answering machine if you won't use it."

Jeanne touched the play button. The machine whirred and clicked and Hannah's deep voice came over the line.

"Come over after school, okay?"

Jeanne pressed rewind.

Teddy thumbed the hollows on either side of the bridge of his nose. "I don't think I'm going to make it to that building committee meeting, Jeanne. You're going to have to do it."

"Teddy, I haven't seen Liz—"

"Go tonight."

"It's board Thursday."

"The building committee won't go past five."

"I promised Edith White I'd listen to the problems the housekeeping staff's having. Those old bathrooms in Senior House are going to have to be replaced. The maids are sick of the mess. The least we can do is listen to their complaints. You want to do that for me?"

"You're the one who speaks Spanish." Teddy sat forward and Jeanne slipped a second pillow behind his head. "Besides, if they don't like the work, they can quit. It's not like there's a shortage of wetbacks."

Jeanne looked at her husband a long moment.

"Sorry, old girl," he said. "It's this headache."

She returned to the dressing room; and, despite the drought, ran the cold water a few seconds and splashed her face until it tingled. She patted it dry and applied a light sheen of lipstick to her wide mouth. She noted that the lines on either side, the parentheses, were deepening and so were those between her green eyes—eyes like peeled grapes, her brother used to tease. She must frown more than she realized. A little foundation might conceal them but lipstick was the only makeup she wore. When she was a teenager, she'd come home with five dollars' worth of Tangee cosmetics, and her mother's inebriated scolding still rang in her mind. *A woman demeans her sex when she paints her face.*

In the bedroom again she asked Teddy, "So what are your plans?"

"If I can get up later, I will. That's about the best I can promise."

Jeanne stood at the door. "I'll bring you back some tapes from the library."

"You're a saint, Jeanne. What would I do without you?"

In the weeks following Billy Phillips's funeral Liz had thought of Bluegang hundreds of times; in a way he was always in her mind in the same way she was always breathing whether she thought about it or not. She had told herself that what happened at Bluegang was an accident, a terrible misstep; and it wasn't her fault, it was Hannah who pushed him and Jeanne who insisted they say nothing. But that was where her memory came unhinged and sometimes Liz felt like she had pushed Billy Phillips down onto the rocks herself.

Time's passage rounded off the sharp angles of memory but it didn't sink to the bottom of her consciousness, it never eroded. It was there like a stone in the shoe, a toothache, cramps, but she learned to ignore it. In time she became good at this—especially after she turned thirteen and got into trouble for smoking down by the old henhouse and kissing Eric Margolis behind the youth center. Her life crowded with new people and ideas and things she knew she should not do—but did anyway. Pretty soon she was kissing a lot of boys and her parents didn't seem to notice so she kept on doing it. Making good grades: that was all that mattered to them. In history she and Jeanne and Hannah read about the Nonintercourse Act, collapsed in giggles, and got sent to detention.

But even when she wasn't thinking of him, Billy Phillips was with Liz, and she was pretty sure it was the same for Hannah and Jeanne because sometimes in the middle of an ordinary moment— sitting on the swings at the park, drinking Cokes at the Burger Pit—Hannah's expression suddenly turned grave and vacant. Her body stayed where it was and she kept on talking, but it was obvious that in her mind she was somewhere else and Liz knew where. It was the same with Jeanne, even tough-minded Jeanne.

The worst of it was, there was nowhere to hide from the memory of what they had done. Or not done. Liz just wasn't sure about guilt and innocence anymore. Reading was no distraction, not even a really good novel like *Marjorie Morningstar.* And in the middle of a movie she would start to see things on the screen that she knew weren't really there. A boy tumbling down a hill. A coyote snuffling around a body.

For a while she had been desperate to talk about it, but when she did, Hannah looked at her like she'd suddenly begun to speak Swahili.

Once Liz started up, "You know what happened at Bluegang? . . ." The three of them had been sitting on the edge of the fishpond in front of the high school wearing their roller skates. It was autumn and still warm. They wore shorts and cotton blouses. "Do you guys ever think? . . ."

As if they were dancers set to move on cue, Hannah and Jeanne had stood up and skated away without glancing back at her. Liz could not forget the sight of their narrow backs and swinging shoulders moving farther and farther away, leaving her behind.

After that she kept her mouth shut and gradually she thought less about Bluegang and more about school and boys and clothes. A hundred memories a day became a dozen and then once or twice a week, and after that she went for long stretches without remembering. Occasionally she wondered if the process of forgetting was the same for her friends and supposed it must be, but she knew if she asked them they would skate away again. And what if they stayed away?

They were teenagers and life irresistibly happened all around them constantly, a dance they had to be half-dead not to join in. The arms of the world had opened up and swept them into lives where everything was a challenge or an adventure or a puzzle. Once in a while Liz saw old Mrs. Phillips and Bluegang came back to her. At such times she thought less of Billy's death than she did of her failure to do the right thing. When her parents asked *Can we depend on you, Liz?* she always said they could but knew it was a lie.

High school was a ball: high grades and student body offices, kissing Mario Bacci, smoking Marlboros in the upstairs girls' bathroom, breaking rules when they could and just for the fun of it. They went to college—seventy-eight percent of the Rinconada graduating class did. Hannah married a doctor and bought a house on Casabella Road and raised two children. Jeanne married her college sweetheart and made a national reputation as an educator. And Liz grew up and led a disjointed peripatetic life and kept on breaking rules in small ways. She became a successful translator of modestly successful books and lived in France, as she had always wanted. She never spoke of Bluegang to anyone until the night, decades afterwards, when she woke, crying, because a coyote had Billy Phillips's icy hand in its mouth and then it was her ankle it held and she couldn't break away or cry for help because she couldn't breathe.

As the flight from Miami taxied into place at San Jose Airport, Liz rewound the tape she had been listening to—Gregorian chants, soothing as tranquilizers. She slipped the Walkman into her oversized canvas tote, stood and inched her way down the aisle toward the exit.

She felt her airport demeanor take possession: a longer stride and straighter back, prouder head, expression not excited, never excited, but anticipatory, expectant, busy-busy-busy. She knew the other passengers and the people lined up at the airport windows watched her as she strode across the tarmac between the plane and the terminal. Gerard said they watched because she looked like

Someone. A woman just back from someplace thrilling, en route to somewhere even better. Though no longer young and never beautiful—her nose was long, a little hooked, and her forehead too high— she attracted more attention now than ever. Gerard said she carried herself with distinction—which was also pretty amusing since she had never felt in the least distinctive. If she had, she would not have had to create her airport personality in the first place.

Once in Heathrow Airport a teenaged girl had asked for her autograph. She signed Amelia Earhart and the girl had said, "I just love your show."

Hannah waited behind the barrier. Her round youthful face beamed at Liz through the glass, glowing with health and excitement. She wore a long cotton skirt and a roomy Shaker sweater the color of orange sherbet and her feet were laced into leather espadrilles. A thick braid overpowered her willful silver blond hair and hung to the middle of her back. Exotic bead and turquoise earrings dangled halfway to her shoulders. She looked like a rich grown-up hippie.

They waved, ran and fell into each other's arms. Let's not talk, Liz thought. Let's not spoil this.

In the car there was suddenly too much to say and no easy place to start so Liz filled up the space with talk about the guest house in Belize, her friends, the way she and Gerard lived.

"While I'm gone he's starting the new kitchen and that'll make life much easier. Trying to feed a dozen hungry tourists breakfast and dinner on a gas stove with two burners is a nightmare. When I get back there'll be a new Aga stove—new to us, anyway; actually we're buying it from a pair of old British queens; one of them's sick so they've decided to go back to England. And while I was in Miami I ordered a double refrigerator with a huge freezer. Plus a bunch of modular cupboards and some Formica. Bright red, can you believe that? Remember when the stuff only came in speckled and sand? God willing it all gets on the right ship and someone finds the energy to unload it." She paused for breath. "You and Dan'll have to quit making excuses and come down before we get too fashionable. Gerard can take you into the rain forest and there's Mayan ruins." She must have said all this before on the phone or e-mail. The important thing was to avoid empty air. "It's super down there, Hannah. In the morning everything drips and the sound of the place is primeval."

"And Gerard? He's well?"

Liz took a photo from her purse and held it out. "I don't think you've seen this one." It showed a tall, dark man, with heavy eyes, strong and vigorous in his sixties, dressed in bush shirt and shorts.

"A hero for the new age," Hannah said. "The Great White Environmentalist." She grinned. "Cool."

Hannah jerked the Volvo into the fast lane and Liz pressed her feet into the floorboards as if the car had dual controls like the one they'd all learned to drive on in Driver Education. Hannah had always been a kind of crazy driver given to last minute turns and tailgating. Liz felt the sonar beep of a headache behind her ears.

In the Santa Clara valley, five years' absence meant a century of change. Going way back she remembered a time when orchards, not silicon, supported the valley. A time when the fruity summer air sang with susurration of bees and yellow jackets and everyone got stung and bit and knew to jump into an irrigation ditch if a swarm attacked. Today there were freeways where she remembered tacky apartments, malls like castle complexes, and cars, thousands of cars. It was worse than Miami. Overhead the sky was yellow.

Smaze, Hannah called it. "The drought just makes it worse." The interior of the Volvo was hot and close and Liz rolled the window down a little. The noise of engines and tires on asphalt was unpleasant.

"I can't hear you over the racket."

"What about air conditioning?"

"I am permanently and politically opposed to it," Hannah said and grinned. "If you have time, I want you to visit Resurrection House with me. There's one little baby, her name is Angel . . ."

"You haven't changed, Hannah. Always a cause. Always the life saver. Vietnam protests, abused animals—"

"I have changed," Hannah snapped. "Don't patronize me because I haven't had your big exciting life. What I do at Resurrection House is very important."

Shit.

Coming home was like swimming in a strange sea. Below the surface there were thickets of tangled seaweed. "But you've got to admit there was a time—" Liz giggled and covered her mouth with her hand. "Remember when you decided it was cruel of Mr. Silva to keep his Japanese quail in that little cage?"

"He was such a prick. He wanted to send me to Juvie."

They were eleven and in school they read about the cannibalism of overcrowded, stressed-out rats.

"I couldn't stop thinking of those pretty birds all pecking each other to death." Hannah laughed. "How was I to know they were worth two hundred bucks each. They just looked like birds to me."

She turned off the freeway at Lark Avenue. The exit ran through a new housing development built in an old prune orchard. The homes were two- and three-story affairs with triple garages and massive brick and stone facades crowded onto lots suited to buildings half their size.

"So much tack, so little time," Liz said.

Hannah braked and idled in a line of cars waiting for a landscape truck to unload a twenty-foot liquid ambar. "Gail Bacci says they're going for more than a million each."

Someone in the line of cars banged on his horn.

"Jerk," Hannah said.

"Who buys them?"

"I don't know. Computer people, I guess. They're like an invading species. We never mix. We're the old-timers. The newcomers think we're frumpy. All they want to do is buy our houses, tear them down and build more of those things." The line of cars moved forward. "You're looking at the new Rinconada. Kids in Ingrid's class drive Lexus SUVs."

"Are they nice kids?"

"Jesus, who knows. The school's got more castes than India. And it's huge. Not like it was for us, the way we knew everyone."

"My parents would have hated it."

Hannah looked at Liz and shook her head. "Your parents wouldn't have noticed."

A stinging wind blew through Liz's mind, plucking the strings of her headache.

When she was seven, she spent the night at Hannah's house for the first time. On the twin beds in Hannah's bedroom with its dormer windows and walk-in closet, the blue satin coverlets had been turned down and the pillows plumped. Liz saw Hannah's sprigged flannel nightie laid across the blankets like a patch of garden and compared it to her own pj's, buttoned up with safety pins. From the distance of several decades the disregard of her distracted intellectual parents still had power to tear her heart. It shouldn't matter anymore, she told herself, but it did.

"It's all so clear in my mind, like it was yesterday . . ." *Say it.* "Remember Bluegang?"

Hannah shuddered. "It's changed too, big time. If I didn't love my house and if the wildwood weren't there like a barrier, I'd move across town. Gail says there are homeless people living in those caves up beyond the swimming hole. There's trash all around and sewage too, I suppose. You'd probably die if you drank the water."

Talk, talk, talk. Saying nothing, nothing, nothing.

Remember Bluegang?

"Gail's always after me to join the group she's organized to clean it up, but I just don't have the time. You know? I give her a big check every year but there's only so much a person can do." Hannah braked and turned into a parking lot.

Liz read the sign painted on the building in front of them: Bacci's Italian Market. In cement planters between parking places, purple and gold lantana drooped under the midday sun. The fragrance of salami, briny olives and baking bread came through the car window.

Hannah switched off the ignition and reached into the backseat for her straw purse. "You want to come in? It'd tickle Mario to see you. He and Gail are coming to dinner Saturday if you'd rather not."

"I'll stay."

Liz put her head back and closed her eyes. Fatigue and apprehension lay on her eyelids like iron coins.

"Were you asleep?" Hannah asked as she opened the door fifteen minutes later. "Do you feel okay?"

"I'm fine." Liz poked in the brown paper bags. "What did you buy me?"

"Salami. Biscotti with walnuts and anise dipped in chocolate. Mindy Ryder makes it."

"What's she doing with herself?"

"That's probably not a good question to ask." They laughed. "She's coming on Saturday too so you can ask her yourself." Hannah pulled out onto Rinconada's main street lined with specialty shops and boutiques with clever names: Bearly Yours, Heavenly Heels.

Liz said, "I was in love with him once. Mario."

"When's the last time you saw him?"

"Fifteenth reunion, I think. It was before I met Gerard."

"Well, let me prepare you. The Italian stallion has eaten a bit too much of his own spaghetti." The car in front stopped suddenly. "Shit."

Liz double-checked her seat belt.

"Gail's made a fortune selling real estate to half of Silicon Valley and they all drive down Santa Cruz Avenue cruising the shops. Jeanne says when Judgment Day comes, Gail's going to burn in hell for what she's done to this town."

"How is Jeanne anyway? Her letters don't give much away."

Hannah drummed her fingers on the steering wheel as they waited for traffic to clear. "She'd say the same of yours."

"Lord, Hannah, I'm an open book."

Hannah's gaze snapped. "Don't forget who you're talking to, Lizzie. I'm the girl who knew you when."

And I you.

Liz asked, "How's the abominable spouse?"

"Still abominable." At a stoplight Hannah signaled right and turned up Casabella Road.

By contrast to Santa Cruz Avenue, Casabella Road had changed little in the years since Liz and her two friends walked it to and from school every day. It began at the Corner Drug Store and, staying level for a while, curved around the little town cemetery before it turned again and ran parallel to Santa Cruz Avenue for several blocks. Beyond St. Margaret's Episcopal Church where Hannah's father was rector for more than twenty years, it veered left and up the long grade old-timers in town still called Queen Victoria's Hill. On either side, restored Victorian homes faced each other like a dowager standoff.

"Stop a second," Liz said. "Pull over."

It had been her intention to fix her gaze directly ahead when the car reached the corner of Casabella and Manzanita. But the wind was blowing hard again, stirring up the grit of memory. The two-storied Victorian stood in the middle of its half-acre lot and called her name.

Hannah said, "It belongs to some people from Rhode Island now. Big computer bucks." The verge board, the bracketed eaves, and the arch of rosettes crowning every window: all had been scrupulously restored and, like the rest of the house, sparkled achingly white in the sunlight. On the porch there was a swing with a bright blue canvas awning.

"If you want to see inside I can call the owner. Her name's Mitzi Sandler. I know her from the Spring Festival Committee. Most of the invaders are two income families, too busy to get into town affairs. She's different. We don't really know each other but she seems okay, better than most maybe."

"I wonder what it was that made my parents buy such a big house in the first place," Liz said. "They never intended to have a family. If they told me once I was an accident, they told me a hundred times. I'm so used to thinking of them as totally a-parental, but this house . . . I mean it's such a . . . grandmotherly house. You know what I mean, Hannah? Maybe there was a time when . . ."

Or maybe the big house made it easier to pretend she wasn't there.

Beyond Manzanita and Greenwood and Oak Streets, Casabella Road leveled out again and followed the shoulder of the hill for a quarter mile then dropped abruptly into a shadowy canyon and a hairpin curve across a bridge over Bluegang Creek. When it rose again, Liz saw a sign, a discreet bronze rectangle: HILLTOP SCHOOL, ONE QUARTER MILE.

Hannah said, "Low keyed and very high priced these days."

At the end of a long driveway Hannah and Dan Tarwater's white country farmhouse sprawled in the shade of half a dozen California live oaks. Hannah stopped at the mailbox and leaned out the car window to open it. She riffled through the bundle of envelopes, advertising flyers, and catalogs. She held a large overnight mail envelope, reading the return address. "This is for you," she said and handed it to Liz, eyebrows raised. "It's from a doctor. In Miami."

Friday

D r. Reed Wallace was young. His diplomas hung on the wall, but Roman numerals confused Liz and besides, she didn't really want to know exactly how young. Under the circumstances, age made no difference anyway. The lab in Miami had provided his name in San Jose and no other.

He entered the examining room, her chart in hand, a few strands of dark brown hair engagingly drooped across his forehead, and leaned against the wall smiling and comfortable as a neighbor chatting over a fence. *Easy for you. You're not going to be east-west in the stirrups, gaping like a Bekins box.* She perched on the end of the examining table and answered his routine questions—her age (advanced), her general health (perimenopausal), childhood ailments (emotional neglect), allergies (good-looking young ob-gyns; they made her blush).

He was tall and slender with excellent teeth and probably wearing contact lenses. Clean fingernails, a discreet yin/yang tattoo on his wrist.

Wallace left her alone in the examining room to strip and don a paper hospital gown. His nurse—a petite Asian woman with a name tag saying Marilu—came in. She weighed Liz, took her temperature and then her blood pressure. Her smile never dimmed from incandescent.

"You can get up on the table now."

Knees up, feet in the stirrups, scoot down, a little farther, a little farther, always a little farther.

Bad as this was, always was and would be because there was no way of doing a pelvic that was not humiliating, physically uncomfortable and emotionally tense, her first exam had been the worst.

She had expected condemnation for wanting birth control pills at a time when the sexual revolution had barely entered the guerrilla skirmish stage. But her lover, Willy, had assured her that in France clinic doctors were worldly and approved of sex. The exam had been carried out in an ill-heated, badly lighted examining room with a speculum the size of a tire jack; and her prescription had come in an ordinary glass bottle, twenty-five at a time. In those days, there weren't even safety caps to struggle with.

On the way home from the dispensing chemist Liz had purchased a little plastic tray divided into seven lidded sections. As she was writing the days of the week on the lids using a laundry pen, she had suddenly remembered Billy Phillips and Hannah's underpants and the mystery of their disappearance. That's how the memory of Bluegang was, a sleeping infection like herpes that awoke unexpectedly and made her miserable a while.

The last thing she had ever wanted was a baby and for years she could no more begin a day without her birth control pill than she could walk out the door without her underpants although occasionally, she did that on purpose, just because she liked the feel of the air and the slightly risky sensation. She always took her pill, but she never quite trusted it to work. Looking back, she saw her adult life patterned by twenty-eight-day cycles of panic and relief.

After fifteen years the pill had become like a credit card she used impulsively, unwisely. She switched to a diaphragm and though occasionally inconvenient, she liked the system better. But the diaphragm made her panic cycle worse. Just to make sure she never got lulled into thinking sex was healthy or fun or even perfectly normal for an adult woman with a thriving body, she obsessed over microscopic holes and visions of deteriorating rubber. Even when she bled she fretted and remembered stories of women who continued to menstruate into their fifth and sixth months of pregnancy, the poor souls who arrived at the hospital complaining of gas pains and delivered healthy twins moments later.

A year ago when her periods had become irregular, and her doctor in Belize told her she was in early menopause, she had misplaced her sense of humor and slipped into a funk. She imagined her body's depleted nest of eggs like last season's potatoes growing mold at the bottom of the bin. One day, feeling a mixture of grief and glee, she cut her diaphragm in half with the kitchen shears and tossed the pieces in the trash.

Dr. Reed Wallace came back into the examining room. As he slipped on rubber gloves, he said, "I've never been to Belize. I hear it's beautiful." He opened the front of her gown and began to palpate her breasts. As he performed this exercise, he didn't look at Liz or her anatomy. He gazed up at the holiday pictures tacked to the acoustical ceiling over the examining table. The travel agent photos of turquoise water and sugar-cookie beaches were there as much for him as for her.

"What do you do down there?"

Same as you, Doc.

"I own a bed and breakfast."

"You get lots of business?"

In my time.

"The rain forest and the Mayan ruins are a big draw."

"It's not exactly Miami Beach though."

"Thank God."

He closed the front of her gown.

"You're okay."

Liz supposed that meant no suspicious lumps.

He sat on a wheeled stool and took up his position directly in front of her, facing the tent of sheet over her gaping legs. He spoke to Marilu, and she handed him an instrument. He raised the sheet, and Liz couldn't see him at all. The whole procedure was less intimate than a root canal.

Reed Wallace said, "I was down in Panama with the Peace Corps."

Liz tensed as she felt the warmed speculum slide into place. She experienced an instinctive and irrational panic that he would split her in half.

"Bocas del Toro. Miserable place."

Something scraped her insides, Torquemada's clamp loosened

and was withdrawn. Liz heard it clink onto a metal tray and the tension drained from her body.

"Next time you might try breathing," Reed Wallace said as he stripped off his gloves and tossed them into the trash. "It's generally a good idea." He had a broad, kid grin. "Get dressed and come across the hall."

He stood up when she entered his office a few minutes later. The old-fashioned gesture made him seem like a well-behaved boy being visited by his great aunt.

"You told Marilu you had a period last month. Have you been regular all along?"

"Pretty much." She asked him the same question she had asked the doctor in Miami. "Isn't this unusual?" Not to mention unfair, biology sneaking up on her just when she'd stopped worrying about it. "I never heard of a woman my age getting pregnant."

"Highly unusual, but we see it every now and then." He glanced at her chart.

For years she had guarded against this occurrence. Once on her way to Orly she realized she had forgotten to pack her pills and risked missing her flight to Copenhagen to drive home like a crazy woman, frightening even the French drivers. And now this, this joke of biology. She imagined her eggs conspiring over time, waiting for the moment when she let down her guard.

"No symptoms at all, huh?"

"My breasts ached but I didn't pay much attention. The man I live with noticed I was gaining weight." She reached into her bag and handed him the envelope that had arrived for her at Hannah's address. "I wanted an American doctor so I went to Miami. When she confirmed the pregnancy they did some tests." She waited a moment, watching him scan the documents in the envelope. "The fetus is perfectly healthy. No genetic abnormalities."

"Good, good," he said distractedly.

"I want an abortion."

That got his attention. He studied her a moment, tipped back in his chair and swung it around a little so he half-faced the window over the parking lot. The tinted window turned the sky an improbable navy blue. "How'd you happen to come to me, Ms. Shepherd?"

"I grew up in Rinconada. I still have good friends there." Liz looked down at the freckles on the back of her hands and then at him. "Will you do it?"

"I think we need to talk about it first."

That word *need*, it cropped up everywhere in American speech these days. Had Americans grown uncomfortable in their luxury and choices, a little ashamed? Did *needing* make them feel less guilty and more like the rest of the world? *I need a four dollar latte.* Well, she *wanted* an abortion and Reed Wallace obviously *wanted* to talk her out of it and she *wanted* him to shut up.

"I'm not going to change my mind." She decided she didn't like him after all. He was only a boy but already he had the medical attitude that announced he knew more and better about her body than she did. Just because he'd taken a look at her clear up to her tonsils didn't give him special rights. "I know what I want and I know what's good for me."

"I'm not trying to change your mind, Ms. Shepherd." He put his hands out, palm forward: *whoa*. "Let's just go slow here, okay? I make it a rule to discuss every surgical procedure with my patients beforehand."

Liz sagged a little. "Go ahead and tell me how it has eyes and ears and already loves rock and roll."

"Maybe reggae."

"Maybe John Philip Sousa. Frankly, I don't care." Liz leaned across the desk. "Let me see if I can make you understand, Doctor Reed Wallace. I'm fifty years old and my health is excellent. My lover and I have been living monogamously for more than seven years. I know that if I'm careful, I could probably have a relatively untroubled pregnancy and deliver a healthy infant into the world in a few months. Hooray for you, me and modern medicine." She stood up without thinking about it. "It isn't giving birth that bothers me. And it's not money either. Even if Gerard left me flat, I have plenty of money. What I don't have," she swallowed, "is any desire to be a mother. I've never wanted children. I wouldn't know how to connect with a child."

"You'd be surprised how many women feel as you do at the beginning. You'd learn, Ms. Shepherd."

"I doubt it." A good shake was what Reed Wallace needed. "Let me tell you, I am the only child of parents who never wanted me. Probably the best thing about dying was they were rid of me for good."

"Ms. Shepherd, I don't think—"

"Just let me say this. They weren't bad parents. They were responsible people who did one irresponsible thing and I was the result. I got what I was supposed to get—haircuts and vaccinations and tennis lessons . . ." Lessons, opportunities, encouragement: she could go on for a long time listing all the good things her parents had given her because they knew in a bookish kind of way everything there was to understand about parenting. Braces and good clothes and shoes that supported her arches. They drilled table manners into her and sent her to camp where she learned how to ride and not humiliate herself on a tennis court.

"But whatever you're meant to do for a kid to make it feel loved and wanted and needed and respected and safe and all the rest?" She took a breath, realized she was standing up and gabbling, sat down. "Well, it never happened for me."

"That doesn't mean . . ."

"I'm not going to bring another accident into the world." Liz took a deep breath. "Anyway, what kid wants a sixty- or seventy-year-old mother?"

"Age isn't so important anymore."

Spoken like a man on the smiling side of forty.

"If you won't abort this, I'll find someone who will."

"Ms. Shepherd, I'm not trying to change your mind about the surgery. It's your body and I respect your right to choose. But I need to make sure you've looked at every angle because there are few things as final and forever as a terminated pregnancy."

"No kidding."

"And at the risk of making you madder at me, I have to say that women who come on as strong as you do, are often the ones who suffer most afterwards."

"Often doesn't mean always, doctor." She waited a moment for his riposte. Nothing. "So, do we schedule the thing or do I go look for another doctor?"

He flipped through his desk calendar. "Next Friday's okay."

"Will I have to stay overnight?"

"In the hospital? No. I'll see you down at the Womancare facility on San Antonio and Third. You'll come in here to the office the day before so I can insert a microscopic dilator. The procedure doesn't take long, but you might feel a little uncomfortable for a day or two afterwards. Every woman's different."

"Pain?"

"I'll see you get a sedative and a local. Unless you're super-sensitive, that should be adequate."

"And afterwards? Can I fly home that weekend?"

"To be on the safe side, I'd prefer you wait a couple of days." He spoke into his telephone and a moment later the Asian nurse appeared beaming in his doorway. "Marilu'll do the scheduling, Ms. Shepherd." He shook her hand. "Just remember you can cancel. Up to the last minute and it's okay."

Hannah dropped Liz at the doctor's office and drove on to Resurrection House in the Alameda district, trying not to worry. Liz looked wonderful, not at all like a person with cancer. But she was being secretive and to Hannah, secrets meant trouble. The night before the three of them had sat up late in the kitchen drinking wine, snacking on multiflavor jelly beans, catching up—not important talk, that took a little time to get into. Liz had seemed distracted, as if there were something she wanted to say but was reluctant or apprehensive to do so. Hannah wanted to ask why she had to see a doctor but knew better than to push. Liz liked to reveal things in her own way, in her own time. Hannah had expected an explanation in the car this morning but instead Liz talked about scuba diving, as if Hannah gave a damn where the best reefs were. The longer Liz kept her secret, the worse it had to be. So if it wasn't cancer? . . . AIDS? Hannah ran a stop sign across from the Swenson Building and a cop came up behind her, flashing his lights. Once she would have explained to the officer that she wasn't actually a careless driver; but her smiling innocence wouldn't get her anywhere now. As far as she could tell, the police academy made sure each girl and boy in blue—this one no more than twenty years old, a protoadult—hated their mothers and considered everyone a felon, even a middle-aged housewife driving a Volvo. She accepted the citation and drove on without saying good-bye.

Mostly she was grateful to the police. Grateful for their willingness to do a nasty job. But she didn't like that she lived in a world needing so much armed control. What would happen if there were fewer laws, fewer cops? Would crime and violence be so much worse? This was an experiment no one would ever be willing to try; but until someone did, how would they ever know if all the money spent on cops and prisons and weapons really made a difference? She thought what good all that cash could do caring for babies, building good houses, planting trees and helping people lead decent and productive lives.

Was she weird for having these thoughts? Did anyone else her age ever consider the possibility that less—of everything—might be better? Jeanne said she was a closet anarchist. She meant it affectionately, but Hannah heard criticism.

Until the late 1950s, the Alameda district had been the enclave of San Jose's rich and influential families. Many of the homes were in the Spanish colonial style, painted cantaloupe and salmon and terra cotta. The others were what Hannah called Iowa homes: built of wood and solid as the Constitution, two- and three-stories with bay and dormer windows, and all enclosed by wide verandas. When taxes and the flight to the suburbs impoverished the neighborhood, the houses had been converted to apartments, offices or group homes like Resurrection House. The district had subsided into gentle neglect. All this before San Jose became the capital city of Silicon Valley.

As she locked the car, Hannah heard from somewhere out of sight the forbidden click-click-click of a rotating sprinkler. At the same time she wanted to knock on the owner's door to deliver a lecture on drought, she wanted to fall into the sound and live in it forever.

It would be nice if once in a while she could just think one uncomplicated thought.

From Junipero Serra Elementary School around the corner, came the noise of children at recess. The clang of a tether ball chain against its hollow pole reminded her of sun-softened playground asphalt hot through the soles of her shoes, and the burn of rope on her wrist as she whipped the ball around the pole. Liz always beat her at the game. Liz was tough, determined as Jeanne in her own way.

Please, God, not AIDS.

A car sped past, stinking the air with exhaust fumes and boomy rap. Its horn blasted. Hannah jumped. Pulse hammering, she leaned against the hood of the Volvo for a long moment. She stood up straight and shook her head to clear it, and Angel moved in to occupy the vacated space. Hannah swung her straw bag over her shoulder and hurried up the sidewalk to Resurrection House.

Set back from the street behind a plot of dusty yard, the style was Iowa, painted dark gray with peeling white trim. Wilty pink, white and cerise ivy geraniums hung in baskets and struggled out of oak barrels on the tired-looking veranda. The house was home to twelve drug-damaged children and their caretakers, residents by special arrangement with the courts and the departments of Welfare and Child Protective Services. Eventually it was hoped the young mothers would come into residence as well and learn to be responsible parents. Hannah believed in the goals of Resurrection House, but she doubted the bit about the mothers.

The screen door had a right angle tear and creaked. Hannah opened it and stepped inside. She smelled the mix of children, food and disinfectant and her spirits rose and her eyes filled with tears of gratitude.

Menopause tears, Jeanne called them. Excessive.

"Well, good morning to you, Mrs. Tarwater." Betts stood in one of the doorways off the foyer, tall and fat. She wore a bright voluminous muumuu and blue rubber thongs. Hannah could not be sure but she thought the perfect helmet of gray bubble curls was a wig.

Hannah held up a paper bag. "Muffins."

"You spoil us." The woman laughed. "If you get me used to eating homemade muffins with my coffee, I'm apt to start thinking I've got a right to them."

"That's the whole point, Betts. You do."

Hannah followed Betts and the slap of her thongs on the hardwood floor into a room furnished with a scarred wooden desk and table, several chairs and a brown leather couch, worn and discolored. On one wall beside a cluttered bulletin board a poster showed a child teetering at the edge of a precipice with a great-winged angel guarding her from behind. The angel had a strong, unsexed face like the Statue of Liberty.

Hannah took a plate from the cupboard and emptied the muffins onto it. Holding one in her mouth, she offered the plate to Betts. An automatic coffeemaker sat on the table and beside it a rack of cups. Hannah lifted the mug with her name on it and poured coffee. At home she'd never tolerate such coal black brine, but at Resurrection House it was part of the shared struggle. While her coffee cooled she opened the closet and sorted through hangers until she found the plain white smock bearing her name tag: HANNAH, VOLUNTEER MOTHER. As she slipped it on, she chatted with Betts about trivialities and overcame her urge to share her concern about Liz. Bett's worry list was long enough already.

Since leaving her convent after Vatican II Betts had worked in whatever capacity presented itself to do whatever good she could. That was how she had explained her work on the day Hannah arrived at Resurrection House having been recommended by Father Joe, the retired rector at St. Margaret's.

"You might find some peace working there, Hannah." His eyes had pierced and offended her with their directness. She thought Dan must have told him she was depressed. She had almost told Father Joe he should mind his own business even if he had known her all her life.

Hannah finished her coffee and muffin and walked to the nursery. When she opened the door, the vertical blinds clacked at the windows and the draft smelled of dust and cars and from somewhere along the street, frying bacon. Four cribs were lined up side by side. In each small bed, a baby lay sleeping.

Angel, the daughter of a sixteen-year-old crack addict, had come to Resurrection House from the preemie ward at County Hospital. Tiny limbs and skin like vinyl, the wizened face of an old woman: Hannah wept when she first saw her. From the start, she had known that Angel needed to be held, to feel a warm body against hers, and the beat of a steady heart. But the baby screamed and recoiled from the touch of a hand on her skin. A sudden noise sent her into spasms.

Betts allowed Hannah to convert the room's old-fashioned walk-in closet into a private nursery for Angel. For weeks the infant slept the clock around in darkness, swaddled tight, with the taped sound of a human heart beating beside her. When her skin desensitized Hannah held her, and they rocked for hours at a time in the blackness. In late spring as Angel finally began to relax, Hannah increased the light in the closet nursery a little every day. At last, near midsummer, Angel looked at Hannah, saw Hannah, and did not turn away.

Hannah knew that wherever her soul went after death, it would take the memory of that moment with it.

Her crib was brought into the big nursery, but Angel still slept more than the other drug-exposed babies. She was fragile though her eyes were clear, and she seemed to like being held and fed. For Hannah, she smiled. Now, at ten months, she was delicately made and chirrupy as a three- or four-month-old.

Hannah watched Angel chew and suck on her dimpled fist. In REM sleep, her eyelids fluttered like moth wings. What did she dream of? A bedroom of her own, a soft-eyed dog asleep on the rug beside her crib? Her brows knitted in a V, and she opened her eyes. For a moment they stared up vacantly. Then they focused and she beamed, displaying two nubby pearls in her pink gums. Her reaching arms jerked around in uncoordinated circles.

"Breakfast time, my Angel," Hannah said. "And then we'll go to the park."

The park was one city block square and planted with old live oak trees through which the sunlight fell like coins. Hannah sat on an iron bench with Angel in her arms, and they watched a pair of noisy boys push and shove each other in and out and over a playground sculpture of wood and rubber provided by a service club. The seats of the old metal swing set beside the sculpture had been stolen, and lengths of useless chain hung from the horizontal bar, limp as wet hair. To conserve water, the city no longer watered the grass and the shrubs and perennials sagged as if despairing. At the edge of the playground, a man with a shopping cart stuffed with green plastic bags scavenged in a trash can.

From behind Hannah a feminine voice said, "Do you mind if I sit here?" Hannah looked up at the speaker, a young woman with a toddler and an infant in a baby carrier. "Your baby's beautiful. How old is she?"

Hannah paused a heartbeat. "Three months." She didn't want to explain why Angel was small and could not yet sit up alone.

Angel eyed the newcomers with interest. The toddler showed her his Tootsie-Pop and she reached for it with normal reflexes that thrilled Hannah.

The young mother sat on the bench and shooed her son off to play. As she adjusted her baby in its canvas carry, she said, "What's her name?"

"Angel." Hannah heard the pride in her voice and added, "Angel Elizabeth Jeanne."

A little make-believe won't hurt.

"Big name for a little girl." The young woman opened her eyes wide at Angel and got a smile for her effort. "She's so petite. What was her birth weight?"

"Five pounds, two ounces." Ingrid's weight. Before the words were out, Hannah wanted them back; but the woman would think she was crazy if she tried to explain why she'd lied.

I'm just pretending a while . . .

"Is your husband Mexican?"

Hannah said nothing.

"I mean you're so fair and she's so dark. Her eyes are really great. I always wanted brown eyes."

"Yes," Hannah said, "he's Mexican."

This young woman believed Hannah was Angel's mother. Why would she think otherwise? Dan might know she was a closet anarchist but to the world Hannah looked like the paradigm of middle-class rectitude. Her word would not be doubted. If Hannah wanted to she could take Angel across the border and they'd fit in easily. Her Spanish was good. They could find a place to live in Ensenada, live for a long time on practically nothing.

The young mother said, "We just moved into that pink Spanishy place near the school. We've got half the second floor. It's not bad but so close to the school and all . . . God, it's noisy."

The idea of mothers complaining about kid-noise made them laugh.

"Do you have other children?"

Hannah stroked Angel's hair. "No."

Forgive me Eddie, Ingrid. I'm only playing.

"You had to wait a while, huh?" It was a tactful allusion and impossible to be affronted by. "Did you have a hard time?"

"She's never given me any trouble."

"Lucky you. This one," the garrulous girl tapped the nearly bald head just visible at the top of the carrier, "took eighteen hours getting born and now he sleeps all day and cries all night. My husband's going crazy. He's in grad school, and he can't study with all the bawling."

They talked about feeding routines and sleeping patterns, the pros and cons of disposable diapers. The sun in the cloudless sky shone through the arms of the great oaks, stippling the playground with light. An ice cream truck went by a half-dozen times playing *Babes in Toyland.* Angel fell asleep in Hannah's arms.

The young mother asked, "Do you come here often? It's nice to have someone to talk to. The parks at home—I'm from outside Cleveland—they're full of moms and kids. Here it's different. More women work." She nodded toward the man hunting and gathering with his shopping cart. "Mostly you see *them.*"

"I'm usually too busy for the park."

"Maybe we could work out a babysitting co-op. I used to do that with my friends."

"I don't go out much."

"You might change your mind. Once the novelty's worn off." She wiped Tootsie-Pop drool and sand off her toddler's face. "What's your name?"

"Hannah."

"I'm Judy." The toddler tugged her pant leg and whined to be lifted. Judy groaned. "No rest, I guess. Gotta go. See ya, Hannah."

"See ya, Judy."

In the distance a school bell rang and from farther away a siren screamed. No harm done. She kissed the top of Angel's head. *When you're mine it'll all be true anyway.*

Hannah made a late lunch of cold meat loaf sandwiches and chocolate chip cookies with milk. After eating she and Liz stood at the sink and put the dishes in the dishwasher. Liz talked about her neighbors in Belize City: the fortune-teller named Divina, the man who drove a Cadillac and sold bananas by the stem door to door, Petula who chartered boats to tourists. She described frogs the size of softballs that squatted on her steps and sang while the rain poured down.

Hannah listened and tried to pretend she was interested. All the while she observed Liz for signs of illness, but the amazing thing was she had never looked better. The years had softened her rather sharp features and she smiled a lot and her laugh came from somewhere deep inside. She must be happy, Hannah thought. Happy or sad, the young were always pretty. But to be a pretty middle-aged woman, happiness was more important than cosmetics or surgery.

If she's not sick, why did she go to the doctor?

Hannah couldn't stand the waiting. "Liz, tell me what—"

"I almost forgot your present. I brought you something special from Florida." Liz went upstairs and in a moment she came back into the kitchen. "Close your eyes and stand with your back to the sink."

Hannah did as she was told. "It's not a bug or anything? From Belize?"

Liz laughed and then Hannah heard a soft unidentifiable squeak and water in a fine spray touched her cheeks and wet her eyelids.

"What? . . ."

"It's rain," Liz said. "I brought it from Florida like you said I should."

Tears again.

They walked down to the barn.

When Dan and Hannah bought the house on Casabella Road, there had been nothing on the lower field but a long, ramshackle old henhouse—a sinister place, thick with webs and shadows and the hint of snakes. Even the Fearsome Threesome, intrepid at eight and nine, had been reluctant to explore it until one hot autumn afternoon when Jeanne led the way and pried open the door with a screwdriver.

They had peered down a long empty space striped by mustard-colored shafts and plates of sunlight entering through knotholes and gaps between the boards. Through a cloud of shimmering motes they saw straight ahead of them, dead in the middle of the barn and spotlighted in dark gold, an oversized wooden chair joined by bolts the size of silver dollars with a high square back and chunky square-edged arms and legs. In a hushed voice, Jeanne said it was an electric chair without the juice. It was easy to believe her.

Years later on the day the builders demolished the old coop, Hannah stayed on the hill and watched, eager to see the electric chair brought out. The workman found a wooden kitchen chair with arms, the kind mass-produced in the Twenties and Thirties.

"It was nothing at all," she told Liz as they walked through the paddock gate and were immediately surrounded by clambering dogs and cats with their tails straight up and quivering. "Just a chair. All those years we were so afraid of it . . ."

Liz nodded and inhaled as if she were about to say something. Now she'll tell me, Hannah thought. *Tell me, tell me.*

Instead Liz gestured toward the animals. "Are they all yours? There must be a dozen cats."

"The dogs and the donkey came from the Humane Society. People just leave cats at the end of the driveway."

"You're such a soft touch."

"What am I supposed to do? Walk away and let them die? Ramon comes morning and afternoon to help. They're no trouble."

Beaten, starved, neglected: the streetwise orphans always kept their distance at first. But gradually, inevitably, they trusted Hannah and learned to come when she leaned on the paddock fence and called. They trembled when she stroked their coats but did not run.

In Levi's and sweatshirt, ancient boots pulled on over a discarded pair of Dan's wool socks, Hannah fed the dogs and measured out oats and forked fresh hay down from the loft. The work was basic and hard, and she felt strong doing it. Liz sat on the gate of an empty stall and gabbed at her, but Hannah only listened with half attention. Liz wasn't saying anything that mattered, not yet. Sooner or later she would have to get down to it but for now . . . well, Hannah admitted, she was just as glad not to go there. Instead of worrying about Liz and her mystery, she preferred to imagine how Angel would love the barn and the animals. When she was four Hannah would teach her to ride. She'd make her a brown velveteen weskit and a matching jacket . . .

Liz had stopped talking.

"What's the matter?" Hannah asked.

"What's going on with you?"

"Look who's asking."

"I know a lot about depression, Hannah."

Hannah waved the word away. "Who said I was depressed?" Hannah hung the pitchfork on a hook. "You're gone for years and now all of a sudden you're back and full of secrets and you know everything." She regretted her tone but did not apologize.

"There's things we should talk about."

"What kind of *things?*"

"Bluegang."

The answer startled Hannah. "Oh. That." She sighed and crouched down to pat a mangy beagleish sort of mutt. Pus accumulated in yellow gobbets at the corners of its eyes. She'd have to call the vet, get some drops.

She stood up and waved her arm in the direction of the creek. "It's right down there, over the hill. If you're so interested, go look at it." She headed out of the barn. "Tomorrow night you can talk all you want to Gail Bacci about Bluegang. It's one of her favorite subjects. That and how much money she's making."

"Please, Hannah. Don't make this hard. I have to talk about it. That's why I've come back."

Hannah stopped. "What about the doctor?"

"That's . . . something else. I told you not to worry about me. I'm not sick."

"I don't believe you."

"I have nightmares . . ."

"The doctor's a shrink?"

"I keep seeing that boy."

Hannah felt her jaw tighten and a brooding ache burrowed in beside her right ear. "We made a deal we wouldn't talk."

"We were children, we wanted it to go away like it never happened. We were scared. But now—. I can't make it go away anymore. And it's crazy not to talk about it. Something like that happens and we have to talk about it."

"Leave it." Hannah pressed her index finger hard into the pain behind her ear and told herself to relax and it would diminish.

"It's not over for me," Liz said. "The last year I've been obsessing."

"You?"

"And I can't sleep."

Hannah laughed. "Who can?"

"I did something terrible that day, Hannah."

You?

"I should have insisted that we tell someone right then. I almost did but I thought how my parents were so busy and how upset they'd be with me."

Hannah's voice broke as it rose in volume. "Did you hear what I said?"

"I knew what was right to do but when Jeanne started talking—"

"I said leave it. I don't want to talk about this." Hannah gestured Liz through the paddock gate and slammed and latched it shut behind them. "And I won't. Period."

Jeanne wove Teddy's Waterman pen between her fingers. On the desk before her, the report from the housekeeping staff lay open, but she could not concentrate on complaints about old plumbing, long hours and low wages. Across the room the bell-curve walnut clock on the credenza struck two. She double-checked the clock against her watch: 2:01.

She had allowed Robby to take Adam Weed into town. Older honor students like Robby were given such privileges on special occasions. In this case, Robby needed to buy his mother a birthday gift. Using the Waterman like a drumstick, she played an irritable riff on her desktop. She had wanted the boys to bond, but maybe it had been a mistake to trust Robby with someone as fragile as Adam Weed.

She could have a drink at five. Five was a legitimate time for a drink.

On the credenza, a little to the left of the clock, was a picture of her father and mother, an enlargement of a snapshot taken one Easter by her brother, Michael, during his photography phase. Against the backdrop of the rose cloister, it showed her father's stubborn chin and wooden back. Her mother's equally unyielding nature was disguised by a floral dress and exuberantly gauzy hat. As far as Jeanne could remember, they had been almost moderate in their habits in those days. The drinking had begun in earnest after Michael died.

There was a knock on the hall door.

Jeanne slipped the pen into her purse, smoothed her bun and tugged down the jacket of her blue wool suit. "Enter."

A frail, delicately featured boy with muddy shoes stood on the threshold.

"Where have you been, Adam?" Jeanne frowned at the footprints on her hardwood floor.

He looked down at his feet.

"Answer me, Adam. I won't bite you."

"Robby and me . . ."

". . . Robby and I . . ."

"We went to the drugstore."

"I know that, Adam." Jeanne smiled. "Was the drugstore muddy?"

"No, ma'am."

"Then how did your shoes get so dirty?" Bluegang and the wildwood were off limits and all the boys knew it from their first day at Hilltop. Nevertheless, the temptation of trees and water and rocks was too much for most of them. "You've left tracks across my floor."

Adam looked at his feet and then up, as if the answer to her question were written somewhere in the far corner of the ceiling.

Jeanne waited. When his gaze didn't shift, she repeated her question with more force but with sweetness too; she didn't want to frighten him. She hoped no teacher had ever frightened James/Mark. She hoped that all his life loving, thoughtful people had surrounded him. She gentled her tone still more. "Where did you get the mud on your shoes?"

He looked out the window.

"Adam?"

"Where the roses are."

"What were you doing in the rose cloister?"

Adam blinked and thought. "Smellin' 'em."

Jeanne considered him. "Where did Robby tell you to take your shower bucket, Adam?"

"Where the roses are."

Was he lying? She couldn't tell. With a troubled, distracted boy like Adam Weed, truth and falsehood were often indistinguishable and by doggedly pursuing the truth she would only cause humiliation and further confusion. As it was the boy quivered with tension and she pitied him.

"Do you like your room, Adam?"

He nodded.

"You're in the oldest wing of the school. Boys have lived in your room since I was younger than you are now."

And before them, nuns in black habits.

Adam blinked several times. She wondered if his eyes had been tested recently and made a mental note.

"I know you've never shared a room before. You might feel a little strange at first, but you'll get used to it. If you have any trouble, I want you to remember that the secret of living with people happily is cooperation and compromise." Adam's gaze was on the ceiling again. She wasn't even sure he was listening. Jeanne made another note to herself: reexamine his test scores. "Roommates are like a little team, Adam. They have to work together."

His face brightened. "My Uncle Louis plays for Chicago. He's the nose tackle."

That stopped her. "I didn't know you had an uncle."

"He plays nose tackle."

"That's an important position. My brother played football. I was very proud of him." She paused. "You must be proud of your Uncle Louis."

Adam nodded.

"My brother played for Stanford back when they were called the Indians. He was a wide receiver."

"Did he go with the pros?"

Jeanne shook her head.

"Uncle Louis played for Wisconsin. He was an All-American and runner-up for the Heisman."

"A nose tackle, huh?" Jeanne took care not to smile. "That's very unusual for the Heisman. Uncle Louis is an unusual man."

"How come your brother didn't go with the pros? Wasn't he good enough?"

"He died his last year of college." For a second her gaze locked with Adam's, and the pain she read there pierced her heart. "I was sad for a very long time after that. I wasn't too much older than you."

"Uncle Louis'll probably be All-Pro this year," Adam said, looking up at the ceiling again. "I'm gonna ask my dad if I can go to Hawaii and watch him play. I might take Robby with me."

Jeanne thought of Simon Weed, so deeply troubled by his son that his eyes grew wet when he spoke of him. The boy had come upon his mother hanging by the neck, and then he walked away and pretended it never happened. Or maybe he had truly forgotten.

Amnesia. Like Young Widder Brown.

"I want you to make me a promise, Adam."

"What kind of promise?"

"Will you come back and talk to me sometimes? Let me know how you're doing at Hilltop?"

He blinked and yawned and scuffed his shoes into the hardwood parquet. Jeanne was merciful and let him go.

Jeanne opened Adam Weed's file and quickly reread the contents. Low academic scores, poor social skills, some vandalism in the year since his mother's death. Increasing signs of vagueness and confusion, inclined to wander off. She keyed his name into her computer and quickly noted the details of their meeting in his file.

Unhappy boys were not a novelty at Hilltop. Most students carried around at least one misery. Even parental suicides were not unknown. But Adam moved Jeanne because when she saw him she saw at the same time his beleaguered father, the tycoon reduced to confusion and clumsy neediness.

Without knocking Teddy came in. He wore light gray slacks and a fashionably oversized black cashmere sweater. His handsome aristocratic face looked tired.

"How's your head?"

"Still hurts."

"Call the doctor, Teddy. You don't have to suffer. There's nothing noble about a sinus headache."

"There's nothing wrong with me a change of climate wouldn't cure." He tossed a manila folder across her desk. "Look that over, will you? Punch it up? It's that book review I said I'd do for the *Journal of Private School Educators.*"

"I didn't read the book."

He shrugged. "I put the bones in, you can flesh it out. Take you thirty minutes."

"I can't do it this afternoon. I'm meeting Liz."

"I only take these assignments because it's good for the school's rep. If you'd rather I didn't . . ."

She looked at her husband and then at the computer screen. In its blue well she saw her blurred reflection with the cursor pulsing on her temple. "What I'd rather is that you finished them yourself." Before he could respond she added, "Just don't expect it before next week."

The clock chimed the half hour. She closed Adam's file and logged off. "There's something else I need to talk to you about before I go."

Teddy prowled from the door to the window and back to the door again. He lifted the cushions on the loveseat under the window. "I wish to hell I could find that pen."

He was upset, she had made him that way. Now, if she wanted to, she could take the pen out of her purse and say *oh, by the way, look what I just found.* And make him happy. Once she took fifty dollars from his wallet and stuck the roll of bills in the inside pocket of his favorite sports coat, then she lay on the bed and watched him go crazy trying to find it and his confusion when he found it after twenty minutes. He kept saying he *never* put cash in that pocket.

Jeanne clicked her purse shut. "Will you stand still a minute and listen?"

He dropped onto the loveseat and grinned like Buckwheat. "Yes, ma'am, Miz Tate. I's all ears."

"I've just had a conversation with Adam Weed. He told me his uncle Louis plays for the Chicago."

"So? I told you his father owns a piece of the team."

"Simon Weed particularly told me that he is Adam's only living relative. No uncles, aunts or cousins."

"So? It's an honorary title. Like Hannah's kids call you Aunt Jeanne. For all we know, little Adam calls the whole team Uncle."

"He came in with mud on his shoes and when I pressed him about where it came from he told me he'd been to the rose cloister. But I'm sure he was lying."

"My goodness, Sherlock, you've had a full afternoon of lies and innuendo haven't you?"

"I let him go with Robby earlier. They used Bluegang as a short-cut into town. It's quicker than the road."

Teddy laughed and she wondered why. If she asked, if she pursued his humor to its motive . . . well, she knew what would happen. Teddy would find a way to make her feel stupid. She let the laughter go as if she hadn't heard it.

"We need a better fence at the edge of the property." She tucked a wisp of hair behind her ear. "One of these days someone is going to be hurt down there and we'll be liable."

"The rules are clear. Every boy knows . . ."

"The rules don't matter. Rules get broken. Bluegang is an attractive nuisance. That's what the law calls it and if we don't have a secure fence we're negligent."

"Jesus-fucking-Christ, Jeanne, don't tell me you've found a way to cram in a law degree."

"Don't swear at me." She forced her voice down. He liked to make her mad; he took it as a victory. As she began straightening her desktop it came to her that there was a secret war going on between Teddy and her, quite apart from the verbal sniping to which she had grown accustomed. He said and did things to get a rise out of her, to manipulate and prove his power over her; and it was for the same reason his pen was hidden in her purse right now. Just thinking of it down at the bottom mixed in with the lint of old tissues and crumpled receipts gave her a pleasant zing of power. It vaguely disturbed her that she had not noted this similarity before. Not having done so must mean something though she couldn't guess what.

Teddy put his hand over hers. "We're talking thousands of dollars, Jeannie. Thousands of dollars that won't do a damn thing to get anyone to send their kid here." He made a comic face. "Can't you just hear Mr. Simon Weed saying, *I want my boy to go to Hilltop because of its high quality chain link fence.*" When she didn't laugh or even crack a smile he said, "Lighten up, will you?"

"If you don't arrange for a new fence, I will. I won't cut corners when it comes to safety."

A long look held them.

Jeanne spun her Rolodex, stopping at W. "I want to ask Simon Weed about this Uncle Louis." She lifted the telephone receiver and punched in a phone number.

Teddy broke the connection with his index finger. "I've already talked to him this morning. Over at the house."

"He called you? At the house? How'd he get that number?"

Teddy sat on the edge of Jeanne's desk and played with a hexagonal cut glass paperweight, peering at her through its facets. "I called him and we had a congenial chat about school finances. He was extremely sympathetic to our lack of a computer facility but he never mentioned a fence. Not once."

"Teddy, what's the matter with you? You can't hustle a parent when his kid only just got here."

"Hustle is your word, Jeanne, not mine." He reached across the desk and lifted the bang of dark hair that fell across her forehead. She started back and he laughed. "Relax, will you? Why can't you take it easy and trust me, huh?"

His hand slid down to her cheek and she pushed it away. "What did you say about Adam?"

"I told him Adam was fitting in fine, just great, and he should stop worrying. I told him boys are my business, just like electronic widgets are his."

"You've never even spoken to the boy."

"Weed's got a business to run. He left us the kid so he wouldn't have to worry about him anymore."

Not true. Simon Weed had not used Hilltop as an expensive dumping ground for his son. She recalled the hunger and confusion in the man's eyes and heard herself promise that at Hilltop School Adam would be safe.

"The kid'll adjust," Teddy said as he walked to the door connecting their offices. "They always do, don't they? Meantime, the happier we make Simon Weed, the happier he's going to make us when check-writing time comes around." He grinned. "Trust your old man on this."

She watched him close the door behind him. The slacks and cashmere sweater he wore today had cost more than nine hundred dollars. He didn't bother to hide the bill from her and why should he?

Liz had been waiting ten minutes when Jeanne met her at Hannah's mailbox. The sun was hot on her arms and legs and at the open neck of her camp shirt; the hard, dry California heat burned her eyes and prickled her skin so she felt the wrinkles forming.

"Sorry, I'm late." Jeanne told her about Adam Weed. "Shall we climb to the flume?" She pointed across the road to a steep trail and set off, saying over her shoulder, "Watch out for poison oak."

Once after a Brownie hike when Liz was eight, a reaction to poison oak had so swollen her throat she had to be rushed to O'Connor's Hospital in an ambulance. She remembered how cross that made her mother and father who had other plans for the evening.

Up the steep dusty trail they went with long-legged Jeanne striding as the lead in hiking shorts and boots, setting a pace that made Liz puff.

Liz had trudged behind Jeanne up hills and down streets, down theater aisles, into restaurants, out of bookstores, watching her dark braids bounce against her back, watching her ponytail, or the comma curve where her hair brushed her shoulder. The time they met in Paris, even there Jeanne took charge. In the Louvre she barely paused at the Winged Victory, aimed herself in the direction of Monet and plowed through the crowds. Jeanne always knew exactly where she was headed. It galled Liz that for years she had compared herself to Jeanne and been found wanting—in courage, in drive, in every category but imagination, which as far as Liz knew, numbered last on Jeanne Tate's list of talents and attributes.

At a level spot they paused. Liz held her side and looked back down the path. "Was it always that steep?"

"You're built like an athlete, Liz, but you never had much stamina."

I'm pregnant, goddamn it.

The thought stunned her and automatically she folded her hands across her abdomen.

"Don't you trek all over the rain forest with Gerard? I thought you two were ecological warriors."

"Not me." Liz wiped her damp forehead with the back of her hand. "I'm just a camp follower."

"Are you kidding? You've never been *just* anything."

This was meant as a compliment, Liz knew; but almost everything Jeanne said had barbs attached. Barbs were her portcullis. Eventually it would lift if the day was long enough and Liz's patience held.

"It's too humid for me to hike much. We have a boat, though. We dive." They talked about Belize, the day-to-day life of Liz Shepherd and Gerard Robin.

"A nice life," Jeanne said and smiled. She was the only person Liz had ever known with naturally straight teeth. "It sounds like a good life."

A perfect life. Since childhood, Liz had trusted no one as completely as she did Gerard, trusted him to take and appreciate her just as she was from day to day, pissy moods and all. She wanted Jeanne to acknowledge how rare and precious such intimacy was, to say that it made her happy that Liz—who had never belonged much of anywhere—belonged in Belize with Gerard. *Fat chance of that.* Being Jeanne's friend meant rarely hearing what you wanted, meant reading between and under and around the lines of conversation. Liz wondered if she and Teddy spoke in this guarded, multilayered way in their private moments. The thought exhausted her more than the steep grade to the flume.

After another climb, the path leveled and followed the curve of the hill. Occasionally the alder and live oak thinned, and Liz saw the gold and green countryside below bisected by streets and marked with houses.

"Rancho Rinconada Estates." Jeanne swept her arm wide. Her fingernails were painted a sheer pink. Jeanne: successful, controlled, professional, and scrupulously groomed. Even on a hike her hair stayed tightly coiled. "The Peninsula's most prestigious bedroom community."

"Jesus," Liz said, wiping the back of her neck with a handkerchief. "Doesn't anyone in this town have any taste?"

How big were the houses? Three, seven, ten thousand square feet? Towers and portes cocheres, swimming pools, putting greens and tennis courts and guest houses and servants' wings.

"They've ruined it."

"Greed rules."

"Our beautiful valley, these hills . . ." Liz felt a bitter impotence. "Once I went with Gerard . . . There'd been poaching in one section of the rain forest. Someone had clear-cut acres . . ." He had covered his face with his hands and wept.

"The Elizabethan one has an indoor pool. For the dozen truly cold days we get in the Santa Clara Valley."

"Silicon Valley."

"Yeah."

They resumed walking and after another fifteen minutes reached the flume that had once carried water to Rinconada from the reservoir in the hills. It was a semicircle of rusted-out metal about four feet in diameter, bolted to V-shaped iron supports sunk in blocks of concrete that raised it a yard or so off the ground. Split and rotten plywood covered the top of the half circle.

Liz pried up a worm-eaten board, peered in, and recoiled. "Stinks."

"Teddy says it's full of rattlesnakes."

Liz stepped back.

Jeanne laughed and hoisted herself onto the flume. She pulled Liz up beside her.

Liz stood with the hot sun in her face and the mating calls of grasshoppers shrilling in her ears. If she closed her eyes, she could pretend she was eight or ten or twelve again. Crows in the distance sounded the same. The sun still burned her skin. The brushy and pungent woods still smelled dry and tickled her nose like Vicks. She grinned down at Jeanne who sat on the edge of the flume, dangling her legs, staring up at her, shielding her eyes from the sun with one hand. She pointed at Liz's leg with the other.

A circle of small red welts clustered between her anklebone and Achilles tendon. "Shit."

Jeanne's mouth tightened. "You and Hannah. Can you communicate without swearing?"

"Come on, Jeannie. I've heard you cuss with the best of us."

"I guess that doesn't happen much anymore."

Liz sat down. "Speaking of Hannah—"

"Were we?"

Don't fuck with me, Liz wanted to say.

"She's depressed. Says she isn't but it's obvious to someone who hasn't seen her in a while. And she's distracted. Her mind's always somewhere else."

"You mean she's not paying enough attention to her house guest?"

"You're the limit, Jeanne. You know what I mean. There's something on her mind." Liz's ankle tickled. Reflexively, she scratched. "Damn."

"Ask Dan to give you a pill or a shot or something. There's great medicine for poison oak. Or we could go over to the school. We keep an ointment for the boys."

Liz hadn't flown in from Florida to let herself be distracted by poison oak. "You see her all the time. What's going on with her?"

"She seems the same to me." Jeanne swatted a yellow jacket. "Older, but we're all that. I suppose it's menopause. She's having a little trouble there."

"Are you?"

Jeanne shook her head. "Sailing right through."

Liz remembered puberty. Pimples. Cramps. The oily unpleasantness, the constant agitation that came of not being hooked up properly to her own body. Now this new change, different but the same feeling of not being hooked up quite right.

"What about you?"

I thought I was in it and so I relaxed and then . . . and then . . .

"No problems," Liz said.

They sat swinging their bare legs over the flume's edge. The parched, breathless scent of autumn dust and dry grasses sucked the moisture from Liz's nose and mouth.

"Does she ever mention Bluegang?" For a long moment Liz's question vibrated between them like a hummingbird.

"Gail's driving her nuts with that cleanup committee of hers. I think it's a good idea and we've given her some money, but I don't have time—"

Jeanne talked about the problems Bluegang caused at school, the need for a fence, her fear that someday a boy from the school would be hurt.

"Another boy."

Jeanne cocked an eyebrow at her.

"A boy died down there and we're the only ones who know the truth," Liz said. "Don't you ever think about it?"

When Jeanne answered the edge in her voice was sharp. Liz knew it as a warning. "Is that why you came home? To talk about Bluegang?"

The deep internal stirrings of imagination, emotion, and memory that directed Liz's behavior, these were alien to Jeanne as far as Liz knew. And if they hadn't been acquainted all their lives, they might not even like each other. Liz wasn't sure they actually liked each other now, that it wasn't their history and shared love of Hannah that bound them.

"For the last year or so, I've had the feeling like it's . . . in my way somehow." She flicked her hand at a yellow jacket. "I dream about it all the time."

"No kidding? I barely remember it."

Liz knew this could not be true.

"I feel like I'm haunted by it."

"So you've come home to exorcise the demon." Jeanne shook her head. "Think I'll pass."

"Are you afraid to talk about it?"

"Afraid?" Jeanne cocked her eyebrow again.

Portcullis down. Drawbridge up. Fortress Jeanne. Impregnable.

"My feelings have nothing to do with fear."

"Well, then, even if you don't need to talk, I do. Can't we? For me?"

"It's not that simple." Jeanne examined her nails, pushing back the cuticle with the pad of her thumb. "When you've flown home to your tropical paradise and your perfect French lover, Hannah and I will still be here. Nothing will have changed for us. Rinconada is where we live and Bluegang runs right through our backyards the way it always has. If we don't want to talk about what happened down there almost forty years ago, to three little girls who bear absolutely no resemblance to any of us today, then I think that's the way it ought to be."

Liz felt the color rush to her cheeks. "Jeanne, I need this."

"You are so self-centered. It's all about what Liz Shepherd wants. Or needs. Or *thinks* she needs. You haven't changed a bit."

Liz jumped to the ground. Tears of frustration flooded her eyes. "You've always been good at making me feel like dog dirt."

"No, Liz, *you've* always been good at making *yourself* feel like dog dirt." Jeanne glanced at her watch. "I've got to get back."

Liz grabbed Jeanne's arm. "If you won't talk about what happened back then, tell me something about now. Hannah's depressed but she says she's happy. What about you? Are you happy? Has life turned out the way you wanted it to?"

Jeanne looked off through the branches and sprays of barbed oak leaves, across the valley. A haze the color of winey mustard veiled San Jose and the eastern foothills and hung low over the vast grid of blocks and streets and the freeway serpentines that wove through and connected the valley, graceful and ugly at the same time.

"I don't think happiness is the point." Jeanne spoke precisely, teacher to student; but the sarcasm was out of her voice and that was a blessing. She wanted to like Jeanne, wanted to love and admire her as she had when they were young. "Just like anybody else, I've had good and bad times. There've been trade-offs, but there's been rewards too. And commitment. In the long run, for me it's commitment that really counts. That's something you and I disagree on—"

"Why do you say that?" The unfairness stung. "How could you possibly know that?"

"Look at your history." Jeanne leaned back against the flume and crossed her ankles in front of her. Such a neat and precise motion, Liz wanted to slug her. "How many men have there been? How many cities?"

And all of them my business, not yours.

Liz had lost count. Forgotten on purpose or accident the one-night stands, the weekends in the country with too much to drink and too many drugs. She had forgotten the men she met in bars who fascinated her for twenty hours or so and the ones she would have liked to know better who didn't call back. And cities? Well, Rennes and Paris and Avignon. London and Florence. Vienna. Now Belize.

"I love Gerard," she said. "That's part of the problem."

"Oh?"

"He wants to get married."

Jeanne grinned and it was clear the news truly pleased her.

"He's not the first, you know." There had been other proposals of marriage, and she had been in love before. But when it came to saying yes, she couldn't do it. Even when she wanted to, she couldn't manage it.

"What's stopping you?"

It had something to do with Bluegang, though it was impossible to explain an intuition that came to her in the middle of the night with the chill clarity of moonlight. During the last year Gerard had helped her by asking the kinds of questions that cornered her and left truth the only way out.

"We shouldn't have left him there."

"Maybe, maybe not. What's that got to do with you and Gerard? And, anyway, it's so far in the past now. We did the only thing we knew to do . . ."

"No. I wanted to tell someone."

"Then why didn't you? Are you saying it's my fault?"

"Not a bit. We all . . ."

"It was an accident, Liz. And what's more, it's one Billy Phillips went asking for. He attacked Hannah. Have you forgotten that?"

Sometimes she did. Sometimes it seemed like Billy Phillips had come after her, not Hannah, and that it was she who had pushed him down onto the rocks. Gerard said she didn't just carry her own guilt, she hauled around Hannah's as well and probably Jeanne's too.

"Teddy and I run a fine school, Liz. We've created something strong and worthwhile together. Once in a blue moon I have a bad day and wish I could run off and join the circus. But it passes. You have to let it pass, let the bad stuff go. I can't believe you're fifty years old and you haven't learned that lesson yet."

"It hangs on to me."

Jeanne took Liz's hands. The unexpected sign of affection brought more tears to Liz's eyes. "Try to understand. If Hannah and I don't want to talk about Bluegang, it's our choice. We're playing our cards the best we can. And you need to play yours while you have a chance. Marry this guy and get on with your life before it's too late."

"But I need to talk about it."

"God, you're a broken record." Jeanne walked away. "Why don't you think about someone besides yourself?"

Liz's throat hurt from the effort it took not to cry. "We were all there."

"Don't try to hang this on us. You've decided you need to talk about what happened for *yourself*. You don't care any more about Hannah and me and Billy Phillips today than you did back then."

"That's not true." Liz scratched her ankle. "I can't believe you'd say that."

"Don't itch, it'll spread."

"Fuck it. And you too!" Liz dropped to the ground and gave in, began to sob. "I didn't want it to be like this. I didn't want to fight."

"We always fight. If you've forgotten that, you've been away too long." Jeanne crouched beside Liz. She took a tissue from her shirt pocket and handed it to her. "Keep your hands off your face. If you touch your face it'll spread."

"I hate you," Liz said, dabbing at her tears. "You always have to be right. You always have to have the last word."

"Yeah," Jeanne said. "It's the cross I bear."

They parted at the road, and Liz walked down to the Bluegang bridge and looked over the edge at the gray stones, dead leaves and litter. She counted three beer cans, an empty Mondavi wine bottle and, under a manzanita bush, a shopping cart tipped on its side, wheels scavenged. How had that gotten all the way up Casabella Road?

Poor Bluegang, she thought. *And good luck, Gail Bacci.* She would write her a check before she went back to Belize.

The feeling after a fight was a weight at the base of her rib cage, resting on her stomach like too much rich food. She and Jeanne had always been quick to spar and then forgive. And sometimes Jeanne's arguments were right on target—like that jab about commitment.

If commitment's what counts in life, Liz had screwed up big time. She hadn't managed to commit to anything or anyone except herself. Until Gerard, home was wherever she built a bookcase and ate the local food. No deep bonds, few responsibilities. And for most of her life she had been comfortable living that way.

Into her mind came the man in Belize City who delivered bananas every week, a refugee from Haiti with skin black and shiny as Italian leather. He drove an ancient Cadillac painted two shades of pink. On Monday mornings she heard him coming from blocks away when his horn sang the first bars of Beethoven's Fifth to warn other drivers that his brakes barely worked. Parked in the sun in front of the guest house, the old Cadillac's chrome acreage blinded her eyes. So wonderful on the outside, the interior workings and the very bolts and screws that held the thing together had traveled their limit. Liz too had gone as many miles as she could manage without an overhaul. She was worn out and cul-de-sacked into the unavoidable conclusion that until she understood what happened that day at Bluegang, her life was on blocks, going nowhere. But it looked like she would have to do it without her friends' help.

She walked to the end of the bridge and climbed around the cement piling and slip-slid down to the creek. Close up, there was more litter. Cigarette butts and cups and condoms. Was there anywhere people wouldn't fuck if the mood struck them? Liz wished for a plastic garden bag and a stick with a nail on the end.

She followed a well-trodden path up the creek toward Hannah's. In some places there was no litter at all, just manzanita and scrub, rocks and poison oak and she seemed to be walking into the past through a wildwood caught in a net of sunlight.

* * *

Now with the steep slope of the wooded canyon to her left, the dry creek bed widening on her right, she looked across to where a bit of frayed rope dangled from a sycamore branch. She remembered the Bolton boys and Jimmy Mesa and his crowd swinging way over the water and dropping into the deepest part of the creek. Some of the girls did it too on those summer days when the town pool closed and Bluegang was crowded with kids; but Liz never had the courage. Hannah jumped and Jeanne, of course. She had the nerve to climb way up the bank and push off hard so she swung far out like the boys did. Liz thought about the varieties of courage and how in her own way she was braver than either of her friends.

In the drought the wide flat boulders where she and Hannah and Jeanne had sunned themselves like pinups stood up in the dirt and sand like gray whales beached. She looked down at her feet and then up the hill at the great California live oak and its saddle of roots. Billy Phillips had fallen to more or less where she stood now. And that's where they left him; that's where the little boys with fishing poles found him the next day.

At breakfast that morning, her father forgot about their special appointment to talk. Instead he and her mother talked about who would be the next president, Stevenson or Eisenhower. They were enjoying themselves and Liz knew better than to interrupt them. As she was washing the breakfast dishes, the phone rang. From the next room she heard her mother's hushed voice; but not the words she said except, "Oh, my God."

Dorothy Shepherd pushed the swinging door between the dining room and the kitchen so hard it banged against the wall. "That unfortunate Billy Phillips is dead," she said. "Apparently he fell and hit his head on the rocks at Bluegang."

Liz had been afraid to speak.

"He didn't come home last night and his mother didn't know what to do. Finally she called Father Whittaker and he got the police out looking." Dorothy Shepherd looked at the wash water in the sink. "Run fresh water. Hot as you can bear. Look at the grease scum." She reached into the sink and pulled the plug.

"That was Hannah's mother on the phone." They watched the dishwater drain away, leaving a few dishes stranded in the sink.

Liz crammed her hands deep in her pockets to hide their shaking. "She thinks—and for once I can't fault her logic—you girls shouldn't play down there again." She fixed Liz with her pale blue eyes, and it was obvious she expected an argument. Liz looked away. She ran steaming water and poured in soap as if the work fascinated her.

"I never did like that place and now I know my instincts were right." Dorothy Shepherd looked out the window over the sink to the backyard where her husband sat in a lawn chair correcting blue books in the shade of a wide-brimmed straw lifeguard's hat crammed down on his head. "This is going to upset your father."

That morning her parents talked outside until almost noon. After lunch Arthur Shepherd called Liz into his study. He took her hands and said, "I want your word of honor that you won't go near that place again, Elizabeth."

"I won't, Daddy." She loved him more than she did her mother. He was no more interested in her than Dorothy was, but in a father remoteness seemed normal.

"Your mother and I are very busy people, and we have to be able to trust you."

"You can trust me, Daddy. I won't go there again." She added, fearing her willingness might betray a guilty conscience, "If you don't want me to."

And until now she had kept her word. What had she expected, revisiting the scene of the crime? A white-light epiphany or a purging grief? A boy had died, a mother had been orphaned, a part of Liz, of her possibilities, had died too. And she felt nothing. Flatline.

He was buried in the town cemetery on Casabella Road in a plot purchased by St. Margaret's Episcopal Church because everyone knew Mrs. Phillips had only Social Security and her husband's Army death benefit. Hannah's father officiated at the ceremony with his assistant, Father Joe. Out of pity and respect for Mrs. Phillips (whose husband had been a hero, Liz heard her father say, at Guadalcanal), everyone along the road went to the graveside and heard Father Whittaker's homily about children being nearest and dearest to God. During the service, Jeanne and Hannah and

Liz stood far apart not looking at each other, and for days afterwards they remained apart. Two weeks elapsed before they talked
on the phone and rode their bikes to see a Judy Garland movie on
Saturday afternoon. Liz couldn't remember the name of the movie
but she did remember this: In the dark of the theater and without
speaking, they reached out and held hands.

Saturday

The clock beside Jeanne's bed indicated it was not yet 6:00, but she knew the cooks were already at work in the school kitchen. Because it was Saturday, breakfast would be pancakes; and because it was October, there would be applesauce. In less than an hour, the housekeeping staff would punch in, and by noon the sitting room and hall of the main building would be full of the fragrance of freshly cut roses, and sometime during the day she knew Edith White would turn to her and say, "End of season blooms always smell the sweetest."

Saturday lunch: make-your-own sandwiches from cold cuts and cheese and—because it was October—bowls full of Pink Lady apples. Intramural or league, all through October and November there were Saturday games Jeanne could count on. If she felt blue, watching the little boys play mayhem soccer almost lifted her spirits. On Saturday nights the senior school had a social exchange with another school or games and movies while the junior school crowded the common room to play board games, watch movies and eat big sticky handfuls of caramel popcorn. In the early days, when the school was short-staffed and struggling they had taken a few boarders as young as six and seven, boys marooned by parents gone off on world cruises, parentless boys put out to board by overwhelmed grandparents. Jeanne was touched by the bravery and stoicism of these abandoned boys who deserved to be at home with siblings, a messy room and a big gallumphing dog. She looked forward all week to the time in her Saturday night schedule when she read aloud to them. For the occasion she dragged out books Teddy told her no kid read anymore—*Dr. Dolittle, The Jungle Book* and *Just So Stories;* and when she looked up from the pages at their intent faces she imagined one of the boys was her own son returned to her by the whim of a perverse god, and that the story of Mowgli encouraged him.

After her brother died and her parents started killing themselves with drink and work, it was Jeanne's salvation that a cook came before six to make the morning meal and that the sitting room roses were fresh. She couldn't control her mother's condemnatory silence or her father's subtle forms of abuse, but she could depend on the school cook—Billy Phillips's mother at one time—could depend on dinner being served in the big hall at precisely six and there was never any doubt that in the fall there would be apples for breakfast, lunch and dinner.

Are you happy?

Obviously Liz was. Hannah worried she had AIDS or cancer but Jeanne didn't think there was a chance of that. She glowed with good health and seemed more confident than she ever had. And Jeanne didn't have to be an expert on the emotions to see the way Liz looked when she spoke of Gerard. She loved him not in some intellectual, theoretical or practical way but . . . powerfully.

Just wait until she was actually married and a few years had gone by.

Jeanne had never spent more than a few moments thinking about what it meant to be happy. Maybe in a philosophy course there had been some determined argument between herself and a professor; it was the kind of thing one talked about in college and then forgot. She lived. She got up in the morning and ate and breathed and worked and did her best and then she went to sleep. She had always been perplexed by the line in the Declaration of Independence about the *pursuit* of happiness and didn't know how a person would do this. She wasn't sure she would recognize it if she saw it running up ahead, taunting her, daring her to chase after it.

She expected to work, to take charge, to be responsible and suf-

ficiently disciplined to control her environment. And whatever re-
sulted from her efforts . . . well, if it was happiness then good.

Liz's question was typical of the emotional thinking Jeanne expected from her and felt compelled to put down. At the same time,
if Liz had changed, Jeanne would have felt the loss keenly. Her
friend's peculiar observations could jolt Jeanne's thinking in a way
she did not like but recognized as, at least theoretically, good. Liz
was in many ways a foreign country to Jeanne; and often their time
together made her feel as she had on the walk to the flume—defensive and slightly third worldish. The years of friendship, the fights
and making up and deep confidences, had never completely dis-
pelled this sense of impoverishment. The sky-ey Land of Liz had
resources of imagination and emotion absent from Jeanne's gravity-
bound world; and though she tried to believe this lack made her at
least Liz's equal and probably her superior, she never convinced
herself for long.

She squinted at the clock beside the bed: 5:45. Too early to get
up. She lay on her back, legs straight, arms at her side and imagined she was lying on the lion-footed bench in the rose cloister on a
hot summer day. The sun would heat her skin and the smell of the
flowers, the drone of the bees, would drown out whatever was in
her head she wanted to ignore. She thought of her brother standing
over her, shaking down rose petals and the sun behind him made a
penumbra of gold around his handsome head. She wished she
could believe in angels. It would have comforted her to know that
Michael hovered nearby, watching over her.

In the spring of his last year at Stanford he and two other football players, drunk on a Saturday night, had become disoriented,
bumped over a median strip and drove down an off-ramp onto
Bayshore Freeway. Going north in the southbound lanes by Foster
City they'd rammed a pickup truck head-on. Everyone died. Five
people altogether.

Jeanne turned in bed and her hand grazed Teddy's back in silk
pajamas. They cost more than two hundred dollars a pair and he
had a drawer full of them in maroon and navy blue and black with
silver piping. Jeanne didn't begrudge him the luxury of silk pajamas and Italian slacks and cashmere sweaters. Hilltop was a finan-

cial success in large part because Teddy was good at managing money and brazen about asking for it. Hilltop's endowment, bank accounts and investments had soared on the Silicon Valley boom. But his gimme-gimme shamed Jeanne sometimes.

She remembered Simon Weed's pudgy dimpled hands. Touching her they would be warm and soft as fresh bread. Almost dreaming, she remembered his kindness like a kiss. It stirred her to think of how he loved his son, and she wanted to touch herself, but she didn't dare with Teddy sleeping beside her. Once he'd caught her, and his teasing shamed her for weeks afterwards. She did not tell him; he would not have understood that some mornings there was a valley of ache in her and she needed to be touched. She reached out and lightly stroked the muscular line of Teddy's hip and thigh. Somehow he found time to go to the gym four days a week.

Jeanne moved her hand around to caress his stomach under the shirt of his pajamas. "Want to?"

"I'm asleep."

"Let me wake you up." Her fingers traced the line of curling hair from his navel to his groin. "Please."

"I said I'm asleep."

"Teddy, it's been weeks . . ."

He hunched off to the far side of the bed. Jeanne laid her palm on the warm place where his body had been.

Her father would say, *Happiness isn't the point.* There were good and bad times, disappointments and victories. Trade-offs. To expect more of life was romanticism, wind in the eaves with no storm behind it. *Get on with business, Jeanne Louise.*

Liz's talk about Bluegang, that had been a surprise; and now, of course, details of that day rose to the surface of Jeanne's mind like the plague of jellyfish that ruined her last visit to Hawaii. The boy's brown blood on the rock and his startled mouth, the space between his two front teeth. Hannah's bright toenails. Liz had brought these memories with her.

Jeanne had never second-guessed their actions on that day. For girls so young, they had behaved with laudatory pragmatism. Silence had protected both Hannah and Billy Phillips's mother. If Hannah had told her story not only would she and her family have suffered, poor Mrs. Phillips would have been shamed and hurt. They had done what was best for everyone.

The school phone rang.

Jeanne reached out to answer it.

Edith White said, "Jeanne, I'm sorry to bother you early but I thought you'd want to know . . ."

"It's okay, Edith." Jeanne swung her legs over the edge of the bed and stood. "I'm up." She carried the phone to the window and watched a pair of mourning doves pecking in the unplanted garden. She wondered, as she always did, if it was true they mated for life.

"It's that new boy. Adam Weed."

Jeanne's back stiffened.

"I was just getting started this morning when I saw him coming across the field."

"Before first bell?"

"Oh, my, yes. Way before. It was just barely getting light. I watched him walk across the soccer field and back into the dormitory."

Jeanne's feet on the hardwood were blocks of ice.

"Did you speak to him?"

"I didn't think it was my place. Not at this stage anyway. Him being new and all."

"He has some learning problems. Maybe he doesn't understand the rules yet."

"What boy doesn't know it's wrong to leave his room in the middle of the night and go wandering all over heaven-knows-where?" Edith asked. "That's more than learning problems, if you ask me."

From her bed in the guest room on the second floor Liz watched a pair of doves side by side on the phone wire, chic in their black-and-white and pearl gray ensembles. They seemed fond of each other. If she said this to Gerard he would laugh and say she was an-thropomorphizing. But he would not try to change her thinking, nor would he be critical in an unkind way. He let her think as she wanted, do as she chose. Once she had believed this tolerance meant he didn't really care for her. It had taken time to realize that

Gerard believed in her in a way she did not believe in herself. He assumed she would do the right thing or as close to it as she could manage at the time. He did not think she needed him at her elbow directing and admonishing. What freedom had come with this. To say what she wanted. To do what she thought best. To make mistakes and to ask advice or not.

She shifted her position, trying to get comfortable. Her pregnancy barely showed but internally her body had changed and there were times like now when she felt possessed by an entity that meant to do her harm. This baby was a freak occurrence that never should have happened. Gerard said it was the evolutionary drive of the body to reproduce itself before too late. As if labeling a disaster made it any less a disaster.

She folded her hands over her stomach. Sometimes she woke in the middle of the night and thought she felt the baby move but the feeling passed so quickly she could not be sure it wasn't just gas, what Hannah's mother used to call cobby-wobbles. She was grateful movement hadn't yet begun. She knew herself. When the bucks and rolls began she would imagine communication, personality, a life would unspool in her mind and she would not be able to stop it.

She wished Gerard were beside her now. After less than a week she missed him and this was unexpected. Without noticing it until now, her affection for him had settled at a deeper level, like rocks and sand and soil at the end of a long subsidence.

Rap reverberated through the wall between Liz's room and Eddie's. The house throbbed and sang with the sound of piped water.

Family.

Saturday morning.

In the big double bed, she stretched her long legs and like a little girl tried to make her toes reach all the way to the end of the mattress. They didn't and her right foot cramped.

Middle age.

She sat up and bent her toes against the cramp until it released. Gingerly she let them go; gently she massaged them. Her fingers touched the poison oak rash. It was dry and harmless now. A dab of Dan's wonder drug had done the job. In the mirror across the room she saw herself and thought, not bad. She might be cramping up like a beached starfish, but for fifty, she looked okay. From across the room she couldn't see the creases around her eyes or the tiny lines around her mouth. If she squinted she looked pretty much as she had the last time she slept in Hannah's guest room.

But I'm still too old to have a baby.

A tap on the door. "I brought you a latte, Aunt Liz." Ingrid held out a paisley printed coffee mug.

"Bless your mother," Liz said, inhaling the aroma of espresso and steamed milk.

The pretty face frowned. "It was my idea."

"Of course it was. What a doll." Liz patted the bed. "Sit down and share it with me."

Ingrid made a face as she settled herself. "Too bitter."

Liz took a long sip. "I think I was born craving coffee with my mother's milk." Not that Dorothy Shepherd had nursed her only child. What a ridiculous thought that was.

"Mom says the first time you guys went to Europe mostly all you did was sit in cafés and drink coffee. She said Aunt Jeanne did a bunch of stuff on her own 'cause she was mad at you for wasting time."

"Here's a word of godmotherly advice, Ingrid. You can tour any time, you can even do it on the Net; but you're only young in Paris for a moment. One hallowed moment."

Between their sophomore and junior years in college she and Hannah and Jeanne had spent a week in Paris bars and bistros, staying up late every night, walking through the neighborhoods, soaking up Paris.

I'll live in the Latin Quarter someday.

Who would you sleep with, Picasso or Hemingway? What about Yves Montand?

French men have sexy eyes.

Simone Signoret must have slept with every good-looking man in Paris.

Frenchwomen are sexy even when they're old.

Liz had wanted to live in France since grammar school when she read *Our Hearts Were Young and Gay* and even more in high school when she struggled through *Swann's Way*. The day after she graduated from San Jose State she was on a plane with a B.A. in French, a minor in Art History, and her parents' distracted blessing

"I'm not even sure I want to go to college. Not right away." The bed creaked as Ingrid got off. Liz watched her roam the bedroom, saw her cast a critical look at her chin in the mirror and try to flatten her long fair curls. Not as curly as Hannah's. More like the ripples in a heat mirage. She flung herself down on the window seat. "I just know I don't want to have an ordinary life. I'll die if I stay in Rinconada. Remember when me and Mom met you in New York last year? Didn't you love it? Don't you wish you lived there?"

"I enjoyed it because I was with you."

"You don't know how awful it is around here. In my high school most of the kids are just so . . . crass. You know? Half the guys are computer nerds and the rest want to own a Ferrari dealership. Can you believe that? Can you imagine your highest aim being to sell cars for a living?"

She groaned and looked so miserable Liz didn't know whether to weep for her or laugh.

"I'd just wither up and blow away if I had to live out my life in this hole."

Liz remembered being sure of the same thing.

"Sometimes Paco and I talk about moving to New York." Ingrid looked over at the bed—quickly, shyly, Liz thought—to see if she was being taken seriously. "He's a terrific writer. Not poetry and all but analytical stuff. Someday he's going to write books about politics. That's what he wants to do."

"What about you?"

Ingrid looked down at her toes painted blue-black. "Promise you won't say anything? I can never talk about stuff like this with Mom and Dad, especially Mom. She would just totally freak if I told her I think I want to be a model. Not like Cindy Crawford because obviously I'm too short and my boobs are too big, but shoes and nylons and stuff." Ingrid stretched one bare leg and foot toward the bed. "This guy's who's a photographer told me my feet are perfect for modeling because they're narrow and the arch is perfect and I've got great ankles. See this toe?" She pointed to the one next to the big toe. "Shoe designers like it if this toe's longest.

Kids used to tease me about my toes but now I see it's an advantage. Plus, I've got good legs, which is absolutely essential if you're gonna model shoes."

Liz saw only a foot, the kind that would probably do all the mundane and essential things expected of it for eighty or ninety years. She wanted to tell Ingrid she could do so much more with her life than pose, but she remembered being seventeen. It was a time all about posing.

"If Mom knew I was thinking about not going to Stanford, she'd go ballistic. She wants me to do everything just the way she did."

"I think she wants you to be happy."

"Right." Ingrid rolled her eyes. "When she thinks about me at all."

She resumed her prowl of the bedroom.

What do you mean, *when she thinks of you at all?*

Ingrid sighed and sprawled on a little upholstered armchair across the room. "See, the thing is, I don't want her in my stuff all the time. I don't want her asking me questions or picking through my drawers, you know?"

Liz nodded.

"But I'd like to think . . ." Another deep sigh. "Well, she just doesn't care much anymore. You know what I mean, Aunt Liz. We never talk. She never asks me what I think. She's always either busy or depressed or talking about that crack baby."

"She cares, Ingrid. When you were born—"

"I know, I know. But I'm not a baby anymore. I'm a grown-up. And grown-ups don't really interest my mom all that much. She thinks she knows me, but she hardly does."

Liz sipped her coffee, burned her lips buying time.

Ingrid began to prowl again. After some moments she said, "Can I ask you a personal question, Aunt Liz? I mean, this is the kind of thing I would, like, never ask Mom and if you don't want to answer, you don't have to. Okay?"

Everything else had been preamble; it was for this Ingrid had come in bearing coffee. Liz pushed her pillow against the headboard and leaned back.

"You won't say anything to Mom?"

Liz crossed her heart.

Ingrid traced the cloisonné mosaic on the back of Liz's hairbrush. "This is pretty. Where'd you get it?"

"Gerard gave it to me."

Ingrid dug a big toe into the carpet. "What's he like?"

"Is that what you wanted to ask me?"

"It's sorta hard."

Under the bedclothes Liz brought her knees to her chin and wrapped her arms around them to contain a burst of silly joy.

"Do you like sex?"

Liz must have looked surprised.

Ingrid's hand flew to her mouth. "Oh, God, I'm sorry. I mean, I just assumed . . . I mean, you do have sex? Don't you? I know you do. Of course you do. Oh, shit." Her round face was scarlet, more seven than seventeen. "Mom and Dad do it. I'm not an idiot who thinks her parents are, like, . . . celibate. But Mom's in the middle of The Change. Dad says that's what's making her so weird. So I'm pretty sure she isn't interested."

Liz could interrupt, take the girl out of her misery; but it was fascinating to watch this display of youth. She had forgotten the importance of sex. Once it was all she thought about.

"I gotta say, you seem a lot younger than Mom. And I thought because you and Gerard aren't married—"

We have sex constantly.

She mustn't smile. It would be so easy to offend Ingrid's dignity.

"Fifty isn't so old, Ingrid."

"I wasn't saying you were old-old. Shit, I didn't mean to make you feel bad."

"And you certainly haven't done that." Liz patted a space beside her on the bed. "Tell me what you want to know. Sex is one of the few subjects I can speak on as an expert."

Ingrid blushed a deeper red.

I love you. You will never know or even guess how much.

Ingrid asked, "Do you really like it?"

"More now than when I was young, actually. Although it doesn't seem nearly as important as it did then. It's not exciting in the same way." An interesting question and difficult to answer candidly. What would Hannah think of all this candor? Maybe Liz should extract a promise of silence from her goddaughter. "The first time—"

"That's what I really want to know." Ingrid leaned toward her. "What was it like for you? The first time?"

The beauty of Ingrid's innocence struck Liz hard where she hadn't been hit before, in a protected place between her head and her heart and she felt a kind of lurch inside. A seventeen-year-old virgin. A maiden. *Why doesn't anyone tell girls to pause and pay attention. Why are we all so eager to be broken?*

"He was a sculptor in Brittany. Young like me and very stormy-minded." Willy.

A bullet to the brain. If he had not died she would never have met Gerard. And gotten pregnant. Couldn't she forget for five minutes?

"I don't want to disappoint you, Ingrid, but not all Frenchmen are great lovers. Sex with Willy wasn't very good. He was learning just as I was, and we weren't either of us any good at it. I think he enjoyed himself, he appeared to; but I basically felt let down about the whole business."

"You didn't love him."

"Oh, I did. Madly."

"Then how could it be . . . a letdown?"

"Because sometimes it is." Liz shrugged. "Sex is a big deal, I'm not saying otherwise. And sometimes love can help make it a *really* big deal. But sex, the basic in and out, it can be tedious."

She watched Ingrid's face as she tried to make sense of this.

"What happened to him?"

"Life, I guess." She shrugged the truth away. "I don't quite remember."

Liar.

She remembered everything about Willy and about Guy who took her from him to Paris. "My next lover was older. He came to Brittany looking for new artists for his gallery. Sex was better with him, but I didn't love him. I loved Willy. Bad sex and all."

Liz felt jaded and parched. "Word of advice, Ingrid: don't settle for less than love."

"You love Gerard, right?"

Liz nodded.

"Then why don't you get married? Mom says—" The blush again.

"Yes?"

"She says you don't think you're lovable, which is totally not true because—"

Liz rested her index finger on Ingrid's lips. "She didn't say I wasn't lovable, honey. She said I don't *think* I am. For some people it's easier to give love than to take it. I think that's what Hannah means." Gerard sang the same tune. Lately it was his favorite ditty. "I'm not saying it's true, Ingrid, but if it is then I've come to the right place, haven't I? Like all those poor dogs and cats and that horse down at the barn? Isn't this the place we all come to feel loved?"

"We *all* love you. Not just *her.*"

"Well, thank goodness for that or I'd have to stay at the Holiday Inn."

"Rinconada doesn't have one. They won't let you build a motel or hotel in the city limits."

"Now I'm doubly grateful." Time to end this before Ingrid saw how she had gotten to Liz. "Let me get out of this bed before I grow roots. We'd see how lovable I'd be with roots growing out of my butt."

Ingrid laughed uncertainly. "I didn't mean to hurt your feelings, Aunt Liz. Honest."

Damn. The girl saw things.

"You didn't hurt them. Not a bit." Liz waved her off. "Now, scoot. Tell your mom I'll be down in a few minutes."

Liz lay back and pulled the bedcovers up to her chin. A crowd of images and memories filled the room and she ducked her head under the blanket to escape them. Silly girl—there in the darkness was Willy, reaching for her with calloused hands smelling of clay. He had adored her in his young clumsy way and had expected her to wrap his love around her and wear it like a Dior. No wonder she'd left him. Guy made love with the hands and body of a man attuned to female chemistry; and when he touched her, she flew into a thousand vibrating pieces. He had understood what Hannah did, what Ingrid could not believe; Liz didn't think she had love coming to her. Guy knew she would give whatever he asked of her;

and the pittance return she would accept with gratitude and surprise. They parted after a year and she did not really care. There
were other men, other buses up and down the avenues of Paris,
London, Rome. After a long time there was Gerard.

Willy's mother had written to Liz in Avignon to say that Willy
was dead. A bullet to the brain. The funeral was scheduled for the
next Saturday. *Come if you can, Elizabeth. He would be pleased.* Liz
doubted this but she knew it would please Madame with whom
she had maintained a Christmastime correspondence since leaving
Rennes. Still, she did not decide to go at once. Her life in Avignon
was comfortably settled in those days. She had sufficient translating work to earn a decent living. Income from her parents' estate
gave her luxuries like a condominium with a view of the Rhone
and a late model BMW, which at the time Willy died was in the
garage having its brakes replaced. Not that she would ever have
chosen to drive to Brittany. Despite her years in France, she had
never learned to drive ninety kilometers an hour rain or shine, day
or night.

Instead she traveled to Rennes by bus and train and arrived exhausted only to learn there had been a mix-up in her hotel reservations. The best the management could do was shrug and offer a
small room at the back, second floor. Liz might have hunted
around for somewhere better if it had not been February and
threatening snow. She had forgotten how bitter cold it could be in
Rennes in wintertime and the old stone hotel, so cheery in its ad
with brass polished and fireplaces blazing, was frigid. What's
more, the management appeared outraged when she complained.
In the hotel dining room she ate too much that night, hoping pâté
and cassoulet and an apple tart with cream might warm her up.
Instead she felt fat and guilty. In the sitting room to which she retreated after dinner clutching a cognac, two men occupied the
chairs nearest the fire. She saw a resemblance between them. The
same heavy, slightly baggy eyes, the long nose and sensual mouth.
Father and son, she thought. Attractive.

The father, serene and dignified in a gray suit patterned in her-
ringbone and perfectly fitted to his slim frame, leaped to his feet
and offered his place in a deep easy chair. Another time she would

have deferred to his age, but that night she thanked him and sank in gratefully.

"I prefer a straight chair," he said. "My back." He carried a wooden chair from the writing table across the room and placed it precisely between Liz and his son. "You do not mind?"

"Of course not."

"I am Etienne Robin and this is my son, Gerard."

"I'm Liz Shepherd."

"American? I would not have guessed it. Your French is perfect."

Gerard said in English, "I thought I could always tell an American."

"Well," Liz said with a little smile, "there you are."

Gerard Robin and his father were also in Rennes for Willy's funeral.

"My father has a large collection of folk art."

"Yes, and Willy's work in the last few years has been quite marvelous. Astonishing garden pieces. Such subtlety of color and glaze and the droll way he had of working in the Breton material. Not in the least . . ." Etienne Robin thought a moment and then grinned. "Not at all kitschy. That is the American word, I think?"

"Yiddish," Liz said.

"I wish I had room for more. In our garden—"

"My parents live in Paris," Gerard said. "They have a weekend house a little north of here, on the coast. He encountered Willy's work in a gallery here in Rennes."

The old man sighed. "He was a troubled man but then, so many artists are."

"Troubled people are my father's specialty. He is a psychiatrist."

Liz remembered that she had read his name in articles debating the relevance of Freudian theory.

Gerard asked Liz how she knew Willy and she told him, an abbreviated and expurgated version. Gerard was a man, he was French, he could read between the lines if he wanted to. He bought her another cognac and when Liz checked her watch she was surprised to see it was almost midnight.

Liz slept poorly that night, clutching a hot water bottle first to her feet and then to her thighs and never really getting warm. In the morning she resumed her place before the fire and drank a cup of milky coffee, wishing she had stayed at home in Avignon. It wasn't just the damp and the cold and the lumpy mattress that had her down. It was being in Rennes again. It was the thought of Willy's brains splattered across his studio.

"May we offer you a ride to the church, Mlle. Shepherd?" Etienne Robin stood in the doorway. "You said last night you do not have an automobile."

Perhaps the day would be easier to bear if she were not alone.

In the years since her departure from Brittany she had not followed Willy's career and had only a vague idea that he enjoyed some success using Breton themes and materials. The crowd in the cold stone church surprised her and the little anxiety she had that she would be conspicuous vanished immediately. There were prayers and testimonials. A choir of children in ruffed vestments sang folk songs in Breton, a language Liz had never heard. Bundled and dumpy as an Eskimo, she sat and stood and knelt between Etienne and Gerard Robin, all the while conscious of the cold and of the flower-decked box in the front of the church. She recalled Willy's boyishness, the way he stroked her head as if she were one of his spaniels. When she chided him for this he did not understand. "But I love them," he said. "And I love you too." She put her hands on the pew in front of her, rested her forehead on them, and wept.

"You must not sleep another night in that dreadful hotel," Gerard said and his father agreed.

"We are leaving for Paris in a few moments. Come with us and stay in our apartment. Tomorrow or the next day you can take the train back to Avignon."

To be invited to stay in a French home on such short and superficial acquaintance was astonishing. She must have looked surprised because Etienne laughed.

It had begun to sleet and the cold froze her bones and made her feel brittle and vulnerable. She didn't want to talk. She wanted to stare into the rain and think about Willy and try to understand why his death made her feel that nothing she had ever done mattered. Her accomplishments, her competencies . . . nothing.

"I would not be good company, I'm afraid."

But the thought of the cold hotel, the lumpy bed . . .

Gerard drove his father's big Mercedes, Liz sat up front beside him and Etienne quickly fell asleep in the back. At the first wide spot in the road Gerard stopped the car and got out. In the rain he opened the trunk and took out an alpaca throw, opened the back door and gently tucked the blanket across his father's lap and legs.

The tender gesture touched Liz and she looked more closely at Gerard Robin.

"Are you warm enough?" he asked when they were back on the highway. "Turn up the heat if you like."

She said she was fine and waited. For the inevitable questions. Why did she live in France and for how long? Was she married? How did she earn her living? But Gerard surprised her. He selected a tape—classical guitar—and set the volume low. For a long time they drove in silence and gradually Liz began to relax. She leaned back and slept a while.

She woke when the car turned off the busy highway near Le Mans and bumped down a provincial road.

"Sorry to wake you but I need something to eat and a cup of coffee," Gerard said. "Will you join me?"

"Your father? . . ."

"He's fine. He took a pill to help him sleep."

The lights of a little bistro brightened the road ahead. Gerard tucked the Mercedes into a parking place between a Renault and an old Citroën and they went in. When Gerard opened the door and the heat and smoke hit them, they looked at each other and burst into laughter. It was a dreadful place and they both knew it before they tasted the bitter coffee and stale bread. But the break refreshed them. Gerard amused her with a running commentary on the clientele and when they returned to the highway and he asked the expected questions, Liz felt like answering them and asking some of her own.

In the middle of the night, thirty minutes out of Paris, traffic stopped for emergency road repairs brought about by the heavy rain and complicated by wet snow. For two hours while they waited for the road to clear, Liz and Gerard sat in the Mercedes and talked about themselves and their families, what they liked and what they loathed; and somewhere before dawn, Liz let down her guard. She had always believed in love at first sight. But after so many instant passions lost their heat in a few weeks or months, burned out like incandescent bulbs, Liz had learned that the love that came on hot and fast could not be trusted. Nor could the men who engendered it. Men who, she had decided, usually knew exactly what they were doing. Experience had taught her to protect herself, but by the time traffic cleared and Gerard was navigating the streets of the Sixth Arrondissement the atmosphere in the car had thickened and grown heavy and sweet with anticipation.

When they reached the Robins' apartment in an ornate old stone building overlooking the Luxembourg Gardens, Gerard helped his father upstairs and told a sleepy-eyed maid to settle Liz in the guest room. He left for his own apartment, promising to see her the next day. In a daze of fatigue and confused feelings Liz stripped off her clothes and climbed into the high bed naked. For an hour she slipped in and out of consciousness, aware of Gerard somewhere in the Sixth in his own bed, and both of them savoring the pull of attraction like a change in gravity.

Liz met Madame Robin the next morning in the front room of the apartment where she sat in a small feminine chair opening mail, facing the windows with her back to a lamp—the only one lighted in the cavernous room. She was a slender woman with an animated heart-shaped face and a precise way of speaking.

"Etienne sees patients down the hall, his office is there. You must not be alarmed if you encounter some wild-haired weeping person. Gerard called. He will see you later today. He must first see about his visa. He is going to Brazil tomorrow night."

Liz thought he must have told her this when they first began talking at the hotel; but because she did not care about him then, the fact had not registered. Now it broke on her like news of an accident. Her thoughts might have shown in her expression because Anouk Robin asked, "Do you know my son well?"

"We met yesterday. At the funeral." Liz remembered her manners. "Madame, you are so kind to take me in. A stranger."

"You are thinking, how 'un-French'?"

Liz had been.

"My husband and I, when Gerard and his sisters were little, traveled a great deal. We lived in Cambridge for a year when he taught at Harvard, and then at Claremont-McKenna." Madame Robin sighed. "I found Los Angeles a challenge, but I have learned to like Americans with the result that our home has always been full of students and visitors. Last year we had a very noisy young student from Australia. Etienne assured me he was perfectly brilliant but I was never sure. He had the most appalling eating habits. I could only satisfy him with steak and potatoes." She looked perplexed, then laughed. "So you see, it is not so strange you are here. Etienne said only that there was an American friend in the guest room, a friend of Gerard's, a friend of Willy's. Is that so?"

"I knew Willy when we were young."

"I liked him so much though when he came to stay I never knew quite what to expect from him. Gloomy." Absently Madame Robin tapped a silver letter opener against her palm. "Willy made me grateful my children are blessed with calm and tranquil natures."

Yes, Liz thought, that would seem to describe Gerard.

The tall narrow windows of the Robins' apartment faced the Luxembourg Gardens, beautiful even in the midst of winter. Liz stood at the glass watching a woman in yellow tights running in the rain with a pair of Afghan hounds beside her.

"It will be so beautiful in a few months."

"I prefer the winter," Madame Robin said. "Tourists exhaust me."

Liz nodded. "Avignon in August."

"Don't misunderstand, I enjoy living at the center of things. When Gerard was a baby we were in my parents' apartment in the Sixteenth. Large enough for all of us and more. But it was too somber there, too quiet. I would take Gerard with me when I went to the chemist and there was no one on the streets. Here there is life, always life on the streets and in the shops. And Gerard lives not so far away, a few blocks. We see him often."

"I used to live off the rue de Buci," Liz said. "And my publisher's apartment is somewhere near here."

"You are a writer?"

"A translator. Nonfiction. Mostly English to French." Liz mentioned a translation of hers that had recently been a best-seller on both sides of the Atlantic. Madame Robin seemed slightly impressed and vaguely encouraging, and so Liz went on to tell her how she had come to France as a young woman out of college, studied at the Sorbonne and worked in a variety of jobs until she made a small reputation for herself as a careful and sensitive translator. She talked to keep from saying what was really on her mind: *When will Gerard be here? How long must I wait?*

"And you live in Avignon now? Why is that? It is a pretty little city, of course, but . . ." Madame Robin raised her eyebrows very slightly, "it is not Paris."

"I find the older I get, the more I need the sun."

"And how old are you?"

The direct question startled Liz. The French were a correct race, private.

"Forgive me," Madame Robin said though it was clear she did not really believe she had misspoken. "I should not have asked. But you are an American. I thought you would not mind telling me."

Liz laughed. "Thirty-eight."

"Young I think. But I know what you mean about the cold." She looked around her. "And this great mausoleum, it is impossible to heat in the winter. Were you warm enough in the guest room?"

"Yes, Madame, thank you."

The deep colors of the Persian carpets and the red and green and gold tapestry upholstering the chairs and couches warmed the gray light that poured through the windows. Madame Robin kept an electric heater beamed toward them; but the cold harried Liz the moment she moved beyond its shallow circle. After coffee and a roll Madame Robin insisted she go back to bed. She slept through the afternoon until the maid brought her coffee and a slice of unfrosted lemon cake and said drinks would be served in an hour.

The family dined together and the talk was of Gerard's upcoming trip. He had been invited by the government of Brazil to visit a remote catchment near the Ecuadorian border.

"How long will you be gone?" Liz asked.

"Six months. Perhaps longer. And then I have been offered a job—"

"Please, Gerard," Madame Robin said.

"—in Belize."

"Do not spoil our dinner."

He explained to Liz, "Maman does not want her only son to leave France. She dictates my comings and goings as if I were a child." It was clear from the way he spoke that this amused him.

Madame Robin said, "Go to Germany if you must. To Italy or even England, but not this place, Belize."

Liz said, "They have wonderful rain forests there, don't they?"

"*Exactement.* There is nothing there but trees," Madame Robin looked at her husband reproachfully, as if she resented his failure to take her side.

Gerard smiled at Liz. His smile crinkled his eyes and drew his brows and his cheeks up so he looked like a boy whose pet project had been encouraged by the teacher. Only she didn't feel anything like this man's teacher. Her stomach fluttered and she smiled back and couldn't stop smiling.

As Madame Robin asked how he would store the books and furnishings from his apartment and Monsieur Robin complained about the farmers, Liz thought about love. She was almost forty and had been in love too many times to think there was anything magical about the process. Chemistry and proximity. By just walking away she could stop the process. It might take a little effort and register as a sacrifice, but it could be done. But, oh, what a waste it would be. This independent and slightly formal Frenchman, humorous and kind to his elderly parents, this man in love with trees and rain, a confirmed bachelor who would often be gone and would never ask for more than she could comfortably give: could there be anyone better suited to her?

She bent her head toward him and a thick swing of dark hair slipped across her cheek. "They call the Luxembourg Gardens the lungs of Paris, don't they?" She swirled the wine in her glass and looked up at him through her lashes, dimly aware of Madame's narrowed eyes watching her. "Isn't that what rain forests are?"

The next afternoon was damp and gray with a wind like a heat-seeking missile engineered to slip between the buttons of her coat, down the neck and up her legs. Gerard gave her his muffler and she wrapped it three times around so he said she looked like she had no neck at all. Liz didn't care. Overnight she had given in; her heart was sinking like a coin in a wishing well. They walked and walked and when the cold became unbearable they nicked inside antique shops and art galleries where the proprietors shot daggers with their eyes no matter how Liz and Gerard pretended to be shopping in earnest. As they stood outside a film revival house reading the bills Gerard took her hand and didn't let go even when they were jostled in the streets crowded with busy urban professionals, dogs, and children in school uniforms clutching their books. At dusk they went up some stairs to a café and ordered little cups of foaming brown espresso.

Liz kept thinking: *At eleven tonight you go. Tonight at eleven you will leave me. Please don't leave me.*

Her thoughts were in her eyes.

"I'll be back," he said.

It was a peculiar love affair. No proximity and no time to become lovers. Instead, they began a long-distance friendship by way of mail and phone. Brazil kept Gerard almost three years and their time in France never coincided. She was in New York or on a much anticipated trip to Africa or doing business in Canada. His parents met him in Rio for a family holiday. And then came an irresistible opportunity in Indonesia. Belize renewed its offer, and he turned it down again. During those years in Avignon Liz watched the mistral tear away the leaves of the sycamores in the park across the street and the new leaves bud and then the wind again. She was strangely patient and confident that when the time was right, she and Gerard would have their long postponed love affair. In the meantime she had an extended romance, unimportant but amusing in small doses, with Bernard, a director of the Avignon Festival through whom she met dozens of artists, actors and musicians; and she translated a book about Benjamin Franklin's years in Paris that earned her a few weeks in the media spotlight. She traveled twice to London to meet with Jeanne and Hannah and once they rented a car and drove up the west coast of Italy from Naples to Genoa. They met in New York, saw shows, ate too much and dished until the small hours.

Often during those years she visited the Robins and eventually she met Gerard's two chic sisters and their families and was invited to spend long weekends and holidays with them all at their country house in Brittany. One day Madame spoke to her using the familiar *tu*, and Liz felt the last barrier between them collapse.

The Robins' country home sat on a promontory in the Gulf of St. Malo, at the end of a narrow seaside road. It was an old stone barn to which they had added several rooms and a porch. In the front a swath of cut grass curved down to the pebbled shoreline. Under a vine-covered pergola the Robin family ate their meals at a table laid with bright cotton cloths, jars of grandchildren-gathered wildflowers and chipped Quimper.

In the Victorian house on Casabella Road Liz had moused from room to room to avoid disturbing her scholarly parents and watched what she said for fear her words would give her away, reveal that she was less than brilliant. For all her effort, nothing she did seemed to please them much, let alone delight them. Not the way the Robins took pride and pleasure in their children and grandchildren. Why had this unusual French family taken her in and made her one of them? Why had this good fortune come to her?

They see in you what I do, Gerard said. And they are determined to get me married before I'm fifty. For such a worthy goal a French family will unbend, even for an American.

At the rear of the house a neighbor farmer grazed a herd of black-and-white milk cows in a field enclosed by a stone wall. The littlest Robin grandchildren begged Liz to walk around the paddock, with them on the wall pretending to be tightrope walkers.

That one, the big one? Is it a bull? If I fall . . .

I'll be here, Mignon (Nu-Nu, Armand, and the others). I will protect you.

She loved the Robin family long before she felt anything but unsatisfied lust for Gerard. Imagination was Liz's gift, what Mrs. Buhler in the sixth grade said she had more of than was healthy, what her father said she must make her servant, not her master. On those summer days walking with the little ones, helping to prepare the meals and at the end of the day in her bed she pretended that Anouk and Etienne were her real mother and father.

Still she expected that when the Robins really got to know her the invitations would cease. She imagined a luxury train had stopped to pick her up, a ragamuffin by the side of the tracks; and someday it would stop again and boot her off.

All this she confided to Gerard in letters and his response was always the same.

You do not appreciate yourself. Maman would not have chosen you for me if you had not been extraordinary. And besides, they know I love you.

But what kind of man loved a woman he'd never slept with? He had left for Brazil too suddenly, and since then they had barely been alone. Kisses, yes, and long, tantalizing embraces, but never time for anything else. This made them laugh. If they were twenty years younger fifteen minutes in a broom closet would give them all the time and privacy they needed.

Another funeral, this time Madame's, a sudden and cataclysmic heart attack as she applied her makeup in the evening. Gerard was somewhere in Indonesia and could not be reached, but Liz attended—almost as a family member—and wept openly, without inhibitions, like a typical American. At the reception afterwards she stood by Etienne and held his hand. It was icy and the skin over the bones slipped beneath her fingers like satin.

"I've decided to take the job in Belize," Gerard said.

They were in Avignon, in Liz's condominium, four years, eight months and two weeks from the day they met. It was winter again and despite central heating and a log fire Liz was cold. Icy rain rapped on the windows and she had stuffed a blanket under the balcony door to stop the draft but it hardly seemed to do the job.

"Will you come with me?"

She wrapped her bulky fisherman's sweater more tightly around her and settled into the cushions of the overstuffed couch.

"For a holiday. See how you like it." He waited a beat. "It is warm in Belize, Liz."

She avoided his eyes. "We barely know each other."

"Think of sunbathing and skin diving."

"How many times have we been together? Barely at all and yet we're such good friends, Gerard. I've never had a better friend." Jeanne and Hannah didn't count. They were sisters, Gerard was not a brother. She feared losing him. He knew her, he was perhaps the only person who did; but if they lived together he might not like what he knew so well. "We've never—"

"We have exchanged letters twice a week for almost five years. We have spoken on the phone. You know my family better than I."

"But . . ."

"Why? Because we have not been lovers?" He laughed and looked perplexed. "I admit, this is unusual. Uncharacteristic. And I mean to remedy the situation as soon as you stop talking." He traced the line of her chin with his index finger. "With your cooperation, of course."

She shivered, not from cold.

"I don't want to lose you," she said. Hackneyed words. Spoken by how many lovers over time? "Don't you think this is kind of perfect . . . the way it is? . . ."

"No. I am lonely without you. I love you, my Liz. I know you. I know you think my feelings will change and that you will be stranded in Central America. But I am set on this, on loving you."

He said come to Belize for a holiday; but he meant come to Belize, pretend you are on holiday, and if you like it stay with me. His expression said: *I know this is outrageous, risky and perhaps foolish, for both of us. But come to Belize anyway. I want you, Liz.*

She told him no, she couldn't. She didn't have the money. Her work was in France. She didn't have the time. *She wasn't brave anymore. She was too old. He'd change his mind, turn away, and then where would she be?*

He held her face in his hands, held her gaze in his dark brown eyes that so perfectly matched her own. And though she told herself to look away again, her heart wasn't in it. Now at last she would know if what she felt for Gerard had been worth the years she'd given to it. Down on the street a horn blared and the wind whipped the sycamores against the roof. She closed her eyes when he kissed her and breathed deeply the faint scent of Bay Rum on his burnished skin. His arms encircled and drew her close. She let his lips open hers and tasted him on her tongue.

An image of Bernard, the artistic director, appeared in her mind. For an instant she saw him strutting and pontificating about music and dance and wine and five-star dining, and she felt a sudden powerful revulsion for her life. She was filled with a sense of adventure she realized she hadn't felt in many years and a desire for risk and hope and a compulsion to leave her old life and begin a new one.

She had been seven years with Gerard. They had known each other, been good friends, for twelve. He was her longest and most committed relationship, and she loved him with a constancy of which she had not thought herself capable. The accumulation of anniversaries amazed her until she reminded herself how well they suited one another. He had his work and she had hers. Even their social lives were mostly independent of each other. Her friends were Divina, the fortune-teller, and Petula, the Englishwoman running charter boats. His were men and women who shared a passion to preserve the forest. They worked together on the guest house, but only when and as it suited them. They were faithful but free to come and go, no rites or documents held them against their will. It seemed to Liz they suited one another as the doves did on the phone wire. She loved Gerard and hoped to stay with him the rest of her life. But why shake things up with marriage? A baby would fatally unbalance them.

In the kitchen Hannah hung up the phone next to the refrigerator and said, "That was Betts. She needs someone to run Angel over to the clinic. She's got a fever of one hundred and one."

Dan said, "That's nothing for a baby."

"For her it is."

"Babies run high temps all the time. You know that." Dan poured a cup of coffee.

"Can you pick Eddie up after practice and get him some new shoes and a haircut?"

Dan added sugar to his cup and sat at the counter opposite Hannah.

"Please, Dan?" She dug in the junk drawer for an elastic to hold back her thick curly hair. "Dan?"

"What happened to Betts's car?"

"The battery's dead. Someone left the lights on last night."

He shook his head.

"Betts needs help and she called me. I'm honored that she feels comfortable doing that." Dan stirred his coffee. "Just tell me, will you help out with Eddie? There are Nikes on sale at Big Five."

"Are you the only person Betts knows with a car?"

She threw down the dishrag. "Why are you doing this? Why can't you just say—"

"I'm serious, Hannah. Can't she call another volunteer?"

"It's Angel. You know how I feel about Angel. What if something happened to her?"

"Your time is already committed. Or do you have more hours in your day than the rest of us? Why couldn't you tell Betts you can't help out because your son is counting on you to pick him up after football? And you've got a houseguest and you're giving a dinner party tonight? Why couldn't you say that?"

"The party'll take care of itself. I've already made the curry."

"That's not the point."

"The point is you don't want me to help Betts. For some reason, you resent the time I spend with Angel—"

"Resent?" Dan laughed and tossed the spoon across the kitchen, clanging into the sink. "If I were to really let go and tell you how I feel, resentment wouldn't begin to cover it."

"What's that supposed to mean?"

"Take it any way you like, Hannah. Just call that woman back and tell her you are otherwise occupied today."

"I don't see why you can't take care of Eddie." Anger thinned and hoarsened her voice; the sound diminished her confidence. "What's the big deal, Dan. He's your son."

"He's yours too, but not so anyone'd notice. Especially not him. You act like he's got rabies. Apart from mealtimes, you haven't had a conversation with him in months. It's like you're afraid to get near him. He tries to tell you something and you ignore him."

"That's not true."

"He loves you and you practically cringe when he's within a foot of you. Don't deny it. I've seen with my own eyes. What the hell's going on?" Dan reached across the counter for her hand. "This is more than menopause, Hannah. There's something the matter and I want you to tell me."

"Don't goddamn doctor me."

Ingrid stood in the doorway. "I could hear you guys clear up-stairs." She walked to the sink and rinsed Liz's coffee mug. "Can't you at least wait until Aunt Liz is gone?"

"This is none of your business, Ingrid," Hannah said. "Unless you want to pick your brother up after practice and take him for shoes and a haircut."

"Dammit, Hannah."

Ingrid gawked at her. "You're kidding, right? That was like some kinda macabre middle-aged joke. Right?"

Hannah saw Dan tug on his earlobe and knew how angry he was. She hated it when Dan was angry with her; the tension clamped her chest like a vise. If she opened her mouth, her voice would sound like terminal laryngitis. But it wasn't too late. She could stop it right now. It didn't have to go further. Dan's temper flared hot and then when it was over, it was over and he never held a grudge. A call to Betts was all it would take to have him smiling again. He was right that someone else could get Angel to the clinic. But Angel didn't need just anyone or someone.

She spoke to Ingrid. "I'm going to San Jose in a few minutes. Angel's running a fever. I told Betts I'd take her to the clinic."

Ingrid stared at her.

"Eddie can wear his old shoes another couple of days. Give him some money and he can get a haircut on his own." Hannah concentrated on tidying the kitchen. The automatic movements—she could load the dishwasher with her eyes closed—soothed her and she didn't have to look at the faces of her husband and daughter. "Ingrid, what are your plans today?" She spoke as if there had been no argument.

"Paco's coming over in a little while. We're going to study at his house."

"I thought his parents were on a trip somewhere. Japan?"

"Korea."

"And they're back now?"

"I s'pose." Hannah didn't have to see the face to know the expression that went with the tone of voice. Pouted lips, sullen brows. "I dunno."

"I don't want you spending the day over there alone." Hannah ran the water hard and scrubbed ferociously at the dishes before putting them in the dishwasher.

"Let her go, Hannah."

"If they want to study, they can do it here. In the dining room."

"And I say, she can go." Dan spoke each word precisely. "You go too. Do what you must. I'll take care of things here. Eddie'll get his shoes. And his haircut."

Hannah stood like a stone, clutching the blue dishcloth so tightly it dripped onto the floor.

"But, Ingrid and Paco—"

He grabbed her shoulders, his face white with anger. "Look, you want to go off and do your thing with Angel and Betts and whoever the hell lives at that place? Okay, you do it. Meantime, I'm in charge around here, and if I say Ingrid can go to Paco's, then she can go. The less time you spend with this family, the less you've got to say about how things get run. Is that clear?"

Hannah's heart contracted. In a fraction of a second, she knew it might be possible to make Dan so mad his anger would flare and not die down again. He could be pushed too far. She wanted to undo the last fifteen minutes, to hold Dan and hug Ingrid until she squealed. She had a quick, urgent longing for Eddie— And then his image repelled her. She didn't want to hold Eddie. She didn't even want to pick him up after football practice and buy him shoes. The thought of his hair, thick and oily and long at the neck, disgusted her.

"Do as you please," she said and tossed the dishcloth into the sink. "I have to go."

Liz settled in the overstuffed wicker chair and put her feet up on the matching hassock. In the sulky light of outdoor flares the party of eight old friends gathered on the patio overlooking the pool and paddock. The sounds of jazz piano came from the CD player in the kitchen. From where Liz sat she saw the silhouette of the wildwood, a black paper cutout against a night sky reddened by the reflection of lights from the busy valley and San Jose. She breathed deep and smelled the creek and wood, the distinctive tang of bay and gum and damp and shadows she knew so well that even in Belize, in her kitchen in the middle of the night, she could summon it. How could Hannah not think of what happened at Bluegang when reminders were all around her?

Liz sensed trouble between Dan and Hannah; but if it bothered Hannah, she hid it well. In a long black skirt, gored and graceful on her slender body, she sat at ease among her friends, her hair curly and wild, barely controlled by silver combs, wilder than any of their mothers would have approved. So feminine, Liz thought. A pretty mouth and wide eyes, and that hair, that wonderful hair, that silver blonde hair. Liz closed her eyes and listened to the sounds of her friends' voices, their laughter and banter. It crossed her mind that she had no business coming back to Rinconada loaded down with skeletons, dumping her bag of old bones at Hannah's feet and expecting her to sort it out. I must be crazy, Liz thought. *At best, unkind.* Hannah—Jeanne too, for that matter—led more or less contented, settled lives. They were not the lives Liz had ever wanted for herself, but that didn't mean she couldn't appreciate them. Bluegang had receded in her friends' minds, and apparently bore no more relevance to this day and place than did the death of Jeanne's brother and her parents' alcoholism, or Hannah's maddeningly mild father and judgmental mother. It was only Liz who could not let the bones rest. *Misery loves company.* Was that the real motivation behind this trip home? Before tonight she would have insisted it was not but now she wondered if she was deluding herself. Maybe Jeanne was right and Liz was just plain selfish and too imaginative. In the middle of the night in Belize she never would have thought this possible; but in this circle of old friends, it seemed if not *absolutely* true, at least *possibly* so. This, she saw at once, was why she didn't like to come back. In Rinconada it took an effort to hold on to who she was now; it was easy to slip backwards and become again that deferential and neglected child, the accident who had disrupted her parents' ordered and scholarly lives.

Mindy Ryder sat beside Hannah on the cushioned bench wearing an ankle length skirt and peasant blouse, an elaborately embroidered shawl across her shoulders. With her long narrow eyes, moody and Slavic, exotic and unlikely above her upturned Irish nose and rosebud mouth, she looked like a gypsy, a description Liz knew would please her.

Teddy and Jeanne sat side by side on a pair of upholstered

Brown Jordan chairs across from Mindy and Hannah. Teddy. Movie star handsome in a loose fitting lime green linen shirt and beige pleated trousers; Jeanne delicately patrician in soft slacks and a light sweater. She wore her hair pulled back and Liz wanted to tell her to let it go, stop looking like a Norman Rockwell schoolteacher. She was on her third drink.

Who am I? Her conscience?

So far that evening they had talked about a best-seller everyone was reading, about a Randy Newman concert and could they still get tickets, about trophy wives, and now the topic was rain. The lack of it.

"If it goes on much longer," Gail Bacci said, "I won't be able to give houses away around here."

They laughed at that.

Gail's homecoming cheerleader features had become marshmallowy with age; but her round blue eyes still sparkled with the energy that had always left Liz slightly breathless. She sat beside her husband, Mario, on the redwood planter seat encircling the trunk of the live oak around which the flagstone patio had been laid. In the half-light Liz could not see Mario's eyes, but she remembered them. Dark brown with flecks of gold and green, dense lashes and half moon eyelids, bedroom eyes high school girls swooned for. Time wouldn't have changed those—or the naughty boy behind them either.

Dan perched on the stone wall beside the steps leading down to the pool. Relaxed, apparently cheerful: like Hannah, he concealed the fact that there was trouble in the family. The years had favored Dan. He was no longer shy and gawky. Like Hannah he seemed perfectly at ease. The pair of them were the weave and fiber of this family and community—schizophrenic as silicon had made it. Liz watched them and listened and occasionally added something to the conversation, but not much and not often. Tonight it took too much energy to fight sliding back into the childhood role assigned to her: Liz the dreamer with nothing important to contribute, one step behind, a little tentative, slightly shabby. Not smart and confident and capable like Jeanne. Not pretty and lovable and well dressed like Hannah. Memory came as a physical sensation, tearing back tissue and making raw again what had never fully healed.

She felt as she never did in Belize: a bolt of burlap in the land of silk.

She accepted another glass of wine. She was among friends and she looked good. Her clothes were right—floaty raw silk pants and shirt in a deep blue that flattered her; her haircut was chic. Why couldn't she relax, play the role expected of her, and have a pleasant evening?

"How much rain do you get down in Belize, Lizzie?" Mario asked.

She never knew the answer to that kind of question.

"I'm surprised you can't give us all the vital statistics," Gail said, laughing. "You were such a bookworm."

Despite her new haircut and pretty clothes and never mind that even pregnant she was at least forty pounds slimmer than Gail, Liz felt pissed on, put down, exactly as she had in high school.

Did anyone ever, really, grow up?

"I'm still a reader." *So there.* "I've made the bookseller on our corner a wealthy man."

"But, my God," Teddy Tate bent toward her, "how do you keep from being bored to death?"

His smugness infuriated her and she tried to recall if she had ever liked Teddy. Maybe for a few hours or days when Jeanne was flush with love, and it had been important that they approve each other's choices of husbands and lovers.

"I have friends. Gerard and I talk and cook together." *And read and listen to music.* "We have satellite TV. We can pick up Miami if we want to. Which we mostly don't." *We go for walks and sail our little boat.* "The guest house takes a lot of work. I'm exhausted at bedtime but it's a good life."

"You'll break my heart if you grow a housemaid's hump, Liz." The torchlight flared red in Teddy's eyes. "Spoil that lovely back."

The way Teddy looked at her made Liz's skin pucker, but she acknowledged his compliment with a polite smile. For a moment, no one said anything. She glanced at Jeanne who had gone over to sit on the wall beside Dan. If she heard Teddy or cared what he said, she wasn't letting on.

"What about Gerard?" Mindy Ryder's slanted eyes glittered. "What's he do? I just want to get a picture of the kind of life you've got down there. I mean, hell, I'm fifty plus and the farthest away I've been is Acapulco."

"That's a crime," Gail said. "We flew over to London for a week; easier than driving down to L.A."

"Gerard helps when he can, but he's often gone for weeks in the field." Liz wanted to bring Gerard alive for these old friends. She could tell them: He knows the name of ten thousand tropical plants, in Latin and English, bird calls too and the history of trees. "He's a consultant to the Minister for Environmental Affairs. His specialty is rain forest management and since Belize has one of the last undamaged forests in the world and the government wants to keep it that way . . ." She didn't describe Gerard. She delivered a prose rendition of his résumé. "He's devoted to his work."

Teddy chuckled. "I thought you went in for the artistic type."

"Managing a whole goddamn forest sounds like an art to me." Mindy said and winked at Liz.

"We should get him up here to tell us what to do about that damn creek." Gail nodded behind her toward Bluegang. "Did Hannah tell you there's a committee—"

"I can't even manage my own life," Mindy said. "Let alone an ecosystem."

"And speaking of your life, how is that girl of yours?" Gail grinned. "Tell us her name."

Mindy sighed. "You know her name, Gail."

"Balthazara!" Gail rolled off on wheels of laughter.

Mindy shook her head and her embroidered shawl slipped a little, revealing plump, tanned and freckled shoulders. "What can I say? She was born in nineteen-sixty-nine. If she'd been a boy I was going to call her Pax. I'm nothing if not a child of my times."

"When's her baby due?" Hannah asked.

Babies. Fifty years old and we're always talking about babies.

"Six weeks."

"Lucky you," Hannah said, "to be a grandmother."

Liz shifted in her chair. The waistband of her slacks cut into her skin. She felt hugely fat with breasts like Dolly Parton. Why had no one noticed?

Because they don't really see me, she thought. Not even Jeanne and Hannah see the person I really am. They see Liz Shepherd the wild girl in shabby clothes and her hair in tangles because her mother never took the time to notice her. Given enough time these people, out of their affection and concern and totally without thinking, would shove her back into the box that had confined her when she was young. She didn't know if she would have the strength to resist and declare: *Look at me. See me. This is me now.*

Of course she wouldn't. That was why she had left Rinconada and returned infrequently and was always glad to leave at the end of a week or ten days. She recalled a visit long ago to the La Brea Tar Pits and saw herself, stuck solid in the mud of time. It could have happened to her so easily. How fortunate she had been in her compulsion to escape.

Mario was speaking to her. "You gotta come in and see the new deli, Lizzie." His handsome features had coarsened and mousse or spray held his gray-streaked comber in place; but her nickname buzzed on his lips and she felt a little of the old electric charge. "I'll give you the grand tour. Let you taste the prosciutto straight from Italy."

"Twenty-two-fifty a pound," Gail said. "Make sure it's a very small taste."

"We had some good times, huh, Lizzie?"

Gail poked him. "Spare us the trip down memory lane, Mario. You're a middle-aged man with four grown children, remember. A grandfather." Gail walked over to the drinks table next to the doors into the dining room. She refilled her glass with chilled white wine. "I was going to bring their pictures, Liz, but *he* wouldn't let me. He made me promise I wouldn't go on about being a grandmother. He prefers you remember him as the Rinconada Wildcats' running quarterback, the dago with the dynamite smile."

Teddy told a story about a boy at Hilltop, something about an imaginary football player. As he talked Liz watched Hannah. She sat with her elbows on the arms of her chair, her fingertips together, drumming gently on her lower lip. Impatient, bored or deep in thought, Liz couldn't tell. Now that the party was established, she seemed less present and to have retreated, content to let her guests take care of themselves. Dan watched her too. Liz couldn't read his expression and that worried her.

Conversation ambled on and none of it was important. The air grew chill and the fragrance of the creek and wildwood more intense. Not unpleasant, simply there, alive.

At the dinner table set with linen and china and ornate old silverware, Hannah ladled curried carrot soup from a tureen decorated with orange flowers and spoke down the table to Mindy, seated on Dan's right. "We were going to eat Italian, Mindy, but Mario'd run out of your ravioli. Sharon Bell says you make the best pasta she's ever tasted."

"And she bakes all my biscotti," Mario said. "I could sell twice as much only she's so lazy."

Hannah said to Liz, "Mindy's a caterer when she isn't at the clinic. Where do you get your energy?"

"Drugs," Mindy said. They all knew she had a long history with cocaine but had not used it in years.

Teddy raised his glass. "Let's hear it for drugs."

"Are you still working at that horrible place?" Gail asked. "You could make so much more . . ."

"Gail, it's not about money. The kids at the center, they're in bad shape when they come to me, really bad. They need me."

"You always were such a good Catholic," Gail said, her mouth prissy from the put-down.

"What's being Catholic got to do with it?" Jeanne's dark eyes glistened and she enunciated every word a little too carefully. She rocked her wineglass on its round base. Liz watched the Fumé Blanc slosh up one side and then the other. "Mindy's right. It's good work."

"I guess I'm just not into good deeds," Gail said.

Everyone laughed at this.

"We love you even if you are a selfish bitch," Mindy said and blew her a kiss.

Gail blushed, looking pleased. Then she waved her hand, brushing off the subject. "Don't you think it's weird how our lives have turned out? I mean, there you are Mindy, you could have been a great artist—or a great caterer—and instead you babysit crazy kids."

"You were going to be a movie star," Mario reminded her.

Gail fluffed her hair. "I make as much money as a movie star."

The table groaned and laughed and groaned.

"Well? It's true." It didn't matter how it came to her, Gail loved attention. "We all thought Hannah would be someone wonderful, like Mother Teresa."

"And instead she's wonderful like Hannah." Jeanne raised her glass in a toast.

"Here, here," Mario said and did the same. They all toasted Hannah.

Except Gail, who was on a roll. "And as for you, Jeanne," Gail pointed a finger, "I would have guessed you'd end up being a judge or an astronaut. Maybe governor. You were absolutely the smartest person I ever knew."

Jeanne smiled delicately, but Liz wasn't sure she was even following the conversation until talk turned to education and Hilltop School and she became animated and pedantic. Watching Jeanne, Liz felt embarrassed for her. Drunk, boring, repetitive. She had always been a little afraid of Jeanne and probably Hannah was too, but her certainty and confidence and control-taking were just a con, a cover-up. To hide what? It was astonishing how little Liz really knew about her best friends. As they had stuck her in a box from childhood, she had done the same to them.

The conversation moved from educating children to raising them. Teenagers in particular. A chill rose through Liz's bones when she thought of the tiny thing inside her grown to a blossoming teenager.

"Meet my mommy. She's seventy."

Jeanne and Hannah cleared the soup bowls and brought in the chicken curry, bowls of rice and trays of condiments.

Mindy sampled the chutney. "Mango. And spicy. Wow."

"It's a hot flash," Teddy said. "Jeanne wakes me up when she has them."

"I do not." Jeanne blushed. "Once I did. Maybe twice."

The women at the table laughed, even Liz who wasn't sure she'd ever had a hot flash. Jeanne's hair had come undone on one side and she kept pushing it out of her eyes with the back of her hand. Liz felt a rush of concern.

Gail leaped to her next topic. "I've got a proposition for you, Dan." If the rest of them wore duct tape over their mouths would she just keep on talking, assuming they all wanted to listen? "When you're ready to sell this wonderful house, just say the word. I could move it in a minute."

"Never," said Dan.

Teddy said, "If you keep making money, Gail, I'm going to get you to endow something at the school."

Jeanne flashed him a poisonous look. Liz looked down the table at Hannah to see if she noticed. She was folding her napkin, pressing the folds with the edge of her index fingernail. Her rice and curry were untouched.

"When Ingrid and Eddie are off in school or married, you're going to be like ants in a paper bag."

"Gail, you have a gift for language," Teddy said and raised his glass again in mocking toast.

He was loaded too. Was that how they tolerated their marriage?

"Maybe we'll have another baby," Hannah said without looking up from the napkin she was carefully pressing.

"Omigod, at your age!" Gail's eyes became slits when she laughed. "What a nightmare."

Are you in there, little creature? Hear what she calls you?

Gail said, "Seriously, here's something that'll interest you, Hannah. I got a new listing today, that little old Victorian next to the house where you grew up. Down on Casabella flats? A coat of paint and some yard work and it goes on the block for a half million minimum."

"Mrs. Phillips's place," Jeanne said and looked across the table at Liz. Shadows circled her eyes and the light within them was like something glimpsed at the bottom of a hole. "She was a cook at the school when I was a kid."

"You should have seen the place when we went in. It was like something in a Hitchcock movie. It hadn't been cleaned in years and inside there were cardboard boxes everywhere all filled with old sheet music and newspapers and magazines. The only clean room in the whole place was the boy's. Billy's. Remember him? Sort of weird, maybe retarded? The old lady kept his room like it was before he died." Gail took a mouthful of curry and kept talking. "There was his pitiful little room with this blue chenille bedspread and a shelf with his little metal cars all lined up like gridlock and no dust on them anywhere. She'd even left his calendar on the wall. I walked in that room and there was Joe DiMaggio staring down at me."

"I remember him," Mindy said. "He died near here didn't he? Down at the creek?"

"DiMaggio died at Bluegang?"

"Shut up, Teddy," Mindy said.

"Someone died at the creek?" Dan asked. "You never told me about this, Hannah."

Hannah shrugged her shoulders. "I guess it never came up."

Mario spooned a fresh helping from the rice bowl.

Gail said, "That stuff's got calories, you know."

Mario said, "Liz and Jeanne and Hannah and me were all in Mrs. English's class when it happened."

"Not to mention your future wife," Gail said. "I got the attendance prize that year."

"Billy was older'n us," Mario said. He turned to the other men at the table. "You guys don't know this story? Dan? Teddy?"

They shook their heads.

"There was this boy, like Gail said, he was retarded. About the same age as your Eddie, Dan. We all knew him."

"Creepy," Gail said.

"Do we have to talk about this?" Hannah asked.

Dan said, "I want to hear the story."

Hannah looked at Liz and then quickly away.

"I remember my dad and his brothers talking about it. Uncle Delio and Uncle Leonard were both on the police force."

"Back then," Mindy said, "they *were* the police force."

"I wanted to be a cop too, so I'd hang around the dinner table and listen to their war stories . . ."

Teddy laughed. "Cops in Rinconada with war stories?"

"What happened was, this kid Billy Phillips apparently fell down the hill at Bluegang and hit his head on the boulders. Some boys found his body the next morning."

"Is this why you're always after me about a new fence, Jeanne?" Teddy asked.

Jeanne ate with determination, focused on rice and chicken and chutney, coconut, peanuts. She didn't look like she was listening but she had to be.

"You remember him, Hannah," Mindy said. "From your old bedroom window, we could see right down into his backyard. One time we spied on him digging up the yard, making roads and bridges and stuff for his little cars. It was so incredibly peculiar the way she let her child tear up the yard like that. You must remember."

"Vaguely."

"Uncle Del said he must have had about two hundred of those Dinky toy cars."

"Some war story," Teddy said.

Dan laughed and walked back to the kitchen with the curry bowl in his hand.

Mario raised his voice so he could be heard in the kitchen. "Lenny and Del didn't think it was an accident."

"Murder?" Gail cried. "You never told me that!"

Jeanne looked up at Liz again and this time there was a slight tilt to her mouth, the bud of a smile.

Mario dropped his voice. Dan came to the kitchen door and listened, still holding the curry bowl. "There was one thing wrong with the accident theory. The kid had scratches on his neck and arms that looked like fingernails made them."

Jeanne refilled her wineglass.

"I don't get it," Gail said.

"Leonard was convinced there was a fight and the kid got pushed."

"What kind of fight?" Hannah's voice was a thin soprano.

"Well," Mario leaned farther forward, "I heard this story. Like a rumor only more substantial, you know? A few months before, someone took out a complaint about Billy Phillips. Some girl said he came on to her."

"Gross," Gail said.

"Let me get this straight," Teddy drawled. "There's a retarded boy and he dies and it looks like murder—"

"No," Hannah said. "Not murder. An accident."

"All right, an accident. But a very suspicious one. And no one investigates?"

"No evidence. Plus, there was only Del and Leonard . . ."

"And back in those days, murder was unthinkable in Rinco-nada," Mindy said.

Hannah said. "It wasn't murder."

Liz held her breath.

"I mean they couldn't prove it. It was an accident."

"I'm surprised you never told me this story, Hannah," Dan said.

She shrugged. "Honestly, I don't remember it very well. It was a long time ago."

"It's not the kind of thing you forget," Gail said.

"You're wrong," Mindy said. "It's exactly the kind of thing you forget when you're a kid. What a shock. I mean, you lived next door to him, Hannah. Knew him all your life. And we played down at Bluegang. Any one of us could have fallen and hit our head."

Had it been so simple? Were Liz's nightmares and sleepless nights no more than a delayed response to an accident that could have happened to any one of them? She looked down the table at Hannah. Her eyes seemed lost in the shadows and she was rubbing the place near her ear she said hurt when she was tense. Across the table Jeanne sat straight in her chair, her right hand playing with the stem of her wineglass. She looked up once and glanced at Liz expressionlessly, then away. Liz's throat tightened and she felt a pressure behind her nose and eyes that told her she could cry without much encouragement. Gerard would say such a strong reaction meant what had happened at Bluegang was important, not simple at all. But maybe he was wrong; maybe it was all just imagination or hormones. Oh, God, she thought. *OhGodohGodohGod*. For a while she had forgotten she was pregnant but now it was back, the awareness of life; she felt inhabited from toes to scalp. And this was worse than Bluegang, worse than seeing Billy Phillips dead and blaming herself.

Mindy was saying, "In severe cases like at the clinic, the poor kids, it seems like their secrets always come back to haunt them. It's karma." Mindy grinned wickedly at Gail. "Bal told me that. She knows all about karma."

A second later, the mood at the table changed as if an east wind had come through the French doors and blown away the smell of Bluegang. Liz realized she had been holding her breath, exhaled, sat back and enjoyed Mindy's description of a set of tarot cards she'd seen at a bookstore. Gail talked about a Ouija board experience and Liz made them laugh with one of Divina's tall tales. Dan refilled his guests' glasses while Hannah cleared the table and brought out plates of salad: designer greens with thin-sliced grapefruit and avocado.

"I don't understand karma," she said when she sat down again. "I'm a volunteer in a place in San Jose called Resurrection House. It's a foster home for children who're born with drugs in their systems—"

"Shall I open another bottle of wine, Hannah?" It wasn't like Dan to interrupt.

"There's one baby, a girl named Angel."

Or like her to ignore him.

"Angel has nothing, nothing at all in the world except me. I go there and I hold her and I talk to her and stroke her and I'm the closest thing she has to a mother. If she could have a home and a good mother—like me—she might have a chance but as it is . . . Did she do something to deserve this? In another lifetime? Is that karma?" Liz saw how she looked down the table from Mario to Mindy, to Gail but not at Dan.

A furrow dug between his eyes.

This is what they're fighting about, Liz thought.

"Let me help you clear, Hanny." Liz pushed back from the table. "It's my karmic burden."

Over dessert, a perfect flan afloat on raspberry sauce, Dan told a joke about a blind skydiver and his dog and Mario went on too long about the 49ers. AIDS was mentioned. There were stories about men they all knew who had been healthy ten or more years and maybe it would not be the pandemic they all feared. Liz felt Hannah watching her and knew she was thinking about her mysterious visit to the doctor. Tomorrow she would explain everything.

Liz talked a little, listened mostly. Nothing new here. Nothing to guard against or prepare for, no one to impress. Her unease had been for nothing. Hormones or high school feelings reborn for an evening. *Zombie feelings. Dead but not.*

After a second cup of coffee, she excused herself. "I promised Gerard I'd call before ten."

In the den, she leaned against the closed door, shut her eyes and expelled a long sigh before picking up the phone beside the couch. It had been a fine dinner but being social took it out of her. She missed Gerard. She missed his silence. She missed feeling like herself. She dialed through to Belize and let the phone ring. Signa, the housekeeper, answered.

"Oh, Miss Liz, he be gone."

Liz's stomach dropped in disappointment.

"He tell me somebody try steal them stone figures out by Limpe Creek. Big meeting all day 'bout how to protect 'em."

"Tell him I called, Signa."

"Sure t'ing."

"How's everything going down there?"

"Pretty good. You better come back here soon, though. We all full up for next month and that new Aga stove not workin' right and Mister Gerard be saying all the time he's not no hotel-keeper."

Liz smiled. She could hear him.

"I'll be back in a few days. Tell him I'll phone again."

Liz hung up and for five minutes she sat without moving, staring at the dark geometric design of the carpet at her feet. The triangles of red and green and blue, the circles and squares and shapes Euclid never named.

She missed him. So why couldn't she just say *yes, Gerard, I'll marry you, I'll be your wife*?

When he asked her to go with him to Belize, she had been reluctant because she didn't trust him or his love. Now she trusted him but not herself and never mind that she had no intention of leaving him. Not ever. She imagined tending to him in his last illness, seeing to his funeral; there was something so sweet in that thought, tears came to her eyes. And if she went first? Gerard would do the same for her. So why couldn't she marry him?

She walked to the window and opened the wooden blinds. In the side yard Hannah and Dan had planted oranges and lemons in three rows of four each. Their drought-bedraggled shapes were etched sadly against the night sky. She rested her hands on her stomach and thought of Gerard dead and of the baby she carried. The den door opened and Teddy looked in.

"I've been sent to bring you back for champagne." There were splotches of red on his cheekbones. Liz stood. "I'll be along. Give me a moment."

"Do I see a tear?" He shut the door and stepped across the room to her. "Not bad news, I hope."

"Nothing I want to share."

He smiled and she saw the handsome young man Jeanne had introduced at a sorority dance. She repented a little of her ill will to-ward him. The wall above the glass-fronted Craftsman bookcase behind him was covered with framed photographs of family and friends. She pointed at one. "There's you and Jeanne at your wed-ding."

He turned, slipped his glasses down on his nose and peered over them.

"I liked your hair long, Teddy. Why don't you grow a ponytail?"

He struck a dignified pose. "Don't forget I'm a renowned educa-tor. I'd lose my credibility with everyone but you." He put a finger to her lips and traced their outline. "Jeanne was an elegant bride. Hannah was Earth Mother. And you had the sexiest mouth I'd ever seen. Still do." He wet the fingertip with his tongue and slipped it between her lips and into her mouth.

She stepped back. "Don't be gross."

"You're the only real woman in this crowd."

This made her laugh. "Spare me the clichés, Teddy." She was embarrassed and furious. "You've had too much to drink."

"I like to think about you down there in the jungle humping your Frenchman. You'd be surprised the effect that thought can have on a man who lives with a woman like Jeanne."

She slapped him. "You're a creep, Teddy. I've guessed it for years, but tonight you hit a new low."

He touched his cheek, smiling slightly. "Girls are such simple loyal creatures."

"And you, Teddy, are just plain simple."

"I wish I'd seen his face," Hannah said later when the guests had gone and they had finished with the cleanup.

"It was a blank, of course. A gorgeous nothing. He probably didn't even hear what I said, he was trying so hard to think of a witty remark to sling back at me." Liz smoothed the dish towel across the handle on the oven door to dry. Over the grind of the garbage disposal she asked, "Do you think Jeanne loves him?"

"A marriage is a strange and wondrous thing, believe me. And the longer it lasts, the stranger it gets. I don't think Teddy could survive without her. And I think she likes that. Needs it. Makes her feel powerful."

"They've both got Ph.D.s, for godsake."

"Yeah, but Jeanne's the brains of that family. Not to mention the energy."

"If I were her, I'd get out while I was young enough to make a new life."

"You don't know, Liz, you're not married."

"Gerard's not a tree. Does that mean he doesn't know anything about them?"

"For some people, being discontented becomes so familiar, they don't want to take a chance on something worse. Plus, divorce is messy and public and our Jeanne likes to keep things orderly and private."

"Are you and Dan okay?"

Hannah looked surprised. "Of course. What made you ask that?"

"I just thought . . . I felt something. An atmosphere between you."

"You and your imagination. We're fine."

Liz had asked the question without expecting an honest answer. If there was to be any truth-telling, it would have to come in Hannah's own time and at the demand of her own need. Not Liz's.

So why am I here? Why didn't I just stay in Florida?

They sat opposite each other in the breakfast nook. Hannah poured the last of the Fumé Blanc and drank her glass quickly. She traced the delicate crystal rim with her index finger. The grandfather clock in the front hall chimed eleven-thirty, and from her bed in the kitchen corner Cherokee woofed softly in her sleep.

"Sometimes I wish I still smoked," Hannah said.

"God, me too."

"Maybe I'll start again when I'm ninety."

"Like one of those decadent old French courtesans."

Hannah nodded. "Like Colette. I'll stay in bed all day, drink champagne and smoke."

"That'd actually make old age something to look forward to, I guess."

In the paddock the waifs and strays barked at something and Cherokee lifted her head and ears and then went back to sleep.

Hannah said, "Mario tells a good story."

"When Gail lets him."

They looked at each other, grinned and said in unison, "Marriage is a strange and wondrous thing."

Hannah held her wineglass up to the light and turned it slowly. "I don't remember scratching that boy."

"It makes sense though."

"I don't like to think about that, about having his skin under my nails." She examined her manicure.

"I think tonight we could have told what happened," Liz said, choosing her words carefully. "and no one at the table would have blamed us."

"You weren't even there. It happened to me, remember?"

"Jeanne and I were part of it. Part of leaving him."

Hannah shook her head as if to say that nothing counted but the doing and the deed.

"You've never told me the whole story." The wine was sour on Liz's tongue. She got up and poured a glass of bottled water. "What did happen?"

The dishwasher purred in the background, a wet velvety sound.

"I don't remember it all that clearly. There are gaps." Hannah's breathing broke into a shiver. "He wanted me to touch his penis." She made a face. "He called it Mr. Pinky, can you believe that? And when I wouldn't he grabbed my blouse, where I had it knotted."

Hannah held the wine bottle upside down over her mouth. Liz watched a half dozen drops fall on her tongue. She put the bottle down. "We were too young for bras so I felt his hands on my . . . skin . . . they were sweaty . . . and it was such a surprise and I was so scared . . . that's when I think I must have scratched him." Hannah spread her fingers wide and stared at them. "How long do you think it was there? A week?"

"It doesn't matter."

"Of course it matters. Would you be here right now if it didn't matter?"

"I don't mean it doesn't matter. I mean—" Liz grabbed Hannah's hand and made a fist of it within her own. "I mean it was another world, and we were so innocent. I don't think I'd ever heard of a boy attacking a girl."

"The thing is, I don't remember scratching him. I suppose I had to though, to make him stop . . . what he was doing."

"He was fifteen."

"And strong, Liz, I remember how I couldn't make him let go of my hand when he held it down to his . . . crotch." Hannah looked at Liz intently, as if to make sure she understood that she had tried to wrest free of Billy Phillips.

"Of course you couldn't. My God, Hannah, you don't have to convince me of that. Plus, you were terrified. That's the whole point. You never had any choice but to do what you did."

I, on the other hand, knew it was wrong to do nothing. I let Jeanne bully me into silence. I was too afraid of my parents to speak up when I knew I should.

"I wanted to tell my mother," Hannah said. "But you know the way she was. And what Jeanne said about publicity, that it would ruin my dad, I believed her. Didn't you believe her?"

"I don't know," Liz said. "I think I let her convince me. I didn't want to get in trouble."

"Afterwards, when I got home, I wanted to tell, but I saw how my mother was and I knew how my father loved St. Margaret's . . . and then time went by and it was one of those things; the longer I waited the harder it was to explain why I didn't tell right away." Hannah gathered the hair off the back of her neck and reset the combs. "Sometimes I wish Mario's uncles had found my underpants; the whole story would have come out then."

"Then you do think about it."

"Not really." A spark of aggravation must have shown in Liz's eyes because Hannah said, "Don't look at me like that. There just isn't that much to think about. Not for me. The whole experience was such a nightmare, I think I repressed it. The details anyway. But if you're asking does it cross my mind sometimes, well, of course, it does. Jesus, Liz, I'm not one of Mindy's basket cases. What happened to me . . . to us . . . it's not the kind of thing a functioning brain forgets. Not completely anyway." After a moment of silence, her voice had a flat eerie calm. "Jeanne must have taken my panties. Before we went back that night."

"Have you asked her?"

"She'd never tell me the truth."

"You're her best friend. She loves you."

"Once, when Ingrid was a newborn, I had this little thing that went around her head, a little pink and yellow bow thing so people would know she was a girl even though she was bald. Jeanne took it."

"No way. She stole it?"

Hannah nodded.

"Why would she do that?"

Hannah shrugged. "I've always thought she blamed me for Billy Phillips's death, as if it didn't have to happen, like I should have handled it better, like she would have."

"God, Hannah, it's not as if you had time to plan. The boy—"

"I think she took the panties so I'd always wonder and be a little afraid. That way she holds one extra card and it's always the trump. Keeps her feeling like she's the strong one."

Sunday

Early Sunday morning Hannah dreamed of walking through pungent fog, a familiar scent she could not identify. Something waits in the fog, something she fears and she wants to run; but her body moves forward, dragged or shoved or by its own volition. A figure emerges from the mist. She sees eyes and chin and mouth. She runs but she is barefoot and sharp rocks and tree roots pave the floor of a vast dark wood. There is a path somewhere but she cannot find it or when she does it disappears and she is back where she started and where are her shoes? She has lost her shoes. Has someone taken her shoes? Her mother will be so angry. She must go back to look for them. She can't go home until she finds them.

She woke drenched in sweat. She touched her face and her palms were hot. She kicked off the blanket and sat on the edge of the bed pulling in deep breaths, feeling her heart beat like a prisoner beating on the bars of her prison. Her nightgown clung to her back and the sweat beneath her breasts steamed. She ripped off the gown and stood a moment to cool herself before the open bedroom window.

In the back garden the bed of white stock she had kept alive with recycled bathwater glowed in the darkness. She closed her eyes and inhaled deeply, hoping to catch a bit of their fragrance. She remembered the dream, the smell of the creek.

Damndamndamn. She did not want this, not any of it.

She took a fresh cotton nightie from the dresser and slipped it over her head. She covered the clammy sheet with a towel and got back into bed. Now she was cold, practically shivering. God, she hated menopause, hated the knowledge that her body was breaking down like an obsolete machine. Dan could say it was normal, but it felt like malfunction to her. Moldering ovaries, rust on the uterus.

Down the hall Eddie got up to use the bathroom. Asleep on his feet, he wrestled the doorknob into obedience.

Mindy Ryder and her daughter, Balthazara, were big into dream interpretation. It would take them about sixty seconds to conjure an analysis of Hannah's dream, but she didn't need voodoo. Her hormones might be wacko, but her brain still worked.

The toilet flushed and in a second she heard Eddie hit the wall as he staggered back to his bed.

She didn't want to think about her dream or Eddie, but the waters of memory rose and there he was splashing around in them: his pudgy babyness, the pointy chin and chapped cheeks, the pink pearl of his lower lip. She missed her little son; she ached for her small boy as if he had died. One morning when Eddie was not quite thirteen she had, without thinking, walked in on him in the bathroom and saw him standing at the sink in his Jockey shorts. He turned around and his outraged gaze met hers on the same level. *"Ma, you're supposed to knock!"* It was after that she began to think about what *forever* really meant.

When her parents died the finality had not struck her deeply, perhaps because she had always expected them to die before her. But now she knew that her baby, her little boy, had died too. She could spend a decade on her knees at St. Margaret's, she could bankrupt the family, she could even kill herself; no plea to God Almighty or sacrifice to a pagan goddess would return him to her. He was dead like her mother and father, vanished like a dinosaur off the face of her earth. Forever.

She pressed her feet against the back of Dan's legs. Perhaps in his own deep dream he encountered an icicle; if so, it didn't trouble him. Encouraged, she squirmed closer. The man slept hot and dry and warmed his side of the bed like a copper pan full of coals.

She remembered listening to *Sepia Serenade* under the covers late at night when her parents were asleep. KWBR Lucky Fourteen. Some nights she had to fiddle twenty minutes to pick up the feeble signal from Oakland. Eventually she always did find it. She longed for the past to be findable in the same way. It buzzed in the ether, invisible as a radio signal, but there, always there, if she could only find the frequency.

She got out of bed and went down the hall to Eddie's room. The door stood half open, the room illuminated by a Junior Seau night-light she'd put in his Christmas stocking that year. She pressed her palm against the door and pushed it open.

She had not been in Eddie's bedroom for several weeks; she preferred to do no more than glance in from the hall, checking for dirty dishes. A few months earlier she had told him he would have to do his own laundry. It was good training and besides she wasn't a servant, but the whole truth was that she couldn't stand to touch his clothes, to be that close to the intimate smell of him.

Tonight she crossed the threshold and stepped over to the bed where he lay. She did not look at him. She focused her eyes on the books and magazines piled on the headboard shelf and told herself there was magic afoot. She would wait an enchanted moment, look down and there would be her baby again, restored to her. But if, like poor love-besotted Orpheus, she looked at him too soon the spell would break.

She didn't believe any of it, of course; but she wanted it to be true and if she wanted it enough couldn't she warp reality with the force of her wanting? In that moment she longed to have her little boy back more than she wanted Dan or Ingrid or good health or a long life. If she could see him as he once was—even if only for a few moments—she would give away years of her life. These thoughts frightened Hannah; but she couldn't help it, she meant them.

She counted slowly backwards from ten, let her breath out and looked down. And there he was: the half-man, half-boy she so disliked. The eyes and nose and chin of the boy in the dream. Pimples, whiskers, the smell of sweat and oily hair. In her worst scenario, she walked into his room and the bed was empty, closet and cupboards too; and she didn't make a move to search for him. Was that what the dream meant? Eddie lost in the fog and Hannah unwilling to go after him? No. The figure had been coming toward her. At least she thought that's the way it went. Funny how dreams evaporated like perfume.

Hannah went back to bed and dozed a little. Next time she woke the digital clock beside the bed told her it was just after five. She dressed in Levi's, a sweater and boots and pinned her hair back and up without combing it. When she entered the kitchen Cherokee greeted her with a thumping tail, but made no effort to rise from her pillow.

"Lazy wretch," Hannah said and stroked the satiny red head.

She made a double cappuccino and sprinkled the top with grated chocolate, grabbed a jacket off the hook by the back door and walked out to get the Sunday paper where the delivery woman dropped it at the end of the driveway. Her boots scrunched on the gravel drive and the clear cold stung her nose and ears and she warmed her hands on her coffee mug. Mist smoked through the scarlet leaves of the liquid ambar trees lining the driveway. Each parched blade of grass shimmered, grateful for the dew. At the base of the mailbox post, she found the paper in its plastic sheath and tucked it under her arm. She was heading back when the sight of her home and garden struck her vision as if she had been away a long time.

The house was built broad and low despite its two stories. The windows were square and generous and the deep, gently pitched rooflines and wide veranda across the front and sides were classic Craftsman. A few earthquake cracks marred the exterior walls and the garage roof needed fixing; the house was getting old but it was solid. It belonged where it was.

Beautiful, she thought. I have everything in the world any woman could want including this wonderful house, but I'm not happy. Liz is right, I'm not happy.

Shame gushed through her and she heard her father insist she be grateful because she wasn't a displaced person or a poor Jewish child with matchstick arms and legs. Make a gratitude list, her father told her; and she told him back that she was sick of painting a generous smile on her face when she was sad clear down to her toes, sick of being agreeable when she was ticked off at the whole damn world, especially the world of Casabella Road, sick of feeling awkward as a schoolgirl sprouting hair and breasts, a puberty-ridden adolescent in a middle-aged body. The only way she was going to make another gratitude list was if her father appeared before her like the Virgin Mary at Fatima.

The day stretched ahead, forty miles of bad road.

She dropped the paper on the back step and headed down to the barn. As she did, Cherokee nosed her way out the pet door and hurried into step beside her. Dogs, cats, broken-down horses: Hannah liked them because she didn't have to pretend with them or second-guess their motivations or look for hidden meanings. If a dog growled, she knew to leave it alone. If a horse laid its ears back, she got ready for trouble. She didn't want to know about their four-footed dreams any more than they cared about hers. She knew when they were happy and when they were not, and if they had a subconscious she hoped to God no one would ever find out about it.

She opened the paddock gate and the dogs rushed to greet her with excited leaps and yips. The cats wove in and out between her legs, tails up and quivering. *Mealtime cupboard love.* She put fresh water, hay and oats in Glory's stall and promised to groom her. Soon. She fed the dogs and cats, and the one-eared burro blinded by a baseball bat.

As she passed out of the barn, she glanced to her right in the direction of the creek. Under cover of the wildwood just beyond the fence something moved; what looked like a small human figure darted from sight so quickly she almost doubted her eyes. Last night Gail had said there were homeless people living in the caves above Bluegang.

"Hey," she yelled.

Cherokee set up a racket and with a gang of orphan dogs behind her, chased to the chain link fence. Hannah yelled after her; but Cherokee had her nose to the ground, her senses keyed to the trespasser. Hannah yelled again and reluctantly the dog came back, the mutts were less cooperative. Hannah held Cherokee by her collar as she strained to be away after her prey. A streamer of fog swirled across the paddock and twined itself among the branches of the trees, obscuring Hannah's view. She breathed in the fragrance of the creek, the smell from her dream: mud and damp and, pervasive, the spicy sour reek of decaying bay and eucalyptus leaves.

At a little after seven Hannah pushed open the gate to the side patio of St. Margaret's Episcopal Church. Father Joe sat on a stone bench by the fountain, drinking coffee; and when he saw her, he smiled and waved her in. Over his slightly rusted black cassock he wore a bulky cable knit cardigan that was the same watery blue as his faded eyes.

"I brought you some flowers for your room." She held out a fistful of white stock. "I'll put them in water."

"There's coffee on the stove."

"Good," she said over her shoulder. "I need it."

Since his retirement, Father Joe had lived in a dinky apartment adjacent to the parish hall, furnished him rent free by St. Margaret's in exchange for his taking the early Eucharist and reading morning prayer during the week, services the current priest—a young father with twins and a disorganized wife—considered burdensome.

When Hannah returned she sat beside him on the bench and held his hand. A little old man's pale hand with big knuckles and spotted by age. The fog had burned off, revealing another clear morning, but it was chilly and Hannah was grateful for her heavy sweater and Levi's. For a time they sat in silence, contemplating the bronze statue of St. Francis that presided over the garden Hannah's mother had laid out before Father Joe came to St. Margaret's. The bushes of yellow marguerite daisies flowered gleefully. With a little drink once or twice a week to dampen their roots, Hannah thought they would happily bloom themselves to death. Some things needed so little care to thrive while others, like Angel, could never get enough. She crouched in the dirt and nipped off the brown seed heads with her fingernails.

Father Joe was a deacon when her mother laid out St. Margaret's garden, and traveled between parishes in the Santa Clara Valley, helping out where he was needed. St. Margaret's was a thriving parish in those days with a Sunday school of more than sixty and a choir that gave concerts up and down the West Coast.

She sat back on her heels and stared at the brown buds in her

palm. "What if it never rains again? Maybe God's giving us the reverse of a flood."

"More like there's a huge high pressure system off the coast,
blocking the moisture. They said on the news last night it's like a
wall keeping the rain to the north of us."

"Maybe it's the Rapture."

"Anglicans don't believe in the Rapture."

"The end of the world then."

"I don't think we believe in that either. At least not the Apoca-
lypse."

"That's the best news I've heard today."

"You're in a cheerful mood this morning, Hannah Tarwater."

She stood and arched her back to stretch it out. What would
Father Joe say if she told him that more than thirty years before she
had killed a boy and abandoned his body to the coyotes. The night
before she had almost told Liz the whole story, but the words
weren't there. She would never be able to tell anyone what really
happened that day, not the full truth.

"Talk to me, Hannah," Father Joe said. "What's eating you?"

She walked across the little garden and tossed the dead heads in
a waste barrel, sat down again. "I didn't sleep well."

"Worrying about the end of the world?"

"I know I'd feel better if it rained." She remembered the touch of
the rain spray Liz brought her from Florida. It made her want to
cry, the memory of rain.

"So what's on your mind?"

"Do you believe in the subconscious, Father Joe?"

"Absolutely. I'm an Anglican. It's one of my vows." She didn't
smile. "Don't you?"

"I don't want to."

"Why's that?"

"I think there's something in mine trying to get out."

Father Joe chuckled.

"It's like I'm the cage and my subconscious is the panther."

"I know the feeling you describe, Hannah."

"What do you do about it? How do you make it go away?"

"I try not to fight it. Embrace it. Let whatever's in there ease out of the cage, so to speak." For a moment he stirred his coffee with a plastic spoon, then he shook his head irritably. "Forgive me, Hannah, that wasn't an honest answer. The true answer to your question is that I *wish* I could calmly embrace the panther. I *wish* I could always and completely trust that whatever's going on in my mind, it's the Holy Spirit at work. I shouldn't be afraid, I should let it out. I pray for that kind of faith, but I don't always have it. Like most people, I use up a lot of energy trying to keep the panther in the cage or trying to convince myself it isn't there at all." He finished the last swallow of his coffee. "Even when it's clawing at me through the bars." He tossed the dregs into the garden. "There's a priest I know up in Millbrae. I trust him so when it gets really bad, we meet halfway, find a church and I make my confession. Maybe that's what you need. It cleans things out, sets things straight."

"That's what my friend says."

"Then you have a wise friend."

That stopped Hannah. She thought of Liz as intelligent but never wise.

They stowed their coffee cups behind a rock and walked toward the church. Hannah remembered Mrs. Phillips.

"Gail Bacci says you went into her house."

"Oh, I'd been in there before. Once or twice a month she'd invite me for High Tea." He laughed. "Being an Anglican, some people always assume I'm partial to crumpets and tea. I never could tell her what I really wanted at four in the afternoon was a cold Corona." He fitted an iron key into the lock on the church door. "She couldn't care for the house or herself anymore, but even so she didn't want to move up to Crestwood. I never really convinced her. Just did the deed. She seems happy now, though." He held the door for Hannah. "You must have known her, Hannie. You were neighbors. Her son was the boy—"

"I know." She stopped on the threshold. "Joe, did she have a happy life?" She hoped for a surprise, a little reprieve.

"War widow. Son died when he was fifteen. That's a lot to bear."

"She was unhappy then? Always?"

"Some people don't have a great capacity for happiness to begin with, Hannah. I think maybe Orna Phillips was one of those."

"I never knew her first name."

"Why all this sudden interest?"

Hannah looked into the gray recesses of the stone church. She felt the truth clawing at her insides.

"I guess I'm depressed."

"For some time."

"I try not to be."

"Maybe too hard, eh? There's no crime in it, Hannah, being unhappy." Father Joe placed his hand on the small of her back. "Go on in, my girl. Down on your knees."

Tears welled against her lower lid.

"When you're ready, Hannah. I'm here."

They stepped into the vestibule of the old church and her head filled with a favorite smell—cold stone and old incense—a smell that meant permanence and quiet and being small again.

"Did I go to the boy's funeral?" she asked, stopping beside the first pew. "I can't remember."

"You were there with your mom and dad. I imagine it was a pretty deep shock to lose someone who'd lived next door to you all your life. And by an accident that could have happened to any of you kids."

"Strange how I remember some things so clearly but the rest is just gone. Why would I forget?" She couldn't believe what Mindy said, that it was normal to forget what caused her pain. If that were true, why couldn't she just forget everything about Bluegang. Why was some of it so clear, so clear it hurt her eyes, her whole head, to look at it.

"You were such an open-hearted little creature, Hannah. Into everyone's business, asking questions all the time. Full of great big emotions. Billy Phillips's death was probably the first time you ever thought about your own mortality. That's pretty heavy stuff for a little kid."

Father Joe left her to change into his vestments and Hannah took her favorite place at the back of the church and knelt to pray. But the prayers wouldn't come and finally she gave up and daydreamed about Angel instead.

The crunch of the Volvo's tires on the gravel drive woke Liz. She had been dreaming of water, of rain and of swimming. She reached across the bed to the nightstand where she'd laid her book, spread eagle, the night before. She propped herself up on the pillows and read for a while. The book was *Justine,* a favorite from college days.

She would tell Hannah and Jeanne about the baby today when they were together at lunch. She put down the book and practiced her dialog. *I have something to tell you both.* Hannah would think cancer or AIDS because her mind worked that way. Jeanne would think that, whatever the news was, Liz was dramatizing . . . because she always thought Liz dramatized. *I'm here for an abortion.* They would be stunned and then sympathize, they might say it served her right after all these years. Hannah would offer to drive her to the clinic.

Not much longer, she thought, laying her hand on her stomach. What should she feel? Odd, this disconnect.

She read a little longer and dozed off again. The house began to stir and she heard zing and ping video sounds from Eddie's room. She got up and dressed for a run. For longer than usual she stretched, feeling creaky and old, bloated and mildly out of sorts. The house seemed awfully busy, awfully early, and she was eager to be off like a dog with its nose to the wind.

Hannah turned from the stove and smiled at her as she came into the kitchen. "Bacon: the breakfast that kills."

"God, I love that smell."

"I'm making a feast. How long will you be?"

"Half an hour?"

"It's chilly out there."

Liz turned left at the end of the driveway. She meant to turn right, run past Hilltop, up and around Overlook Road; but instead and without thinking she went down Casabella Road toward town. She glanced at her watch: 9:20. Seven minutes down and twelve back, allowing for the hill.

The road swung into the hairpin turn at the Bluegang bridge and then up a rise and to the right. The air seemed to crackle in the arid cold, but the sun warmed the back of her neck; and when she rolled her head to the left and then the right, the stiffness melted out. Casabella swooped into a wide turn and sloped down the hill past more old houses, villas and cottages and all of them perfectly restored. The street was an architectural gallery. Three blocks. Two blocks. One. And there it was, her house. A woman in running clothes sat on the front steps reading the newspaper.

Liz stopped. The woman looked up.

"Mrs. Sandler?" Hannah had told her the woman's first name but Liz could not remember. She stopped at the edge of the property. "I'm Liz Shepherd."

Mrs. Sandler smiled and waited.

"I used to live here."

"Oh. Shepherd. Of course." She put out her hand. "Glad to meet you. I'm Mitzi."

"The house looks wonderful."

Had it always been beautiful? It troubled Liz to think that she had lived seventeen years of her life oblivious to the beauty around her. What she remembered most clearly was being embarrassed by the busy-faced, old-fashioned house in the unfashionable part of town. She had wanted to live in a shake-roofed ranch house out by the country club, like Gail.

She pointed up. "That was my bedroom. We called it the turret."

"The corner tower." Mitzi Sandler folded her paper, *The New York Times*, and stood up. "We've turned it into a playroom for the kids. Our daughters."

Liz nodded.

"Would you like to see inside?"

Liz looked at her watch.

"Actually, I'm staying with Hannah Tarwater—"

"I know Hannah. She's terrific."

"We've been friends—"

A buzz came from the cell phone on the steps.

Mitzi looked apologetic and reached for it, saying as she did, "Look, if it's not convenient now, I'd love to show the old girl off another time. Can you come back later in the week? We're going to be working in the basement but—"

"Thursday?" Liz asked.

Mitzi Sandler nodded, smiled and punched a button on her phone and said, "Hello."

*   *   *

Jeanne preferred the 10:30 service at St. Margaret's and always sat up front. "For the theater," she told people. By which she really meant "for the mistakes"—like the time the acolyte dropped a plate of consecrated wafers and the priest had to eat every one of them while the congregation pretended not to notice. Most mistakes were more subtle and only noticeable to those who, like Jeanne, had participated in the Anglican liturgy all their lives and knew it well enough in all its rites to let her mind drift and think of other things.

God and church didn't have much to do with each other in Jeanne's mind. God seemed like wishful thinking but the Church made excellent sense. Jeanne did not like to think of a world minus the Ten Commandments, minus reward and punishment.

She genuflected and crossed herself, never missing a beat. She said the words of the Creed and Thanksgiving while she thought of all the things she had to do before the end of next week. She knelt for the Confession, resting her hands on the back of the pew in front of her. She laid her head on her hands and closed her eyes.

A hangover drilled at the inside of her skull.

She had only intended to soften the edges of the evening. A few glasses of wine was like applying an airbrush to the guests at Hannah's table. Their flaws disappeared. No moles, no wrinkles, no unsightly hair. Nobody bored her, not even Gail. But it hadn't worked. The more Gail talked, the less she said; and Teddy, glossy and smug, had laughed at every joke. He meant it when he said he planned to ask her for money. His fawning irritated Jeanne like a burst of poison oak she couldn't stop itching. And as if that were not bad enough, Mindy—who by all the laws of life should have been a bitter, neurotic, drug-addled ruin of the Sixties—was contented and self-acceptant as the Buddha himself. All Mario did was remind Jeanne of the past. Like every other girl at Rinconada High School, she had adored him.

The thought of love powered the drill in her head.

Which was worse? Drinking on purpose or trying not to drink and still doing it? Either way she went, she mirrored her parents. Her father had been a slow, purposeful, daily drinker who took a shot of Jack Daniel's every hour or so from midday until bedtime the way some people dose themselves with aspirin for constant pain. By nightfall he was a zombie but still able to lay down the law. Her mother had regularly tried not to drink; but eventually, after a week or a month of white-knuckled abstinence, she succumbed, drank and wept and blamed herself for her son's death, blamed Jeanne for daring to live on, and took to her bed.

The usher touched Jeanne's shoulder. Old Mr. Applebee. Since his wife died he seemed to have forgotten how to comb his hair. Jeanne smiled at him, rose, genuflected in the aisle, then stepped back to let the boys she'd brought from school go before her where she could keep an eye on them. She imagined her own boy at the same age as these. Adam Weed had stayed behind at the school; his father had said they were not churchgoers. Teddy was afraid Simon Weed would take his son out of school at the first hint of trouble. Teddy the Know-it-All. Teddy Mr. Big Bucks. Jeanne knelt at the altar rail, crossed herself and lifted her hands for the Host. She wished for once Teddy would get what he deserved. She grabbed the chalice when the priest offered it.

At Hilltop Jeanne parked the van in the transportation shed and the boys ran off, yelling, to change their clothes and meet in the dining hall for a baked ham dinner. Sunday was a free day for the older ones; but after a quiet hour following dinner, the younger boys were required to play organized games. According to the Hilltop Method this encouraged cooperation and healthy competition. Late in the afternoon there would be study hall and story hour followed by cheese on toast and tomato soup.

A memory smacked her.

Billy Phillips's mother, when she was cook at Hilltop School, had instigated the Sunday night tomato soup and cheese on toast. It had been a year for tomatoes, the plants drooped from the weight of them. Jeanne had been sent into the garden with a bushel basket, hauling it back into the kitchen and stopping every few yards along the way because it was heavy and she was—what?—eight or nine, no more than that. Mrs. Phillips had shown her how to blanch the tomatoes and slip off the leathery skin and moosh the fruit with the potato smasher, simmer the pulp with a little chicken broth and then push it through the ricer. Mooshed, smashed and riced tomatoes, evaporated milk, salt and pepper; the cooks still used Mrs. Phillips's recipe. She had been finishing her kitchen shift on the day her son died. Jeanne, out of breath from running, had passed her coming out of the kitchen on her way home, clutching her straw bag filled with leftovers.

Slow down, Jeannie. There's fresh cobbler in the pantry.

Jeanne could have told her then.

Coulda, shoulda. Damn Liz for bringing it all up again.

Hard to believe, but Jeanne was older now than Mrs. Phillips had been back then. She thought how the burden of being a war widow with a young son, a problem child, must have burdened her. And then he was dead and she was alone and Jeanne supposed her widow's pension was enough to live on alone. In some ways her life was probably better without him. She had stopped working at Hilltop and from Hannah's bedroom window the girls often saw her sitting in a canvas chair in her backyard knitting. Even in summer she knit.

Jeanne locked the van and slipped the keys into her purse. Her fingers touched Teddy's Waterman. Ahead she saw a trash can. She dropped it in and gave the can a kick so the pen dropped to the bottom.

Jeanne detoured around the administration building, and crossed the lawn to the rose cloister where she stopped a moment to sit on the lion-footed bench, postponing. Dawdling, her mother would have said.

The glory season was over. Tomorrow Mr. Ashizawa would spend the day pruning the plants back to the wood. Few blossoms remained from Saturday morning's cutting and those that clung were sadly overblown. Petals carpeted the ground beneath the plants. In some places the covering looked inches deep. She had read that Cleopatra and Antony made love in a chamber filled with rose petals. The lovers waded to one another through rose petals and fell upon them like silken sheets.

Jeanne wondered if Teddy would ever make love to her again. And if he didn't, how much did she care. She imagined making love with Simon Weed. He would have a small penis, she guessed. But capable.

When she passed through the oleander hedge a few minutes

later, she found Teddy on the patio drinking a gin fizz and reading a paperback.

"Hair of the dog?" he asked, holding up his glass.

"I'm having brunch with Liz and Hannah."

"Lucky you to be so popular."

"Do you have a headache?"

He shook his head. "You?"

"I feel great," she said.

Jeanne walked past him into the house. When she emerged thirty minutes later she had changed into a peach-colored pantsuit with a bright scarf at the neck. Her hair was loose and curling about her shoulders. Teddy raised his glass.

"I see there's life in the old girl yet."

"Do I look okay?"

"Do you care what I think?"

Her spine stiffened. "Teddy, can't you just answer me straight? Does everything have to be a punch line? Do I look all right? Maybe I'm too old to wear my hair down. What do you think?"

"I think you're showing off for Liz."

Jeanne walked away.

"Don't do anything I wouldn't do."

That gave her a lot of options.

The restaurant was called La Vache and it tried for the French country look. On the second floor dining terrace, round tables covered in rough cotton cloths and shaded by green-and-white umbrellas overlooked the dusty oaks and shedding sycamores of the town park. Potted flowers, artificially crumbled stonework: the effect was pleasant but not like any France Liz knew. Dress at La Vache was casual for which Liz was grateful. She wore a black tunic over pants with an elastic waistband. This would not be an easy meal. She had to be able to breathe.

Liz and Hannah ordered sparkling water from a waitress in a pushup bra and talked about Jeanne while they waited for her to arrive.

"Have you ever told her she drinks too much?"

Hannah rolled her eyes. "A couple of years ago."

"And?"

"What you'd expect. She got that arch superior look, lifted her eyebrow, the whole thing."

"What did she say?"

"Something like, '*I can handle it.*' Very cool. Made me sorry I cared."

"She's formidable."

"Sometimes we go for a walk in the morning and I can smell it on her breath."

"She told me she never drinks during the day."

"I think she tries not to and she can be super-controlled—"

"What else is new?"

"—and then something happens and she loses it."

"Sounds like her mother."

"Did you know they drank?"

Liz nodded. "My mother used to talk about everybody in the neighborhood. Being superior gave her permission to be a gossip."

Hannah tore a morsel from her French roll. "I've thought about suggesting an intervention but I don't have the guts to do it alone and Teddy wouldn't help. He loves it that she has a weakness." She brushed bread crumbs into her palm and dumped them in a potted plant. "Her parents died drunk. You weren't here but by then everyone in town knew. If Jeanne and Teddy weren't running the school they would have lost it."

"And now she's headed the same way. How'd she get like this, Hannah?"

"How did any of us get to be the way we are?" Hannah spoke as if first causes were of no interest to her, as if their conversation the night before had not taken place. They were back to "making" conversation, twirling and pirouetting over Billy Phillips's grave.

Liz said she had seen Mitzi Sandler that morning. "I'm going to go into that house. I'm going to force myself."

"Your parents did the best they could."

"It isn't just them, Hannah. You know that. The house, the creek, Billy Phillips, they're all part of the knot I've got in my stomach."

Hannah looked wary. "You're not going to start on Bluegang again, are you? Wasn't last night enough?"

"It's the elephant in the living room, Hannah."

"If there's an elephant in anyone's living room, it's in Teddy and

Jeanne's." Before Liz could respond Hannah went on. "Over the years I've given a lot of thought to those two and I'll tell you, Liz, I'm sure there's a secret there. A nasty little secret our Jeanne's too ashamed to talk about."

Liz had sometimes thought the same thing. "What do you think it is?"

"Haven't a clue. But it's there. Buried way back probably. I'll bet Teddy knows."

"Whatever it is, he probably holds it over her."

"Such a jerk," Hannah said, shaking her head.

"But he's still handsome."

Hannah laughed. "For a scumbag."

"That was a beautiful shirt."

"He spends more on himself in a month than Jeanne does in a year. Two years." Hannah glimpsed Jeanne talking to the hostess and waved. "Here she is."

Jeanne's hair was loose around her ears, shiny in the autumn sunlight and the peach pantsuit brightened her complexion or, Liz thought, she might have brushed on a little color. For some reason, this effort, which in another woman would have been unremarkable, made Liz terribly sad; and there were tears in her eyes when she stood up and hugged Jeanne.

"What's that for?"

Liz shrugged. "I guess I love you."

Jeanne looked as if she expected to hear a qualification. After a beat she smiled and hugged Liz back.

"Sorry I'm late." Jeanne dropped into the chair next to Hannah. "The kids had to get their God-fix." She poked Hannah. "Did you make it to eight o'clock?"

"I couldn't sleep. I've been up since five."

"You're a better woman than I."

"No argument there," Hannah said.

The exquisite La Vache buffet scarcely tempted Liz.

Jeanne eyed the sparse fare arranged on Liz's plate. "You dieting?" Her own plate was segregated into neat vegetarian piles. "Try the crepes."

Hannah said, "You know at our age, it really isn't a good idea to diet. I read an article that said there's estrogen in our fat cells. God knows, we need all of that we can get." Hannah put her elbows on the table—her about-to-tell-a-story position. "Last summer I was in Nordstrom buying a shirt for Dan. It was the middle of summer, heat wave outside and the air conditioning going like crazy, and right then, while I was talking to the sales boy, I felt myself begin to flush. Like mercury rising in a thermometer? And these great rivers of sweat started to pour down my face." She rolled her eyes. "Cataracts."

Liz laughed sympathetically; though she had not had the experience herself, it would come. "At least in the tropics you can blame the humidity."

"I don't want to blame the humidity. I'm not ashamed of being middle-aged." Hannah sat back, straightening the lapel of her lemon-colored blazer.

"Hannah's a bit of a zealot on this subject," Jeanne said.

"I just refuse to be humiliated because I have a normal, healthy, fifty-year-old body." Hannah wagged her fork at them. "I went through puberty, now I'm going through this. So?"

Methinks she doth . . .

"You on HRT, Liz?"

Just at the moment she seemed to have all the hormones she needed, quite naturally.

"What kind of doctor do you have?"

"Regular," Liz said. "Nose to toes."

Jeanne said, "I read in the paper about how writers of a sex education curriculum had to change all references to vagina to 'down there.' Penis stayed penis, but vagina became 'down there.'"

"One of Ingrid's friends used to call it her Christmas purse." Hannah was the only person Liz knew who could eat and talk and laugh at the same time and not look disgusting. "Before you go back, you should go in and see my doctor." She put down her fork and added with forced carelessness, "I forget, the doctor you saw on Friday, was it a woman? What was that all about, anyway? Hormones and stuff?" Hannah pushed her plate away and put her elbows on the table again, ready to dish. "Why were you so secretive? You told me not to worry but it's hard, you know? Don't tell me you were embarrassed to talk about it." She looked at Jeanne and barreled on. "See, this is what I mean. It doesn't matter how much education a woman has, there's this kind of shame—"

Stop talking, Hannah. Breathe, Hannah. Quiet and distracted last night. Wound up like a spring doll today. *What's the matter, Hannah?*

"So who was this doctor?" Jeanne asked.

"A clinic in Miami recommended him. It's not about meno-pause. And it's not cancer." Liz felt the beat of her heart, the flick of a feather up under her ribs and imagined she could feel another below it, keeping time. "I was going to tell you both today. I'm pregnant."

"Oh. My. God," Hannah said.

Jeanne sat back and stared. "I can't believe you'd be so careless. After all these years . . ."

"Shut up, Jeanne. She's going to have a baby." Hannah sounded like an announcer declaring a lottery winner. "I'm so happy for you, Lizzie."

"Don't rush out and buy me a layette, Hannah. That's why I came home. I'm having an abortion while I'm here. Friday."

Silence. Liz watched a hummingbird pierce the heart of a potted fuchsia on the railing behind Hannah.

"You can't do that. Why would you do that?"

"Hannah? I thought you approved of abortion. In fact, it seems to me you had one yourself."

"I was a college student. I wasn't married. I hadn't even met Dan. It's a totally different thing. You're fifty years old and you're going to be a mother." A light had gone on beneath Hannah's skin. Liz recognized the glow from peace marches and campaigns to save whales and polar bears and wolves. "It's a miracle, Liz. You can't abort a miracle."

"They're all miracles," Jeanne said quietly.

"I know it's a miracle but that doesn't mean I want to be a mother. And anyway, Jeanne, you don't even believe in miracles." Liz's head had begun to spin. "This is unreal. I particularly remem-ber conversations we all had. I can remember you saying—"

"People change," Jeanne said.

Liz felt sucker-punched. "I guess I'm finding that out."

"I'm a vegetarian because I don't believe we have the right to kill anything with a beating heart." Jeanne put her hand on her chest as if she needed to demonstrate that she qualified. "I also oppose the death penalty and war and abortion. Killing is killing is killing and I'm against it all."

"Is that why you won't talk about Bluegang?"

"Don't change the subject," Hannah said.

Her friends had vanished and been replaced by strangers. "Of all the people in the world, I expected you to support me, Jeanne."

"Well, I'm sorry. I just know you'll regret it. You'll grieve."

"How do you know? Have you been fifty years old and pregnant?" She let out a short breathless laugh. "When this is over, I'm going to celebrate."

"Why can't you keep it?" Jeanne asked.

"I can't believe you'd ask me that. I've never wanted a family. I can't remember ever once thinking to myself how grand it would be to play mommy."

"Why do you have to use such an insulting tone? There are millions of women who'd—"

"Shit, Hannah, this is about me, not you or millions of other women. You know what it was like when I was a kid. If my parents remembered to say good morning, I thought I was being spoiled. When I had my first period, it was your mother who explained it to me."

Jeanne said, "You'd bond. It's instinctive."

"This is bizarre, Jeanne. There's no such thing as the mothering instinct. It has to be learned and, frankly, I'm never going to get it." She turned back to Hannah, desperate for support. "If you've got troubles with Ingrid now, how would it be for my child when she's seventeen and I'm almost seventy."

"She?" Jeanne said. "It's a girl?"

"I don't know and I don't want to."

"If you have a good relationship, age won't matter."

"Jeanne, you're blowing smoke. You don't have any more experience with mothering than I do. You've never had a child."

"She's had a whole school full," Hannah said.

"I know it's wrong to kill a living soul."

Soul. Did the fetus in her womb have a soul? Liz did not think so. Not yet, anyway. And if it did, would it be murder to abort it? Again, she didn't think so. If there was such a thing as the soul, it was spirit, immortal, not rooted in the flesh it inhabited. Abortion could never destroy a soul, only flesh and blood.

"I'm free to disagree," Liz said quietly. Not because she was calm, because if she didn't control herself she would scream. "Free to choose."

"Since when does anyone have the right to choose murder?"

Liz wanted to throw down her napkin and walk out. But where would she go?

Hannah spoke up. "What about Gerard? What does he think? Maybe he'd like to be a father."

"Does he know? Have you told him?"

"Of course he knows, Jeanne."

"And he wants you to have an abortion? What kind of a guy is he?"

"He wants me to decide for myself." The air fluttered in Liz's lungs as she rushed to Gerard's defense. "He knows it's up to me what I do with my body. He loves me. He wants to marry me."

Hannah laughed and her hands dithered in the air. "What a day! A baby and a wedding. Oh, Liz—"

"I didn't say we were going to do it." Liz sank back in her chair, flattened by the weight of so much explaining. "We've done well, all these years. Why mess up a good thing?"

"I don't get it." Jeanne pushed her plate away. "You come up here and you tell me you want to talk about Bluegang, about how you should have done this or that, all kinds of talk about taking responsibility, and then you tell us you're getting an abortion. Isn't it just more of the same? Isn't it more Liz putting Liz first?"

Hannah said, "What's Bluegang got to do with—"

"If you want to make up for Billy Phillips you should do the responsible thing. Have the baby. Marry Gerard and have the baby."

"One child is not equal to another." Liz moved her plate aside and leaned forward, speaking quietly. "And as for responsibility, Jeanne, it would be totally *ir*responsible if I went ahead and had this baby out of guilt or romantic notions of motherhood or to make up for something that happened years ago. And my bet is, if we were talking about someone else—say Mindy got pregnant—you'd both feel just like I do. It's because it's me, Jeanne."

"And you, of course, are the most important person in the world. How could I forget?"

Hannah grabbed Liz's hand and squeezed it. "Jeanne, you're being mean. Stop it." She held on to Liz's hand. "I believe in a woman's right to choose, Liz, you know that. You can choose not to have this baby but you can also choose to have it. Choice goes both ways. In all the rhetoric, you seem to have forgotten that."

"I haven't forgotten." Liz sighed.

"You're being a hypocrite," Jeanne said. "If Billy Phillips haunts you now—"

"We can't weigh lives, this one for that one." Liz held up her hand, asking for silence. "We should have told our parents what happened that day. I knew that but I didn't push it and that's the deep shame of my life. I knew it was wrong to leave him there on the rocks for a couple of kids to find, wrong to make his mother worry all night long. That poor sad woman who had nothing else in the world but her one boy. I'm ashamed of letting that happen. But having a baby at my age won't undo any of it."

And I'm not going to let you bully me into doing what you want. Again.

Hannah said softly, "He would have raped me. I pushed him away. It was an accident."

"Of course it was. You know I don't blame you. And I don't blame Jeanne either. You both did what you thought was right. The only one who didn't was me." She took a deep breath. "I did what I knew was wrong."

"More Liz thinking first, last and always about Liz."

"No, what's wrong is forever putting yourself *last*." Liz had had enough of Jeanne. "What's wrong is wasting your whole life married to a man you don't love. It's never saying to yourself, *I have the right to be happy*. What's really, really wrong is letting your husband drive you to drink."

"Oh, boy." Hannah sat back.

Jeanne stared at Liz and then down at her hands clasped in her lap. At the table next to them a man told his companion if she would just learn to focus, her golf swing would improve seventy-five percent.

Jeanne's eyebrow shot up. "Have you two been discussing this between you?"

Hannah and Liz looked at each other and nodded.

Jeanne smiled.

Her composure was frightening, a body of water thick with snakes whose movements made not a ripple on the surface.

"I'm glad you care about me, but honestly, alcohol just isn't a problem. If it were, my work would suffer. But the school is thriving. My father was an alcoholic and near the end of his life, he let the school run down. But there's nothing like that going on with me. I know my limits."

It was bullshit, but it sounded so damn logical.

"And as far as my marriage is concerned—"

"It's none of my business. I shouldn't have said anything."

"But you always do. You ask questions, you have your theories of how I ought to live . . . Teddy and I have had our down times, Liz. But we've made a contract and we've produced something worthwhile out of the terms of the contract. He's not the man I thought he was when we married; but then, I'm not that starry eyed Phi Beta Kappa either. The point is that change doesn't nullify the contract. Or make the results any less worthwhile."

"That's the saddest thing I've ever heard you say."

Liz wished she could go away somewhere and cry for an hour or the rest of the afternoon. Instead they went back to twirling and pirouetting. They were old friends and they had argued before—though never so intensely over matters so personal. They went back to the buffet for dessert. They talked about Gail Bacci and wondered aloud about Mindy's sex life. Anyone passing their table would have thought they were having a good time. Jeanne ordered a second glass of wine as if to spite them.

In the middle of a reminiscence about Mario, a laugh burst from Hannah. "I just got the most wonderful idea. It takes care of everything." She leaned forward. "You don't have to have an abortion. You can have the baby and I'll raise it for you. You can be its mother and Gerard can be its father, but it can live up here in Rinconada with Dan and me."

Liz stared at her and took a long drink of iced tea.

"Dan's a wonderful father. You know that, Liz. You already love him madly and you could totally trust . . ."

"Thank you. Thank you, for that."

She looked from Hannah to Jeanne and back to Hannah. Her oldest friends, the best friends she would ever have. Yet to call them friends was a misnomer for they were neither friends nor family but some category of relationship between the two. The first time she saw Hannah, Liz and her mother had been standing in line to enter the first grade classroom. *'I'm late for my lecture,' her mother said to the mother of the curly haired blonde girl in front of her. 'Would you mind taking Elizabeth in?'* Jeanne, when Liz met her, was punching a black leather bag hung from the branch of a prune tree, wearing Buster Browns and a faded dress with puffed sleeves. She drove her fist into the bag; it swung away and her braids swung too.

So what if they didn't really know each other anymore? So what if they didn't seem to get that she was a grown woman, and able to make her own choices in life. Maybe what counted most were the memories and shared experiences. Hannah had said it an hour earlier, speaking of Gail and Mario. *They've been together so long, they'd be lost on their own.* Liz wanted to go on believing what they had was something extraordinary and profound. It was either that, it seemed, or let Jeanne and Hannah skate away. She couldn't bear the thought, not for a moment, but neither could she return to the box where they obviously wanted her kept.

She took their hands in hers and brought them to her lips, shaking her head.

"That is the kindest offer anyone ever made me. But it wouldn't work, Hannah. My mind's made up."

It was almost five when Jeanne walked through the oleander hedge and into the house. On the kitchen counter she found a note from Teddy telling her to come down to the school right away. She drank a glass of wine, brushed her teeth and gargled, changed her clothes and went down.

"Where the hell have you been?" he said when she entered her office. The air conditioning was on but sweat slicked Teddy's forehead. "I heard the car thirty minutes ago."

"What's happened?"

"It's that goddamn Adam Weed. I wish to hell you'd consulted me before you accepted his application. We have enough to worry about with normal boys—"

Jeanne made herself take a deep breath. "What's wrong with him?"

"The little bastard's disappeared. No one's seen him since games." Teddy sank into a chair and looked up at her. "You should have been here, Jeanne. It's not like I can run this school alone, you know."

She took a seat beside him and asked again, more gently, "I need to know what you've done, Teddy."

"That friend of his, his Big Brother, Robby: I told him and his pal to look for him."

"Where?"

"Where do you think? Around the school."

"Did you tell them to check Bluegang?"

"I wish you'd been here, Jeanne. You know I'm not good at this kind of thing."

"We'll find him, Teddy. He'll be okay."

He smelled sour and she was glad to move away from him, glad to go to her desk and sit down. She turned on her computer and called up Adam's file.

"It said in his records from Wisconsin that he hates games. He's so small and uncoordinated." Speaking to herself she said, "I should have known he'd do something like this."

"A little late to think of that now." Teddy's tone made her look up. "You should have warned the staff the kid'd bolt if he had to play sports. It was your responsibility. But if something happens to him, I'm the one gets the blame." He paced. "You realize that, don't you? You can fuck up royally, but I'm the one who has to take it in the ass."

Jeanne picked up the phone.

He grabbed her wrist.

"We can't call the police. If the police find out we've lost a kid, it'll be in all the papers . . ."

"I'm only making an intercom call." She pulled his hand away from her wrist finger by finger. "It's what you should have done in the first place. We need to alert the resident staff and have a meeting. Someone must go down to the creek."

There was a knock and the office door opened a crack. Robby McFadden looked in. "Found him."

Teddy strode to the door and swung it wide. Adam stood behind Robby and another boy.

Jeanne stood up. "Where was he?"

"Just walking in the hall," Robby said.

"Going back to his room, I think," the other boy added.

Teddy grabbed Adam by the arm and jerked him into the office. "Where were you?"

"Teddy. Let him go."

The older boys gawked at the scene. Jeanne turned back to them and said in her business-as-usual voice, "Excellent work, boys. Now you must go over to the dining hall and find cook." She wrote a quick note and held it out to Robby. "There's a lemon coconut cake in the pantry and some Cokes."

"All right!"

"You can have all you want," she added before they rushed away. "If I hear anything about this matter, any gossip at all during the week, even a hint of it, I'll know one of you is responsible. If that happens, I'm going to be very unhappy." She cocked one eyebrow. "Do you understand me?"

They said they did and thought they meant it, but Jeanne knew schoolboys. In the midst of Hilltop's routine and order, they were starved for novelty. They intended to keep their word but the tasty morsel of gossip would be irresistible. By midweek the news of Adam's disappearance and Teddy's panic and rage would be the talk of the school. Eventually the story would reach a few parents who would have to be assured their children were adequately supervised at Hilltop School.

"Just who the hell do you think you are, young man? You think you can run off any time you want?"

For now the most important thing was controlling Teddy's temper. "This school's got rules, mister, and you're going to follow them or you're going to be out on your keester."

"Keep your voice down, Teddy."

He jabbed Adam's chest with his index finger. "Learning to play games is part of learning to be a man. You want to be a sissy—"

"Stop it, Teddy."

"—all your life, Weed? And hear this: if you ever leave school again without permission, I'll set a cane across your backside. Your father signed a paper that said I could do it—"

"He never!"

"—and you better believe I'll do it. Boys are not allowed to leave the school without—"

"Didn't leave the school."

"Don't lie to me."

"Didn't." Adam made fists and pressed them against his thighs. *There's mud on his shoes. Like last time, he's tracked mud across my floor.* "Where were you, Adam?"

He pointed out the window. "Like you said I could."

"What's he mean?"

"He likes the rose cloister. I gave him permission to go there." Jeanne didn't really believe Adam had been in the cloister but she wanted to protect him from Teddy.

"Why wasn't I told about this?"

Jeanne counted silently before asking in a measured voice. "Did anyone check the cloister?"

"Why would I think of that?"

"I asked if you'd done a thorough check. It's right out in front."

"You believe him?"

"He has mud on his shoes." She pointed at the caked Reeboks.

"What were you doing there?"

"Smellin' 'em."

"Jeanne? . . ."

"It has a wall. It feels safe and private. I went there when I was little." She knew she was convincing herself and that was all right. More than the truth, she wanted Teddy to know he'd bungled the search and that in doing so he had put the school at risk. "Send him back to Edith. He's missing his supper."

"He can't get away with this."

"Go get your dinner, Adam."

Jeanne shut off her computer and stood. She walked to the window and looked out across the expanse of withered lawn to the cloister. Overhead crows cawed and wheeled, black against the darkening sky. In the rose garden, the blossoms were finished. Mr. Ashizawa had cut them back to the bone and there was nothing to smell but earth.

"You overrode me, dammit." Behind her, Teddy had begun to pace.

"It was going nowhere."

"I don't care, you can't just reverse . . . Actions have consequences, Jeanne. Isn't that what Hilltop teaches? Isn't that what it says in the brochures? Didn't your father? . . ."

"Yes. Yes to everything."

"Well, then?"

Anger suited Teddy. Emotion put color in his face and animated him out of his irritating insouciance. But his good looks had no more power over her than his anger. If she gave in to his bullying and apologized, if she did his bidding, soothed and coddled him, would he return the favor by becoming the partner she yearned for, the friend and lover she could depend on? No chance. A day of smiles and flattery and then back to the same old thing.

In an album somewhere there was a picture taken of her on their honeymoon. She is on the beach, leaning back, her arms straight behind her and the wind blows hard enough to whip the hair across her cheek and she glows, she is incandescent with joy. Carmel beach and she and Teddy were newlyweds. She had been pregnant and waiting for the right moment to tell him. Actions do indeed have consequences, but it had taken her this long to see how the rule could apply to her own life.

That night Hannah read in bed and waited for Dan to come home. It was after eleven when she heard his tires on the gravel and a moment later the sound of Cherokee dancing on the kitchen's tiled floor. All evening Hannah and Liz had been like strangers in line for concert tickets, polite, forced by proximity to make the smallest of small talk. Hannah could not believe Liz didn't see what a perfect resolution to her problem had been offered. Not that babies were problems, Hannah would never say that. She would say they were a gift from God. And especially this one. Dan might not accept Angel into his home—too risky, too much baggage—but how could he object to raising Liz's baby?

Dan was pulling off his tie as he came into the bedroom. "A boy. Eight pounds, nine ounces."

"I have to talk to you."

"And he was mighty reluctant. I'm bushed." He stripped off his undershirt. "Let me get a shower. We'll talk after."

"Then you'll be too sleepy to listen." She patted the bed. "Please."

He gave her a wary look, but he sat. "Five minutes. After five, I pass out."

"Liz told me something wonderful today." Hannah sat beside him. She slipped her arm around his waist and made her voice steady. "She's pregnant."

"I thought she might be."

"You knew? And you didn't tell me? Why didn't you say something?"

"None of my business."

"She's going to have an abortion if we don't stop her."

"I'm pro-choice, Hannah." He pulled away. "I thought you were too."

"This isn't about that."

"Honey, I'd leave this up to Liz if I were you." He started to get up.

She grabbed his hand and held on tight. "Liz is our family. When we were kids she was like my sister." He hadn't interrupted yet. Maybe he wouldn't. Maybe he guessed what she was going to say and had already decided to agree. He was the sweetest man in the world, the most generous and flexible, and he had always given in to her requests when he knew they were important. Always. "I told her if she'd go ahead and have it, we'd raise it for her." She held her breath until her chest hurt. Dan leaned over and unlaced his shoes. "Say something, Dan. What do you think?"

He took off one shoe and threw it in the direction of the closet.

He took off the other and threw it in the same direction only harder. He stood and unbuttoned his shirt. Hannah jumped up and put her arms around his waist from behind. She rested her cheek against his warm, bare back.

"Weren't those good times, Dan? When the kids were small? You liked having babies in the house, you know you did, you told me you did. And we were good at it. You said we made a good team. Remember?" *Please, remember.*

He turned and grabbed the top of her arms. Her shoulders lifted. It was the way he held Eddie the time he crashed his bike riding double down Overlook grade, not wearing a helmet. Love and fear and rage.

"I'm not saying it'll be easy," she said. "But think about Angel . . ."

"Angel!" He pushed her back on the bed.

"Don't be angry, just listen, okay? A baby like Angel needs special parents who can understand . . ."

"You've got one minute left."

"Dan, let's take them both."

He looked at her and sat down, collapsed.

She knelt before him. "These babies need me and I need them. I can't explain it but I do, I need them. I promise they won't be any bother to you. I swear they won't. I'll never ask you to do anything . . ."

"Get up, Hannah."

She wouldn't. She wrapped her arms around his legs and laid her cheek on his knees. His calves felt solid as timber. "Please, Dan. I don't think I can live without this."

After a moment, he expelled a deep breath. She felt his hands touch her hair, smoothing and combing with his fingers the ripples left by her braid. She closed her eyes and began to relax.

"Have I ever told you about my fantasy?" he said. "I've always wanted to learn to fly fish."

"You can do that. There's no reason—"

"I imagine you and me learning to fly fish and going up to Canada, flying into some remote river and wading into it up to our thighs. I see me cleaning the fish and cooking them while you read poetry aloud. And then I think about making love to you under a mosquito net a thousand miles from the nearest telephone or hospital." He lifted her chin and looked into her eyes. "Kinda pathetic, huh? You're dreaming about babies and I'm dreaming about you."

His words damaged her. She didn't know how exactly, but they marked her. "You make it sound like I don't want to be with you. You know I do."

"How would I know that, Hannah? Even when you're here, your mind's somewhere else."

"We can go camping anytime." She stood up, mad because he'd suckered her in with his talk of fantasies, cheated because she had thought he was going to say yes. "The woods aren't going anywhere and neither are the fish. God knows there'll be mosquitoes until the end of time. But Liz's baby comes with a time limit."

"It's a fetus. Not a baby."

"She'll kill it."

"Hannah, that's her right."

"I know but this one's different."

"Dammit, Hannah, listen to yourself. It's too much. The way you feel about Angel and now about Liz's pregnancy, it's too much. It's not normal."

She stood up. "You think it's biological." The hard tone of her voice surprised her as much as a stranger's would at that time, in that room. "Menopause, empty nest."

He took a moment to answer. "If it were that simple, I wouldn't be so worried." He rubbed the back of his neck. Hannah saw exhaustion in the gesture, but she had no sympathy for him. "I wake up in the middle of the night and worry about you, Hannah."

"Poor you."

"There's a psychologist in my building, I like her . . ."

"No. Absolutely not."

"Hannah, there's no shame attached to seeing a therapist. She's a nice woman, skillful."

"If I needed a shrink, I'd go to one."

"People do it all the time."

"Well, not this people. I'm not going to let some Gen-Xer with letters after her name tell me I'm sick because I care what happens to unwanted babies."

"Why does it frighten you so much? What do you think you might find out?"

"I thought you were going to take a shower."

"If you won't go for yourself, go for Eddie."

"Him?"

"You've got to do something about your relationship. You're breaking his heart."

She made a sound like a laugh and pulled back the bedcovers. "Help me fold the quilt."

"Don't try to change the subject." He took the heavy quilt from her hands and dropped it in a chair. "Eddie's fifteen. I remember what it's like to be a boy that age. It's not great, Hannah. He looks in the mirror and he sees his skin's lousy and none of his features fit together. He's awkward and shy and embarrassed by his own thoughts. He's caught between being a boy and a man and it hurts. He needs you to love him and admire him and make a fuss over him so he can get through this time without losing all the confidence we worked so hard to build when he was little. You reject him and you know what he thinks? He thinks if even his own mother doesn't love him, then there's got to be something really wrong with him."

"Of course I love him. He knows that. And I don't reject him. What an idea." In the bathroom she brushed her hair without looking in the mirror. "Besides, Eddie's not the point. He's a distraction. I want to talk about Angel and Liz's baby . . ."

"If you can't be a mother to your own son, what makes you think—"

"I'm a damned good mother and you know it."

"Not to Eddie you're not. Not anymore. You neglect him, you reject him, you make him ashamed of growing up."

"You son of a bitch."

She threw the hairbrush across the room, missing him by an arm's length. It hit her bedside table, shattering a little crystal water jug and glass she kept there. With a cry she dropped to her knees and covered her face with her hands.

For a moment Dan watched her cry, then went to his closet and took out his shorts and athletic shoes and socks. "I'm going for a run." He stood at the bedroom door. "I don't want to hurt you, Hannah. I never want to hurt you. Only I've got to be honest, the way you are right now, I just can't stand to be around you. There's a limit to what I can take, Hannah. The way you are now, it's breaking my heart."

Monday

By the light Liz judged it was early, probably before six. Gerard would have eaten breakfast hours ago and depending on his schedule he might be in the Jeep heading up country or under the guest house laying out rat traps or holed up in their suite with a stack of professional reading. He might be down at the quay griping to Petula about tourists.

This time next week I'll be home too.

It had been a mistake to come back to Rinconada. She had brought trouble with her.

The night before she had tried not to listen but the bedrooms shared a wall. She had heard something break and an occasional angry word or sentence came through. *There's a limit to what I can take.* She wanted to forget the way Dan said it. Anger by itself would have been bad enough, but Liz had heard as well despair and exhaustion, the voice of a man ready to give up. She thought what only a few days before had been unthinkable. The trouble between Hannah and Dan might be serious. The idea of them apart tore at her heart.

Dan wanted Hannah to see a therapist.

And maybe that's what Liz should have done. Instead of coming back to Rinconada and lugging trouble with her, she could have stayed in Florida, had the abortion and then gone to a professional to talk about Bluegang.

Jeanne might be right. Liz was such a narcissist she had to drag everyone in on her troubles.

She rolled over onto her stomach and punched the pillow, closed her eyes and told herself go back to sleep. She turned again and stared up at the ceiling, and then at the window, at a cobweb in the corner like a cheesecloth swag with the light behind it.

When she first went to Belize Gerard had taken her for a walk in the damp forest just as the sun rose. As light hit the treetops he tilted her chin up and she saw the canopy festooned with jeweled spider webs shimmering in the warm wet dawn. She had known then that she would stay in Belize. Divina read the cards and said she must stay, she and Gerard, they were *simpatico. Liz did not need tarot to tell her this.* They understood each other's moods and weather and she knew a baby that demanded and deserved centrality would forever disrupt the atmosphere between them. Because Liz remembered what it had been like before Gerard, she knew that when things got rough and if they stayed rough too long, she would cut and run. If this meant she was a coward then so be it. Thank God after a long life's struggle she wasn't fighting who she was anymore. She could never explain this to Hannah and Jeanne. She could talk until she needed a respirator and they would cling to their memories of the girl she had been. Perhaps this might be in the nature of long friendships. Or maybe just theirs.

Hannah lay still and alert, listening to Dan's movements around the bedroom and bathroom. A weight the size and temperature of Antarctica lay across her chest as she recalled the night before. When she thought of talking to a therapist, she couldn't breathe. It wasn't logical and she didn't understand it; but she couldn't breathe and she absolutely couldn't tell Dan because if he knew he'd say it proved his point. She heard him go downstairs and out the kitchen door without taking time for breakfast. The tires of the BMW snarled on the gravel.

The night before she had pretended to be asleep when he returned from his run. She lay without moving, listening to him shower, feeling him move about on the bed beside her, getting comfortable. He was like an old dog going round in circles to find a comfortable spot. She'd never kick a dog but she'd like to kick Dan. She'd like to beat on him until he cried mercy, raised his arms—*I surrender. You can have Liz's baby and Angel too and what I said about Eddie—*

She hated him for saying that about Eddie.

What was so terrible about being unhappy? She'd been in and out of moods all her life. Being unhappy wasn't any reason to see a shrink. People who yukked it up all the time were the ones who needed their heads examined; it wasn't normal considering the state of the world. But it was typically male to have so little insight, to assume that because Hannah grieved for Angel and Liz's un- wanted baby, because she craved something he did not and was willing to fight for it, she must have some kind of terminal illness of the psyche. Well, she wasn't losing her mind and if Dan didn't know that then he needed *his* head examined.

By the time Hannah got up, the children had left for school and the house was empty except for Liz, still in bed, thank God.

Once when Hannah was down with the flu, she lay in bed and watched a morning interview program about abortion. Three women faced the cameras with the moderator, an excited man in an expensive-looking suit, standing on the steps between halves of the audience. Throughout the show the audience—every one of them at least as rotund as Gail Bacci—hectored the guests and sometimes each other. One of the guests claimed to be a theologian but looked like an Ivy League coed. She said a fetus has no soul in the womb. No one asked her how she knew this, but never mind, she rattled on. She said the soul hovers near a pregnant woman until the instant of birth. She said it had to be that way otherwise there would be two souls in one body at the same time and for some reason that was impossible. After birth the soul entered the body of the newborn; connecting up and settling in took a day or two.

Hannah didn't think much of the theologian but she liked her theory even as she laughed at it. She had looked into Eddie's eyes when he was only a day or two old and seen someone or some- thing very wise gazing back at her. Soon after, his eyes were only baby eyes; but she never forgot that fleeting glimpse as if for an in- stant she had spied upon eternity.

Hannah was not opposed to abortion on any moral grounds. An

abortion might be many things—a sorrow, a waste, a great relief—but it wasn't murder even if the theologian's theory was only New Age blab. But a baby with Liz's hair and dark brown eyes, the thought of that particular baby trashed . . .

Hannah considered herself a feminist and would argue for any woman's equal rights with a man. But the Movement, as it had once been called, angered her because it demeaned what she did best. Not that people like Gloria Steinem and the other one, the homely one who wrote the book, ever meant to put motherhood down. Hannah had never believed that. But it happened anyway; and now, because she had never wanted a career away from home, Hannah had no place, no stature, not even daydreams to sustain her. From early childhood she had fantasized being a mother and last night Dan as much as said that proved she needed psychiatric help.

Hannah didn't need a therapist, she needed babies and they needed her. She was a mother; this was her particular skill only no one wanted her to use it. Which was a big part of what was wrong with the United States of America. Motherhood was treated like a stage meant to be survived—like menopause or adolescence. A woman born to nurture and raise a big family got labeled wacko because she cared. And never let her dare admit the fun of being a mother, never let her say how she enjoyed the challenge. Especially don't use the word *challenge.* Compared to closing a big real estate deal? Be serious, Hannah Tarwater. Get your feet on the ground. You're going through a syndrome. *Empty nest.* As if she were a stork, a chickadee, a goddamn ostrich.

At Resurrection House she parked the Volvo and went inside, noting as she opened the door that the screen had been mended. Betts met her in the hall.

"Get a cup of coffee and come on into my office, Hannah."

Alarms rang in Hannah's head. In the common room she poured a coffee under the outstretched and protective gaze of the guardian angel and felt imperiled.

"Last night I got a call," Betts said when Hannah joined her in her office. "Just move those papers off the chair."

Hannah sat.

"From Angel's mother. Shannon."

Hannah sat so straight her back ached between the shoulder blades. *Shannon.* She had not imagined a name so innocent.

"She said she wanted to see her baby so I told her to come over this morning." Betts jerked her head in the direction of the nursery. "She's in there now."

"How can she come back here like nothing's happened? Where does a person get that kind of nerve?" Hannah jumped up and charged around the office. She was vaguely aware of looking over-wrought but didn't care. "You've read Angel's chart. This Shannon person smoked crack right up until she went into labor. She was probably a hooker, Betts. It's a bloody miracle Angel is even alive with all the crap she's got in her system."

"You know the law." Betts took off her glasses and rubbed her eyes, nodding. "I can't break the law. I have to let her spend time with her child."

"What if she wants to take her away?"

"If Shannon is trying to stay clean and make something of her life then she can go to court to get Angel back. That's always our goal, to put families back together, better than they were." Betts stood up. She looked formidable in her long black-and-white muu-muu, a floral tank running right over Hannah.

"What about the child advocate?"

"What about her?"

"She wouldn't let her go."

"Hear me, Hannah: If Angel's mother can show she's ready . . ."

"Fat chance."

"Don't forget the name of this place. It's not called Foster Mother House. It's not an orphanage. It's called Resurrection House. Resurrection means forgiveness and a second chance. If we can give a baby and her mother an opportunity to get a new start in life, then we're doing what we aim at."

Hannah wanted to slam her fist through the wall. She'd had about enough lectures from people who did not know the first thing about what it meant to be a mother. Or care that it was what she knew best.

"Does she have a place to live? A job?"

"She's staying with a friend."

"Oh, great." Hannah went into the little bathroom off Betts's office. She looked at herself in the mirror over the sink. *Obsolete.* Splashed water on her face and washed her hands and returned to the office. Betts had not moved, and as soon as Hannah sat down she began talking again in her kindly patient way.

"I know it's not a good situation, but this girl does seem determined to turn her life around. I've talked to her and—"

"What did she think of Angel?"

Betts rolled her eyes. "Her first words were, and I quote, 'How come she's so scrawny?'"

"Damn."

"But the truth is, Angel *is* scrawny. You and I, we know what she used to look like, what a wonder her development is. She's come a long way in ten months and that's what we notice. But Shannon sees her the way she really is." Betts settled back in her chair with a heavy sigh. "Angel isn't your baby, Hannah. Caring for her doesn't give you any rights."

Talking about the welfare of a baby as if they were all the same and their lives could be settled by a line in a law book. Hannah refused to cry. "Don't worry about me. I'll learn the drill." She stood up and walked into the common room. She pulled on her smock as Betts looked on.

"I don't want you to minimize how you feel, Hannah. And I don't want you to think I don't appreciate you. Not just me, all of us here. You have a great deal of love and so much to give. The connection you've made with Angel is a wonderful thing, a blessing for both you and the child. You've probably saved her life. I'm only saying, you mustn't hold too tight. Stop by the chapel and say a little prayer before you meet Shannon. It might help."

Hannah looked down at the hand that took hers. The fingers were short and thick and practical looking, the veins stood up like a trail of molehills. In one she saw a pulse beating.

"Light a candle, Hannah."

"For Angel."

"No. For Hannah."

The chapel—once a butler's pantry—had been fitted with a pair of kneelers, an unadorned and ecumenical altar and a shelf of votive candles. Hannah didn't go in, but as she watched the flickering candles a thought came to her. Something Liz had said during their conversation on Thursday. *The world's not bad, it's just more complicated than it used to be. But for Ingrid and Eddie and kids their age, it's just the way it should be because they've grown up with it.*

Was that a hopeful thought? Or profoundly depressing?

At the end of the nursery a thin young woman with fair, raw-looking skin stood looking down into Angel's crib.

"You must be Shannon," Hannah said in her best Rinconada-doctor's-wife voice.

Shannon's large eyes peered at Hannah's name tag and she laughed nervously. "'Volunteer Mother.' You don't have kids of your own?"

"Two. A boy and a girl. Grown up."

"She's my baby." Shannon pointed at the sleeping Angel. "Kinda funny lookin', huh? I expected different."

Hannah remembered all the rules of conduct her mother had taught her. *Smile at people you don't like. Make strangers feel welcome. Be tolerant of those less fortunate.*

"When she first came here from the hospital, she couldn't even be in a lighted room. She had so many seizures we had to keep her tied down for fear she'd hurt herself."

"I didn't know she took fits." Shannon's expression registered alarm and disgust.

In spite of herself Hannah felt sorry for the girl. The scope of her ignorance was as real as if it stood beside them banging on a drum.

"Crack damages the brain. Didn't you know that?"

Shannon lifted her shoulders and let them droop. She was so thin her shoulder bones stuck up like tabs on a paper doll. "There's not much I don't know about crack."

"Are you still using?"

She shook her head.

"How long has it been?"

"A month."

"Not long."

"Feels like forever."

"Do you have a job?"

Another head shake. "But I'm gonna start lookin'. There's a

place over the east side does mass mailing. You know, like junk mail?" Shannon paused. "When's she gonna wake up?"

"We let these babies sleep as long as they can. Sleep is precious to them."

"Yeah, I'm with her." Shannon snickered.

Hannah wanted to grab this girl and shake her; she wanted to hold her; she wanted to wring her neck on the spot.

"It's not because she's sleepy. Her nervous system needs as much downtime as it can get. It's so messed up by the drug that she can't relax like a normal baby. When she came here from the hospital she couldn't even cry."

"Shit."

Hannah nodded. "Shit."

After a moment Shannon drew a chair near to the crib and sat down so she could just see over the top of the slats.

"I never meant to hurt her, you know. I was just stupid."

And you're not now?

Shannon put her arm across the horizontal bar on the crib and rested her chin on it so she could stare down at her baby.

"I'm getting it together though. I'm gonna make it."

Hannah turned away.

In the hall Maryann labored with a laundry hamper almost as big as she was. She gushed gratitude when Hannah volunteered for wash duty.

Maryann said, "Angel's mom's applied to live here. Did Betts tell you? Remember that grant proposal we wrote last winter?"

Hannah had typed it on her own computer. She had even paid to have it copied.

"The city's giving us enough money to have four mothers onsite. They can learn how to keep house and take care of their kids while they're getting it together." Maryann glanced back over her shoulder into the nursery. "She doesn't seem like a bad kid. Just sort of dumb, you know?"

"But she won't be approved? . . ."

"We have to start with someone, hon. If we wait for a Rhodes Scholar we'll never get the program going."

"And it's a good program," Hannah said. She really believed

this. But not for Shannon and Angel. For everyone else, but not for them. She lifted the laundry basket to her hip. "I'll start the wash."

On the back porch she unloaded the clean laundry that had just finished cycling through the machine, emptied in the dirty, added soap and bleach and checked to make sure the water setting was at HOT. Lifting the basket of wet clothes, she pushed through the screen door and walked out across the dry grass to the carousel clothesline at the back of the yard. There was a dryer on the porch beside the washer, a noisy old thing; but it was only used when the weather was wet.

Which it probably never will be again.

Hannah ran her hands down the sheets and pillowcases she pegged to the line, feeling still the warmth from the machine as she smoothed the wrinkles and straightened the edges.

A redwood playground apparatus filled one corner of the big hedge-enclosed yard. A contribution, a tax deduction for the man-ufacturer. The sandbox had chicken wire spread across it to keep the cats out. In violation of the law a plumber friend had rigged the pipes from the washing machine, diverting gray water into the vegetable garden. Tomatoes and beans and pepper plants thrived there surrounded by a frame of bright green grass.

She thought of Shannon and Angel living together at Resur-rection House. She imagined seeing the girl every day. She saw in her mind how Angel's eyes would light when her mother was near . . . The unfairness stung her. No one as irresponsible and dimwit-ted as that girl—She stopped in midthought. Shannon was old enough to be a mother, but she wasn't far removed from being a baby herself. Maybe no one had wanted her. Perhaps she had been so abused and neglected that the sight of her face would have wrung a younger Hannah's heart in the same way Angel's did now.

Think what others have suffered. Her mother's voice sawed through her head. *Put yourself in the other person's shoes.*

Back in the house she hauled the old Electrolux and all its cum-bersome attachments out of the upstairs hall closet and began to clean the bedrooms. She hated vacuuming above all household chores, but forced herself to do it because her father had told her that doing difficult things was good for the soul and she had a feeling her soul needed help today. In the dayroom she found May who, like Maryann, had been with Betts from the beginning. Surrounded by several children she sat cross-legged on the floor, building something out of blocks.

Hannah asked a boy about three years old, "Are you building a tower?" The boy looked at Hannah, then at May, then he pushed over the blocks. The other children began to cry. He got to his feet and walked away. By the window, he stood and kicked the peeling baseboard again and again and again.

Hannah made an apologetic face and May shrugged.

In the hall Hannah leaned her forehead against the wall and pressed hard. The house vibrated with the boy's kicks and the children's rising wails. Even if Shannon stayed off drugs and alcohol and got a job, she wasn't going to be able to change what the chemicals had done to Angel's brain. Too soon she would be that boy's age. And though now she was learning slowly and responding to stimulation, school would be a nightmare. Researchers agreed about crack babies. They would struggle all their lives and probably die young.

Monday morning and Jeanne's head hurt.

Actions have consequences. Don't buy the goods if you can't pay the price.

How old do we have to be before we stop hearing our parents talking in our heads?

As always the new week had begun with a full-school nine a.m. assembly conducted by Teddy. He said the weekly gathering of the student body gave purpose to the week ahead. What he really liked was the audience and never mind that Jeanne needed the time at her desk to manage problems that had arisen over the weekend. She was required onstage beside Teddy. Mr. and Mrs. Chips.

The pain stretched across her eyes and forehead like a blindfold. She wished she could rip off the front of her face.

Back in her office by nine-thirty if she was lucky and no teachers snagged her on the way off the stage, Jeanne learned what had gone wrong since Friday: inevitably toilets had backed up and fuses blown. Equipment lost, stolen or abandoned under the bleachers.

Adolescent nicotine fiends to be lectured at. This Monday there was the particular problem of Adam Weed.

Edith White waited in Jeanne's outer office.

"He's a deceitful one," she said, standing at Jeanne's elbow while she unlocked the door. "All that nonsense about being in the rose cloister yesterday."

Jeanne poured a glass of water from a carafe on the credenza and swallowed four aspirin as Edith eased her muffin-top backside into the chair opposite the desk, pursed her lips, folded her hands, and sat as primly as a schoolgirl visiting the principal.

"Can't trust him."

"How do you know that, Edith?" Evidence is too much to hope for, Jeanne thought as she sorted through and ordered the papers on her desk.

"Used my eyes is all. His shoes were covered with mud. He went and tracked it all over that pretty Chinese carpet in my little foyer."

"Perhaps he stepped in a puddle somewhere on campus."

"In this climate?"

Jeanne joined several documents with a paper clip and put them in an upright file on the corner of her desk. She glanced at a pile of pink phone memos—at least a dozen from parents. Had word of Adam's disappearance already reached them?

"I won't accuse a boy of lying without proof, Edith."

"Jeanne, you know as well as I do, there's not a drop of mud on these school grounds except around those rose bushes of your father's."

"And that's where he said he was."

"Someone would have found him there."

"What's your point, Edith?"

"He was down at that blasted creek, that's my point." Edith leaned forward. "Saturday a.m. when I called you, that's the direction he was coming from. That creek's trouble waiting to happen with only a bitty old fence—"

"Assuming your guess is right, what would you have me do?"

"For starters, the boy needs a good talking to." Edith preened a little in the spotlight of her opinion. "And a little detention time wouldn't hurt either. Then, if he does it again, I suppose Dr. Tate ought to take the paddle to him. You and me, I know we disagree on this. But to my way of thinking, a rich boy like that, he's probably been spoiled silly. A lick or two wouldn't hurt him. Actions have consequences and some of them hurt the backside."

Jeanne examined her hands and counted slowly.

"And you got to do something about that fence before some little tyke ambles off down there and takes a fall. I tell you, Mrs. T., there's going to be a tragedy down there, mark my words."

You're a few decades late, Edith.

Jeanne stood up. "You're a great help. As always."

Edith White, looking pleased with herself, waddled out of the office and Jeanne stared after her.

The night before she had been awake until after three A.M. Unable to sleep, her mind full of Liz's revelation, their argument and the problem of Adam Weed, she'd found a bottle of pinot noir in the liquor cabinet and taken it into the little study where the TV was. Sometime after midnight she watched a movie about a woman terrorized by a mysterious hitchhiker who kept appearing at the edge of the road. Bluegang was like that hitchhiker. Lately it seemed to be waiting for her around the curves of every conversation. It and James. Why had she been mean to Liz when she knew so well what happened to unwanted children? When he was born abortions had been hard to come by, dangerous, and tainted with shame. In any case, Jeanne had never considered having one. She was a married woman. She and Teddy were starting the family she had thought they both wanted.

She called up Adam's file and typed in what Edith White had told her. At the top of the file was the number where Simon Weed was staying through the month. She lifted the telephone receiver and was halfway through the number when Teddy came through the door talking.

"I guess I'm going to just go out and buy myself a new pen." He stretched out on the leather couch under the window, hands folded behind his head. "I thought I was rather inspirational this morning, didn't you? I would have made a good preacher. There's a feeling I get—" He sat up. "You're not listening to me."

"I've been thinking about Adam Weed."

"Christ, that brat." He lay down again.

Jeanne laughed a little. "The cussing's got to stop if you want to be a preacher."

"There was a time when I could have been anything I wanted."

Jeanne waited. He sat up again.

"You know, before I met you, before I transferred to Stanford, I was going to be an actor."

"I saw you do Lysander at Montalvo, remember?"

"And I was good, wasn't I? The silly little bitch playing Hermia was an embarrassment but I was damn good. Onstage I had presence. You can't learn that kind of thing. You've got to be born with it."

He stood, his legs slightly spread, rocking back on his heels. The applause of two hundred and fifty boys gave him an amphetamine buzz. "I had it all, Jeanne. Talent. Looks. Mom always said I never went through an awkward stage like most kids. Like my brothers. Thank God. Mom wanted me to be an actor but my father said he'd die first." He turned his back to Jeanne and stared out across the driveway toward the rose cloister. "The old bastard never wanted me to do anything or be anything that wasn't absolutely ordinary and exactly like everyone else."

It was the thousandth variation on a theme she knew by heart. She had always listened dutifully and made sympathetic noises because that was their contract, hers and Teddy's. Teddy gazed out the window at the sunny day, rocking on the heels of his Italian shoes. "When I was talking to the boys this morning, I got the old feeling I used to have onstage when I knew I had the audience where I wanted it. Here." He turned and thrust out his fisted hand. As suddenly his hand dropped to his side and he sagged at the middle. "I gave up a lot for this school."

What would happen if she lost her temper? An exquisite orgasm of pent-up rage and then sweet sleep? She asked the question and she knew the answer. If she got really mad at Teddy she would lose the moral high ground self-control gave her. She smiled a little and raised an eyebrow.

"No one ever starts out wanting to be a teacher, Jeanne. Teaching is always something you end up doing. I only went to Columbia grad school because it was the closest I could get to Broadway."

"You went to Columbia because Harvard and Chicago turned you down."

He stared at her then laughed. "Your memory's unusually sharp this morning."

"I was accepted at all three schools. You were accepted at Columbia. Period. Chicago offered me a full ride and that's where I wanted to go. But you said you wanted us to go to grad school together. You painted a picture of what it would be like, how we'd curl up on the couch and study, share the same desk..." Jeanne paused and held her breath for as long as it took for something to release in her. She stood up, lightheaded.

"If you didn't want to be a teacher, you could have gone off and been Laurence Olivier and I wouldn't have minded. I loved you, Teddy. You could have danced naked down Broadway, and I would have found a way to accept it. If we're going to talk about sacrifice, why don't I start listing the things I've given up?"

Teddy grinned and winked. "There's still fire in the old girl, huh? Reminds me of before. You were a hot little ticket. I would have said and done anything to get in your pants."

She knew this must be the way he talked to his girlfriends.

He walked across the room and stood behind her. His hands on her waist were warm through her blouse.

"Go away, Teddy. You wear me out."

"You should have listened more closely to my talk this morning. You wouldn't be so crabby." He touched her shoulder and she shoved his hand away. He reached around and slipped his other hand down the front of her blouse. "Nipples are hard. You know what that means."

"It means I'm angry!" she cried, turning, shoving her hands against his chest, pushing him backwards into the credenza. "Don't you get it? I've had it with you. There's a limit! Even for me there's a goddamn fucking limit."

When Liz heard Hannah's car start and knew she was alone in the house, she got out of bed and went down to the kitchen. As she read the note left for her, Cherokee shoved her cold nose under

Liz's hand, demanding attention. Liz knelt beside her and pressed her face into the dog's silken throat. Cherokee pulled back and licked her face.

"At least you love me."

She made a cup of coffee and left the kitchen, crossed the dining room and opened the double doors onto the patio. The morning was bright and warm. Liz took off her dressing gown and sat in the sun with the hem of her nightie pulled up above her knees, her feet stretched out in front of her and her head tilted back. After a while she fell asleep. The ringing of the phone awakened her. The message machine clicked on and she heard Dan's voice.

"You there, Liz? Pick up, will you?"

She ran into the kitchen and answered, breathless. "I was outside."

"Hannah gone?"

"She's at Resurrection House."

"I want to talk to you."

She recalled the overheard conversation and believed she knew why he was calling.

"I'm at the hospital now. How 'bout if I swing by the house on my way back to the office. Give me twenty minutes."

"What's this about, Dan?" She wanted to hear that he was planning a surprise party for Hannah or that he needed her to help him pick out a special gift for her.

"Twenty minutes, half hour max."

Liz had met Dan Tarwater in the fall of her senior year. For weeks in advance Hannah had been calling from Palo Alto to rave about him. Palo Alto to San Jose was a toll call but Hannah said screw the bill and her giggle came down the line like bubbly. "He's fabulous, Liz. I've found the perfect man."

What a surprise to meet him at last and discover that perfection was tall and skinny and kind of shy, with an off-center nose and hair that needed trimming.

"Don't you just love him?" It was half-time of Big Game; the stadium quaked under their feet as they climbed the bleachers on their way to the bathroom. "Isn't he absolutely fabulous?"

Hannah's shining eyes, the electricity in her hair, the flash of her straight white teeth in the sharp autumn light—Liz remembered these.

"Just wait," Hannah had said with a certainty that filled Liz with envy. "Years from now when we're all ancient and haggard, you'll look at me and say in your croaky old voice, 'Hannah, that Dan Tarwater is a fabulous man.'"

Turned out she was right.

Thirty minutes after his call as they sat facing each other on kitchen stools she told him what Hannah had said that day.

Dan blushed like a boy. "Fabulous. Like something out of a fable?"

"An honest-to-goodness Prince Charming. Last of an endangered species."

"I'd rather be a magician or a wizard." His eyes widened and his expression became open and wounded. "I could do with a little magic right now. A crystal ball maybe." He spoke about Hannah. "Menopause is a complicated biological process. Some women sail right through and others have a hard time. It's not always the chemicals by themselves, medicine can deal with that."

"She's always been emotional, Dan." She wanted him to laugh. "She cried at Coca-Cola commercials."

"It's getting worse and when I bring it up, when I ask what's bothering her, she either looks at me like I'm hallucinating or says I'm trying to make her miserable."

"I told her I thought she was depressed."

"Bet she loved hearing that. What did she say?"

"She denied it, of course."

"I thought you might know . . ."

Something happened to Hannah a long time ago. To all of us, really, but to her most of all.

A story like Bluegang had life in it. If Liz revealed it to Dan it would eventually burrow up in the middle of a conversation like one of those tropical worms that entered the body in one place and emerged months or years later in another. Hannah had to realize for herself that the incident at Bluegang had warped the trajectory of her life, that it had damaged her as it had damaged them all.

A boy died because Hannah pushed him onto some rocks. She didn't mean to but she killed him and she's never really faced it.

Saturday night after the party Hannah had taken the first steps toward freeing the secret held so long and so close. In time she would find whatever courage she needed to tell Dan the story. But if Liz told him, Hannah would never forgive her. Their friendship could withstand almost anything, but maybe not that.

Dan said, "And there's this Resurrection House thing, it's like an obsession for her now. She wants to adopt this baby, Angel, she's been working with. Yours too. Jesus God, Liz. Hannah wants us to start all over again."

"She's a rescuer."

"Yeah, well maybe, once upon a time, but it's gone beyond that now. She's got this thing about Eddie. Sometimes I think she actually dislikes him." He dragged his hand across his mouth. "I want her to see a therapist."

Liz laughed. Dan looked at her sharply and then he laughed too.

"Talk to her. Please."

"She won't listen to me. She's angry with me because of the abortion."

"Try anyway." Dan glanced at his watch and headed for the front door. "Maybe there's nothing you can do. Or me. I don't know. I think I just needed to talk. After last night . . ." He stopped. His chest lifted in a great sigh.

She said what she didn't quite believe. "It'll be okay, Dan."

From his expression she knew that he didn't quite believe it either.

"Hannah says Gerard's asked you to marry him."

Liz nodded.

"Do it."

"I'm not built for the long haul, Dan. Eventually, I cut and run."

"Says who?"

"I always do. I always have."

"Not here you haven't." He came back inside and put his arms around her, kissed her on each cheek in the European fashion and then held her at arm's length, his eyes all kindness. "No one could ask for a more faithful friend, Liz. I don't know why you came back. We both know you could have had the procedure in Florida. It doesn't matter why, I'm just glad you did."

When he was gone Liz made another cup of coffee and sat on

the patio looking down toward the barn. For the first time she could remember she examined the assumption on which she had based her whole adult life: *I'm not built for the long haul . . . A quitter . . . I cut and run.* What was the proof of this? Bluegang. She had been faithful to her friends, to Gerard and his family. To her own aged parents she had shown only care and consideration. Editors admired her reliability and every author she collaborated with praised her willingness to work until the translation was perfect. But long ago she had abandoned Billy Phillips when she knew better. She had cut and run from Bluegang. And that single incident had shaped her choices for more than thirty years. She could see that this was illogical, made no sense; but when you examine it, what in life did?

Eddie came home when Liz was watering the bedraggled nicotiana gangling in pots by the kitchen door.

"You're early," she said and followed him into the kitchen. "I was about to go over to Jeanne's but I thought I'd recycle the rinse water first." She opened the refrigerator. "Want a snack? There's leftover lasagna."

Eddie dropped his backpack in the middle of the kitchen tiles and sank onto a stool at the counter.

"I got cut."

"Where? Show me."

He turned away from her, disdainful of her ignorance. "Football. Coach said I should bulk up over the year then try again if I want." He sneered. "Prob'ly wants me to shoot steroids for good old Rinconada High." He mimed pumping a hypo into his arm.

"Don't even pretend."

"Who cares anyway? I never did want to play football." He grabbed an apple from the basket on the counter and bit into it.

"Your mom told me you liked it."

"What does she know?"

"You should do something you like."

"Oh, yeah." His upper lip curled like a tough guy in a B movie. "What I like."

"Why'd you start football in the first place if you don't like it?"

"She wanted me to."

"You mean Hannah?"

"Who'd you think I meant?" He glared at Liz. She stepped back and threw up her hands in defense.

"Hey, kid, don't aim your guns at me. I'm Liz. Your godmother. No blood kin at all." Thank God. "Just an innocent civilian."

"You don't know what she's like. All the time talking about how it was when she was in high school, how much fun you all had at the games—"

"She's only making conversation, looking for something you can have in common. It's hard on a mom when her boy isn't little anymore." How did she know this? His expression of hurt and defiance touched her heart and she felt a click somewhere inside, like tumblers in a lock. "In some ways you're a stranger to her."

"And she likes it that way."

"Oooh, that's cold."

"So? Forget I ever even said it." He eyed the kitchen sink and shot the apple core into it. "What do I know?"

"She loves you, honey."

He scratched a pimple on his chin and examined his fingernails. Like an ad for teenage despair, he dug in behind a bunker of resentment and picked his face. Hostile and hurt, defended and vulnerable: Eddie was all these at once and Liz was a soldier ducking grenades, dodging land mines, fired on by snipers.

Welcome to parenting, she thought. Battlefield Tarwater.

"Try to imagine how it is for her: one day you're three years old and you're the center of the world for each other. When she looks in your eyes she sees herself reflected. Next thing she knows you're fifteen, five feet ten and all the things she did best for you, you don't want." He stared off into the distance. Liz put her hand on his cheek. Under her palm, she felt his terrible skin but she didn't pull back. He resisted and then submitted to the pressure of her hand. How long since anyone had touched him there, in that way? He turned his troubled face to her.

"This is a hard time for her too, Eddie, but it'll pass. I promise you."

He jerked away and headed for the hall.

She called after him. "What would you like to talk about, Eddie. What interests you?"

He stopped. From the set of his shoulders, she read his indecision. He turned back to her and said, with a note of challenge, "I collect football cards. Maybe that makes me a nerd compared to all those guys on the team, but I don't care. I'm not a head-banger. I think you gotta be an idiot to do that shit for free."

"Tell me about your card collection."

"I got more than ten thousand cards since back when I was in elementary school." His tone dared Liz to be interested. "And my fantasy football team's beating out Sean's, big-time. I won seven bucks off him yesterday."

She recalled that the day before when Liz and Hannah returned from lunch Eddie and Sean were watching football on the den television, switching channels every few minutes, hooting and cheering.

"Tell Hannah. Show her your card collection."

"Great." He polished another apple on his Levi's.

"Just say you want to talk. She loves you, Eddie. She'll listen."

"No way." He fired the words. "If I was to tell her I don't want to play football, she'd go all serious and say something like how if I quit I'll miss out on So. Much. Fun." A barrage of mockery backed up his anger. "She'd tell me about the time Mario Bacci ran for three hundred yards and what a great night that was and how no one'll ever forget it. Then she'd look at the clock and tell me she's going to Erection House and I should do my homework and don't forget my chores and have a nice life whoever you are." He exhaled a deep breath and stared at his half-eaten apple. "Oh, yeah, she'd ask me if I washed my hair. She asks me every day. She knows I do. I can't help it, I got oily hair." Eddie was a killing field of emotions.

"You're making yourself miserable, honey, and you don't have to. Tell her she has to listen to you. We all want to be needed, Eddie. We all want to be important to other human beings."

He listened, fidgeting and making so-what faces but standing in one place.

"If you don't tell her, the time'll pass and you'll be left with a big old scar in the middle of your gut and it'll never go away. It'll be there whenever you want to love someone or trust or . . . you know."

She took the apple core from his hand, eyed the sink, and dished it in over her left shoulder. Surprised by herself, she laughed and raised her hand to Eddie. Their palms slapped together.

An hour later, Jeanne and Liz were on the patio, hidden from Hilltop School by the oleander hedge, stretched out on the lawn furniture drinking Mexican beer. Jeanne wore shorts and a T-shirt and no bra. Her hair was down and she couldn't remember when she'd last combed it. It was early for beer, but she had decided to make an exception because Liz was there, because it was only Corona, and because she had been feeling almost giddy since her blowup at Teddy that morning. True, she had lost the high ground when she lost her temper; but she felt so good remembering the omigod look on his face.

"I love my guest house," Liz was saying, rolling a peanut between her palms to break the shell, "and I'm proud of what we've done with it, but it's not the same as a school. A school matters."

"That's because children matter."

"How come you never had any of your own, Jeanne?"

Other years, other visits they had talked about politics and economics, women's issues, books and clothes, gossiped and recalled the time they stole golf carts and spent half a summer night tooling over Rinconada golf course, the summer they learned about sex from the little green book Jeanne found in her father's bureau, barely recalled boyfriends, parties, scandals, the way things used to be. But this trip it was babies, all babies.

She said, "If you want to feel like you belong to something, like you're connected . . ."

"Don't start, Jeanne."

Jeanne smiled and tipped her head back. The sky was a terrible clear enamel blue. If she reached up and laid her hand on it, the surface would be hard and slick like tile. No wonder it never rained. There was a tile barrier between the earth and sky. If the army shot holes in it, the rain would pour through like a showerhead.

She said, "I had a baby once. A boy." James now Mark.

Jeanne felt Liz waiting.

"I never told anyone. We were in New York."

The light on the patio became more intense, draining the color from the blossoms on the oleander bushes. She thought of the sun as an interrogator's weapon focused on her. But no one had forced her to tell Liz about James. There was no third degree going on. Maybe holding the secret had become worse than the secret itself. Maybe this was the only way to convince Liz not to have an abortion. Maybe—probably—she'd had too much to drink.

"We put him up for adoption. Teddy said . . ." Jeanne watched the bubbles rise to the surface of her glass. Garrulous, confessional Mexican beer was at work here, and she wasn't going to fight it. She wanted to talk, to blab, to tell all her nasty secrets, every one of them. If Liz could do it, if Hannah could . . .

"You were in grad school—"

Jeanne shook her head.

"But I thought—"

"I quit. Teddy said it was too much." Teddy, Teddy, Teddy. She closed her eyes and made a sound that came out a groaning laugh.

"I think I should get you something to eat, Jeanne. And how 'bout some coffee?"

"Don't take care of me. I can take care of myself."

And now that I've begun, don't give me an excuse to stop.

"I've always taken care of myself."

That's what happens to the children of drunks. They either fall apart or they become most marvelously self-sufficient.

Jeanne said, "My soul craves a Marlboro."

"Uh-huh."

"Go look on the end table in the living room, will you, Liz? There's a Russian enamel box with cigarettes in it. Get me one, okay?" Jeanne laughed at the look on Liz's face. "For godsake, it's not the end of the world. I want to smoke, so let me smoke."

Liz returned with one Marlboro, holding it at arm's length between her index finger and thumb.

"I'll buy you a gun but I won't load it. If you want a match, you'll have to find one yourself."

Jeanne stood up, steadied herself on the back of the chaise, and made her way around an arrangement of glazed Mexican flowerpots to the gas grill. She lifted one end of the plastic cover and found a box of safety matches. "Ah-hah!" She scraped one on the grill, stood rocking slightly, the cigarette in her left hand, the match in her right, weaving before it.

I feel too good to kill myself, she thought and blew out the match. *I feel wonderful.*

She broke the cigarette in half. "I don't believe I care to smoke after all. But I do want another beer."

"Jeanne . . ."

"Lizzie, don't. I choose to get a little tanked, unburden myself at long last and reveal my dirty secrets, and all of a sudden you're Mrs. Grundy. Will you cut me no slack?"

Liz lifted her arms in a show of resignation. "Just stay put so you don't hurt yourself." Jeanne let herself be maneuvered back to the chaise and pushed gently down.

She had come home from lunch and had two shots of vodka from the freezer. She'd drunk three?—four?—maybe she'd had five?—beers. But she'd been drunk before and kept her silence. Something else had nudged her over the border into a new country.

Liz came back with the beer and set it on the table beside Jeanne's chair.

"I made you a sandwich."

"I ate."

"If you're going to drink, you have to eat."

"What kind?"

"Just eat it."

Ham and pepper cheese with iceberg lettuce.

She ate the whole sandwich, aware that Liz was impatient. "I've never told anyone this before. Teddy'd kill me." She grinned, imagining his face.

"Just so you don't wake up with a hangover, blaming me."

"Just listen, will you? You know you're dying to hear this." Jeanne slurped the foam off her beer and wiped her mouth on the back of her hand. "I was pretty sure I was pregnant when we got married, but I didn't tell anyone, of course."

Hard to believe now the power of the taboo against unmarried mothers. Even going to the altar a little thick at the waist was a mortification to the family

Liz said, "It sure would have put a crack in your image."

"My image? What was my image?"

"Same as now." Liz shifted, brought her bare feet up under her on the chair cushion. "Always in control. You always know what's happening."

"My father—"

"Actions have consequences," Liz intoned.

"Right." Jeanne stared at the bright Corona label for a minute. "I threw up for three months. Teddy was furious when I finally told him."

Jeanne heard Liz mutter something, but it was only background noise.

Not once in twenty-five years had she considered telling anyone what really happened in New York. Now that she was about to, she was perplexed to find the story no longer either vivid or all that shameful. What was Liz going to do when she heard it? Run from the house screaming, *"Shame, shame"*? And what if she did? Compared to the rest of her life would that be so terrible?

"He wanted me to have an abortion, but I wouldn't listen to him. I was sure he'd love the baby once he saw it. And I had this superwoman image of myself. I was going to go to grad school, raise a baby, fix gourmet meals and be perfect."

"Sounds about right."

"Teddy said I was one of those people who had to learn the hard lessons by living through them. And if I wasn't going to get rid of the baby, he was going to make me pay. So he cut me out of his life. For a few weeks he moved in with another grad student, a dancer. That was the consequence."

"What a prick."

"He started to have trouble in school and that's when he came back. Columbia was hard for him. Not that he wasn't smart enough, but there were so many distractions. Teddy loved New York."

She'd seen him with the dancer once. Jeanne was walking back from the early service at St. John the Divine and saw them ahead of her, still dressed in Saturday night clothes. Teddy was doing a little dance step and the girl had hold of him by the waist. Looking back now, Jeanne knew it might have been better for both of them if he had stayed away; but in those days the idea would have burned a hole in her brain.

"He came back to me so I'd help him get through school. I ended up doing his work and mine."

"Why didn't you tell him to take a hike?"

Jeanne reached down and picked up one of the cigarette halves she'd tossed away.

"Look. If you decide to sail a boat across the Pacific, you have to sail it in bad weather and good. You don't get to stop in the middle of the ocean and say, Gee, I don't think I'll do this anymore." She paused to admire the metaphor and hiccupped. "We have a contract."

"Yeah," Liz said. "And he broke it."

"That didn't give me permission to do the same." *And I loved him.* "All my life, I'd never imagined anyone would ever want me and then there was Teddy. He was smart and you remember how gorgeous he was and he had so much flair . . ."

"You can love anyone you like, Jeanne. You don't have to explain."

Jeanne split the thin cigarette paper with her nail and laid the half cigarette open like a patient at surgery. "Things were okay until around Christmas. I got sick and the doctor said I had to take it easy for the baby's sake. Teddy said it was too stressful for me to be in grad school and pregnant at the same time and that's why I got sick in the first place. He said the best thing was for me to drop out and then I could help him get his degree. I could go back afterwards."

This part of the story did shame her. Teddy this and Teddy that and Teddy everything: couldn't she think for herself in those days? The daring and resourceful always-to-be-trusted-and-relied-upon Jeanne. If she wasn't running after her father's approval, she was going for Teddy's.

"But, Jeanne, you have a degree. I've seen it on the wall in your office."

Jeanne removed bits of tobacco from the paper and blew them off her fingertips a few at a time.

"Fake." She held her breath and waited for the world to end. "We bought it in New York from a man who forged passports and green cards. It cost a bundle, let me tell you. I always planned to go back to school eventually. Meantime, Teddy said it didn't hurt anyone if I just put it up on the wall. He said it wasn't any worse than beefing up a résumé."

"But he got his."

"Fair and square." She smiled. "More or less."

"How could you let him talk you into something like that?"

"Why'd you fuck that Brazilian soccer player?"

"Who?"

"You told me you never had one word of conversation. He couldn't speak English and you—"

Liz groaned. "At the time . . ."

"Exactly."

"That guy was one night, Jeanne. What we're talking about now is a whole life. Your life."

"I wanted him to love me. Haven't you ever wanted anyone to love you? I wanted his praise. I was afraid of him." Afraid of the final consequence, the consequence never spoken of but implicit in every conversation with her father. *Do what I want or I will abandon you.*

Like we abandoned Billy Phillips, Jeanne thought. Like we walked away and left him in the dirt because he frightened Hannah, because he was dim and strange and did not please.

Liz leaned forward and asked softly, "What happened to the baby, Jeanne?"

Jeanne tried sighing to relieve the pressure under her rib cage, but it stayed in place like a stalled weather front.

"He had a squashy little nose and his hair was almost black— like my brother's. Beautiful."

"Omigod, why didn't you tell anyone? Did your folks know?"

Jeanne laughed shortly. "You must be kidding me. They would have counted backward. You know the way it was then."

Liz lifted her hands and let them drop, stared at them, shaking her head.

"He was a colicky little thing. Not really healthy in that drafty old apartment. And he cried so much he interrupted Teddy's sleep—"

"You brought him home from the hospital?" Liz's face registered horror and pain at the same time.

Jeanne's tongue seemed to have swollen to the size of a bath sponge. She drank the last of her beer. "We only had one bedroom and Teddy wouldn't let me put the cradle in with us because he said it was bad for babies to sleep with their parents. So I made him a little nook in the living room, behind the bookcases. I made him a mobile with smiling faces dangling from it and hung it right over him so when he woke up he wouldn't feel lonely.

From the instant I saw his squashy little nose and puffy eyes, I loved him more than I loved myself.

But not more than she loved Teddy.

"He couldn't study at night. He said the baby and I were driving him out of the house, making him fail.

"Even when James was quiet he made little noises to himself, and Teddy said those irritated him more than yelling. Down the hall the Jamaican students partied five nights a week and that never troubled Teddy, but the little snuffling whimpers of a baby . . .

"In the end he wore me down with arguing. It took almost three months."

"Three months." Jeanne heard the break in Liz's voice. "He recognized you. He must have been smiling."

"Teddy said it was gas."

"Christ, what a bastard."

"I was worse. I just couldn't stand up to him."

"Like me and Bluegang."

"Aw, shit, I suppose."

When he told her not to pick the baby up because she'd spoil him, she did as she was told. When he said that nursing would ruin her figure and he hated saggy tits, she put James on formula. When he said James was a cross baby, a tense baby, a sickly baby because she was an uptight mother, she believed him. She was being selfish, he explained. She was cheating Teddy out of a good degree, cheating James out of a happy family, cheating some infertile couple that longed for a baby. James was driving him crazy and he couldn't stand it much longer and she'd have to choose . . .

"So I chose."

Between Teddy and James, between returning to her father with a baby, no degree and no husband. Or. A husband and His-and-Hers degrees. Mr. and Mrs. Theodore Tate: the perfect couple.

"He went to a good home, Liz. I made sure of that. In Rye. Probably better than any we could have made for him."

"Have you tried to contact him?"

She spoke about her trip to Berkeley.

"He's a grown man. You should know him."

"He'd never understand."

"Give him a chance."

She knew she wouldn't. A small part of Jeanne hoped James/Mark did not know he had once had different parents from those who raised him. Life would be easier for him if the truth were hidden. If he knew the truth it wouldn't matter how good his adoptive parents were, nothing compensated for abandonment. She'd seen this demonstrated countless times among her boys at Hilltop. And she never wanted to explain how she had rejected him for a man she didn't even like anymore. He had appeared happy and healthy when she watched him in Berkeley. Better he stay that way than know the truth.

"Have you told Hannah this?"

Jeanne shook her head.

They sat, heads back, staring into the empty sky.

Liz said, "I've never really known you, Jeanne. Not since we were kids anyway. I thought that you didn't know me, but it goes both ways. This is such a huge thing to keep secret."

"We each have a Rosebud, don't we?" A sled. A rejected baby. A dead boy. "I'm not proud of what I did, Liz."

"But you were so young."

"That's no excuse. I knew what I did was wrong."

"Yeah. Me too."

Without being asked, Liz went into the house and came back with two more beers. They drank in silence.

"No wonder you want me to have the baby."

"I don't want you to give up your chance, your last chance."

Liz walked to the edge of the patio where scarlet and gold bougainvillea, thriving in the drought, grew in neon profusion. She brushed a branch with the palm of her hand and the bracts disengaged and floated down like bright hot flakes.

"I wasn't going to tell you this, but now I've heard your story,

I've changed my mind. I think you have a right to know. If you don't already." Liz sat again. "Saturday night, when I went in to use the phone after dinner, Teddy came in and made a pass at me."

Jeanne raised an eyebrow. "Don't let it go to your head. You're not the first."

"Why do you put up with it? And don't tell me it's a contract because—"

"I love him. Or something like that."

"Oh, Jeannie."

"I wish I didn't. Life would be easier if I didn't. But he needs me and in that way I guess he's kind of like James. My baby."

"But he's not a baby. He's a man. And not a very nice one."

"If I give up Teddy it means I gave James away for nothing."

They heard footsteps on the gravel and Turner, the P.E. instructor, came through the oleander hedge.

"Adam Weed's had an accident," he said. "He's in the infirmary."

Hannah left Resurrection House in midafternoon. In Rinconada she stopped at Mario's for onion focaccia and coffee beans and she was on her way up Casabella Road when, on a whim, she turned into the old town cemetery and parked her car near the caretaker's shed.

"G'day to you, Mrs. Tarwater." Brian, the caretaker, an Irish transplant who had never lost his brogue, spoke to her from his potting shed. "I was over by your parents this very mornin' and they're looking fine. But I'm sorry to say that veronica you put in last spring, it's gone and died. I dug it up and put in a plug or two of new grass. We should be sayin' novenas for rain, if you ask me." To Brian the cemetery was more a garden than a graveyard.

Hannah thanked him for his work and strolled up the hill to where her parents were buried. She sat on the granite square marking her father's grave and propped her feet against the edge of her mother's stone.

At Resurrection House Betts had called her in for another talk. She wanted Hannah to understand that having Angel's mother as a live-in resident was the best thing for both mother and child. She outlined the pros and cons as if all that mattered was logic, as if a baby girl were a number in an equation. Hannah hadn't bothered to argue. If she said, "I'm the only hope Angel has," Betts was sure to deliver one of her gentle lectures on maintaining distance. Under most circumstances Hannah would agree with her. But Angel was a special case, and nothing Betts could say would change that.

Hannah felt the cold of the granite stone through her jeans and the wind was up and the air full of leaves. She pulled her jacket across her chest and shifted her position on the stone. Pins and needles chased each other down her leg. Overhead the sky was hard and bright and hurt her eyes. As she walked back to the car Hannah caught sight of Father Joe leaning against a tree, smoking a cigarette. Not far from him an old woman knelt by a stone. As Hannah approached him Father Joe put a finger to his lips.

"You asked me yesterday about Mrs. Phillips." He tipped his head toward the old woman. "I bring her up here from time to time so she can tend her boy's grave."

Hannah stared at the bent figure in a brown coat, brown shoes and heavy stockings. She was the size of a child with a narrow back and bent shoulders. As she weeded the gravesite, the wrists poking out from the cuffs of her coat looked thin as pencils. She wore a hat with faded yellow lilies drooping around the brim.

"Pretty spry for more than ninety, huh?"

"You shouldn't smoke."

"I'll introduce you. She might remember you."

"Another time, Joe."

He stopped her exit with a hand on her arm. "How're you doing today? How's the panther?"

"What?"

"You said there was a panther in you, trying to get out." Father Joe had small intense eyes that fixed Hannah directly, daring her not to hold the contact. "I liked your metaphor so much, Hannah. If I still gave sermons, I'd use it. I can't believe you've forgotten it."

Hannah laughed and Mrs. Phillips turned around, poked her head forward and pushed her eyeglasses up on her nose. One hand fluttered a greeting.

Hannah looked away, her eye sockets throbbing.

"Don't forget what I said about confession. If you'd prefer, I can arrange it with a priest you don't know. There's a woman over at St. Paul's—"

"I must go. Really." Hannah hurried down the path. "I have company waiting."

She ran across the parking lot and jerked open the door of the Volvo. Getting in she hit her hip on the steering wheel and cursed and then her slippery fingers fumbled with the keys.

Billy Phillips shoved his hot hand under her Brownie shirt and touched her breast and giggled, a greasy-haired, pimply sound that made Hannah's stomach lurch. He grabbed her hand and pulled it down to his crotch. What was she feeling? What was that? She looked down and saw the hard bulge of his penis straining against the zipper of his jeans. She jumped back with a jerk and when he came at her she put up both hands and shoved as hard as she could against his chest. He lost balance and his arms pinwheeled. His breath—quick shallow inhales, body at a backward slant, heels digging into the mulch of oak and bay and his eyes getting round and white and his mouth round and pink and then he wasn't there anymore and after she heard his body hit the rocks, she heard his voice. Help. *She inched forward and peered over the saddle of roots down at the creek.*

"Hannah." Father Joe was coming toward her.

She waved her hand in his direction. As she pulled out of the parking place in front of Brian's potting shed, she saw the caretaker bustling toward her with a tray of seedlings in his arms. She kept driving and he gestured for her to stop.

She folded in the middle.

"Glad I caught you, Mrs. Tarwater." Brian held out a flat of impatiens seedlings, lemon-green and limp. "I thought you might find a place for these up at your place. Poor wee fellas need your touch. Think you can help them?"

Help them.

Help me. *Billy Phillips lay on his back, his arms and legs spread wide. His eyes were open and his lips were moving.* Help. Me. *She watched his mouth make the words a third time. His arm move a little and his hand lifted toward her.* Help.

She turned her back on him.

Help. *She heard him say it one more time before she covered her ears with her hands and began to cry. When she cried she couldn't hear his voice.*

"You okay, Mrs. Tarwater?"

She looked at the tiny plants but instead of seeing them bent and feeble as they were, she saw them growing strong and tall on firm stalks, their leaves spread flat and wide to capture the light. She saw them blossoming in vibrant red and the sweetest, softest baby girl pink.

It came to her then what she must do about Angel.

Tuesday

Jeanne dreamed she was with her son at Bluegang, swinging on the rope. Huge goldfish swam below her, kissing the surface of the silvery water. They stood on their tails and turned like dancers while their great unblinking eyes stared up at her. *Go ahead*, James cried, only now he had become her dead brother, Michael. *Let go of the rope, Jeanne. Let go.* She did it.

Jeanne sat up in bed. "I dreamed I was flying."

Teddy stuck his head out the bathroom door, his face half covered with shaving cream. "Did you say something?"

She lay back and closed her eyes. For a split second after waking she had understood—as Einstein must have, in one stunning moment, suddenly and with his whole being, comprehended relativity—that the secret of human flight had nothing to do with wings or hollow bones or loft; no equations were involved. It was simple and elegant as sun reflected on water. A switch existed in her mind, and that was that. In the nanosecond after waking she had known where that switch was found and how to lift it.

"Are you planning to go to work?" Teddy's tone was not quite sarcastic. Since her explosion the day before his manner had been careful.

She threw back the covers and slipped her feet into the slippers set beside each other next to the bed. She reached for her dressing gown and found it at the end of the bed where she laid it every night.

"I talked to Simon Weed's secretary," she said. "He's in Tokyo until tomorrow night. But she said he'd be at the school late Thursday without fail."

"I still think we can handle the boy."

Jeanne shot him a look.

"You want to coddle him, Jeanne. We need to work out a plan of firm and consistent guidance."

She shook her head. "I'm going to tell Simon Weed to take his son out of school, hire a tutor and then keep the boy with him as much as possible. I'm also going to write him a refund check for his tuition."

Teddy's head jutted forward. "You can't do that. You'll be setting a precedent. It says in the agreement he signed that tuition checks aren't refundable. We can't change the rules for Simon Weed."

She walked past him, into the bathroom. Standing at the vanity mirror, she smoothed cream into her skin while Teddy watched.

"Tucker and his stupid rope drills," she said. "Hilltop isn't a Marine Corps boot camp. I want you to tell him that."

"None of the other boys have trouble—"

"None of the other boys found their mother hanging from a hayloft."

"We've been through this before."

"And the pitiful thing is, Teddy, Adam tried to climb the rope. Tucker goaded him until he had no other choice."

"How was he supposed to know—"

"You saw the advisory I sent out. Everyone on staff got a copy." She spoke through a mouthful of toothpaste. "It said Adam Weed had been severely traumatized and should be handled carefully. If Tucker ever emptied his mailbox—"

"Can we at least agree the kid goes back to his own room today?"

"No." She spat into the sink. "I want him in the infirmary where the nurse can keep an eye on him. I'll tell her to give him some audiotapes. Robby can visit him."

"Why not bring him over here? Put him in the guest room and give him his meals on a tray? Maybe you'd like to wait on the little prince yourself."

She turned her back and lifted her nightgown over her head. Before he spoke she felt his eyes on her.

"You're still a good-looking woman, Jeanne." She did not like his tone of voice, the purr that was under it. She stepped into her panties and hooked her bra behind her back.

"Good-looking as Liz?"

"She's a little intense for my taste."

They regarded their images side by side in the big mirror over the dresser. She in her bra and panties, he in a brocade dressing gown with velvet lapels. Like some decadent nineteenth-century count.

"I'll be glad when she's gone. You've been in a snit since she arrived. I miss my old Jeanne."

She chuckled. "I'll bet you do."

"Did you hear yourself? That tone?"

"What about Margie Scolero?" Margie and her husband operated the Barnes & Noble bookstore in Willow Glen and lived up Overlook Road.

"What about her?"

"She's not intense. She's Ms. *Town & Country* perfect size eight, trim as a toenail."

"So?"

"So, I'm trying to figure out what turns you on. Liz is intense but you came on to her Saturday night. And last Christmas at Martarano's party, you pushed Ms. Perfect down on the bed and climbed on."

"Where do you get this shit?"

"Be man enough to admit to your own hard-ons, Teddy."

He gawked at her language.

"I saw you with Margie. I was getting our coats and went in the spare room by accident. You hadn't even bothered to close the door."

"Oh, that! That didn't mean anything." Teddy rolled his eyes and laughed. "I was drunk, Jeanne. Those things happen when people drink too much. Besides, Margie's a prick teaser."

"Liz too?"

"If she told you I made a pass, then she lied, and she's sicker than I imagined. She's jealous. She wants to make trouble between you and me." He watched her debate which sweater to wear. "The red one. It brings out the color in your skin."

She chose the black and pulled it over her head.

"Don't tell me you're going to believe Liz before me?" He looked yellowish around the mouth and eyes as if he had eaten something that didn't agree. "You hurt me, Jeanne. You really do. After all these years . . ."

She eyed him speculatively. "I don't think I could hurt you if I put a gun to your head."

His mouth opened, then closed. "I don't have to put up with this, you know."

"You're right, Teddy, you don't." The balls of her feet tingled. "As a matter of fact, I don't think you should put up with me or the school anymore." She rested her hand on the dresser top to steady herself. "From what you've told me in the last twenty-four hours, you don't really want to be here so why don't you just pack a bag and go?"

"Careful, Jeanne." Moisture appeared on Teddy's upper lip. "Watch what you say. You might not like the consequences."

"You don't like me, you don't like the school, and you never wanted to be a teacher in the first place. You were meant for the stage so go on, do it. Move to New York."

"We've been together a long time, Jeanne. We've built something worthwhile here."

His voice dropped a note, took on a velvety menace; and she felt like prey, a pheasant discovered in the high grass where it had nested, safely camouflaged its whole life, caught now in the gaze of a mountain lion.

He said, "Don't start something you can't finish. If I were to leave you, I wouldn't come back. You should think about what that would mean. You know you can't run this school alone. Sooner or later someone'll get wise to that phony degree."

"Maybe I'll throw the degree out. Maybe I'll sell the school. Gail said some Tibetan monks are looking for a retreat. Why not Hilltop?"

He snorted. "You wouldn't do that."

"Wouldn't I?" Jeanne giggled. "I think I could do anything, Teddy. If I wanted to." *Even fly.*

Her amusement was a slap in the face though she saw him struggle to keep from showing it. He charged away from her and dressed fast, talking through his teeth about how little she knew of the world and how she didn't have what it took to succeed without him. He ripped the paper strip off his laundered shirt and flagged it at her.

"You're bright, Jeanne. You're diligent and you're orderly. I'll give you those qualities. But you know who gets the prizes? The one with flair." He snapped his black-and-white checked suspenders down on his shoulders and shrugged his arms into an unstructured sports coat of gray-green wool. He adjusted his floral tie and smoothed back his luxuriant hair with the flat of his hand.

"You're right, Teddy. You definitely have flair. I'm rigid, yes, and not very imaginative. I admit it. But I wasn't always this way." She said the words and did not believe them herself. In truth she had been hiding in the tall grass all her life. But it had become worse after she married. The stakes were so high, the possibility of shame and scorn had felt like a death threat sometimes. She had spent years hunkered down, holding her breath. "The day I married you, I started discounting myself, giving myself away in bits and pieces: my degree, my baby . . ."

"Jesus Christ, Jeanne, is that what this is about? No one forced you—"

She left him looking at himself in the long mirror and walked through the shadowy living room and out onto the side patio where the morning smelled of dust and oleander. From the school she heard the eight o'clock bells. What would it be like to begin the day without them? She passed through the gap in the hedge and approached the rose cloister. The day before Mr. Ashizawa had pruned every plant to the wood. Jeanne liked what she saw. With its garden of sticks, unplanted borders and stiff grass the school landscape had a wide-open, bony beauty. Nowhere to hide. She was going to sit in the cloister and think about Teddy and James and Bluegang until the clutter in her mind was pruned away and only the truth remained. The sky was full of birds moving south at this season. She would watch them and try to figure out how they did it.

* * *

Hilltop's eight o'clock bells were ringing as Liz stepped onto the patio with her second cup of coffee. She thought about Jeanne getting ready for another day with Teddy, and the sadness that had been with her since yesterday rose in her throat and she had to swallow hard to keep the tears down. Hannah stood near the oak looking up.

"Sheep in the sky. Mom used to say that meant rain. She was usually wrong but she kept on saying it." Without glancing at Liz she went back into the kitchen.

Liz had expected this visit to Rinconada to be a difficult one, but the difficulty so far exceeded her expectations it might as well be something altogether different. Less like a potholed road, more like driving backwards over a line of parking garage spikes. But yesterday's conversation with Jeanne had redeemed it a little. She and Jeanne understood each other now as they hadn't before. But, oh God, Hannah. What to do about Hannah? Liz followed her inside.

Hannah knelt on the kitchen floor, half inside a low cupboard.

"We have to talk," Liz said to Hannah's back. "You keep walking away from me but sooner or later—"

"Sooner or later it'll be done and over with. What's to talk about?" The depths of the cupboard muffled her voice. "Your mind's made up, isn't it?"

"I don't mean the abortion."

Hannah pulled out of the cupboard and looked at her. "I have other things to think about today." She stuck her head and shoulders back in the cupboard.

"What're you burrowing for?"

"A gizmo to make baby food. A little plastic thingie."

Liz wanted to scream. Instead she accumulated eggs, cheese, a green onion and a bit of tomato on the counter. She said with false brightness, "Shall I make you an omelet? They're my specialty."

The response from the cabinet was an echoing triumph. "I knew it!" Hannah held aloft her trophy, a small white plastic food grinder.

"Early Cuisinart?"

"You put the cooked food, zucchini or peas or whatever, in here and then slide this thing on top and press down while you turn the handle. Comes out pureed. Simplest thing in the world. I used it for Eddie."

"Speaking of Eddie," Liz cracked an egg on the edge of a ceramic bowl, "we had a good talk yesterday. He's a terrific kid."

Hannah put a baby bottle and the food mill into a cardboard box.

"I'm amazed. You still have all that baby stuff."

"I never expected to stop at two," Hannah said. "There's a car seat and a crib in the attic."

"Why did you stop? At two?"

Two deep lines formed between Hannah's eyes. She spoke distractedly. "I don't think we meant to. It just kind of . . . happened." She sorted through a stack of neatly folded baby clothes. Liz watched the way her hands lingered, stroking the nap on a pair of velveteen short pants with an embroidered bib front.

"What did you talk about?" Hannah asked.

"Who?"

"You and Eddie."

"I should let him tell you."

Hannah laughed shortly. "You're kidding, of course." She walked into the laundry room and emerged a moment later dragging a cooler with a blue top.

"Are we having a picnic?"

"I'm taking some stuff to Resurrection House."

"He calls it Erection House."

"Isn't he clever."

Liz poured beaten eggs into the hot frying pan. "Have you talked?"

"Who?"

Liz had noticed the first day how Hannah's concentration wandered. It was worse now, flying off in all directions like a toss of butterflies.

"We were talking about Eddie."

"Oh. Yeah. I mean, no, he hasn't talked to me." Now Hannah had the classified section of the *San Jose Mercury News* spread on the counter. "What's up with him this time?"

"The coach cut him. Told him to come back next year when he's stronger."

"The boy lives and breathes football. He must be devastated."

"Not quite." Liz tilted the frying pan, letting the egg mixture spread out to the hot perimeter.

Hannah looked up. "What's that supposed to mean?"

Liz stared at the eggs solidifying in the pan and felt sick to her stomach. In a psychology book Gerard had given her to read she had come across a term for what they were doing now: *triangulating*. Eddie and Hannah needed to work out their troubles together; they would not benefit from her interference. But she was already so deep in the triangle, two triangles: one with Eddie, one with Dan. She could not extricate herself.

"What he loves is football cards. And fantasy football—whatever that is. He says he doesn't want to play the actual live game at all."

Hannah's eyes rounded indignantly. "That's not true."

"He said he's tried to tell you but you won't listen to him."

"I don't need someone to explain my son to me."

"I'm not explaining him. You wanted to know . . ." She slid the omelet onto a plate and hoped it smelled and looked good enough to distract Hannah who was obviously geared up to be really pissed at her.

Hannah folded the newspaper, pressing hard on the creases with the side of her hand. "There's not one used high chair in the classified. Can you believe that? Not *one*. This is such a throwaway society. Maybe I should go out to the landfill. There's probably a whole mountain of high chairs out there." Hannah giggled and her eyes seemed to lose focus for a moment. "Do you remember the time we had to walk through the dump to get to—"

"That wasn't me, Hannah."

"Sure it was. I remember—"

"I don't know who you walked through the dump with, but it wasn't me." Liz ground pepper over the omelet. "We were talking about Eddie."

Hannah blinked. "Don't you think I know what we're talking about? I'm not crazy, you know. You were telling me how much better you know my son than I do. That being the case, why don't you give him a message for me? Tell him he ought to be damn glad to have me for a mother. Tell him he might not always be so lucky."

"Hannah!"

She strode across the kitchen and shoved the newspaper into a bin marked for recycling. "He and Ingrid both think I'm totally obsolete. Like some rusted out high chair . . ."

"They don't. Where does that idea come from?" Liz looked at the omelet on her plate, groaned and dropped her fork.

"What's the matter with you?"

"We've got to talk about what's really going on here."

"We *have* talked. And talked and talked and talked. I'm fucking sick of talking." Hannah stared at her hands smudged by newsprint. She rubbed them on her Levi's and looked at them again. Her eyes brimmed. "I've tried to convince you. And Dan too. It isn't like I haven't tried, really tried hard. But neither of you understand." Tears spilled onto her cheeks. "You just don't see things like I do. You and your abortion and him and his . . . whatever. Neither of you realize what's important."

"Oh, God, Hannah, it's not just the baby. It's not just Eddie or Bluegang."

It's you, my dearest sweetest friend, little girl grown up and old. There's something happening in your head and you have to stop and take care of it. You have to let us love you and help you.

"Remember Mrs. Vogler?" Liz asked. "How she went on a retreat and didn't come back for four months?"

"What about her?"

"When she went my mother said, 'If a woman's going to lose it, she'll do it during menopause.'"

Laugh. I'm joking with you. Please laugh.

"You've been talking to Dan."

"We love you."

"What a load! If you really loved me you'd stop nagging about Bluegang and you'd let me have your baby." Tears again. "There is nothing peculiar about wanting to help a baby!"

"This isn't about helping anyone."

"Of course it is. That's what a mother does. She helps. And there's nothing wrong with wanting to be a mother either."

"You're not making sense, Hannah. You already are a mother."

"It's not the same."

"But it is."

"I'm not crazy."

"No one thinks you are."

"Yes, you do. You and Dan."

"Hannah, Ingrid and Eddie need you—"

"Oh, for godsake." Hannah kicked the base of the cupboard viciously. Liz stepped back. "Ever since you got here, you've been stirring things up. First it was the business about Bluegang and then the baby. And now you're meddling with my son. We were all just fine before you came, Liz. Just peachy." Hannah struggled to close the flaps of the cardboard box. "Why don't you go back to Belize and leave us alone?"

Liz had not expected this and at first she couldn't think what to say. She could not believe that Hannah meant what she said. She was angry, emotionally caught up in something that had nothing to do with Liz. So don't bite, Liz thought. Don't let her goad you into saying or doing something we'll both regret. But she was sick of tiptoeing around whatever was eating Hannah, weary of trying and failing to force a dialog that Hannah was determined not to have. The effort suddenly felt like so much bullshit, and Liz could not make herself be either patient or tolerant. "I'll pack my things." She was human, after all.

"Don't be so melodramatic." Hannah blew back a strand of hair fallen across her face. "No one's asking you to leave. It'll all be over after tomorrow."

"The operation's not 'til Friday."

Hannah looked confused.

"The abortion. Isn't that what we've been talking about?"

"Oh, that!" Hannah tossed back her long braid and began to wipe out the cooler with a sponge. "You'll do what you have to do. I can't stop you."

Hannah made sure the animals had plenty of food. She turned out Glory, gave him a chance to stretch out the kinks. He walked stiff-legged for a few moments then broke into a trot and then an easy lope. The dogs ran after him barking. On the far side of the ring he stopped to smell the ground, bent his knees and dropped into a roll.

Hannah looked up at the house, graceful and country-elegant even from the rear. Who would expect that people living in a house with such wide windows could hide so much? On the second floor, one down from the guest room, was Eddie's window. If she were a mockingbird in the citradora looking in, would she know her boy better than she did as his mother? Fantasy football. Fantasy. Who was Eddie? Apart from the fantasy boy in her head?

Abruptly, she turned her back on the house and walked across the paddock to the far fence where the day before she had glimpsed a figure hiding. If she believed in ghosts she might say it had been Billy Phillips risen up from Bluegang and through the wildwood, come to haunt her. Still begging the help she had refused him. But she didn't believe in ghosts and she barely believed in Billy anymore. If Liz hadn't come back she would have managed not to think of him more than once or twice a year for the rest of her life.

Hannah opened the gate. A few steps and she was on the edge of the canyon looking down through the wildwood to the creek. Gail had said it was mostly dry but she thought she saw a glimmer of light on the water fifty feet below. And there was the path, overgrown but still visible. If she walked down it she would find the great oak at its base. The same saddle of roots. The rocks would not have moved.

If Hannah had walked up to Mrs. Phillips in the cemetery yesterday and said, "I pushed your son, I caused his death and when he asked for help I turned my back," would the words have penetrated the fog she lived in, would they have given the old woman a life?

Of course not, what was over was over and so what was the use of thinking about it anymore? Hannah was sick of thinking and talking, of mincing the past into smaller and smaller pieces. Pureed past, she thought and laughed. She knew what she wanted now. She wasn't a frightened little girl anymore and the mistake she made once, she wouldn't make again.

In the early afternoon, Liz knocked on Hannah's bedroom door. "I won't disturb you," she said, looking in. "I just want to know if there's a rental car place in Rinconada or do I have to call San Jose."

Since that morning, they had kept their distance from each other. It was a big house and easy enough to do. But the tension was an atmosphere, present as static before an electrical storm.

Hannah stood with her hands on her hips gnawing on her lower lip as she considered the clothes piled on her bed. She still wore her Levi's and sweatshirt, and she hadn't changed out of her work boots when she came up from the barn. Dirty footprints marked a trail across the pale rose carpet.

"You're wearing your boots."

Hannah looked down. "So I am." She laughed as if she hadn't tracked mud all over a carpet she would have to vacuum, as if she didn't loathe vacuuming above all household labor. "Why do you need a car?"

"I have to see the doctor on Thursday. He inserts a dilator to relax the cervix."

"I can't drive you."

"I don't expect you to."

Hannah picked up a skirt, examined it and tossed it onto a discard pile at her feet. "I would if I could but I can't." She dug in a dresser drawer and pulled out a gray hooded sweatshirt. She looked at it critically. To Liz she appeared to be debating with herself. In the end, she tossed it on the bed.

"That's why I want to rent a car."

"Look in my address book by the kitchen phone." Hannah waved her away. "Under C, I think. Maybe R. Or A."

In the kitchen Liz found the number of the rental agency under A and called. There was no one in the office. The message machine told her to leave her name and number and she did.

Returning to her own room she propped the door open on the chance that Hannah might come down the hall and see it as an invitation to talk. She wondered if these really were the final days of their friendship. In the future would she write to Jeanne, meet Jeanne for occasional holidays, call Jeanne for hour-long phone talks and wait for her to reveal some bit of news about their mutual friend, Hannah Tarwater? Would Ingrid move into Liz's life, a substitute for her mother?

She lay down, her body suffused with a dull ache like a total body migraine. The breeze through the window was cool. She drew up the comforter and slept a while.

Ingrid woke her. "A guy called from Drive-Right," she said from the doorway.

Liz yawned and stretched.

"Are you okay, Aunt Liz?"

"I've had better days."

"You want me to get you something? Coffee?"

"No. Thanks."

Ingrid slouched against the doorjamb, waiting to be invited in.

"How come you need a car?"

"I have some errands on Thursday."

"That's half day. Paco and me'll drive you wherever you want to go. He really wants to meet you."

Liz could pat the bed beside her and Ingrid would be there in a flash but the thought of a conversation with this girl who seemed to hold in potential so much of what Liz had lost—well, she could barely face the day let alone that.

"I need the car on Friday too."

"What about Mom?"

"It's more convenient if I drive myself."

"But Thursday Paco'll take you around, okay?"

"Ingrid—"

She took a few steps into the room. "You'll love him, Auntie Liz."

If Liz asked her to go Ingrid would do it, but she would be hurt and confused; she would think the rejection of her company was about *her*. That's the way it was at seventeen. Everything was about you. Liz stared down at her hands, at her fingers laced across her stomach the way the shell of an oyster protects the pearl. Maybe that never changed. She did not want to speak to Ingrid because it would be hard on her, on Liz. She sighed and patted the bed beside her. "Sit down, honey, I've got to tell you something."

Ingrid perched on the edge of the bed.

"I need the car to go to the doctor . . ."

"You have cancer." Ingrid's body wilted into itself. "That's why you came back here."

"No." Liz waited for the moment to pass, for another world to come into being so she could avoid telling Ingrid what she must. "I'm pregnant."

The information took a second to register. "Omigod, that's fabulous." Ingrid began to talk, sounding like her mother off on a tangent of plans.

Liz put her hand on Ingrid's forearm. "No, it's not great. I came here, to Rinconada . . . I wanted to see you all, but I also . . ." She closed her eyes a second. "On Friday I'm scheduled for an abortion." Ingrid didn't seem to hear her. The pronouncement flew over the girl like sheep galloping across the sky.

"Did you hear what I said? I'm not going to have this baby. I'm going to have an abortion." Liz waited a moment for the truth to register and when it still didn't seem to make it into Ingrid's head, she added, "I don't want to be a mother."

That got Ingrid's attention. "Why not? You'd be amazing."

Liz shook her head, tired of having to convince people of what she knew in the heart of her being.

"What about your boyfriend? Gerard?"

"It's complicated."

"You didn't use birth control?"

"I didn't think I could conceive. I thought I'd started menopause."

"It's like a miracle."

"No, Ingrid. It's like an accident."

Ingrid stared at her. Liz thought, yes, look, see me as I am. Know me. *If we come through this . . .*

"How can you love a guy who wants you to murder his baby?"

She was stunned for a second and couldn't think what to say. "Ingrid, an abortion isn't murder. It's many things but it is not murder."

"You don't know. Not for sure."

"It's my body and I know what's inside it."

"My friend says babies have souls. Even in the womb."

"And she's free to believe that. But I don't. This . . . thing inside me . . ."

"It's not a thing," Ingrid cried, "It's a baby. A real live baby."

Liz raised her voice. "It is nothing like a baby. Not yet. It's barely anything at all." Liz reached for Ingrid's hands but she pulled away. "Listen to me. In your life you're going to hear a lot of stuff about abortion, about how it's wrong or it's right and maybe you'll end up being one of those women who thinks it's wrong. And that's fine. If you don't believe in abortion, don't have one. But before you make up your mind, I want you to use your intelligence. Don't get seduced by answers that make everything seem easy, black and white, yes or no."

Ingrid twisted a lock of hair around her finger and stared at it.

"Honey, none of the big questions have simple answers. And the older the world gets, the more that's true. We all just have to learn to live with shades of gray. No matter how much we long for black and white."

Ingrid stared. "How can you live like that?"

"Just the way you do—or will, the way your mom and dad do. I weigh the good and the bad, the consequences of my actions. I use my brain to look ahead, to think about those consequences. I decide." She heard her words and thought that it was never that easy. She took Ingrid's hand and wouldn't let her pull away. She placed it flat on her stomach. "This is an embryo, not a baby. It doesn't exist apart from me. If I died tomorrow, it would die too. Right now, it's a mass of cells growing in my uterus. Against my will."

"You make it sound like cancer."

Liz opened her mouth and shut it.

"If Gerard loved you, he'd want you to have your baby. I mean, it's his too, isn't it?"

Liz wanted to explain that she and Gerard were happy as they were: a pair. But of course Ingrid would think that selfish because she was more like her mother than she could yet understand. Love and family and children were all of a part to her.

"And if you loved him you'd think his baby was the most wonderful, miraculous, fabulous thing in the world. You'd be excited."

"Is that the way you feel about Paco?"

"Well, I would if . . . you know."

"What if you had sex and you got pregnant?"

"I wouldn't. We'd use protection."

"Just suppose."

"I can't suppose. It would never happen, we'd be careful. We aren't stupid."

"But just suppose it did happen to you. Would you want to get married and have the baby, raise it?" Ingrid started to answer. Liz shook her head. "I don't want you to answer me. I want you to think really hard about what it means to bring a child into the world. All the levels of responsibility, all the possible consequences."

In the moment that followed Liz was conscious of Ingrid and the bedroom in which they talked but her senses reached beyond and engaged the house and the yard and the garden. The tang of the wildwood filled her nostrils and the back of her mouth; down in the paddock Glory whinnied, the dogs barked and somewhere in the house a radio played. The narrow, silver-green leaves of the citradora shivered in the wind and a mockingbird sang on a swaying branch. The fullness of the world, its richness and variety tightened her throat and she felt such love for Ingrid as she would not have believed was in her.

"The point is, you have to do what you believe is right. If you don't, if you go along with the crowd or follow someone else's sense of right or wrong, you're betraying yourself." Liz folded Ingrid into her arms. "That's the worst thing you can do, honey. Betray yourself. It can take a lifetime to get over that."

"You were such a good boy," Jeanne said and tucked the infirmary blanket tighter around Adam Weed's small body, the palms of her hands warm with the pleasure of the simple task. "Nurse Judy says you're very brave."

"She gave me a Hershey Kiss."

Jeanne dug in the pocket of her sweater jacket and brought out another silvery Kiss. She held it out and Adam took it.

"Thanks."

He unwrapped the foil, put the chocolate in his mouth and lay back. Jeanne took the paper from his hand and set it on the bedside table beside a glass of water with a bent plastic straw. Next to the little table, a window opened onto the back common where a half-dozen students tossed Frisbees and footballs. Adam stared at the ceiling. Jeanne watched him and became aware that he was con-centrating hard on something.

"I'm counting," he told her. He pointed at the acoustical tiles overhead. "There's twelve in all the rows 'cept one's got eleven." His forehead wrinkled. "I mighta lost count 'cause I had to blink."

"Have you tried counting the dots?"

"My eyes get all burny."

"Would you like a book to look at instead? Maybe a magazine or something to draw with?"

He shook his head.

"Nurse Judy says you broke your ankle. Does it hurt?"

"Uh-huh."

"Have you had some aspirin?"

"Uh-huh."

"You're going to learn to walk on crutches for a while."

He looked interested. "Cool." He looked up at the ceiling again.

"Why'd you let go of the rope, Adam? You were almost to the top."

He said nothing. She guessed from his long stare that he was trying to figure out how much he could trust her.

"Uncle Louis said."

"He told you to let go and fall?"

Adam nodded and then sighed.

"Do you always do what Uncle Louis tells you?"

He put his hands up to cover his ears. She pulled them away gently.

"Uncle Louis lives in your mind, doesn't he?" His hands wrig-gled in hers. "I'll tell you a secret, Adam."

He looked at her.

"Mostly you don't get to know this until you grow up." She dropped her voice and looked from side to side, a cartoon spy. "It's a very grown-up secret."

"I won't tell."

"Promise?" He nodded the smallest possible nod. "The things you hear in your mind, they're not always true. Sometimes the mind lies."

Adam stared at her then looked away and up. His lips moved as he began to count the tiles again.

"Never mind. Everything's going to be okay. Be patient a little longer." She touched his cheek and imagined it was James she caressed. What would it be like to touch her own son? "I talked to your father's office a little while ago. He's in Tokyo. Japan. But he'll be back on Thursday and then he's going to come down here and get you."

"Uncle Louis says Daddy's mad at me."

"Uncle Louis is a liar."

Adam looked as if he expected momentary murder and mayhem.

"Your father wants you to be happy. And so do I. You don't have to stay at Hilltop if you're unhappy." She lifted a lock of hair off his forehead for the pleasure of touching him.

Adam closed his eyes, ignored her and pretended to sleep. Jeanne stayed beside him. She watched his face and after a few moments the tension melted from it. His breathing deepened and beneath the light infirmary blanket his narrow chest rose and fell.

Outside the infirmary she stood on the side porch watching the boys on the playing field. She knew each by name, his parents and his special needs. When the Frisbee dropped near her feet she picked it up and bent her arm back, sent it sailing on a gust of wind. Once years ago there had been talk of making Hilltop a coeducational school, but she had opposed the idea. At the time Teddy asked why she cared so much; and her answers had been scientific, based on sound educational theory. Children did learn better when boys and girls were separated. But really, she saw now, her arguments had been to rationalize nothing more than wanting to be surrounded by boys standing in for James, variations on her son.

She would tell Simon Weed to follow his heart. He must not let his boy go to strangers, even Hilltop strangers. Hire tutors, the best in the world. Kid-friendly shrinks, as many as it took to sideline Uncle Louis.

When Hannah and Dan made love that night they kissed as if they were inventing kisses, as if kissing might save their lives. Afterwards Dan stayed inside her and they held each other for a long time before slipping apart and over to their own sides of the bed.

Hannah took care not to wake Dan when she went into the bathroom. The luminous digital clock ticked over the minutes after midnight. Her body ached for sleep while her mind churned and made sleep impossible.

It was Wednesday at last.

Barefoot in her white terry robe, she moved through the house like a ghost. In the den Cherokee lifted her elegant head from the couch and thumped her tail. Hannah sat beside her and switched on the television. She found an ancient black-and-white movie starring a pallid young man with a pencil mustache and Myrna Loy, skinny and smirky as always. They guzzled martinis and called each other darling. She watched for a few minutes, then flicked to a channel where a swami preached circles in a singsong voice, flicked again to the skin care secrets of a woman with kumquat-colored hair. On MTV a boy in sequins gyrated while fans screamed.

While the images danced on the screen, Hannah walked around the family room absentmindedly straightening the bookcases and tidying a pile of papers left by Eddie on the project table. On the cover of a blue binder he had written with care, using stencils, THE RINCONADA ROCKETS. Inside neatly tagged dividers with typed labels separated the pages. In the first section there was a typed list of players, the roster of the Rockets with all their personal stats: size, weight, college team, position in the draft. The second section held the players' trading cards encased in plastic for protection. Hannah stared at the mostly African-American faces and repeated the names to herself. She recognized a few as stars. The third section was all statistics, a formidable array of numbers translated into percentages and ratios. Yards on the ground, yards in the air, attempted passes and completed passes, sacks. Math. And laid out as clearly as a Fortune 500 stock report. The next divider set apart a precise reckoning of how much money the Rockets had won for Eddie so far that season. Twenty-three dollars and thirty cents. The last section held typed articles about the Rockets signed with the byline Ed Tarwater. She read one entitled "Rockets Fizzle in Third Quarter" and found no errors.

He made her proud, this boy, smart as he was in his special way. But he shamed her too. While hiding who he really was—the owner, manager, coach, and even the journalist of a winning team—he had tried to play football at Rinconada High School because she wanted him to. Her skin prickled with regret and then with irritation. She never demanded he play. He could have refused.

Hannah's throat and jaw tightened. She pressed her fingers to her temples. He loved her and she had been awful to him.

"It isn't that I don't love you, Eddie. Ed. It's just I can't . . ." Her words feathered off into the silent house.

The boy would be better off without her.

Deep in a bosky dream, Cherokee thumped her tail.

Hannah turned off the television and made her way to the kitchen where she warmed milk for cocoa. The clammy tiles stuck to her bare feet. Outside the branches of the olive tree scratched the kitchen windows, and she was aware for the first time of the wind breaking through the trees. She opened the back door and stepped outside into a rush of cool air. Clouds tumbled and chased across the sky like children playing. Gooseflesh rose on her arms and she rubbed it hard. There was weather on the way at last.

Wednesday

"You're early, Hannah." Betts looked up from her paperwork. She glanced at the clock on the wall over her desk, stood and gathered a stack of papers into a bulging file. "I didn't expect you until ten."

"Couldn't sleep." Hannah found her cup and poured coffee.

"Everything okay with you?"

"The weather's made me edgy."

"The guy on Channel Ten said rain by noon. That high pressure system seems to have moved."

"A big storm, I heard."

"I'm due at the staff meeting this minute. Want to sit in?"

"For a while."

Staff meetings at Resurrection House were held in what had been the mansion's dining room in the glory days. Hannah found a seat on an ancient overstuffed couch near the door and folded her legs under her. In more optimistic times the home's dilapidated rooms had inspired her with all that soap and water, paint and time, energy and commitment could accomplish. That was before she learned about percolating damp and mold and cockroaches four inches long. Overhead fecal-brown water stains the size of hubcaps marked the ceiling. Underfoot, the carpet remained a grimy brown despite vacuuming and whirring carpet cleaners. Everywhere she looked she saw symbols of a futility progressed far beyond the reach of suds and paint and willing volunteers.

Hannah knew each of the eight other women in the room but

today she said nothing, greeted no one as she sat with her legs curled under her, holding on to a cup of bad coffee with one hand while the fingers of the other beat on the arm of the couch. She wore sweatpants, a plain gray sweatshirt, and running shoes. Her hair was in a ponytail, and she'd left the house without applying makeup—not even lipstick. Her plan had been to look anonymous. An unremarkable middle-aged housewife, a suburban frau born to shop at Wal-Mart 'til she dropped, unnoticed.

Betts addressed the group. "We need to move along this morning. Sheila and Lupe are minding the store for us but let's not take advantage of them." She opened the notebook on her lap. "I have only three agenda items."

She mentioned the problem of cigarette smoking. Maryann moved that the screened laundry porch be designated a smoking area. Someone else said outside on the front veranda. A vote was taken and the veranda won.

The next item of business surprised Hannah.

"Shannon came by yesterday to tell me she's got a job."

"I hope you didn't take her word for it." May's laugh was caustic.

Hannah shifted her legs out from under her and planted them on the carpet. Inside her running shoes her toes began to wriggle impatiently.

"I called the company and they verified. Apparently she was completely candid with them about living with us and having Angel. The man I spoke to said he thought she was a good employment bet. Highly motivated." Betts checked her notes. "The company does bulk mailing. Third class stuff."

"A real career opportunity," May said.

Betts shot her a look. "It's a start and that's all we're asking at this point. I've gone over the house contract with Shannon. She knows the rules and she told me she'll follow them."

Maryann asked, "Where you going to put them?"

"The room at the back, the one that overlooks the side yard," Betts said. "There'll be plenty of room for a crib."

Betts: so determinedly optimistic, so everlastingly cheery. And so wrong, so completely blindly wrong.

Hannah had read Shannon's core as surely as a psychiatrist decoding responses to a Rorschach test. Shannon had beguiled every woman at the meeting—except perhaps May—with her girlish smiles and promises, blinded them to her shifty, restless, sideways eyes. Angel needed commitment and sacrifice, a lifetime of devoted and selfless care if she was to rise up whole and bright. Shannon didn't have it in her.

Betts began to speak of another girl who had applied to live at Resurrection House. Her baby was still in the preemie ward. She stopped in midsentence. "You okay, Hannah?"

Hannah picked up her purse and rose from the couch. "I need some air," she said and managed to smile. The folding doors squeaked as she pulled them back. She shrugged apologetically to the group. "Hot flash."

Benign smiling faces watched her out the door.

It's so easy to fool them, she thought.

Hannah went immediately across the foyer downstairs and along the hall to the nursery where it was quiet except for baby sounds and the scratch of an oak branch against the eaves. Swaddled in a blue blanket, Angel lay on her back sucking her fist. Her open eyes stared unfocused at the ceiling.

"Hello, baby girl."

A blink and then Angel recognized her and squirmed excitedly. Hannah picked her up. At ten months the bundle in her arms felt more like three or four. Small splayed hands batted her face. Hannah grabbed one and kissed it. Pressing her face against the baby's warm damp neck, she whispered, "Angel, my Angel."

With Angel in her arms Hannah left the nursery and went quickly to the front of the house. From behind the closed dining room doors, she heard laughter and the sound of paper shuffling. She scribbled on the chalkboard: *Gone to the park. H and A.*

She grabbed her jacket from its hook and hurried out the front door and down the steps, across the yard and around the corner to where she had parked the Volvo out of sight of the house. She shifted Angel to her hip and rummaged in her bag for keys. She opened the back curbside door. Eddie's infant car seat was anchored in the back on the side opposite the driver. To fit Angel, Hannah had to loosen her blanket and then adjust the angle of the seat to an almost reclining position. The lever stuck. She needed both hands to budge it. She laid the baby on the backseat and groped under the car seat. Her hands were slippery with sweat. Behind her a door slammed and a dog barked. She turned around expecting to see Betts or Maryann hurrying toward her, but it was only a woman from the building next door retrieving her newspaper.

The lever released with a jerk, sending a startled squirt of adrenaline through Hannah's system. She brushed her hair back off her face and rested her forehead against the roof of the car until her heartbeat slowed and her hands stopped shaking. Then she settled Angel in the car seat, closed the rear door, went around and opened her side, got in and turned on the ignition. The engine fired and immediately Angel began to cry.

Hannah smiled because tears were exactly what she had expected. The movement of the car and the purr of the engine would lull Angel to sleep. But she had forgotten how a baby's raw screams take on substance in a car's interior, filling up the space with a noise like shards of glass. She laughed and felt young and pleasantly harried and entirely competent.

She focused on the road ahead. Angel finally quieted. Hannah craned her neck around to check if she was breathing. Of course she was, there was no reason for her to stop breathing. But once Hannah started worrying, she couldn't stop. It had been the same with Ingrid and Eddie. At the next exit she pulled off 101 and switched the car seat to the front passenger side.

Angel cried again, barking shrieks of distress Hannah could not silence with touch or talk. This was exactly the sort of problem a girl like Shannon would not know how to handle. She would probably end up hitting Angel out of frustration, but Hannah would never do that because she understood any break in routine overstimulated a crack baby. The next few hours would be difficult for Angel, but Hannah had prepared for that. She kept one hand on the wheel and the other stroked Angel's thin arm. A few miles down the freeway the baby's tears subsided again into woeful snuffles, and at last she fell asleep. Her long black eyelashes glistened and every minute or so she shuddered, shaking off the last of the tears.

To the right of the highway a mass of plum-colored clouds insinuated itself eastward over and through the passes of the Coast Range. Drained of color under a heavy sky, the parched landscape of live oak, eucalyptus, fields and orchards lay in dun desolation. In the wind the trees arched their spines like ballerinas; and beside the road, a string of fishing lakes shone like pewter plates. Hannah checked the rearview mirror. A blue-gray wake of empty road stretched behind the Volvo, and she imagined she was looking back at the receding shoreline of her old life. Reflected in the rearview mirror she saw an untidy middle-aged woman with too much frizzy hair. She smiled at herself. Everything was going according to plan and expectation.

Once she saw a highway patrol car on an overpass, and for an instant a cold clarifying wind keened through her mind, and she knew she should turn around. But the thought passed as quickly as the scenery.

Hannah knew what she was doing. The flight with Angel was kidnapping and literally against the law, but she had thought this through and right and wrong could not concern her anymore. What jury would convict her for saving a baby's life? In Hannah's care Angel had a chance, with Shannon she did not. Simple. True.

The day before Hannah had shopped for supplies and cashed a large check at Wells Fargo. By the time Dan learned how large, she would be gone. The cooler was in the trunk full of ice and basics. In one cardboard box were the cans of soup she had got for herself and the jars of baby food Angel would need until they settled somewhere in Mexico and Hannah could puree fresh produce as she had for Eddie and Ingrid. In another box was an old microwave she hoped still worked. The first night they would stay in a little housekeeping motel she remembered in the Carmel Valley. It was off the road and quiet, sparkling clean and smug in its plain utilitarian style. The next day she would trade the Volvo for a used car, pay cash, and drive to the border.

Hannah tried not to think about Dan and her children, but everywhere along the road she saw things that reminded her of those she had left behind. In a paddock a man stood beside a horse, and she knew she could depend on Dan to feed Glory and the foster animals. She imagined him beside the mare, resting his forehead on her neck. At first he'd be too worried and confused to be angry. Then he would beg God to help him understand why she had left him. He would fight off anger until, exhausted, he had to let it in. For a while it would take over his life. But some part of him would never give up hope that she was coming back. He would be a good father and a comfort to the children.

She pushed down the faces of Ingrid and Eddie when they came into her mind; but like buoys in rough weather, they popped to the surface again. Someday she would write them. *I love you, I will always love you.* She shook her head to clear away the syllables. *You two gave my life its meaning.* She clenched her teeth until her jaw ached.

At the age of six or seven Ingrid's favorite book had been *Peter Pan in Kensington Gardens.* Peter returned home and found the window barred and bolted and saw his mother with a new baby in her arms. Ingrid asked to have the chapter read aloud to her again and again and sobbed as if she would die—then put herself to sleep planning revenge on Peter's behalf. Ingrid would hate Hannah for leaving home and would dream of retribution. Eddie would make her a stranger and be sure she had never loved him, from the beginning.

Flying down the highway, she heard their baby fists rap on the tightly closed car windows and their voices begging to be let in.

Liz ran down Casabella Road, daring the rain to come. Her joints creaked and her muscles stretched like old bubble gum. She had woken in a slough, glum to her toes. Running sometimes helped. The sky was low and gray and misty on the edges, spilling down the hills like water over rocks.

She detoured left on Las Robles. It had been an oak-strewn hillside sloping down to Bluegang when they were kids. Now manorial edifices of stone and brick rose on quarter-acre lots, surrounded by bright green lawns despite the water shortage. *I'm not against new houses. I'm not against change.*

Nothing is forever, Liz thought as she skirted a place in the road dug up for underground power lines. Everything dies eventually, and friendships sputtered out from inattention, dishonesty and cowardice. The incident at Bluegang comprised but a fraction of a day in childhoods otherwise rich in light and laughter; no wonder she and Jeanne and Hannah had believed they could coast through the years on what they had agreed to remember. Their complicit silence had been a way of denying time and change. If Liz had not been visited by nightmares blacker than any secret, if Gerard had not been there to counsel her, if she had not come back demanding that they talk about Bluegang, if she had not come back to get an abortion—so many contingencies, so many opportunities to reconsider or turn back—they might have floated on down into old age reminiscing like codgers in a sentimental movie. But she had returned to Rinconada and now, while Liz hoped she and Jeanne might have taken their first tentative steps outside the box and begun to truly see and know each other, she and Hannah were estranged as never before.

She recalled the fierceness of their childhood fights, always them against her and rarely over anything more important than a whim: notes passed around her, snubs and giggles and whispers and Liz left in the dust as Hannah and Jeanne rode off on their bikes. Two in the box and one outside longing to be invited in. A classic pattern and, inevitably, Liz so hated being left out she would apologize even if she didn't always know what she'd done. She'd make something up and say how sorry she was and please, please, please would they be her friends again? The apology always satisfied Hannah and Jeanne and they magnanimously forgave her and moved over and let her snuggle back into her own warm corner of the box. She had wanted to be Hannah, to be Jeanne, to be anyone but who she was and her place in the trio had been based on that. Recalling now her willingness to play the timid underdog, her heart ached for the girl she had been.

The visit to Rinconada had taught Liz some things. For one, being Liz Shepherd suited her fine and she wasn't timid anymore, not a bit of it. She had become a woman brave enough to confront the shame of her past, sure enough of who she was and what she wanted to make a painful choice. Proud enough to ask that others see her as she really was. But she had not dreamed the cost of self-knowledge could be so high. Was it worth the loss of Hannah? The question jabbed her in the ribs, and knocked the air out of her.

Down Hernandez now, a long straight downhill where the houses were old again and most of them in some stage of remodeling. She got her breath back. Her legs were strong, her strides long. In front of Miss Rigby's house the sidewalk buckled over knots of oak roots. Liz stepped off the curb and onto the road where the surface was smooth underfoot and she flew like a girl, her joints lubricated now, her muscles warm.

In Belize City there were fortune-tellers everywhere, and Liz had been to a half dozen of them over the years until she settled on Divina who also sold lottery tickets and knew where to score good ganja. Divina said relationships to people and places carried over from lifetime to lifetime. So maybe Liz and Hannah and Jeanne had been friends in another life. Maybe sisters. If so it didn't matter that she and Hannah couldn't make connections anymore. They would come together again in the next life. Or the one after that.

This was not a comfort to Liz.

Angel woke, crying again, and Hannah was glad for the distraction from thoughts of Dan and the children. They were at Morgan Hill. She checked her watch. It was almost forty minutes since she'd left Resurrection House. Soon Betts would begin to expect her back. After an hour she might send Maryann to the park to see if something had happened to delay them there. Maryann would look around for the Volvo and report it gone; and Betts—clever Betts—would see the stroller still in the closet and figure it out in a second.

Hannah said to Angel, "You're a hungry girl, aren't you. Mommy'll give you a bottle in a few minutes."

Hannah left the freeway and drove west, crossing old 101 and continuing into the hills. She rolled down her window to vent Angel's shrieks. Here, on the leeward side of the Coast Range and far south of the Bay, the effects of the drought were most apparent. Leaves lay thick around the woebegone gum trees and their bark spiraled off in sheets. A patina of velvety, smoke-colored dust lay over everything. Three or four miles into the mountains, Hannah came to a little roadside park: a pair of cement picnic tables and a blue portable toilet under sycamores beside a dried up creek bed. She stopped the car, got out, went around to the passenger side and opened the door. When Hannah unbuckled the seat belt restraints Angel thrashed and screamed louder.

Hannah had expected this.

She gathered Angel into her arms and tried to hold her close. The feel of heart beating against heart could soothe a crack baby's distress. "Hush, my baby girl," she crooned. "It's going to be all right, all right." Angel did not want to be held close; she twisted her torso and kicked into Hannah's breast.

"You're starving." Hannah laughed because it was simple when you knew what you were doing. "Just a minute now, hold your horses."

She sat Angel in the car seat. She closed the door and went to the trunk, opened it and brought out the bottle she had made early that morning and placed in the cooler. Angel was not going to like the cold milk at first, but it wouldn't hurt her.

Angel's screams rose a decibel. Hannah rushed around and peered in the window at her. She was not strapped in and had managed to twist her body sideways and stretch herself across the little seat. She kicked against one side and arched her back over the other.

Hannah ripped open the door and gathered the screaming baby into her arms. She hurried to the rear of the car where she had left the bottle perched on top of the closed cooler. The bottle fell from her shaking hands into the dust and rolled under the rear end of the car.

"Shit." Hannah dropped to her knees. The bottle lay between the rear tires and beyond her reach. Angel kicked against her ribs and inches from Hannah's ears, her cries scraped like a surgeon's saw.

"Shut up, Angel, for Chrissake."

She went back to the front of the car and put the baby in the car seat. This time she buckled a strap across her middle. Down on her hands and knees, she still couldn't reach the bottle. She lay on her side and scooted under the car. Her fingertips touched the plastic and closed around it. She looked up and saw through the space between the front tires that she was not alone in the park. A teenage boy stood under one of the sycamores near the creek, watching the car.

* * *

Jeanne asked, "Where did you sleep last night?"

"My office," Teddy rubbed the small of his back. "Either we kiss and make up, or I buy a new couch."

Jeanne tilted in her desk chair. Her mind was empty.

Teddy's voice took on a teasing, caressing tone. "What can I say? What do you want me to say? I drink too much, I get a little ... you know." Teddy smiled. "I like women, Jeanne. You know that. But I'm better than I used to be. That's true, isn't it?"

How strange. Your husband as good as admits he screws around and you find you have nothing to say. Jeanne stared out the window behind Teddy, but she did not need to see the mounding gray and violet clouds wounding the sky to know heavy weather was coming.

Teddy sat on the edge of her desk. When this familiarity did not break the silence, he moved off and lounged on her couch under the window. On the credenza the bell-curve clock ticked. A gust of wind threw a handful of barbed oak leaves against the window screen.

Teddy knelt on the couch and closed the glass.

"You better announce we'll be on rainy day schedule," Jeanne said. "I'll ask Jorge to move all those folding chairs out of the old rec hall. We can have movies."

"And we can quit schlepping gray water."

"It's been a good exercise for the boys."

"Some positive feedback from the parents."

"And Mr. Ashizawa says the roses are as healthy as he's ever seen them."

A bell rang. Jeanne glanced at the clock. "Do you want to take lunch or shall I? It's fried chicken."

"I'd just as soon pass."

Jeanne pinched her lips. "Suit yourself."

"Look, Jeanne, I really am sorry about coming on to Liz." He leaned forward, resting his elbows on his knees.

"Simon Weed will be here tomorrow," she said.

Teddy looked as if he were about to say something else then shrugged. "So I heard."

"And I called about the fence."

Teddy sighed and sat back. He ran his fingers through his hair, acting the role of the beleaguered husband, principal, whatever.

"Adam's been going down to the creek every chance he gets. Edith says there was manure on his shoes, which means he's been visiting Hannah's."

"Tell her to get fifty thousand dollars' worth of chain link fence."

"His mother was a rider. They raised Appaloosas."

"So?"

She would not be drawn into explanations. "The contractor'll be up here next week to measure for an estimate."

"So this is how I pay? I let you drive the school into bankruptcy?"

She laughed, reached back and undid her knotted hair. It fell across her shoulders and she felt something let go inside.

"Do you have any idea how expensive—"

"I don't care what it costs." Jeanne combed her fingers back through her hair and stood up. "I won't let a boy get hurt down there because you're—"

"At least this means I get to sleep in my own bed again, right?"

"There's plenty of room in the house. Use the guest room. No one ever visits us and there's a new mattress on the bed."

"Is this Liz? Has Liz been filling your head—"

"I just know I don't want to go back to the way it was. I can't." She sat beside him on the couch and took his hands. "This is my life, Teddy. The only one I get. And I don't like it." She gestured toward the far wall. "Look."

There was a faint outline above the clock where her forged diploma had hung.

"Wait a minute," Teddy said, instantly on the defensive. "I'm not taking the blame for that thing. I never forced you to quit school."

"You persuaded me to want it for myself."

"That makes it my fault you don't like your life?"

"And you persuaded me to give James away."

"Jesus-fucking-Christ." He started to stand up but Jeanne held him.

"I'm not blaming you, Teddy. Honestly, I'm not." She wanted him to understand this because it was more than important, it was the heart of the whole conversation. "I let you persuade me. The actions were mine and now so are the consequences."

"So are you through with the school? Through with me? Christ, Jeanne, what are you going to do? Sell out to the monks, change your name and join the Peace Corps?"

Her thoughts danced off, distracted by possibilities.

"In case you've forgotten, California's a community property state."

She stood. "I don't know what's going to happen. Maybe this is the end, maybe it's the beginning. How does anyone know these things?"

Hannah stared at the boy and she was sure he stared at her. She scrambled backwards on her knees and rose, brushing the dust from her sweats with one hand. She rinsed the baby bottle in the icy water that had accumulated in the bottom of the cooler. She looked up and saw that the boy had not moved.

Hannah sat in the backseat with Angel cradled in her arms. The baby rejected the nipple at first, tossing her head from side to side. Cold milk dribbled out over her lower lip and got lost in the pleats of flesh under her chin. Hannah wanted to shove the nipple into her mouth and felt instantly ashamed. If Hannah, who had made a study of crack babies and worked with Angel for months, could lose her patience, how much more difficult it would be for Shannon. She concentrated on relaxing and counted her breaths, making them deep and even. Angel began to suck.

Through the space between the front seats Hannah observed the boy. He wore Levi's, a T-shirt and heavy black boots like a biker. She was sure he had moved a little closer to the car. Now she could make out the design on his shirt. A cobra and skulls.

The memory of Billy Phillips, his all-but-forgotten face, blew threw her mind and was gone.

This place is dangerous.

She took the bottle out of Angel's mouth. Her small face pinched and the tears began again. Hannah got out of the car and rested the bottle on the roof against the luggage rack. She strapped Angel in the car seat, closed the door on her tears, rushed around to slam the trunk of the car, took her place behind the wheel and locked her seat belt. In a spray of gravel, she pulled onto the road and drove west, deeper into the hills. She did not look at the boy in the rearview mirror.

She passed a side road, braked, backed up, and peered at the sign. The old Cutter Dam Road would take her up to Mt. Madonna Pass.

"I can get over to the coast this way."

The sound of her calm and sensible voice saying calm, sensible words restored her confidence as it soothed her nerves. She looked at her watch. After noon. By now Betts had probably called the police and alerted the CHP.

"But no one will ever think of looking for us on Cutter Dam Road."

She felt clear-headed and confident again as she reached over to smooth the hair off Angel's damp forehead. If only she would stop crying everything would be perfect. Her screams ricocheted around the interior of the Volvo; the four sides vibrated with neon sound.

At a fork in the road Hannah braked and stopped. The wind was high now and buffeted the car, weighted with leaves and grit and occasional raindrops. The road to the right led back to Rinconada by a circuitous route. Hannah took the narrower left-hand road that wound toward the Mt. Madonna summit. A sign said WATSONVILLE, 48 MILES. Fifty yards later another sign warned of hairpin curves ahead.

At the first wide spot after the second sign, Hannah stopped the car again and got out. She smelled dust and damp and darkness on the cold wind that cut through the weave of her sweat clothes. Around her the coast redwoods rose in stoic dignity. Even on a sunny day the woods would be dark, but today their dim silence held the heavy air in stasis and time hung in weighted suspension. It seemed to Hannah that she had taken a wrong turn from the real world into a shadowy realm. A voice in her head told her *Go back, Go home.*

"I can't. It's too late."

She opened the trunk to get Angel's bottle from the cooler, but it wasn't there. She searched the trunk, she looked under the front and backseats and on the floor. And then she remembered placing it on the roof of the car, wedged snugly against the luggage rack so it would not roll off while she buckled Angel into the car seat. The bottle was on the road somewhere. Perhaps that boy had watched it drop and picked it up out of the dirt. A pink plastic bottle in the shape of a bunny . . .

Hannah got back in the car, into the noise, and reached across Angel to the side pocket in the passenger door where she kept maps bundled together with a rubber band. She sorted through them until she found one for Northern California. After a minute, she located Cutter Dam Road. With her finger she traced it all the way to Watsonville on the coast, hoping to see some other town along the way but knowing that she wouldn't. The south end of the Coast Range was wild as it had been for hundreds of years. A drop of rain hissed as it exploded on the warm hood of the Volvo.

She felt a shiver of relief.

Angel cried louder and threw up on her Snugglies. A line of mucous spread from her nose across her red cheek. The reek of urine and feces filled the car.

I have to think about this.

She could go back to Morgan Hill but the CHP might be watching for her. She had to think of another alternative.

But the noise made it nearly impossible.

Stupid.

That boy had made her run and now everything was getting messy when it should have been easy.

What have I done?

What she had to do.

She slammed her safety belt in place and drove with furious care, hunched over the wheel like an angry little old woman. Her head ached and a sibilant ringing in her ears would not stop. The atmosphere inside the car was thick with the smells of urine and sweat, baby shit and milky vomit. She opened the window again and rain gusted into the car. Her hair, wild about her face, dripped moisture down her cheeks and neck. She cranked the window up halfway and turned on the windshield wipers. She applied her brakes and the Volvo's tires skidded on the oily road.

She thought of her garden soaking up the rain, of the bulbs sighing as they resettled in the damp soil, the eucalyptus, the oaks and

madrones and alders and acacia, the fruit trees and the ornamen-
tals, the olive tree, the line of liquid ambars all quivering with pleasure as the water reached their roots. Rain gave Glory the jitters;
she would run and toss her mane and whinny to the wind and the
poor little donkey would stand still and let the water soak through
its woolly coat. A benediction, that was what the rain was. A sign
that God had put his anger away, that he had turned his head toward them again at long last. She imagined Father Joe standing by
the statue of St. Francis, his arms outstretched, palms up. Rain
meant there would be a spring Hannah could hope for and count
on and plan for.

She thought of planting vegetables and a huge bed of pansies,
Johnny-jump-ups and nasturtiums. She rounded a curve fast, braked
hard; and the Volvo's rear tires slipped and squealed. The ringing
in her ears was the singing in her cells, the song of atoms and elec-
trons vibrating toward critical.

Oh, God, what have I done?

She began to cry.

She would not plant a garden this year.

Near the summit she drove through squalls. The windshield
wipers swooshed back and forth, clicked like a metronome, ticked
like that noisy old clock in Jeanne's office. She swerved to miss a
tree that had fallen across the road. Rain. Tears. Slow down. She
blinked and rubbed the steam off the inside of the window. Put on
the defroster.

Shut up, Angel. For five fucking minutes, shut up.

She must stop. She could not see the road enough to drive. She
must either pull off to the side of the road and wait out the storm—
it would be hours and what about Angel? She was hours beyond
her last feeding. Maybe by now Betts had called Dan and he was
home. The police might be with him asking questions.

I could go to jail.

She had only done what she had to, what she was born and designed to do—care for babies, make them healthy and happy. It
was what she did best, the only thing she knew how to do really
well. Hannah sobbed and beside her, Angel screamed.

A shadow loomed in the road ahead. The second before Hannah
slammed her foot on the brake, she thought of the poster of the lit-

tle girl and the angel in the common room at Resurrection House. She heard the tires shriek and felt the car swing out. The Volvo spun, throwing Hannah's head hard against the door. The last thing she remembered was the screams: Angel's, the tires, and her own.

Liz got caught in the rain and broke all records running back up Casabella Road. She burst into the kitchen, her shorts and T-shirt cold and clinging to her.

"Hannah," she called to the big house, "you home yet? Can I fix you some lunch?" They were going to talk things through if Liz had to tie Hannah down to make it happen. Their friendship would change and it would grow again. *I will plant myself in this house and I won't leave until it's restored.*

She stripped off her wet things and stuck them in the dryer. Padding across the kitchen in bra and panties she told Cherokee, "Looks like it's thee and me, sweet pea."

She went to her room and changed into Levi's and a bulky sweater the blue-green of the water where she and Gerard went scuba diving. In socks and sandals she scuffed back to the kitchen and made herself a tuna fish sandwich and a cup of tea. The phone rang once but when she picked it up the line was dead. While she ate she stood in front of the refrigerator looking at the clutter Hannah kept in place with magnets shaped like animals, vegetables and fruits. She took down the schedule for Eddie's football practice, balled it up and tossed it toward the sink. She read an article about the infertility clinic Dan was running with the help of a local psychologist. There was a note to Ingrid dated the week before: *Clean your room, under the bed too.* The number of the car rental agency was behind a yellow plastic pineapple.

She stared at the number for so long without moving, her foot went to sleep. She remembered the receptionist's voice, nasal and sweet, *You might be more comfortable in a midsize, ma'am.* A syrupy foursquare voice, Hannah would say. Centuries of female rage behind an armor of sugar. If she knew Liz were renting a car to go for an abortion would she refuse her business?

Liz walked around the kitchen until the pins and needles in her foot went away. At Hannah's desk she stopped a minute to look at the framed photos. There was one of Jeanne with pigtails to the middle of her back and her mouth full of shiny braces. Liz remembered her as a bossy and opinionated little girl; but now she must add to the description hurt and scared and trying not to show it. Like heavy weather Jeanne's sadness descended on Liz and she accepted it as if it were part of her own.

Her mind churned. She thought of everything. She thought of nothing specific. She put the picture down, picked up the phone on the desk and called Belize.

Eventually Signa answered. "Dis is Palmetto Guest House. Signa Cassasola speakin'."

"Signa, it's me. Liz."

"Miz Lizbet. How you bin keeping?"

"I'm fine actually. Good. How're you all doing without me?"

"I tol' Mister Gerard, I won' cook no more on dat old Aga stove."

"Bad, huh. What's it doing?"

"What it *not* doing. Las' night oven go way hot, tonight too cold so tomorrow I be makin' my special pork stew for dinner."

Liz imagined Signa watching herself in the mirror as she spoke, preening like one of the peacocks living wild on the grounds of the old governor's mansion. "Is Gerard around?"

"Oh, yes, yes. I fetch him come to the telephone." Liz heard Signa's long musical call and a moment later Gerard's voice floated down through the lines of air and wire and in through her ears and down into the warm pit of her stomach.

"How are you, my Liz? Nothing's wrong? When are you coming back?"

"I'm worried about Hannah. I may need to stay a little longer."

"As long as you must, chérie."

"Signa says the Aga's gone wacko. What about the trouble with the ruins?"

"It goes on. Greed."

"I guess I didn't leave at a good time."

Silence and the sound of Gerard's breath from thousands of miles away.

"I'm glad I came, but it's been hard."

"But you are talking? You and your friends? About what happened?"

"It's been . . . more difficult than I expected." Silence. "I've decided something." And more silence. The sense of his waiting was so strong he seemed to be in the room with her. "I want us to get married."

He laughed.

"I'm not promising I'll be good at it, but I want to try."

"You make me happy, Liz."

"Let's do it soon, okay? But no big deal. Just us."

"And the operation?"

"Day after tomorrow."

"Ah." A single syllable into which she read sorrow and regret and relief and love all at once. "Come home soon, my Liz."

She stared at the photographs on the desk. Jeanne. Dan. Liz and Hannah and Jeanne together. Hannah with Eddie and Ingrid in the big padded rocker, another of the two little ones riding Glory. And half a dozen of herself—timid child, wild teenager, off to Europe with matched luggage—all her incarnations except the one that mattered most. The woman she was now. She thought of Jeanne, her rigid spine bending at last. Her school, her students, and James. She thought of Signa at the airport waving her parasol and looking saucy for the customs officers. And she imagined Gerard in his broad-brimmed hat and his walking shorts and his muscular legs the color of toasted almonds. She saw him holding out his arms. Knowing her and wanting her, the real Liz.

Hannah parked the Volvo at the side of the house and got out. She hobbled around to the passenger door, opened it and looked down at Angel who was asleep at last and unhurt thanks to the restraints on Eddie's old car seat. Hannah barely felt her own injuries though there was a rough scrape on her left temple where it had banged against the car door; and every step sent a spasm of deep pain there and through her back and left shoulder. She gathered the baby into her arms and dashed through the rain for the kitchen door. She slipped her key into the lock, turned it, and realized the door was open.

She had forgotten Liz. Suddenly she felt weak in the face of what was to come, like a prisoner being carted through the crowds to the guillotine.

Liz turned from the kitchen sink and saw her. Across the kitchen the phone rang.

"Don't answer." It would be Betts of course.

"Whose baby . . . is that Angel? Why's she with you?"

A third ring.

In Hannah's arms Angel began to fuss, and her heart-shaped face pinched toward the center like a cushion.

"No matter what, don't pick up."

On the fourth ring the answering machine clicked on.

It was Jeanne. Liz answered. "I think you better get over here." She hung up.

"I told you not to."

"She needs to be here."

Angel wailed.

"She looks sick," Liz said.

Hannah handed Angel, belting out her misery again full volume, to Liz.

"Jesus, Hannah. What's wrong with her?"

"She's hungry. There's formula out in the car and there should be a glass bottle in my vet supplies in the laundry room. Boil the nipple first. Anything else you need's in the car."

She opened the cabinet over her desk. No aspirin. She limped toward the hall.

"You're hurt. What happened?"

Hannah waved her hand dismissively.

The phone rang again.

They looked at it.

Hannah shook her head.

This time it was Dan, laughing. "Can you believe this, Hannah? We've had almost an inch in the last hour. Turn on the Weather Channel. The guy says there's eight storms lined up across the Pacific."

Hannah lifted the receiver. "I'm here." Her voice sounded flat, like a computer generated message to remind her of a doctor's appointment. She made an effort to sound interested. "There's a big washout on Casabella, just before the bridge."

"We're going to have flooding everywhere."

Hannah nodded.

"I thought you'd be excited."

"I am."

"You okay?"

"I'm fine."

"You're sure?"

"Yes."

"You don't need me up there?"

"I said I'm fine, Dan."

"In that case, I'm going to stay in town until it lets up, okay?"

"Sure."

"Typical California, huh? The weather's either perfect or a disaster."

"Uh-huh."

Angel's wails kicked up a level. Hannah waved Liz to the far side of the room.

"That sounds like a baby."

Hannah watched Liz pat and rock and murmur to Angel. Nothing made any difference to a hungry baby.

"Hannah?"

"It's Angel."

A moment of quiet and then, "Shit."

"I thought Betts would have called you."

"I'm still at the hospital." A long moment of silence. "What have you done?"

She laughed. "Oh, God, Dan, I've been really stupid."

"Do you want me to call her? Or do you want to tell me yourself?"

"I'll give you the number. Tell her Angel's safe."

"Why wouldn't she be?"

Hannah turned as Jeanne came through the kitchen door, her hair plastered to her head despite the umbrella she carried. As she rested the open umbrella on the floor on its spokes she looked from Hannah to Liz and Angel and back to Hannah and raised an eyebrow.

"Hannah," Dan said, "why wouldn't Angel be safe?"

Hannah sat down. "I lost it, Dan. I thought I could take her somewhere and get a job and . . . have a . . . life."

"You have a life."

"See, her mother—Shannon—she's so young. She can't . . ."

"Don't go anywhere. Stay put. I'm coming home."

"No, you don't have to. I'm okay. Now. Liz and Jeanne are here and when the rain lets up they'll take me back to San Jose."

"Oh, Hannah." The parched syllables blew through her head like the dust of old bones. "When's this going to stop?"

"It's not a disaster. Don't make it sound like a disaster. I made a mistake but—"

"I'm coming home."

"Please, don't, Dan. I'm . . . too embarrassed to see you. I'm ashamed. Just call Betts for me. Please?" She started to hand the phone to Jeanne. "I love you, I love you so much and I've been such a . . . flake. Don't give up on me. You won't will you? Promise."

"No. Never."

She gave the phone to Jeanne who became instantly efficient. "She's all right, Dan. And so's the baby."

Hannah imagined her husband's voice broken with concern and love and frustration. Breakdown. Kidnapping. Worryworryworry.

"We'll do our best," Jeanne said. She pressed the disconnect. Hannah asked, "Is he coming?"

"Not unless someone calls him."

"Thank goodness, I couldn't stand it." The look on his face, the brokenheartedness.

Angel's screams rose up the scale, louder and shriekier. God, Hannah would be grateful for silence. She took the baby from Liz who looked relieved. "Go get the formula. It's in cans in a grocery bag in the backseat." Amazing how, in the midst of breakdown, kidnapping, worryworryworry she could still assume the role of mother. She should be handcuffed in a squad car; or on the bed, zombied by Valium. Instead she was ordering her friends about for Angel's sake. Mothering. It was her gift. "Jeanne, I need the car seat too."

"Jesus," Jeanne muttered and headed out the door after Liz.

It took ten squalling minutes to get organized, but once Angel had the bottle in her mouth, the silence in the kitchen was profound. Hannah sat in the rocking chair, her feet propped up on the windowsill and looked out at the falling rain. Billowing and cloudy sometimes or lashing the window, other times plumb straight and almost solid like a sheet of aluminum. This was what she had dreamed of. Rain and rocking Angel in her own kitchen.

May as well enjoy. You're going to pay for it.

Hannah felt a hand on her forehead and the touch of a damp cloth.

"You might need stitches," Jeanne said as she dabbed at the wound. "Where's the Bactine or whatever?"

It took a moment to focus. "In the linen closet. Top shelf. Will you bring me some aspirin too?"

She looked up at Jeanne and smiled.

Thank you, she thought, for not asking questions. Thank you for waiting until I can explain. Dan would have talked, but her friends knew when to be quiet. Their silence comforted her.

Liz brought her a glass of orange juice to take the aspirin. Jeanne sprayed Bactine on her forehead and blotted away the drops that rolled down her cheek like tears. Through all of it, Angel sucked contentedly.

After a while Hannah began to explain. "I wanted to take her away and live in a new town, be a new person. A mother again. I thought she wasn't safe without me. That I was her only chance." Angel's dark eyes closed in ecstasy. Cherokee wandered over and sniffed the tiny feet, looked up at Hannah, and then went off into another part of the house.

"I had an accident on Mt. Madonna. There's a housekeeping motel in the Carmel Valley. I was headed there."

"Why didn't you go down 101?"

"Are you sure you don't want Dan?" Liz said. "There could be internal—"

"I'm going to be stiff. That's the worst of it."

"If you'd gone 101 you probably would have made it."

"But I thought maybe Betts had called the police and they'd be looking for the Volvo." Hannah felt herself droop. "I don't know. I'm not cut out to be a crook."

"You need to get some help," Liz said. "When Angel's taken care of. Just talk to someone."

Hannah shook her head. "I need to talk to you two."

"Maybe so, absolutely. But you need to see a therapist too. This isn't going to go away, all these feelings you have."

"Liz's right," Jeanne said. "There are times when . . . well, it's not a sign of weakness to ask for help."

Hannah snarled, "Traitor."

She lifted Angel to her shoulder and patted her back. The baby burped and her little body relaxed. Hannah put her in the car seat with a blanket tucked around her. Her dark lashes fluttered like flags of farewell. Hannah watched her sleep and might have stood a long time staring and memorizing Angel's features if Liz had not touched her arm.

"Sit, Hannah. She's sleeping now."

Hannah did as she was told. She looked around her at all the familiar objects in her kitchen and should have been comforted by them. She had made it home in one piece, somewhat battered but more or less whole. So why wasn't she comforted by familiarity? Because she felt lost, separated from herself. She wasn't Hannah anymore. Hannah had vanished in one extraordinary and incredibly insane afternoon. "When I was coming back, after the accident, it took forever the traffic was so slow. And I just kept asking myself why I'd done it, how I could have been so stupid."

"You aren't stupid," Liz said. "You weren't thinking clearly."

"What made me think I could start all over again? She wore me out, the sound of her. In the car, crying."

The phone rang.

"I wanted to belt her."

The voice on the answering machine was Betts. "We've been frantic down here. But we didn't call the police, Hannah. I knew you'd come back. Dan says you're bringing her back and if she's okay—I'm sure she is, I know you didn't mean her any harm—I'm willing to just let this thing go. But you understand, I can't have you here after this. I can't trust . . . Hannah, I know you're there and I want you to listen to me. You need to get help. That's what I told your husband. There's no shame in it, Hannah." They listened to Betts's breath on the answering machine. "I'll expect to see you when this rain lets up. Okay? I know you're listening to this. Just get Angel back here."

Click.

Silence.

Liz said, "I need a drink."

"Oh, what a dandy idea. Allow me." Jeanne walked into the dining room. Hannah heard her open the door of the wet bar, the sounds of ice cubes and glassware. She returned a moment later with a shaker of Manhattans.

Hannah said, "I haven't had one of those in years."

Liz said, "Remember the time—" and stopped herself.

"I want to give a toast," Jeanne said. She lifted her glass. "To the three of us. Coconspirators. Friends forever. The drunk, the kidnapper and the—" Jeanne looked at Liz. "You still having the abortion?"

Liz nodded.

"What a trio."

Hannah drank the Manhattan fast and held out her glass for another. She watched her hand shaking. Something was growing in her, swelling up inside her, taking her over, filling her head, fattening her up like poor Hansel. She wasn't herself anymore. The hand that shook . . . to whom did it belong?

She laughed.

Liz looked concerned. "Hannah?"

Jeanne poured another drink from the silver shaker. A drop of condensation fell on the back of Hannah's hand and she watched it spread.

"While I was driving, trying not to hear Angel, I started thinking about Billy Phillips."

"You don't have to talk about this now," Jeanne said.

"Yes, she does," Liz said. "Go on."

"You guys don't know what happened." These were the words Hannah had never spoken. This was a new language, terrifying to master. "He didn't die right away." She looked at them. Why weren't they shocked? Well, she'd give them something . . . "And he asked me . . . asked . . ." She closed her eyes and bit her lip, saw him on the rocks, his wet red mouth opening-closing, making the words, begging her. She tasted blood on her tongue and giggled. "I let him. Die."

"Don't be ridic—"

"Shut up, Jeanne." Liz crouched at Hannah's feet and took her hands. "Go on, Hannah."

She couldn't stop giggling, which she knew was crazy and

meant she was wacko, ready for the loony bin because she didn't think it was funny, not the least little bit, so why was she laughing, so why couldn't she stop?

Liz squeezed into the chair beside her and wrapped her arms around her.

Laughing now, crying a bit, laughing, crying. Sobs scraping the back of her throat like a dry shave. Hiccupping. "That's it. I let him die. The same as if . . ." Right behind the sobs, a burning gagging sweetness, ". . . as if I killed him on purpose."

"It's not the same," Liz said. "You were a frightened little girl and you did the only thing you knew to do."

Swallowing down the bile, the tears, shaking her head, speaking through her hands clamped across her mouth. "I knew . . . but I couldn't . . . stand to look at him."

Jeanne sank into a chair and muttered, "All these years."

Hannah rested her head on Liz's shoulder. She heard Jeanne start to say something else and Liz's irritated shush. The rain blew against the patio windows, waves of it driven by the wind. She imagined the trees in the wildwood thrashing and whipping against each other and the rush and swirl of the Bluegang waters. Over the pebbled shallows and around the boulders, the flood cutting out the soil under the roots of the oak saddle. One day the soil would give way, the roots would lift and the great tree would fall and turn to dust. But the boulder where Billy Phillips lay would remain and bear in its molecules forever the memory of his blood. The kitchen clock clicked over the seconds. Angel snuffled in her sleep and Cherokee came back into the room and rested her head on Hannah's knee and gazed at her woefully.

Sicko. Wacko. *Looney Tunes.* Hannah didn't think she was any of those things but she supposed she would have to find out now. Dan wouldn't let her get through this experience without dragging her off to some kind of shrink. After the accident, with the Volvo facing into the embankment, a front fender deeply dented and rubbing against the tire, one headlight broken, all she could think of was to pray. *God get me through this and I'll do anything.* A child's prayer, a frightened child's promise. But she supposed she would have to keep it now. She tried to imagine herself talking to a stranger about Bluegang and Angel. She could do it, supposed she would do it if forced.

Hannah knew Dan so well, knew exactly what he would say. *This isn't all about you anymore, Hannah. It's us too. And the kids. Our life together. If you want us to have one, you'll do this.*

She stood unsteadily and walked to where Angel lay in Eddie's old car seat, fast asleep. Scrawny, Shannon had said and Hannah saw it now too. She watched the trembling of the tissue eyelids, the sucking movement of her lips.

"She's dreaming of food," Hannah said. The Manhattans made her head spin.

Jeanne and Liz came and stood beside her and together they watched Angel sleep and after a moment Hannah began to cry and in the silence, she reached for her friends' hands.

Thursday

L iz woke to rain and a silent house. The clock beside her bed glowed: 8:15. Not for years had she slept so late but then she hadn't had many days like yesterday either. The urgency, the excitement, the crying and laughing. It was like being in high school again. No wonder they had all been so eager to grow up.

Hannah, Jeanne and Liz had sat in the kitchen all afternoon until around five when the rain eased off—no blue in the sky, just a break between storms. Jeanne made more Manhattans and Liz, seeing that no one would be sober enough to drive Hannah and Angel back to San Jose, switched to coffee. They turned on the Weather Channel and a pregnant broadcaster with a broad Midwestern accent showed them the radar picture of storms queued up over the Pacific, one after the other like women waiting for a stall in a public bathroom.

During the calm Jeanne had run up to the school for her car and they all piled in with Angel and Hannah in the backseat, Liz driving. Just beyond the Rinconada town limits the rain began again, harder and colder than before. They made it onto the freeway, but there the forward progress halted. Branches of trees from the suburban yards behind the freeway buffer walls littered the six-lane freeway, and in low places storm sewers had overflowed into lakes several inches deep. Cars and utility vehicles, even trucks and a school bus were stopped on the shoulders, and between Lark Avenue and Curtner they encountered half a dozen accidents. The lights of police and paramedics swam through the rain like red-eyed fish. Traffic lined up behind the accidents and rubber-neckers stalled and inched forward. Liz felt like she was in a civil defense movie demonstrating what not to do in an emergency.

They didn't talk. What would they say even if they had been able to hear themselves over the tattoo of rain on the roof of Jeanne's Mercedes? They were friends and they knew enough to keep quiet.

At Resurrection House finally, Liz asked, "Do you want me to come in with you?"

Hannah said no. "Park somewhere. Across the street. You can make a U-turn. This may take a while."

Liz did as she was told. It was cold in the car and the windows steamed up. Jeanne retrieved from the trunk an ancient army blanket frayed at the edges. Liz remembered Gerard that night on the way back to Paris, the tenderness with which he had tucked the blanket around his sleeping father. She and Jeanne climbed into the backseat and wrapped themselves in the old blanket. The car reeked of sweet bourbon breath. Half an hour later Hannah ran across the street, dodging fallen branches and crashed into the backseat with them.

"Will somebody please just drive?"

Liz's body ached from the continual tension of yesterday. She got out of bed and stretched for a few minutes, but the best way she knew to get the kinks out was exercise. She ran in the rain in Belize all the time. She supposed she could do it in Rinconada too so she dressed in tights and shorts and a double layer of shirts. In the hall closet she found a short snug slicker and a hat belonging to Dan. She carried these into the kitchen. On the counter she found a note written in thick Magic Marker, held in place by a framed photo of herself aged twenty.

Guess where Dan's taken me? Fuck it. Dinner you, me, Jeanne, alone.

The signature was Francis Scott Key. Liz thought that was a good sign.

She made a cappuccino and spread Hannah's homemade plum jam on a toasted English muffin. Even in tights, her legs were cold, her thighs especially. She checked the thermostat and upped it to seventy-five and in the cupboard under the window seat she found a wool throw and wrapped it around her and settled into the rocking chair to eat her breakfast.

Dan had been home when they returned from Resurrection House. When she saw his car Hannah had said only "Shit." Jeanne had dropped them off. As they ran for the door Liz heard the grind of the Mercedes' big tires grabbing for traction on the wet gravel and she imagined Jeanne was glad to get away. Dan and Eddie looked up from a dinner of eggs and bacon eaten at the counter.

"Ingrid's staying over at Paco's," Dan said. "And yes, his parents are home."

Hannah nodded. To Liz her smile looked tentative.

"Where were you, Ma? You think the bridge'll go?"

"I don't know, maybe. It's made it through other storms."

"If it washes out do I have to go to school?"

"I'll take you up Overlook when I go to the hospital," Dan said.

"The guy on the TV said this is the worst storm in fifty years."

Hannah nodded.

"Where were you, Ma?"

Liz wondered now, as she watched the rain and drank her coffee, how much of the story Eddie would learn. In time, all of it probably. Ingrid too. Family secrets sifted down through the cracks in the silence, slowly reconstructed themselves a few degrees further from the truth. Would Eddie think his mother was loony? Liz imagined he would be sympathetic in a male sort of way. Ingrid less so. Her mother's crackup would anger and frighten her—as Liz's decision to have an abortion had done. But years from now she might understand both events. She would get how one day a switch went off in Hannah's brain and she went crazy—not forever but suddenly and brilliantly like fireworks splashing the sky in the middle of an empty night.

Liz carried her cup and plate to the sink. She pulled the rain hat down over her head, zipped the slicker to the throat and peered outside. Cherokee padded up and stood beside her.

"Not you, girl."

Only knowing how good she would feel afterwards made Liz step into the storm and pull the door behind her.

She ran down Casabella Road, over the Bluegang bridge, which might not hold if the rain continued to wash away the soil under the piers but looked safe enough for the time being. The road was awash and in minutes her feet were wet through the socks. She splashed for the pleasure of it and once her muscles had begun to warm up she enjoyed jumping the litter in the street, the rubble and fallen branches. On the ridge the elegant Victorians hunkered down glumly. She waved to a woman tying down an outside awning and a dog barked at her from the protection of a front veranda. She splashed down Queen Victoria's Hill and saw another woman running on the road ahead of her in navy blue spandex tights and hooded jacket. Her form was good: her torso upright, shoulders relaxed and arms pumping close to her sides. She ran across the street and up the front steps of a house. Liz saw that it was Mitzi Sandler and the house was hers. Under cover of the veranda, Mitzi turned. Liz waved and Mitzi lifted her arm and gestured for Liz to come up on the porch. Liz crossed the street and took the steps two at a time.

"I thought I was the only maniac around here," Mitzi said.

"I like to run in the rain."

"Me too. Reminds me of back East." She opened the screen door. "Want to come in? I've got something to show you."

"I don't want to get cold."

"I'll give you a jacket." She looked at Liz. "And a hair dryer."

"I'm in kind of a rush." Liz looked at her watch and thought about her appointment with Dr. Reed Wallace in two hours. "I've got a doctor's appointment."

"Just come in for a minute. I've been hoping I'd see you." Mitzi Sandler turned and headed down the hall toward the back of the house. She opened a cupboard door and handed Liz a red towel. She stood a moment vigorously drying her hair with a blue one.

The house was nothing like Liz remembered it. Her parents' dark old Oriental carpets had been replaced with bright area rugs in geometric designs. The walls were painted in trendy shades of grape and burnt orange; the butler's pantry, just glimpsed, was now a deep rose.

"We went mad with color," Mitzi said. "The folks who bought it after your mom and dad had everything white. It was horrible.

Like a hospital." She opened the basement door. "One reason we bought this house was the basement. During the Loma Prieta earthquake the houses on either side slipped off their foundations but this old girl held solid."

Liz's father had predicted that would happen someday. She wished she could tell him he had been right.

Mitzi opened the basement door and turned on the light switch. "Watch your step. We haven't replaced these stairs yet."

"It had a dirt floor when my parents bought the house." Liz recalled being told that her father had laid the cement floor himself.

"That's what I figured. We were down here with the contractor when we found it."

"Found what?"

Mitzi laughed. "You're going to love this."

Liz could not imagine loving anything in the basement. It was a part of the house she had always avoided.

"We're going to put in a rec room for the kids so we had a contractor over to look at the place yesterday." Mitzi flipped another light switch illuminating a large empty room. Cement walls and floor. No windows. Liz wished she hadn't accepted Mitzi Sandler's invitation. She was cold and felt her thighs tightening.

"This room was full of old stuff from when we moved in years ago, but we had to clear it out so the contractor could see what he had to work with. The whole room, you know?" In the corner she bent down and gestured for Liz to do the same. "Look at what we found."

It was a footprint less than six inches long and beside it, a handprint small and finger-splayed.

Mitzi looked at her expectantly. "Read what it says."

Neatly printed in the cement beside the foot- and handprints in a style Liz recognized as her mother's, were the words *Our Precious Liz, aged two.*

The three friends met for dinner Thursday night at Capretti's, the only family-style Italian restaurant left in Rinconada. Jeanne remembered being taken there by Hannah and her parents to celebrate her eleventh or twelfth birthday and again when she was fifteen and had won a coveted speech and drama prize. It was the sort of place her own parents never went; come to think of it, she could not remember them ever dining out as a family. Certainly not in a restaurant where waiters in spaghetti-spattered aprons yelled to the cook across the small dining room in rapid-fire Sicilian and Calabrian dialects. At Jeanne's house mealtime was a linen, silver and china, silent affair. By dinnertime her father had been nipping at the bottle all day and was virtually comatose, shoveling food in and swallowing it down by kinetic memory while Jeanne's mother, seething silently, sipped her own drink and said nothing. Jeanne would happily have eaten anytime, anywhere with Hannah's family, but Capretti's held especially warm associations for her. On her birthday Hannah's father ordered a pizza the size of a car tire and the waiter kept refilling the pitcher of root beer and telling her to *mange, mange.*

The restaurant was located where it had been for forty years, in a long narrow space between the Rinconada movie theater—an art house now, of course—and a bar called the Black Watch, another holdover from the days before boutiques and high-end import shops lined Santa Cruz Avenue. These days Capretti's required reservations every night of the week. Hannah had asked especially for one of two tables snugged in the bay windows on either side of the entrance.

A good spot, Jeanne thought. The distraction of the passing parade might make what she had to say easier. Then again, maybe lightning would strike one of the trees lining Santa Cruz Avenue and cut the dinner short. She'd never have to tell Hannah the truth.

"How are you?" she asked Liz after she had ordered a martini up.

"Dilated. He inserted some kind of thing."

"Can you feel it?"

"If I try."

Jeanne sipped her drink. "Well, I've been thinking and I realize I can't let you go to that place on your own. I'll drive you."

"You don't have to," Liz said. "I rented a very snazzy little Mustang. We drove it down here tonight."

"But tomorrow you're not going to feel like driving," Hannah said.

"It's settled, then," Jeanne said. "We'll both go with you."

Liz sat back, looking shocked. "I thought you guys didn't approve."

"I don't," Hannah and Jeanne said, in unison. They laughed. "Then why? . . ."

"Because," Jeanne said, "when all's said and done— It's your body. I don't approve, but . . . shit, Lizzie, you're my friend. It's your choice. I won't deny you that."

"What about you, Hannah?" Liz asked.

"Well, I agree, of course. Except . . ." Hannah lifted her glass and stared through the ruby liquid at the flickering candle at the center of the table. "If I could just understand why . . . To me being a mother's the most wonderful . . ." Her voice faded to a deep sigh. "I guess that's not entirely true. Maybe."

Jeanne and Liz listened without interrupting as Hannah told them about her first session with the therapist in Dan's building.

"It's the most peculiar experience. Actually, I think I may get to like it. I started opening my mouth and talking and it seemed pretty simple, kind of nice to have someone listen to me talk for an hour. But after we got through the easy stuff and she asked me to tell her what I felt—about families and babies and all—nothing I said made very much sense. I felt like I was babbling."

Jeanne did not say what she was thinking, that therapy and therapists were for the weak-minded and undisciplined. This had been her father's opinion, seconded by her mother and since the events of the last week, Jeanne wasn't sure she believed it anymore. It worried her to think she had taken the opinion on without examining it. What else did she only *think* she believed?

"She's so young," Hannah said. "I almost walked out when she opened her door and there she was in her size six Ann Taylor suit, not a line on her face. Gorgeous fingernails. And she doesn't have kids. I asked her that right away. So how can she understand someone like me?"

Hannah described feeling awkward at the start of the therapy hour; for the first time in twenty years she had wanted a cigarette, a whole pack of Marlboros to hang on to. Jeanne knew just what she meant. Gradually, however, she had relaxed and started gabbing about Angel.

"And then—I don't know how it happened but I kind of segued into Eddie and Billy Phillips and Bluegang."

She leaned forward. "I amazed myself, all the details I remembered. I've been hoarding that memory inside, whole, all these years."

"What a surprise," Liz said.

"Did you cry?" Jeanne imagined Hannah bawling inconsolably.

"Not much really. Which when you think about it is also weird except I feel cried out, you know?" Hannah poured more wine for herself. "Last night Dan and I stayed up talking, that's when I cried. Did we keep you awake, Liz?"

"Dan gave me a pill. I was out in five minutes."

Lucky Liz. Jeanne had been on-and-off awake most of the night. The wind drove the rain against the bedroom window in sweeps and though the bed was warm, she was cold, missing Teddy's warm bulk in the bed beside her, wondering if he was asleep, wondering what James was doing. What did her boy dream of? What did he long for, what did he fear?

"What I think is I've been trying to save Billy Phillips all my life," Hannah said. "I love Angel but more than anything I think she's been a way to assuage my guilt." Hannah colored. "Does that make sense? Tamara—the therapist—said it does."

Liz said, "And I think when you look at Eddie—"

"I know, I know." Hannah's eyes filled with tears. "I'm so ashamed."

That morning Hannah had stopped Eddie on his way out the door with Dan. The bridge over Bluegang had not gone down but the way was blocked on both sides by black-and-yellow striped sawhorses with blinking orange warning lights. The only way into town was up the Overlook pass, a tortuously narrow and twisting county road.

She described the conversation to Jeanne and Liz.

"I'll drive you, Eddie," she said. "Go ahead, Dan."

Eddie had looked wary, like a half-savvy animal being baited to a trap.

"Please, Eddie." *We need to talk.* If she said that he'd take off running. "It doesn't matter if you're late."

"I'll take your car," Dan said. "Drop it off at the garage. I'll get you a rental and come back for your appointment."

"We could skip it," she said, before she could stop herself.

Dan laughed and shook his head. "One-thirty, Hannah. Your appointment's at two."

"What about me?" Eddie wailed. "What about school?"

"You stay, son. You need to talk to your mom."

"Shit." Eddie flung himself onto a chair and stared sullenly out the window.

In the middle of the night it rained hard and the windblown drops had sounded like pellets thrown against the house, but in the morning it fell softly and steadily and the drops seemed to weigh barely enough to answer the pull of gravity. It was the kind of rain that would soak in deep and do the most good, Hannah had thought as she stood behind Eddie's chair looking at the barn and paddock, the bedraggled line of the wildwood edging the slope down to Bluegang. If she could just get through the winter, in the spring there would be green everywhere, the tender chartreuse of new growth that always lifted her heart with hope. She told herself that she must cling to the promise of hope even if it was purely intellectual at this point.

Several moments must have passed. When Eddie spoke his irritation did not completely conceal the alarm in his voice.

"What is it, Mom? How come you got me sitting here? It's almost first period. I'll miss—"

"This is more important," Hannah said.

"What'd I do now?"

"Nothing. Don't be frightened."

"Who said I—"

"I'm not angry with you. You've done nothing wrong." She swallowed. "It's me. I've done something wrong."

He scratched his head. "Is this about what happened yesterday?"

Hannah told Jeanne and Liz, "I was sitting on the windowsill facing him. The old casings let in a draft that found the space between my wool sweater and the waist of my jeans, but I didn't want to get up for a jacket or to bring a chair around for fear of losing Eddie's attention." So she stayed where she was.

She said to her son, "You know how I never let you play at Bluegang? You did, of course, I couldn't really stop you."

"It wasn't just me, Mom." He was on the defensive immediately. "Ingrid used to go down there and take sunbaths on the rocks. Her and Margaret."

"I didn't know."

"There's lots of stuff you don't know, Mom. When I was little they used to pay me not to tell on them." The idea that this conversation might be about Ingrid and not him appeared to lift Eddie's spirits.

Hannah said, "I told you not to go down there because I wanted to protect you." The only way to tell the story was to leap into the middle of it, heart first. Make a big splash and get his attention. "Something terrible happened to me down there."

Liz said, "You told him?"

"Everything," Hannah said.

She told him about Billy Phillips and the day when there were no new polio cases and the town pool opened for business, leaving Bluegang Creek to the crawdads and crows and a twelve-year-old girl with her shirt tied around her midriff like Debra Paget. Eddie fidgeted at first but her story captured him and he soon grew still.

"He died?"

She nodded.

"He attacked you. It was self-defense."

"Maybe. But the thing is, the bad thing is, I could have helped him but I didn't . . ."

"You were scared. Who wouldn't be? You were a little kid."

She nodded again and waited for the next, the inevitable question.

"So, what'd you do?"

She took his hand, turned it and stared down at the hair sprouting on the backs of his fingers. A man's hands soon. But she wouldn't think about that. She would think about it when she saw Tamara again. "We went home."

He looked at her.

"And until now, we never told anyone."

He looked down at her hand holding his. "God, Mom. You let him just lie there?"

And if she hadn't? If she had run home and told her parents and her mother had called an ambulance and her father had gone next door to see Mrs. Phillips, what would have changed in her life? She probably would have gone to Stanford, met Dan and married him. They might not have bought this house, but then again, it was such a lovely house and she liked being near Hilltop. So nothing major would have changed but in the deep core of her where the guilt and shame had taken hold and produced their poison, she would have been fundamentally different.

"It was wrong, awfully wrong, but I just . . . let him . . . lie there."

He could look at her again, she was grateful for that. And there were tears in his eyes.

"You were scared. I would've been too. I probably would've done the same thing."

She blessed his generous, forgiving heart, his innocent and uncomplicated view of the world.

"I've been unfair to you, Eddie."

"No way, Mom."

"I looked at you and saw that boy. I didn't know that's what I was doing but it was and after a while," her voice faltered and she tightened her hold on his hand to steady herself, "after a while I stopped looking at you at all."

He was embarrassed now and wanting to get away.

"All that football stuff . . . I made you up, in my mind." She smoothed back his hair and rested her hand against his cheek, turning his face so their eyes could meet and hold. "I made you up instead of seeing my very own, real-life, beautiful boy."

Jeanne listened as Hannah talked about Dan and Tamara and Eddie and what might lie ahead for them. Thoughts of her own son in Berkeley distracted her. She wondered what to do about him. She nodded absently when Hannah asked her if she wanted the night's specialty, canneloni. The waiter took her martini glass and filled her wineglass, went away and in a moment returned with a wooden salad bowl.

Jeanne watched Liz and Hannah serve themselves. She took a breath, held it a minute and said, "There's something I have to tell you, Hannah." She forced herself to look right at her, not to blink, not to glance away.

Hannah looked up from her salad, her fork holding a tomato wedge in midair.

"I took your underpants."

"Jesus," Liz muttered and ripped a slice of sourdough bread in half. "It never ends."

"If you don't want to listen—" Jeanne snapped.

"It's not that. It just . . . it never ends."

Hannah said, "I always suspected you had them."

Liz said, "How could you do that and then never tell her? Let her worry all her life?"

Jeanne speared a lettuce leaf and looked at it. She wished Liz would just be quiet and let her tell the story her own way. Liz had come from Belize demanding disclosures and confessions and seemed to think this had earned her a superior moral position, at least the right to orchestrate the revelations. As if they had not all been at the creek that day.

"You want me to be quiet," Liz said, reading Jeanne's thoughts. "You want me to act like *oh, this is just more business as usual.* Well, Jeanne, I don't just shut up and follow the leader anymore."

Jeanne stared at her.

"Okay, okay," Hannah said, waving her fork still bearing the tomato wedge. "We've all changed, inside and out. Let's agree to that, okay? And get on with what happened to my panties. I can't believe you did that to me, Jeanne. Why would you be so mean?"

Jeanne shrugged. "I couldn't sleep, the night after. I kept thinking we'd forgotten something, a clue that would lead the police to us. And then I remembered you said Billy had your underpants and I remembered how your mom used to write your name on the elastic with a laundry pen. I wanted to protect you."

"Thank you so very much," Hannah said acidly. "For saving my reputation. All these years I thought some boy from Hilltop was going to blackmail me. One day there'd be a knock on the door . . ." She stopped. "No, that's not true. After the first few days, I knew it was you. But I was afraid to confront you."

"I meant to tell but then I knew you were upset and I sort of . . . liked that."

Would Hannah forgive her for enjoying the tiny illusion of

power those secret panties gave her? Where were they now? Hidden in some box of mementos along with other things she'd taken over the years: her mother's checkbook dated 1954, her father's favorite cuff links. She could still hear him storming through the house, raging at the housekeeper, accusing her of theft. And she remembered the feeling that gave her. Pity for the maid, a university-educated refugee glad for a job while she waited for her documents to clear. Excitement. Strength. Power.

"I was a kid with no control over anything."

"No kid has any control," Liz said. "That's why they call them kids."

Jeanne cocked an eyebrow at her. "I'm not excusing what I did—you're right, Liz, it was mean—but this is the only explanation I've got. So do you want to hear it or not?"

Liz sighed. "I know, I know."

"My mother and father were drunks. My brother died in a freak accident. When I was a kid I felt like my life could just spin out of orbit at any given moment and I was hanging on for dear life. Knowing where those panties were made me feel like I had a little power. Over something. Someone."

"It doesn't matter anymore," Hannah said.

"I still take things sometimes." Jeanne couldn't help grinning. "When I'm mad at Teddy."

Liz laughed. "You just redeemed yourself, old girl."

"I don't want any more talk about me going to a therapist," Hannah said. "You're as sick as I am."

Liz said, "We're all sick."

"Omigod," Hannah said, "the voice of authority."

"As it happens, I am. This is all I've thought about for the last year."

"And so you came here to force us to think about it too. I hope you're satisfied."

Liz nodded.

Hannah looked at Jeanne. "What about you? Is it all out now?"

Jeanne nodded slowly, asking herself: How do I feel? Not shamed or humiliated as she had always expected. The only word that came to her mind was *empty*. At first this made her unhappy and then she saw that it was good. To be empty was to be ready—for change, a fresh start or a new take on a bad start. She held up her glass in a toast. "To us—"

"Battle, Murder and Sudden Death," Hannah said.

"—We survived."

It was after ten when Jeanne parked the car and walked to the house through the oleander hedge. The rain had stopped and patches of star-studded night sky were visible between the clouds. The cold night smelled sharp and tangy. She opened the patio door and stepped into the kitchen. Teddy surprised her, standing in the dark, wearing his blue satin pajamas.

"I thought you'd be asleep," she said.

"I wanted some juice." He opened the refrigerator. "How 'bout you? Orange? Cran-grape?"

She didn't think juice would mix well with martinis and wine. She'd had too much to drink again. This was something she was going to have to worry about eventually, but not now; she thought she might need liquor for a little while longer.

"A bottle of water."

"Such restraint. I am impressed." He handed her a cold plastic bottle. She handed it back to him and he tore off the plastic seal.

Jeanne sat down and gestured to the chair across the old wooden table. "I think we should talk a while."

She hadn't planned or practiced a speech. She just knew there was something important that had to be said.

"I know where James lives. I've seen him."

"You've talked."

"No. But I'm going to." She looked at Teddy and in the un-lighted room she could not read the subtleties of expression that would have given her a clue to his thinking. She had to ask him, "Well? What do you think?"

He breathed deeply. "I think you'll be sorry. I think you can't go back."

"This isn't about going back. It's about moving forward. In my life."

"Sounds selfish to me. What about him? I think you'll be sorry."

"Why?"

He leaned forward, resting his arms on the scarred tabletop. "You can't just turn yourself into his mother, just like that, because you've got some menopausal last chance panic. He already has a mother. He's a man now and he's lived his whole life without you. Why would he want you?" He meant to hurt her and he was on target.

"Aren't you even a little curious?" she asked when she could speak evenly.

Teddy shrugged.

"I know why."

"Why what?"

"Why you have a son and you don't care."

"And now you're going to tell me."

"You're the only one who interests you, Teddy. No one else really matters."

"I don't think that's fair."

"But it's true. And I . . ." She stared out the window at the rushing sky that was almost clear now. ". . . I don't want to be around a man who isn't interested in me." A thought struck her. "Were you ever, Teddy? Interested in me?"

He opened his mouth and closed it. She made out the creases in his forehead, the two indentations between his eyes.

If she waited long enough, he'd say he loved her. Experience had taught him this worked to bring her around when she was out of sorts. And maybe he would mean it. Teddy's version of love might be one of the more peculiar varieties: Here today, gone yesterday and the year before, but from this day forward constant as seasons and school bells. More likely, if he said he loved her it was because he didn't want to think about changing his life. She didn't want to think about it either. Separating, divorcing, selling the school, keeping the school: it flattened her to think of the consequences that might arise from this conversation.

"I think we ought to try again," he said. "We've built something fine here, Jeanne. Hilltop is an excellent school."

She nodded, vaguely impressed that he had resisted saying what he did not mean.

"But it's taken both of us to build it. If you tried to run it alone . . ."

"I might sell it. There are those Tibetan monks."

He snorted. "And what would you do then?"

She shrugged. "I don't know. Maybe marry Simon Weed." Even in the twilight she saw his incredulous expression. It made her laugh. "Don't worry, Teddy, I haven't been coming on to him. But astonishing though it may seem, someday, someone might actually want me."

"Give me a chance. You owe me that."

She didn't owe him a damn thing. If she stayed with Teddy it would have to be for herself. She had given him more than twenty years of submission borne of her fear that he would abandon her if she did not please him. So now what? Should she see what would happen if she were no longer cowed and submissive? How would Teddy react to a new Jeanne?

"Will you come with me to meet James?"

He answered quickly. "No. I can't do that."

"What about after, when he knows why we gave him up. If he wants to meet you?"

Teddy put his elbows on the table and pressed the heels of his hands into his eye sockets. "Maybe. I don't know, Jeanne. I don't know."

She looked at him and all at once she knew, without his ever saying it, that Teddy was ashamed, that like her, he had grieved for the loss of their boy. And like her he was proud and ambitious and determined to make a good life. She felt pity for Teddy because it was dawning on him—slowly, to be sure, but consider the size of ego the light had to penetrate—that he wasn't going to get through life well groomed and unscathed. Like her, like Hannah and Liz, the mistakes made were not the kind that could be ignored forever. Eventually, truth broke through and when it did it burned. Her instinct—or habit?—was to comfort and assure him that she understood and everything would work out fine. But she made herself stay in the chair.

Things would work out, she was positive about that. But how or in what way particularly, she could not guess.

Dan put his arms around Hannah and spooned her into him. "How'd it go today?"

Hannah felt like knifing her elbow into his ribs. Reason and love prevailed, however, and she relaxed against him.

"You mean with Tam-a-ra?"

Dan chuckled, puffing his warm breath against the back of her neck.

"She seems okay."

"I want you to know, Hannah, what goes on in her office, it's just between the two of you."

"Got it."

"But—" he paused dramatically.

"Yes?"

"Did she tell you? Are you crazy?"

This time she did jab him and he rolled away laughing. She pushed him onto his back and lay across him. "I am not only crazy, Dan, I am dangerous. A menace."

"Well, I knew that already." He pulled her head down to his and kissed her. His lips and tongue tasted of toothpaste and his skin smelled of the herbal soap he showered with.

How could I have wanted to give this up?

She felt him harden against her and she slid down to take him in her mouth. As she did she heard the sounds of her small world settling in for the night. The drip of water from the gutters, the occasional gust of wind brushing the olive trees against the house. From Ingrid's room the sound of music, electronic bings and bangs from Eddie's. At the edge of the wildwood an orphan dog barked and far down Casabella Road the Millers' beagle bugled back.

She raised her head. "I love you, Dan. I love our life. We're going to be okay, aren't we?"

He groaned and knotted his hands in her hair. "Ask me that in fifteen minutes. I'm having trouble concentrating."

She didn't have to ask him, she knew the answer for herself. And she knew why.

Thank you, Liz. For being brave. For coming home.

Florida

Unexpectedly Gerard was waiting for her at the airport in Miami. As Liz came through the door from the transfer vehicle into the chaotic terminal she was thinking of him and there he suddenly was as if she had conjured him. Wearing a blue work shirt and shorts, he leaned against a concrete pillar, his muscled brown legs crossed at the ankle. He was looking down at a book open in his hand and didn't see her right away. She stopped to admire him—the obvious strength and power in his body, the large head and slightly shaggy salt-and-pepper hair. She stood still and enjoyed the moment of anticipation, irritating the tourists and travelers surging up the ramp behind her.

"What are you doing here?"

"The Aga." He took her carry-on bag.

His resigned shrug, the pleased expression that tilted his mouth and crinkled his eyes, the kiss aimed for her cheek but jostled to her earlobe by the crowd, blended with the sights and smells and distinctive South Florida sound of the airport, and lifted Liz almost off her feet with happiness and relief. She looked around her like a tourist, saw everything from the signs advertising rum and condominiums and the Dolphins to the bright shirts and dresses of the crowd as if for the first time. The music, the Latin beat that was everywhere in the background in Miami: Liz grabbed Gerard's hand, spun out a little and twirled. She didn't like Miami and she particularly didn't like any airport anywhere, but today it all felt like home.

"What happened?" she asked as they hurried through the crowd.

"Who can say? The thermostat, I think."

Liz laughed. "Bet Signa was unhappy. What'd you do?"

"Mariscos from Timothy's. Barbecue."

"Can it be fixed?"

He shook his head.

"You bought a new stove?"

He nodded, smiling a little. "Red Wolf."

"Omigod, that's fabulous." She stopped in the middle of the crowded terminal. "But how can we afford it? They cost thousands. We'll have to postpone screening in the porch."

"Maybe yes. Maybe no." He put his hand on her elbow and they walked again.

Liz thought how amazing it was. They were walking through the Miami airport talking as if no time had passed, as if her whole take on life had not undergone a profound shift in the last week.

She stopped again, opposite a bathroom. "Be right back."

It was a long narrow bathroom tiled in aquamarine with black sinks and a large mirror on one side, a dozen stalls opposite and at the end a fold-down table. When Liz came out of the stall a young Hispanic woman, fat but pretty in a bright tight dress, came in carrying an infant against her, pushing a little girl in a stroller and talking in scolding tones to a toddler in a T-shirt, diaper, and miniature Nikes. She laid the smallest on the changing table and while she dug for a diaper in a red-and-white canvas bag the girl in the stroller banged something metallic on the stroller tray and the toddler ran from stall to stall flushing the toilets. His mother snapped at him and he ignored her. The girl in the stroller banged louder and began to cry. The mother yelled at the boy and he ran the length of the bathroom, arms out at his side, banging on the stall doors and making what Liz assumed was an airplane sound.

Liz stood at the sink, washing her hands, watching the scene in the mirror. As she turned to dry her hands, the boy streaked across the narrow room, his mother yelled a stream of Spanish, he spun around and careened into the back of Liz's legs. She bent like the flap of a cardboard box and dropped to her knees, on the way down hitting her chin on the edge of the sink. She cried out, and the boy leaped back and began to wail and ran to his mother, hiding behind her. A woman towing another toddler walked in, noted the racket, turned around and left. Liz pulled herself to her feet and blinked at her reflection. There was blood on her lips.

The young mother asked in heavily accented English, "You okay, lady?"

Liz looked at her and nodded, smiled, and then, confusing both of them, she began to sob.

The mother's face reddened and she began to speak Spanish too fast for Liz to understand. She yelled at the little boy and his cries joined the racket.

Liz waved away the distressed mother. For some reason, she couldn't remember a word of Spanish. "Your children . . . take care of them. I'm fine. Fine." It occurred to her that she should be embarrassed leaning against an airport bathroom wall, bawling like a toddler. But she wasn't.

This was what had been put aside, postponed; this was what she had not done and had to do before she could move on.

Eventually the mother and her children left with the boy hanging on to his mother's hand, sniffling and craning his neck around to stare at Liz until he turned the corner. She wet a paper towel and applied it to her eyes. Blew her nose and smiled at the blurred mess that was her face.

When she left the bathroom Gerard was across the concourse leaning against a window, reading again. He looked up and saw her and his face creased with concern.

"What has happened. Are you ill, my Liz?"

"Can we sit down and talk?" She wanted to tell Gerard everything and then get on with life. "I'm not sick. I just need to talk now. I don't want to wait."

"Of course," he said without much enthusiasm. They walked across the flow of the crowd to a row of plastic seats under a window. Gerard drew her down beside him. "The abortion, Liz, tell me. Was it so difficult?"

Thousands of feet over the Bible Belt she had wondered why it was so often difficult to tell the truth. She was a translator sensitive to the nuances of words; but the language of feelings defied her and if she could avoid using it, she knew she would. So now, while it was in her mind to speak, she must make herself do it before the inclination passed. While the impulse was upon her and before the memory faded, in a crowded airport with a thousand people passing only a few feet from them.

Gerard narrowed his eyes and tilted his head toward her. "You changed your mind?"

"If you mean about the abortion, no. I didn't. I am no longer pregnant. But in a way the trip did change my mind. When I went up there, I knew I didn't want to have a baby because I was positive I'd make a mess of it. *Merde.*" Without thinking, she began to speak in French. Her story came more easily in the language that was not fully her own. The inherent formality of French and the reflexive voice put a little distance between her words and their content. In French, the words and the feelings behind them seemed manageable and less confrontational. All this might be a mind game but it didn't really matter because at least she was talking now, telling all before she began to forget. Her memory of what had happened in Rinconada would sift down into the storehouse that held not only Bluegang but Mario and Gail and Willy, Brittany and Avignon and the apartment overlooking the Luxembourg Gardens. It would become part of what made her in the same way sunlight and water and soil mixed and became trees and drew down water and were the lungs, the life and breath of the world.

She rested her cheek against Gerard, smelling Signa's strong soap on his work shirt. "I found out my parents loved me." And so did Jeanne and Hannah and Dan and Eddie—even Eddie, who had hugged her hard the last morning and whispered *you're the best.* Ingrid had hung back until the last moment and then burst into tears and clung to her.

"I thought I didn't know how to be a mother and I found out I did. I could be a good mother, Gerard." She saw from his expression that he had known this all along.

"Then why? . . ."

"Babies are for the young, *mon cher.*"

He looked sad, maybe a little for himself but mostly for her.

"It's okay. Honestly it is." She touched his cheek, loving the faintly bristly feel against her hand. "I think this must be the last stage of growing up, the time when you learn that there's a price to pay for everything. A consequence."

She watched the people going by—men, women and children—and thought of their lives like individual solar systems burning with energy and events; and the vitality of life filled her with the sense of limitless possibilities. "Life is generous with second chances, but sometimes . . . we just run out of time. We don't get to have everything we want. But it's okay because we get something else. And it means what we have, we have to enjoy all the more."

A female voice over the loudspeaker announced the last call for a flight to New York. First in English and then in Spanish.

"So, I missed my chance to be a mother. And I have to grieve for that, I guess. I do grieve because I know . . . now, I would have . . ." Liz realized she was repeating herself. "But what I have . . . here and now . . . with you . . . is so precious to me. If I hadn't gone up there and had the abortion and if there hadn't been all the trouble there was, I'd never have realized. I might have let you drift away. When I think how lucky we are to have each other and how easily I could have lost you . . . I could take off, I feel like flying."

"I will catch you by the ankles and never let you go." Gerard wrapped his arms around her and pulled her close to him. "My Liz, there are children in Belize. If you want to adopt—"

"I don't. Or maybe I do. I don't know what I want." His face, his breath and the scent of his skin were unspeakably dear. "Except you, I want you."

That night at bedtime Gerard turned off the air conditioning and opened the balcony door. Far down at the bottom of the hotel canyon someone played the marimba and there were sounds of a party by the pool. The air in the room became heavy and tropical, Liz felt her skin grow buttery and it was as if the humidity penetrated even to her muscles, softening her where she had been taut and resistant only hours before. Perhaps it was just being with Gerard again, back where she felt most easy. They made love to each other with their mouths and hands and there was such tenderness in this mutuality that Liz fell back against the pillows filled with a deep satisfaction. *Change. What has changed in me?*

She turned, rested on her elbow and watched Gerard sleep. His forehead was completely relaxed, not a line on it. His mouth was open slightly so she could see the moist pink gloss of his lower lip, succulent as a fruit. His lips moved a little as if he were saying something in his sleep. Perhaps I love you. Because he did love her and she loved him. She didn't think she would have been able to think this as forthrightly a week ago.

What has changed?

It might only be imagination—with Liz that was always a possibility; but why not believe what her heart told her? Surely after all these years she could trust her heart when it spoke so clearly. She and Gerard had been good together from the day they met, from the night they walked into that smoky stinky bar near Le Mans and simultaneously laughed out loud. Liz had thought it couldn't get better for them, but with her willingness to trust that what they had would endure, what was a partnership had become something else. A picture mounted and framed. A jewel set in gold. Two parallel lines had joined to make a circle large enough to hold them both. It was a variety of love Liz realized her parents might have had and which they had sought to preserve all their married lives despite her. *Our Precious Liz* had tried to make a triangle of their circle but they had not let her.

Liz fitted her body against Gerard's, inhaled his sleeping smell, a warm, burrowing, home smell, and closed her eyes, contented. She would never have a mother and father who were not distracted, she would never have a chance to save Billy Phillips, she would never have a child of her own. But Hannah and Jeanne, she would always have them. Their love for each other had passed safely through foul weather into fair. And there was here and now this tender and warm-skinned man. And here and now these were enough.